The Power of Love
The Two

Ross J. Kinnaird

ISBN: 978-1-0686863-3-7

For more info on The Power of Love Series

www.thepowerofloveworld.com

First edition: December 2023

First Print: December 2023

Edited by Imogen Howson – Inkwell

Cover by Ardel Media

DEDICATIONS

To the Ones who, in time of need, come to rescue the most vulnerable souls. They, in the darkness of their painful memories, grasped a glimpse of the greatest understanding of them all:

Love is all we need.

To Simon, a friend, a confidant and someone who proved me many times over, how determination and faith can change our lives, our world, our destiny.

CONTENTS

Chapter One
A Difficult Truth

∞

If I had known how deep the pain would go, right inside my heart and my bones, would I have chosen this path anyway? If I had owned the power of my own sister, would I have taken the risk, knowing that I could have healed from the blow I inflicted on myself and on the ones I loved? Would I have kept John that close to me, risking losing him, losing the Daniel I was, losing what we had together in the remote chance I could bring us back to who we were?

Two weeks had passed since Anita, Noah, and I had returned to the ordinary, familiar world of our loved ones. We had left Runae with new discoveries and new feelings, and now we were struggling to find the painful balance between what we had and what we were destined to have, between who we were and who we had become. We all had our own challenges to face, different truths we had to come to terms with.

Anita was still struggling to accept that what she had experienced was indeed real. Her memories hadn't returned, despite the effort we had both put into digging for them. She could feel the joy and the pain, the fear and the excitement, like ghosts of an ancient past coming to haunt her days, but she still couldn't believe. Noah had sent a few texts a couple of days after he had gone back home, saying he didn't know where to start. His past was simpler but blurrier than mine. There was no artefact to trace back, no lead to follow. He had nothing that could lead him through.

As for me, I had tons of memories, evidence of who I had become, and with those, the difficult conversations with John multiplied. I had decided to go all in. If I had to face the challenge of sharing the complicated truth, I was going to do it fully. All my secrets had been exposed in the open, been revealed the same day I had come back home. There was no easy point to make. Every piece of information was painful for him and for me, every detail was difficult to grasp. If learning that I had been in another world was incredible to believe, the fact that I had experienced it with someone else, another man he knew nothing about, was impossible to digest. The worst came when I told him how Noah and I were somehow bound together.

'So, is this a very convoluted way of telling me you fell in love with someone else?' he replied at some stage. John's words were filled with resentment and fear.

'I didn't fall in love with anybody! I'm telling you what I discovered. This has nothing to do with you and me, do you understand?'

'How can you tell me you met a man, that the two of you are "connected", that you feel each other's feelings and thoughts, and at the same time, tell me this has nothing to do with you and me?' He had a point.

'Whatever this is, it's not me doing it. It happened to me, not done by me…' But I knew that was a subtle difference to grasp.

'And what is falling in love? You're telling me that the two of you, and by the way, I don't even know who this individual is—'

'*Individual*.' He reminded me of Anita, the first time she said, '*This Noah…*' to keep the distance.

'—are the two halves of something? How can you expect me to not feel like you're just…in love with him?'

'OK, let me explain it again.' I had to make it clearer. 'My feelings for you are the same. I love you. That hasn't changed and probably never will. Now, I found out why all that madness was happening to me. I know it's impossible to believe, and I don't believe it myself, sometimes. But I have seen it with my own eyes, and I have felt it in my head, in my skin. This "thing", as you called it, includes a shocking truth about me and Noah. Do I want it? No. Can I stop it? I don't think so.'

John went quiet. That was the third or fourth time, within the space of a week, that we had argued about it. He was sitting on the couch in our sunroom, and I was about to let Daisy back in through the patio doors. In between going in and out, it felt strangely symbolic of what my life had become. The fight had erupted out of nowhere, as if he had been fuelling it in the background, an explosion waiting to happen at any moment.

'What are we doing now? What am I supposed to do? Wait for the day you tell me you two are meant to be together? It's not easy to hear that you have this…mental connection…this…whatever this is, with another man.'

'I told you everything because this is something that has happened to me. That is happening to me. It doesn't mean anything for the two of us. We are together. I want things to stay this way.'

That was my fractured truth. I knew I couldn't be certain about anything any more, but I wanted to believe that he was the man I would grow old with, the one I would have a life with, regardless. Little did I know back then that my will didn't matter. I was part of something bigger, something written long before I was born as Daniel. It was a destiny I didn't want, but I couldn't run from it.

A few days later, Anita came to visit with the latest updates on her and Patrick. John was working in his workshop in the garage at the back of the house.

'You have to understand, this is not easy for him,' she said at some point. We sat on the bench outside, and Daisy was asleep in the, shade next to us, finding some relief from the unusual warmth.

'I know that. I barely understand it myself,' I replied.

'Yes, but you lived it. Nobody else in here has,' she said, as if she had no part in it, almost like she was the female version of John.

'Anita,' I answered, exhausted. 'You did. You were there with me. I know you can't remember, but why would I lie to you? You were with me every step of the way!'

'Yes, you told me that. And of course, I believe you,' she said, moving closer to Daisy and rubbing her coat. 'But I understand why John doesn't. If I didn't feel the things I feel, I would probably be reacting the same way as him.'

John had seen Anita coming in through the gates, so he paused his work to say hi and joined us on the bench. His face showed the same pain and hostility it had since the moment he had learned the truth. He wasn't just coming to greet Anita, he was looking for someone to blame. This was his chance to finally confront the one who was supremely complicit in all my recent mistakes.

'So, it looks like you had your little adventure too...' His tone dripped with sarcasm.

'As far as I can tell...' She stood in a difficult position, torn between protecting me and empathizing with him.

'Well, if what he says is true, you must have formed an opinion on all this crazy talk, right?' He was ready for a full-blown confrontation, armed and ready. His eyes blended beauty and anger, his sandy hair falling on his forehead like guns in the hands of a war angel.

'John, please,' I said, trying to prevent things from escalating further.

'No, I want to know now. I've been waiting to meet you for what? Two weeks? I want to know.' He wasn't even looking at me.

'It's OK, Daniel.' Anita refused to be cornered by John. Whatever she had in mind, she wouldn't let him speak to her like that. 'John, I understand how you feel, more than you can imagine. I don't have memories of what happened, *but*,' she said before he could interrupt her, 'I do remember how it felt. It's blurry in my mind, but it's real in my heart.'

'Is this enough? How can you believe it?'

'Because it's Daniel! You should know he wouldn't lie, especially about something so painful. Would he risk you, me, and his life for an unbelievable fantasy?'

Her memories might have been left behind, at the gates to the two worlds, but her faith in me remained steadfast. John looked at me, his face releasing its grip on anger and disbelief. Anita had struck a chord in his mind, and now, right in front of us, he was questioning his own thoughts.

'John, please,' I said again. 'You can't be mad at me because you don't believe me and, at the same time, because you do. If you don't believe me, then OK, I'm crazy. I'm losing my mind. Let's make decisions based on that. But if you're mad at me because you do believe me, then let's face the worries that come with it. Fighting on both sides isn't helping, and to be honest, it's not fair either.'

'This is why I was hoping Anita could shed some light, help me believe it, even if it hurts.' He looked back at her, waiting.

The answer remained the same. She couldn't help him trust me. She had her own similar demons to face. Eventually, her practical side resurfaced.

'I told you, John. I don't remember. But I can tell you this: I've been thinking about what happened. We were gone for days and days. I've lost weeks of my life, and I don't know how. How do you explain that? If Daniel has an answer, I trust him. I know he would never lie to me or to you. So this is it. We were gone, in another world, another dimension, I don't know. I do believe Daniel and Noah had the power to bring themselves and me somewhere else. Whatever happened there, I don't know.'

'So let's say this is true. What happens now?' John was nearing his defeat, but he still resisted it.

'We are waiting for Time's instructions. In the meantime, Noah is looking for another piece like the one I showed you, in the box with the shell. Also, Time said something about Anita, something like "Make sure she knows", as if he knew she would forget. I'm trying to help her remember. Other than that, I don't know what's going to happen next.'

'What about you and this…Noah?' he asked, repeating the same question again.

'The only "me and Noah" that I know of is the two pieces together. I have mine finally. He needs to find his. Apparently, that's important for whatever we'll need to do. But there is nothing else between me and Noah,' I repeated, hoping Anita would confirm it.

'John…' Anita tried to get his attention. His gaze had drifted far beyond our heads, his mind grappling with the enormity of that difficult truth. 'It's going to be OK. We are back home. You are Daniel's home. That's all that matters now.'

The fifteen minutes we spent outside with John felt like hours. Anita was ready to leave, but John returned to his work, his mind melting. So she decided to stay a little longer.

'Tell me about you and Patrick,' I said after John had left. This time I wanted to force the conversation. I knew Anita hadn't shown any opening to that painful topic, but I desperately needed to talk about anything other than me.

'There is no me and Patrick, I'm afraid. Oh, he was worried about me being gone. He wanted to know what happened, and of course, I lied. I told him I needed some time to think, and I had asked you to come along...' She still held on to that secret pact we made on our way back from Noah's Bridge.

'Oh, I see. Did he think we're nuts?' I replied, smiling.

'Well, either that or...' she hinted at our journey to Runae, 'I guess I went for the easier one.'

'Did you talk about what's going to happen between the two of you?' I kept pushing.

'A bit. Of course, it's Patrick we're talking about. There's no talking about feelings, commitments. How far can a conversation go with someone like that?' She was somewhat cold towards him, towards the idea of fixing their problems.

'So you're not going to get back together, I assume.'

'I don't think so. He doesn't budge from his spot. Everything is so...shallow. It's like he can't go any deeper than that. And to be honest, I was OK with it until a few months ago. I guess I've changed, and he's not going to bridge that gap I've left.'

'What about "his crazy ideas"?' I still remembered what she had told me while we were sitting by the mountains, after passing through hell in the Valahan Mogs, waiting to rescue Noah from the Crimson Queen. 'Did you tell him how you feel about it?'

'Sure! That's the main reason we had so many fights lately. He never liked his family, always complaining about it. He wanted to be independent and be independent with me by his side. Then, one day he decided he wanted to leave the country, start a new life, start a new business…'

'You never told me that?' I was shocked.

'Because it didn't make any sense! I thought he was joking. But then he started to get closer to his family again. His sister, Aoife, do you remember her? Her boyfriend lives in Germany. He had a business plan, some crazy project about an e-commerce for cheap stuff. And she was going with him, and Patrick's family wanted him to go too, to be part of this "adventure". I'm telling you, nuts!'

I couldn't believe my ears when she had told me about Patrick randomly moving from one idea to another. I didn't realize she was talking about something so extreme.

'OK. Let's leave this project aside for a moment. What about you?' I asked.

'About me, what?' she replied, still angry just by talking about it.

'You in this picture! Did he, at least, ask you to go with him?'

'Of course not! It didn't matter. I didn't matter. So I knew it wasn't just his inability to show emotions. I don't think he has ever felt them, for me.'

'So he is going to go?' I couldn't believe it still.

'Yup. Next week. He was going to go sooner, but his "stupid ex-girlfriend decided to disappear"…' She quoted him, and I was astonished by what had happened to her, right under my nose. I had no idea. I started to think I hadn't been a great friend if I wasn't aware of her struggles, but I knew Anita wasn't exactly talkative about things that hurt her. We were surrounded by unwanted, difficult truths. Both of us were dealing with changes bigger than us. We were both finding ourselves at a crossroads, where people would come and go without stopping by. Although her situation was not supernatural in nature, it was still hard to accept.

'Did you have any other episodes?' she asked, as if I were a victim of some sort of disability. It was like the time we had spent in the other world was gone, and we were back to when she would ask me about my dreams.

'Nothing. Since we came back, it has been quiet.'

'Good,' she said. 'Don't worry about John. He will come around.' And she took her bag, ready to go. 'You know, there is something very strange in this house…' And her eyes moved across the fields, the house, my world.

'What do you mean?' I asked, following her as she was getting in her car.

'I'm not sure. This is not the first time I felt it. Do you know that feeling of being watched? When you walk in the streets, at the shops. Sometimes you can tell when someone's eyes are on you? It's like that.'

'You know this means something, right?' I asked, hoping the Anita that saw through history and its mysteries would come back to me soon. 'Can you see what is it?'

'No, I can't. It fades quickly before I can even focus on it. Anyway, I'm going. Don't worry about John. It will all be OK.'

Despite the situation, Anita and I were still playing the game. Two best friends who tried to keep the ball rolling against the odds, against the uncertainties of our lives. Somehow, the fact that she was still the same, even without her memories, was reassuring. If my problems with John could have been fixed as Anita hoped, the issue with my unjustified absence from work was getting worse. I had attended a few meetings with my manager and HR to go through the reasons why I had skipped work without informing anyone for three long weeks. The morning after Anita's visit, I was again facing the inevitable series of questions about my reasons and my whereabouts.

I wasn't expecting any positive outcome. After all, in their eyes, I had breached my contract. My behaviour was considered unacceptable, but somehow my excuse protected me from a harsh judgement. I said I had gone to Italy to see my grandma, who had suddenly got worse. Once again, my lies were mixing with a reality that few others could have understood. My apologies broke through the wall of dismissal, and I came out victorious, but with a severe warning. There wasn't much to celebrate, but considering the risk I faced, I felt spared. However,

Harry couldn't just accept my version of the story. Although he wasn't going to affect my life in any way, he was determined to pass a sentence of bad friendship and unreliability.

'You should consider yourself lucky! If that were me, they would have fired me on the spot!' he said as we were sitting outside in the outdoor dining area at work. Without me even noticing it at first, he had started to smoke. The idea that I hadn't had a cigarette in weeks had just popped up in my mind.

'They didn't go as easy as you think, Harry. I'm still in by a pure miracle,' I replied, not wanting to engage in his argument because it was always the same. I was the lucky one, the one who didn't really work that hard.

'Yeah, a miracle. If we were in England, you would be long gone now,' he replied, not even looking at me.

'Hold on a second now. You're obviously mad. I don't understand if you're mad because I'm somehow safe, or it's because I was gone for three weeks without telling you,' I said, carefully choosing my words. I was still the sinner, and my right to be treated fairly felt weak.

'No. I don't know,' he stuttered. 'Yes, it's because you were gone. People were worried. Here, they were worried and started to ask me questions.'

'I told you already that I'm sorry. What else do you want? Do you understand it was something that took me by surprise?'

'Well, you had the time to tell Anita and bring her there with you… Not enough surprise in there, is it?' he retorted, and there it was. The reason behind his anger was who I had chosen to bring with me, to support me in what, in fact, was a lie.

'Believe me, she is not happy either. I actually spared you from the trouble,' I replied, and once again, my lies were almost true. 'Did you meet any special girl while I was away?' I clumsily changed the topic, using Harry's self-centeredness.

'No, it's the same story every time. They say they are looking for something special, but then they are really not. And they say us men are the insensitive ones. I'm growing tired of this country to be honest. There is not one thing that goes my way.'

'It's not the country, it's the people, Harry. And not all of them. Just a few rotten apples can't make you feel like everything else should be thrown away?' Immediately after saying it, I pictured myself in a basket full of bad apples. 'You'll find someone, soon I would imagine.'

My attempt worked. Harry went on and on for a good five minutes, taking the rest of my break. I was happy I had managed to put the issue away. I was also glad he wasn't trying to inquire about my trip to Italy and all the questions that were left unanswered. The heavy day passed, and coming back home was just a relief. Daisy was the only one left in my life who was giving me a good time just by seeing me. There was no 'Where have you been? You left me alone. You did me wrong.' It was just pure and simple love, the same she had shown me since the day we had brought her home.

John, on the other hand, saw me coming home but decided to stay in his workshop, a clear sign he was still processing his thoughts and feelings for me. Right before I decided to go and see him, asking what he wanted for dinner, a message popped up on my phone.

Noah

How are you?
Three weeks now, and I'm still looking…

Daniel

Did you not find anything at all?
A lead?

Noah

Nothing really. My mother had a journal
she was keeping. I had no idea it existed.
I've started to read it, but it feels like I'm intruding…

Daniel

Do you think she was your Praetorian?
Like my grandma was for me?

Noah

I'm not sure. I'd say yes, she was.
She mentions a few names of bad people she
met in the early years. She calls them Harpies..

Daniel

It really sounds like bad people.

Noah

Did you get fired?

Daniel

Not for now.. I have to go make dinner
Text me if you find anything.

Noah

Alright. Is John OK?

But I didn't answer his last text. Somehow, talking to him about John felt weird. It felt like I was being unfaithful to John by talking to Noah and unfaithful to Noah by talking about John. Finally, the Artist decided to come back home, right after I had put my phone on the kitchen table. His body brought the cold front of an early ending summer, and I was unprepared to face another storm. I smiled, told him I was making dinner, and avoided saying anything else.

Chapter Two
The Awoken Ones

∞

Waking up by myself in what once was our bed was a daily blow to my heart. Since I had come back, John had decided to sleep in the spare bedroom, away from me and my madness. Whatever his mind was plotting, his signals were clear. He didn't want to be close to me, near me. In the rare moments when I could set aside my guilt, I could see much more in his actions. He wasn't just upset with me for my disappearance, the things I had told him, or Noah. It went beyond that.

Occasionally, I had a sense that he was unhappy about no longer being the centre of my world. I had embarked on a solitary journey, leaving him behind. John was like a blend of Harry and Anita. He couldn't fully comprehend what I had experienced, and he resented me for venturing on that path alone. Victory wasn't on the horizon for me.

Several days had passed, and things hadn't improved. A stubborn, deafening silence had settled between our hearts.

Finally, one evening, circumstances pushed us closer together. I had prepared dinner for both of us, hoping John would join me at the kitchen table, giving us the opportunity to discuss anything other than me. However, Daisy's growling at the front door interrupted our plans. Oblivious to the commotion as I was far from her, I was surprised when John entered the room.

'Can't you hear Daisy?' he said, once again employing a tone as if I had failed even that simple task. 'She has been going mad at the front door for a few minutes now.'

'What? Is she hearing something outside?'

'I've checked. There is nothing. And she's still at it!' he replied.

'OK, wait a moment. Let's go and check again,' I said, setting aside the food on the kitchen island.

We stepped outside; the sun had long disappeared, and darkness settled in. With the outdoor lights on, we walked to the front of the house. However, unusually, Daisy didn't follow.

'Come on, girl, let's go. Show me!' I urged, looking at her. But she wouldn't move. Her snout was fixed on something behind me, in the pitch-black night, beyond the tall magnolia trees.

'Come on Daisy, let's go for a walk!' John added, trying to be more convincing.

'She won't come out, that's weird...' I said to John, who was looking at me, ready to blame me for that too.

We spent a few minutes walking around the house, from the closed gates to the hill at the back. The lights from the poles scattered around forced the shadows of the night just inches away, but they failed to give us any clues about what we were searching for. Then, everything went dark. The lights inside and outside the house simultaneously went off, and we stood there, as if we had lost power as well.

'What's going on?' John exclaimed, a few feet away.

'Let's go back inside. Come on, I'll check the switch box,' I replied, moving towards the house.

'Girl, calm down!' John said, raising his voice as Daisy's barking grew louder, echoing through the fields. 'What the hell?'

John's eyes focused on the large trees behind me. A shadow, darker than the encroaching night, moved from one part to another. Like a blurry grey cloud, it expanded slowly, filling the empty space. For a brief moment, I thought a spectre had somehow survived and managed to cross the node, finding its way into my home, my life.

'John, get back in the house,' I said, slowly moving backwards. 'Now!'

'What is that?' he asked, defying my request.

'I'm afraid it's a spectre. I thought they were all gone...'

'Watch out!' John shouted.

The malevolent presence rapidly grew larger, advancing towards us. Even if I was mistaken and it wasn't a spectre, the imminent threat to our safety couldn't have been clearer. I could feel it in my skin, my hair tingling in the air. I knew it had come for me, to harm me. A high-pitched whistle pierced our ears just as I turned back to push John inside the house. Before I could close the door behind us, the shadow attacked, exerting its oppressive weight on us. I'd grabbed John and pulled him into my arms, shielding him from the pain we were about to feel, when a bright white flash emerged from inside the house. The long-forgot cloak I had received from a mysterious benefactor materialized, positioning itself between us and our aggressor, shining brilliantly. As if it had a life of its own, it emerged from the spare bedroom, standing there to protect us, protecting us from the sufferings we weren't meant to endure. Moments later, the magical glow vanished along with the attacker. The cloak slowly descended onto my shoulders, covering my body and head, silent and lifeless.

'It's true…isn't it?' John said, still in my arms, his gaze directed at the floor where Daisy now sat silently.

'It is, John… I'm sorry,' I replied, releasing him from my embrace. My attention shifted to the long, white garment adorning my back.

'So I guess this wasn't something from a Connemara gift shop?' he asked, looking at me.

'I suppose not…' I felt embarrassed once again. I hadn't told John that he was mistaken in thinking I had bought it during my trip to Noah's Bridge. 'But I have no clue how or who sent it. The morning you found it in the kitchen was the first time I saw it too.'

'Is that…thing gone?' John's gaze drifted outside, behind me. 'What was it?'

'It appears so. I'm not entirely sure what it was, but I know it wasn't a spectre. I need to text Noah,' I said, not fully thinking how that would sit with John. 'If that thing found me, it might find him too, and I don't think he has a cloak like this.'

I took a final glance outside, ensuring that the evil presence had truly vanished, then returned inside and closed the door behind me. John lifted Daisy and locked the door, adding another layer of protection. Little did he know that those creatures could employ their magic to break through any powerful barrier, let alone a wooden door. He followed me into the kitchen, standing by my side as I texted Noah. The events had rapidly reshaped his perspective, forcing him to confront the terrifying reality he had refused to believe in. We had been thrust out of our usual dynamic, where I used to follow him everywhere, seeking attention. Now, I held the reins, and he was too scared to challenge it.

Daniel

Something tried to attack us at the house.
We managed to send it away. I don't know
what it was, but I'm worried it could come to
you next. Please, text me asap.

John was silently looking at my phone while I continued texting. His thoughts could have drifted to our recent fights, our heated conversations about another man entering my life, but I didn't care. Once again, I found myself straddling the blurry line between these two relationships, and I couldn't bring myself to feel guilty about it.

'What about Anita?' he asked.

'What about her?'

'Wouldn't she be in danger too?' he added.

'I don't think so. It's me and Noah they're after. Anita's more like you, just got dragged into it. But yeah, you're right, better safe than sorry. I'll text her,' I replied, sending a similar message to Anita.

'It's petrifying to know we can be attacked just like that, out of nowhere. Are we safe now? Are we safe here?' John expressed genuine concern. This was the first time he had confronted my truth head-on.

'I don't know what to say, John. In Runae, everything was magical. Eventually, we became accustomed to the idea that all those beings possessed powers beyond our imagination. Here, on Earth, we don't have such thing. If that evil has reached me here, it must have come from another place…' I tried to make sense of my own words as I spoke.

'But you're here… There is magic here too, isn't there?'

That question hit me like a sudden awakening, a slap in the face. I was drawn into a mystical realm of beings I had never truly felt I belonged to. It was the first time I realized that I wasn't just a victim of events. In John's eyes, I was one of them, at least to some extent. It was also the first time John and I discussed the topic without anger, guilt, and misunderstanding. That experience was traumatic for him, but it brought him closer to me, Noah, and Anita. He could now sense and understand the things we had felt, and he could finally see with his own eyes some of the truths I had been telling him. Anita's reply came swiftly.

Anita

Are you alright? Is it John OK?

Daniel

We are OK. Somehow, it was what John needed to understand. We are talking..

Anita

Good. Shall I come over or will I let you two sort things out? Do you need me?

Daniel

It's OK. Don't worry. Do we meet tomorrow after work?

Anita

Sure. I finish at 4 on Fridays.

Daniel

Please let me know if something weird happens there.. I'll come right away!

Anita

I will, don't worry. Night x

That night, John returned to sleep in our bed. I wasn't sure if he was reconsidering our relationship or simply afraid of being alone in the spare room. Either way, I didn't comment when he joined me. We had managed a longer conversation over the cold dinner that had been waiting for us. John was gradually becoming more accepting of the significant secret I had buried in my past, and that I had never meant to hurt anyone. Noah's name came up a few times, but we never truly discussed my connection to him or how it made John feel. Before falling asleep, I checked my phone again. Noah still hadn't replied, and my calls had gone unanswered.

'Still nothing?' John asked, lying in bed. Even though he was facing the other way, he knew I was still waiting for a response.

'No, nothing. I'm sure he's OK. I'm just worried...' I replied.

'He'll text you...' Those were his last words before drifting off to sleep, and I could feel the weight of his heart, his struggle to set aside his emotions for the sake of something greater.

The next morning, on my way to work, I received a message from Noah saying he was OK and that he had worked through the night at a nursing home and had left his phone at home. Relieved to hear he was fine, I informed him about what had happened, hoping he'd be better prepared if a similar situation caught him off guard.

Noah

I have an idea about what that might have been. I spent the last few nights reading my mother's journal.

Daniel

What did you find?

Noah

I think she might have known more than I thought. There are a few details that you might want to read too..

Daniel

Shall we get on a call tonight?
I'm seeing Anita at 4.

Noah

I work tonight too. But I start at 6. Let's do that. Call me when you get to her. I feel we might need her again.

Now I was looking forward to knowing more, and the day at work felt longer than usual. I met Harry at our usual spot in the canteen, and we discussed how long it had been since we were all together. While he danced around the question of when we would do it again, I couldn't help but think about how we could be around him without revealing what we all knew. How would we keep him in the dark about our secrets, our many whispers in the shadows? Somehow, I felt like I was betraying his trust in me, in our friendship.

Despite my numerous mistakes, I couldn't say no to the idea of getting together for dinner over the weekend, pushed by Harry's sincere and kind intentions. I agreed, but with the condition of rescheduling if John and Anita couldn't make it. With the afternoon nearly over, I hopped in my car and drove to Anita's place. I texted Noah, letting him know I would call him soon.

Anita was sitting outside on one of the squeaky chairs where we used to sit and smoke cigarettes. She had managed to avoid falling back into that bad habit, which was another sign that whatever she had experienced with me had to be true. With a glass of red wine in her hand and a pair of sunglasses on her face, she greeted me with a big smile. She looked like she was caught between work and bedtime, still wearing a fancy top but with pyjama shorts on the bottom. As I drove by her house, the loud, joyful chattering of children playing at the nearby beach welcomed me in the open. Along with it came a strong scent of the salty sea, snuggling comfortably into my nose.

'Well, that was an effort!' I said, smiling as I sat beside her.

'Yeah, I'm exhausted… I just got back. I saw the sun was out, so I thought I'd put on something light and rest a bit. You can't imagine how crazy these past weeks have been for me, but luckily, people aren't asking too many questions about where I was.'

'Oh girl, it feels like we're back at the beginning. Us sitting here, about to talk about all the crazy things happening to me and you… I hope I didn't get you into trouble with work,' I sighed.

'Not at all! I run that place. They were more worried about not knowing what to do without me. Anyway, did anything else happen after your text?'

'No, thank God! Well, John slept back in our bed…'

'Well, that's a good sign, isn't it?' She smiled.

'Yeah… It means he's losing his mind! Anyway, Noah texted this morning. He said he has news. I told him we'll call him before he goes to work. He might have some updates.'

'Cool. I have news too!' she exclaimed, standing up. 'Patrick is gone. He left the country…'

'So he actually did it!' I replied, astonished.

'Yes, he did. It makes you wonder how strong his feelings were if he could make such a decision just a month after we broke up. Anyway, let's move to the backyard. I don't want the neighbourhood to know our business.'

I wasn't sure if she was referring to Noah's business or her own. Knowing that she would allow personal topics to be discussed only for a few minutes, I was afraid she would change the subject by the time we reached the other side of the house. So, I kept the conversation going as we moved from one area to another.

'So he left everything behind and just…moved? His friends, his family, his job?'

'Everything. I don't know… When my parents left to go to Australia, they did it for a reason. They were both retired, and they wanted to live close to their families. I can understand that. But him? At his age, with things and people he claimed to love right here, how could he manage to leave everything behind? It's beyond me,' she sighed.

'Mad! I just can't understand how people can just turn off their feelings like that. Love more than any other feeling. Where does it go? Does it turn into something else or just dies off? I really can't understand how something so powerful can't be also permanent,' I exclaimed.

'Mad indeed! Do you want some wine? Let me get you some, and then we can sit outside and call Noah,' she said, almost dismissing my questions. 'I think we often mistake the need of companionship as love. For some reasons we get so entangled with our worries that whatever we have in our hands must be *it*. It becomes our only way to keep us going.'

'You mean it might not be love at all? What is it then? Hope? Don't you have anything without alcohol? I'm driving…' I added, moving away the bottle of wine she had just placed on the kitchen counter.

'Oh, sure, what was I thinking?' Anita seemed strangely distracted. 'I wish it were hope. I think it's anything that can fight against our fears. Look at me, for example. What is the thing that upsets me the most?'

'Shannon?' I replied, smiling.

'Funny,' she smirked. 'Questions with no answers! And this is what Patrick was able to give me. No questions. Everything was flat, normal. Day in, day out, over and over again.'

'So you never loved him in the first place?' I knew her argument was valid, yet I still couldn't accept it.

'I don't know. Am I mad? I'm not sure if I'm upset because I love him and he left me, or because he finally did something crazy and this is now raising a question I can't answer. Anyway, let's change topic. I'm getting sad and I'm drinking wine. Not a good combination!'

A few minutes later, we sat outside in the same spot where our journey to another world had begun just a few weeks before. We were talking about the cloak that had luckily protected me when the vision of our recent past came to my mind. I could still see it with my own eyes, how the events had unfolded, how we had left and come back to that very spot. Anita was still unaware of our past actions in Runae, but I could see her mind struggling between not knowing and remembering.

'You do remember something, don't you?' I asked, seeing her staring into the empty space.

'I don't know… I remember the sound of broken cups. I think we were drinking tea? There's this vast sea in my mind, and a feeling of flying, like I had my own wings…but there is something else entirely, something that feels much older than a few weeks ago. I see like…angels everywhere? Well, I don't know.'

'Yes! It's coming back, I can sense it!' I said, encouraged.

'Let's call Noah, shall we?'

We immediately dialled Noah's number. He had been waiting since the moment I texted him. He was at home, lying on his bed with the journal on his lap and a few sheets with his notes beside him.

'So, I managed to read more than half of my mother's journal,' he said, his voice coming out of the speaker. 'At first, I thought I had never seen it before, but I think I had read the first few pages once, in my other house by the lake, after she was gone. However, back then, they didn't seem relevant to me, so I forgot about it. Somehow, it feels like I'm violating her privacy…'

'That's normal, Noah. I've been in situations like this, almost every time I do some research for work,' Anita replied. 'At least it's your mother's journal, not a complete stranger's business.'

'True, but I still preferred it wasn't my mother's...' he said. 'She doesn't mention how I came to be. She doesn't talk about being pregnant with me, but she doesn't talk about adopting me either. That piece doesn't seem relevant to her. But she mentions someone she calls Dõron, who came to her and told her that I needed to be safe...'

'Does she say if Dõron is a he or a she?' I asked.

'It's a she, a woman,' he replied. 'She writes, *God had sent me Dõron, a kind, spiritual woman, to remind me that I need to protect my son from evil*. Then, a few pages later, she talks about some bad people she called the *Awoken Ones* or *Harpies*, who were coming to test her will and strength. I don't know, some parts seem quite odd. There are pages with only a few sentences, as if she was just writing them down for her own piece of mind. Obviously she wasn't trying to leave me...leave us a map.'

'Harpies?' Anita asked. 'In history, Harpies are usually evil entities that bring bad omens.'

'Yes. She calls one of them *the Snake*, a man who tried to convince her that she had to give me up through lies and fear. This particular individual tells my mother that she is actually one of the Harpies herself, called *Athymos*, and that's the reason why she had to give up her son. *He said Athymos is the one who destroys love, taking it away from people's hearts*. But she couldn't believe it and *refused to listen to his wicked words*.'

'Noah, does she mention anything about a crowned heart so far?' I was deeply interested in the contents of the journal, but our main goal was still pushing through my thoughts.

'I don't think she had it, and I don't think she knew about it either. My mother never mentioned it.'

'If she was your protector, whatever she wrote about what was happening to her must have some correlation with everything else. How far have you got with the journal?' Anita asked.

'I'm halfway through. I've been reading it at night while watching over some patients. If what you say is correct, we can assume these Harpies are still around?'

'I think so,' I said without even thinking. 'And I have a feeling that's who paid us a visit last night.'

Our conversation went on for a good hour. I told Noah again what had happened to me the night before, and we speculated about the connection between the event and his mother's writings. We discussed our next steps. It was crucial that we knew what the journal said up to its final page. We also had to ensure that whatever was threatening us, we could quickly find a way to be safe.

The evening passed, and I let Noah go to work. I informed Anita about Harry's plan, and though she wasn't completely happy about it, she decided to give it a try and come over for a nice dinner at my place. As I headed home, John was the next one on the list to ask. Hopefully, he would be in a good mood and say yes.

Chapter Three
In Between Two Men

∞

Harry's plan shaped quickly. We were going to get together at my place for a barbecue and drinks. The invited guests would be the usual ones. Although I didn't feel like throwing a big party with more than just the four of us, the idea of having more people was comforting. We would be too many for our conversations to revolve around the heated topics of the past few weeks.

Anita had given up on the idea that Shannon and Mark would come. She had briefly complained about Shannon's presence, fearing questions about Patrick. She didn't want anyone to know. The topic had to remain as secret as our trip to Runae. John had invited his best friend, Theresa, whom we hadn't seen since the fake birthday dinner, and everyone was going to bring something to drink so that the festive atmosphere would last throughout the day.

I had a weird feeling that we were making a mistake by gathering together while holding on to so many secrets. We were all friends, but at times, our strong and conflicting personalities clashed. John and I had not fully resolved our issues, and the same went for Harry and me. Anita and Shannon were constantly on rocky ground, so stepping together onto a minefield would be traumatic. However, we desperately needed some real-life experience, something that would make us feel normal, even if that normalcy consisted of our usual, standard arguments.

As if our barbecue lacked juicy issues to discuss, Noah was going to become part of our heated conversations. He was free for the weekend and eager to share his recent discoveries. He had told me he was coming over for a deep dive into his findings and asked Anita to be present for the conversation as well. When I had shared my concerns with her, she had said it was actually a good idea. It was time for John to seriously meet Noah, understand that he wasn't a threat, and get some answers to the recent perplexities. Unconvinced, I had reluctantly agreed and brought up the topic with John the night before the big gathering.

'I can't say it makes me happy,' he replied.

'I know. I know what you think and how you feel about Noah. That's why I want you to be there when we talk. I need you to understand what dynamics are at play so that we might be able to move on,' I weakly attempted to persuade him.

'So, he is coming tomorrow, along with the rest? How are you going to explain to the others who he is and why he is here?' he asked, trying to set a trap.

'Anita has kindly offered an excuse. She'll introduce him as a work partner on a project regarding Noah's Bridge,' I said, thinking that she had really studied every inch of the village's history. Once again, my lies were twisting the truth.

'In other words, you're going to lie to your friends. You're asking me to lie to Theresa,' he pointed out, scoring several valid points. I was losing the battle.

'I'm not happy about it. What else can I say? Look, I understand it makes you uncomfortable. It makes me uneasy too. I would never force you to lie to Theresa. If you feel you want to tell her the truth, you can do that. But please, tell her to keep it to herself. I don't want other people to think I'm going mad, and more importantly, I don't want people to get hurt. We don't know how far the danger can crawl.'

'So, let me be clear'—he reluctantly came to an agreement—'he will be here, with our friends, in our home. We will pretend he is not who he is and go along with it. Then what? What happens next?'

'When everyone else is gone, we will sit and talk. You, me, Anita, and Noah,' I concluded.

The plan wasn't perfect, and John would rightly challenge it even if it were. The only move available to us was to hope for the best. I knew the risk. We were carrying a painful burden and openly exposing ourselves to danger.

The following day, I woke up to a bright sun peeking through the window, and I felt a bit more positive. I spent the morning cleaning the garden at the back and setting up the table under the gazebo for our guests, while John went shopping for dinner. Daisy seemed to have forgotten how long it had been since we had enjoyed the sun outside. She ran from one place to another, playing with some of her toys scattered on the grass. The day was starting beautifully, and my hopes were high.

In the early afternoon, Anita rang the bell at the gates. John went out to greet her before I could leave the barbecue stand, and to his surprise, she was bringing her 'work partner' with her. John stopped in the middle of the pathway, his eyes fixed on the passenger seat.

'She picked him up, or something?' he asked as I ran up to his side.

'Yes, at the train station.'

'You must be happy your friends are getting so acquainted,' he sarcastically remarked after days of silence.

'John, please. Keep an open mind, for me? Please?' I begged.

My last words slipped through the smile I had falsely put up, trying to make Anita and Noah believe that nothing was going on between the two of us. Anita got out of the car, carrying two big bags of food and drinks. Her smile was more genuine than mine, or at least, her effort to pretend was better placed. Noah approached, his hand ready to shake John's, but he found the counterpart resistant to the welcome. I had brought home my other one, and that threesome in esoteric absentia wasn't working.

'Hi, I'm Noah. You must be John. I've heard a lot about you.' His hand still hanging in the air.

'I've heard a lot about you too, unfortunately,' John responded, making a statement in his usual proud way.

'I'm sorry to impose in this way,' Noah continued, retracting his unwanted hand. 'I hope I get the chance to explain the events. I don't want to cause any trouble.'

'Let's wait and see,' John said, taking Anita's bags from her hands and moving inside. The greetings were over.

Anita looked at me, smiling. From her point of view, the fact that John hadn't pulled a gun and shot Noah on the spot was a victory. Not feeling the same optimism, I said nothing to the two of them, my mind screening all the possible future outcomes, looking for potential killings.

The few minutes the four of us spent in the house before the rest of the crowd arrived were met with an awkward silence, broken up only by a few sentences Anita threw here and there, trying to get a conversation started. Thankfully, Harry arrived earlier than expected. His usual mood was on; he was coming in, conquering the world.

'Mister!' he shouted at John, a big smile on his face, hands ready to hug him. He had come back from a session at the gym, his hair still wet, and a minty scent of cheap shower gel wafted across the kitchen. 'I haven't seen you in ages! How are you keeping?'

'All good!' John said. It was like he had transformed into another person. His entire personality had shifted. 'Are you just back from your boxing?'

'Of course, my friend!'

That genuine 'my friend' was like a strike. It wasn't uncommon for Harry to call John like that, but in that circumstance, it added weight to the harsh line of friendship. If the war had broken out, Harry would have taken John's side.

Soon enough, the house was full. Theresa arrived, bringing the most random stuff, from whiskey jams to weirdly shaped potatoes she had been growing in her own garden. Theresa could have been defined by many as a *strange woman*, but her mind and beauty had a sort of simplicity that would have made anyone comfortable. Shannon and Mark arrived *last and late*, as Anita had pointed out. The meat was already grilling on the barbecue; Harry once again was leading the tasty cuisine, while the rest were chatting away, moving inside and outside. Daisy didn't move from Harry's feet, clearly hoping a piece of beef would casually drop on the ground, and everyone was commenting on how beautiful she was—an evident attempt to fill the conversation gaps left by the factions at war.

John pretended Noah didn't exist, while the latter didn't really know anybody but me and Anita. She ignored Shannon at any cost, and I juggled between making Noah feel welcome and not giving too much away, making John mad because of it.

Just before sitting at the table, Theresa started a whispering conversation with John in the kitchen, by the sink. They were confabulating something, and I was worried he was going to spill the truth. On my way to get fresh drinks from the fridge, I heard random words like 'the shop, customers, money,' and I felt some relief understanding they were talking about Theresa's bistro. Eventually, the conversation opened up to everybody once we sat to enjoy our meal. The seats ironically reflected the status quo. John sat g beside his best friend; I had Anita on one side and Noah on the other. We could have easily been back at Runae, at Reela's table, among more friendly strangers. Harry was the partition line between Anita and Shannon, and lastly, Mark was squeezed between her and John, almost invisible.

'Where is Patrick?' he asked. A few words brought him right into the spotlight. From ignored to being annoying, the jump was sudden.

'Patrick is in Germany at the moment,' Anita calmly replied, as if she had just talked about the weather. Then she whispered to me, 'I bet she fed that question to him.'

'Don't be so judgemental. Shannon seems OK today,' I replied, while chewing to hide my response.

'For now...' She expected the worst, like I was about John and Noah.

'Where is everyone going these days? First you'—Shannon pointed her fork right at Anita's face—'then Daniel, now Patrick.'

'I could have gone too if someone had asked me,' Harry intervened.

'Not now, Harry...' I said.

'How's your grandma, by the way?' Theresa asked, genuinely interested to know. She had no idea she was igniting a bomb that I had no way to stop from exploding.

'To be honest, she could be worse. Thank God she is still OK,' I replied, hoping someone would come and rescue me.

'Is this why you were gone? I thought Patrick told you Anita wanted to go somewhere to take some time off,' Shannon asked Mark, who had just looked at us, waiting for a clarification.

Harry gave me a weird look, as if he was also waiting for an explanation. I had told him I had to go and see my grandma, and Anita had come along. Now her version of our lie was leaking out.

'Well, timing sometimes is our best friend. That's why Anita went with Daniel. She needed a break, and he needed someone on the spot. I'm sorry I could not leave my work.'

I couldn't believe my ears. John, whom I had thought would never come to rescue me from my misery, had jumped in and corroborated our clumsy lie. *Is he trying to show me he is by my side, after all?* I wondered. I couldn't be more wrong. A few minutes later, as I went back inside to refill our drinks, John came along to get some cheese. He moved closer, making me believe he was going to tell me he was OK with the situation.

'Whatever I did, it wasn't for you. Just to be clear. I did it because I don't like when people put their noses into others' business. Sometimes, your friends get on my nerves,' he said, annoyed.

'Oh, so now they are *my* friends? I see you are keeping your distance, and it's getting even wider.' I reacted to his words as if I were genuinely hurt, but deep down, I knew the current situation was entirely my fault.

'You are widening the distance by bringing strangers into our home!'

'Again? When are you going to sincerely give me a chance to prove you wrong? Or am I wrong just because it's me?' That wasn't the right time for a fight, but I couldn't control myself. The tension built up so quickly that releasing it was all I could think of.

'What's going on with the two of you?' Theresa had just come in, bringing the empty wine bottles. She looked at us, surprised. Her red hair filled the room with the same random madness that agitated our hearts.

'It's nothing, Theresa. Just a bad mood,' he replied.

'Is everything OK?' She looked at me as if it were obvious I was the culprit of all the sins in the world.

'It would be if *your friend*' —now I was the one remarking the distance—'put his pride and his own selfish behaviour aside for a second,' I let out without thinking.

'What happened?' she insisted.

'It doesn't matter what happened. What matters is that John understands that some situations are difficult to solve. That we are not bad people only because we are struggling, and suddenly we are not revolving around him any more.' And with that said, I walked out with drinks in hand.

Whatever they were going to discuss, it wasn't important any more. Secrets and lies had become unbearable. *I'm tired of feeling responsible for who I am; tired of feeling ashamed to be someone else's problem. I'm not the problem. They are. They want me to be the person they've decided I am, nothing more.* In my mind, I was back being fifteen, trapped in my mother's cult, constantly judged for being different, rebellious, and gay. I had made a promise to myself never to be manipulated into being someone else ever again. And now, I had just realized I was making the same mistakes over and over. I had to be the person John wanted. I had to be the one Noah urged me to become. I had to be the one Time said I had always been.

Back at the table, Shannon drove the conversation, talking about her efforts to become an influencer. She complained about the competition, the absence of public support, and how people failed to recognise that hers was a legitimate profession. At first, I believed she remained as shallow as I remembered, but my pain and scars told me otherwise. That was simply who she was, and I had to accept her for it. I refused to shift from being a victim to becoming a perpetrator. Thankfully, Anita was busy trying to bring Noah up to speed on all the people sitting at the table, having no time to engage in any challenging conversation with her.

The afternoon passed without any major incidents, as if we had struck a balance between enjoying ourselves and avoiding any more conflicts. Here and there, genuine smiles and laughter lifted my spirits. As night fell, the doorbell rang. Surprised and aware that the gates were closed, I glanced at John, perplexed.

'They're all here. Who could it be?'

John raised his shoulders, as if wondering the same.

'I'll get it! I have to go and check my phone anyway,' Theresa said.

The only person missing was Patrick, and there was no chance he had changed his mind, come back from Germany, and decided to be there with us. A few minutes later, Theresa returned.

'There is a man at the door, asking for John?'

'Who is he?' I asked, standing up.

'He didn't say. You better go and see what he wants. John, I have to go. The new girl at the shop is about to get a big delivery, and I want to be there in case she needs help. Thank you very much for today. It was fun!'

Outside the front door, a middle-aged man stood waiting to be invited in. His hair was shining grey, his eyes were black like the darkest hour before dawn, and a silvery short beard encased his square face. The moment I showed up, he smiled. Somehow, I had the feeling we had met before, but I could not tell where and when.

'Hi! Is John home?' he opened up.

'Yes, and you are?' I replied, still surprised he had jumped over the gates to come to our door looking for John.

'I'm Lëo. I've commissioned some work from John.'

His words were slow, like he was calmly looking for the right thing to say, his eyes exploring my mind and our house. His way of talking, his name, everything was telling me I knew him, but how, I could not recall. Theresa came behind me, her purse in hand, ready to leave. After kissing my cheek and with an empathetic expression on her face, she whispered:

'Try and relax the tension. Both of you. It will all work out!' And she left.

'Oh, apologies if I interrupted the party,' the man said, after hearing some laughs coming from the back of the house.

'It's OK, please come in,' I replied, showing him outside at the back where John was sitting with the rest of the crew. At the sight of the new guest, Daisy barked loudly, her defences raised.

'John, my dear, how are you? Hello, everyone!' the man said. The tone in his voice sounded warm and friendly. He looked like a younger, more attractive version of Santa Claus. His Irish accent was very strong, but his words were still slow and clear.

'Oh, hi!' John replied, his expression perplexed. 'Calm down, Daisy! Excuse me, do we know each other?' That question took me by surprise.

'You are so funny! You should be a showman, not an artist. Anyway, I'm here for your other talent. Remember I commissioned you for a work for my office?'

'Sure, sure! Oh God, forgive me, I must have drunk a little too much today!'

How John could forget the man who had requested the work he had been occupied with for weeks was beyond me. The idea of John having a sharp, smart mind cracked a bit in my head. *Do I have anything to do with it?*

'Can I see where you're at?' the man asked.

'Well, sir,' I interjected, 'you should know, John doesn't show his work to anyone before it's finished.'

'Well, I believe it is finished, or it will be very soon, isn't that right, John?' Again, his words were slow. It was like he was feeding his talk to John, trying to persuade him, trying to persuade me.

'Yes, yes! Let me show it to you!' John's response was unusual. I couldn't stop thinking about who that man was to have such authority over someone with a strong will like John's. That was the first time I had seen him responding so passively to someone else, without challenges, without refusals. *If this man is his commissioner, he must be paying him a lot,* I thought.

'Who's that?' Anita asked after the two left the dinner table and moved to John's workshop.

'I have no idea. This is the first time I've seen him. He does look familiar. We might have met him the night of the show in Dublin? I would say it has something to do with John's work,' I replied.

'I have to be honest, he gave me the chills, and seeing John that confused, or maybe even threatened, it's something else...'

'Isn't it?' I replied, looking at the far side of the garden where the two of them had disappeared, entering the workshop.

Less than an hour later, John was still away, and tiredness had pulled our guests up from their seats, and one by one, they all had left. Harry was the last one to leave. He had been waiting for John to come back to say goodnight, but eventually, he had given up. Anita, Noah, and I were the only ones left, still sitting at the table.

'Is he coming back?' Anita asked.

'I hope so, eventually. It's work. You know I don't put my nose in his stuff,' I replied, smiling.

'Maybe you should?' she continued.

'Sure… I've already screwed up our dynamics. Let me try this as well. Who knows, maybe it will finally kill us off,' I laughed, trying to hide my sarcastic suffering.

'Is he like that because of Runae or because of me?' Noah asked, pouring some water into his glass.

'Everything, and goes even beyond that,' Anita replied, preceding me.

She was unusually involved in the matter. Although I knew she cared deeply about me and my problems, she typically wouldn't step in unless pushed. We understood each other's limits and the right moments to intervene, and she would never have forced her way in by answering for me on such a sensitive topic. I sensed she was trying to protect me, being kind enough to shield me from even having to answer that question—*but why now?*

A few minutes later, the pair returned, speaking quietly as they made their way to the table. It seemed the strange man was explaining something to John, suggesting changes while maintaining an air of secrecy around their conversation. His hands moved through the air as if he were recounting the greatest story ever told, and beside him, John listened intently, like an enchanted child captivated by a bedtime tale.

Once at the table, John invited his guest to sit down and keep us company. His words sounded forced, as if he didn't genuinely mean it; he seemed compelled to extend the invitation, as if some sort of respect was expected. A few moments later, after settling beside John, the strange man clasped his hands together on the table and began to speak.

'Now that the uninterested parties are gone, I'm glad we can have our little moment here,' he said. We listened intently, each of us trying to grasp what he was hinting at. 'The girl here, Anita, is it?' he asked, taking her by surprise. No names were exchanged. How did he know? 'You are not really part of this, a bit like my friend John here. But still, something tells me you have been pulled into this…crazy, absurd fantasy… Yes, there is something buried deep in here...'

'Who are you? Why are you here?' I asked. I didn't know where he was going with that, but I clearly understood what he was talking about.

'I'm here to help you…to help you and Noah,' he said.

'So you know? Who are you? You look familiar. Have we met before?' Noah echoed my same questions.

'I told you,' he repeated, and a strange smile appeared on his face. 'I'm here to help you…to let go, to get back to your real lives, to forget everything about it.'

With our shocked faces turned towards him, filled with questions, fear, and curiosity, we were left astonished. The man leaned back, relaxing his shoulders against the chair, opened his hands, and asked:

'Shall we begin?'

Chapter Four
A Thousand Lies
∞

My eyes were fixed on that strange man. His look was charming, his words were sharp yet attractive. Something in his voice was pulling me in, like warm water on a freezing day. I was eager to know more, to find peace for my senses. He pulled a chair away from the table and moved closer to us, his entire presence growing larger. John was left in a corner, as if his interest in him had vanished. We were now the subjects of his attention, the ones in need of medical care. Something in my head told me he must be a psychiatrist. *How did he get to know us?* I wondered.

'What you have experienced is extraordinary. John had the chance to share his thoughts, his worries with me several days ago,' he started, sitting in front of the three of us. 'Oh, there is no need to be mad at him. He had good intentions, just like you. And intentions are all that matter in life, aren't they?'

'Who are you?' Anita asked, hesitant.

'How can I explain it to you? Let me see,' he said, softly touching his beard with his right hand. 'I'm a sort of expert in lies, in the stories our mind fabricates in times of need.'

'Are you implying that we have been lying? Sir, you have no idea what you are talking about!' I said, ready to stand up and ask him to leave.

'Oh no, not at all,' he replied, his voice calm, like balm on deep wounds. 'I've been working on cases like yours all my life. Believe me, there is no judgement in what I'm about to say. I trust your point of view. It's because I trust you that I told John I was happy to come and help.'

'Can you help us?' Noah asked.

'I can. I'm sure I can. You see, you and Daniel have experienced what I call extreme painful occurrences. You had to come out of your journey victorious, and in order to do so, you had to find a way out. If not in this world, maybe in another.'

I wasn't sure where he was going with that. His words were deliberately vague, applicable to any possible scenario. It felt as if he wanted us to believe he was talking about our journey to Runae, but somehow, I was certain he was referring to something else. We didn't have to wait long before the true meaning of his words became clear.

'Extracorporeal experiences can be driven by many factors. A troubled life, extreme and painful experiences, and chemical imbalances can give rise to what you have felt, like the adventure of your life,' he explained.

'Are you saying we imagined it?' I felt a mix of conflicting emotions. I wanted to reject his statement, feeling offended, but I couldn't resist the pull of his voice.

'Not really. For you, it was real. For everybody else, it wasn't,' he replied.

'That explains why Anita can't remember anything,' John chimed in.

For a good hour, the strange man gave us tons of details about his truth regarding our visions, our cracked reality. The longer we listened, the weaker our beliefs became. It was as if he was able to strip our minds of our certainties, one by one, replacing them with something more reasonable, more comfortable. The space around us fell silent. There was no interference, only him. If we had the chance to see ourselves from the outside, we would have seen four puppets, four enchanted dolls, with dull eyes and amplified ears, captured by his psychological spell.

The charming stranger who had unexpectedly come to us was bringing the only gift we could ask for: the chance to return to the normal life we were meant to live. Whether his words were the pure truth or a deceiving lie, it didn't matter. If he could make it happen, that would be the only truth worth believing. We would no longer be outliers; we would be purified from any disease that was tearing us apart.

As his trick neared its goal, he added more, emphasizing the importance of detaching ourselves from any connection to our past for the sake of a full recovery and happiness.

'Now. It's important that you distance yourself from any possible variation of the truth you have learned to believe in. I can take care of any memory and any physical items that can remind you of your bad experiences, your troubles. I know you have some sort of chest, a box that you believe can bring you to other worlds? You need to get it out of your life! I can take care of it, if you hand it over.'

He was giving us the opportunity of a lifetime. We could forget everything that had happened, freeing ourselves from an unknown and difficult future. I found myself drawn towards the dream of a peaceful, normal life, and I moved inside the house, reaching for the artefact I had cherished and protected. Within moments, I was outside again, holding my grandma's box, ready to hand it over to that charming man in exchange for the closure we longed for.

However, as I approached the stranger with the box, the ground began to shake, and a blinding light emerged from behind him. Someone familiar, someone we had learned to forget in the past hour, appeared just a few steps away from John, who stared in disbelief, petrified.

'Stop this forgery!' a voice shouted.

The man sitting in front of us raised his shoulders, surprised and scared. He knew who had come to stop him and, in fear, he withdrew his hands from mine. Without turning around, panic evident on his face, he stood up and searched for a quick escape.

'I know you, evil! You have done enough damage with just the power of your tongue! I believed your kind was long gone! How did you come back from the land of the dead? How did you learn about them? Speak now, Harpy!'

We felt as if we were suddenly awakening from a long sleep. Our senses returned, and the effect of the stranger's subtle spell began to fade away.

'Time? You're here!' I exclaimed.

'Daniel, how did you come to know this…disgusting being?' Time questioned, but I didn't know what to say. Was it really John who had brought him so close to us?

'We know him, don't we? Who is he?' Noah asked, his hand on his forehead as he tried to see Time, who still shone brightly.

'His name is Lëogan. He is a Harpy. The master of a thousand lies. A snake, a manipulator of realities! You have seen him in the Ancient Mirrors. He is the one who originally corrupted the minds of the Aqualymphs, Humans, against the Leonty!'

'It's him!' I shouted, looking at Noah, finally remembering the brief vision of a man walking through the node in Runae. 'He told Aura he had come from Earth. So you really do come from our world… I thought Una had killed you!'

'How is this possible?' Noah asked, echoing Time's question.

'How long has he been here? What did you tell them? *Answer me!*' Time thundered.

But the man was paralyzed. He wouldn't move, his eyes darting from side to side, searching for an escape. John remained seated, gripping his chair in fear, just as terrified as the man he had allegedly brought into the house. Finally, the master of lies turned around, a wicked smile acknowledging and welcoming Time.

'He knows…he knows you're back, so he knows they're back…' His voice had changed. It was no longer a pure charming melody. His tone became rough and harsh.

'Did he send you? You were dead! How did you come back?' Time demanded.

'We don't die from a mortal end. We answer to Death himself as his children. We know what to do and when to do it. We have been waiting for generations…we have been stopping you all this time… Now, we'll do it once more. It's too late for you, for them.'

'Where is the rest? *Where are the others?*' Time's patience was wearing thin. The answers were being kept from him.

'You know I won't tell you… You won't wake him up, nor Soul, nor Love…' The stranger laughed, a horrifying sound.

'You're useless!' Time swiftly moved from his place to Lëogan, gripping his shoulders. 'The evil's magic may allow you to come back as he pleases, but not if I trap you between death and oblivion! Only one good act was carried out by the hand of the Crimson Queen. I'll make sure it stays that way!'

'Speaking of which… tell me, if you're here, who is protecting your world?'

But those were Lëogan's last words, his final attempt to corrupt Time's sense of security. In a blinding, vast light, he vanished, disintegrated by Time's unchallenged power.

The moment he was extinguished by our saviour, the invisible bubble of oppression and insecurity released its hold, leaving us free.

'Why do I feel better now?' Anita asked, looking at her own body as if she had been chained to her spot.

'It was his unpleasant sorcery, keeping you down, to crush your will. His power was very similar to the one Una held in her mind. You know now the extent of it,' Time replied, looking at Anita. 'I'm happy to see you are still in the picture. Good. Very good!'

'Time, this is John,' I said. John was still silent, muted by another, stronger splash of truth.

Time turned around and gave him a soft smile. In my head, I wished that would be enough to let John believe in everything I had said. But not only that. Somehow, I hoped he could feel the way I felt, standing by Time. Feeling protected, safe, hopeful. The God of Runae was exactly as I remembered, his cloak still draped over his shoulders, the hood partially obscuring his eyes.

'Thank you for rescuing us, once more,' Noah said, moving closer to Time.

'You did the same for me. It is a debt that I will never manage to repay. Tell me, did you find your other half?'

'Not yet. My past is lost in fog and smoke; I can't find a trail that leads me to it.' The fear of disappointing that magical being was vividly displayed on his face.

'Don't worry, you will. In one way or the other, it will draw your soul to it.' Time replied.

'Did you know we were in danger? Is this why you came?' I asked.

'Yes, but there is more. I found Soul. I mean, I know where—well, when—he is, but I can't free him just yet. It took a while before I could find the right moment when he existed, freely, but I'm afraid we can't rescue him right away. Runae is vulnerable right now. You have heard what that thing said. We have been detected. 'I'm not surprised by it, but I was hoping we could have more time.' The brief smile that appeared on his face felt out of place. He brought challenging news, yet he looked pleased.

'So what are we going to do next?' Noah once again projected into the future.

'I need you to hurry up. It's vital you find your artefact. The window of opportunity is going to be very small, smaller if we delay,' he continued. 'I'll get back to Runae immediately. We don't know when the evil might strike. In the meantime, please be careful. The other Harpies are much more powerful and wicked than the one you have just met.'

'Time?' I asked before he could vanish from our world. 'Was it you? Did you send me the ivory cloak?'

'The what?' He sounded surprised. 'You have the Great Healing cloak with you? The conjurer of supreme protection?'

'It looks like yours.' John finally joined the conversation, still afraid to say too much. 'It came to protect us, recently.'

'This is incredible!' His expression showed a surprising rejoicing hope. 'If she hasn't come out yet, there is a reason. Let's leave it for now…' And Time suddenly paused.

'What's wrong?' I asked, moving closer.

'I'm just…baffled. You have only half of Love's artefact and you are obviously a very long distance from your node. However, I landed by your side right as I crossed it. Something strange is at play here. Something I'm not aware of…' And Time's gaze moved from us to the house, the fields and, once again, back to me. He was silently searching for an answer in between space and time.

'There is a node on Earth as well?' Noah asked, looking at me and Anita. We knew we had reached Runae through the designated, supervised spot. It suddenly made sense it would be the same in our world.

'Of course! There is…well, there was a node in each of the worlds,' Time replied, his eyes still fixed on me. 'Please, remember. Be careful and please hurry! Oh, one last thing. Make sure she wakes up. It's important…no, it's vital that she comes back.' And after a brief look at Anita, he was gone.

His smile was the last thing we saw before Time dissolved into nothing, right before our eyes. John stood up, unable to believe what he had just witnessed. Anita, who had forgotten our past experience, was unexpectedly calm, as if she were familiar with the recent events. Her face puzzled, her hands on her chin, she mentally put pieces together—thoughts, feelings, beliefs.

'Now I know,' she started. 'I'm sure I've been there. I know him, I remember how it felt seeing him for the first time. The door that locked him away, with the clepsydra carved into it.'

'You remember! You remember everything?' Noah interrupted her, smiling.

'Not yet, but I remember him!' Happiness came right through her eyes.

'John,' I said, looking at him. 'Are you OK?'

'Does this always happen in this way? They just show up and leave out of the blue?' I could see in his eyes his thoughts coming together, finding a proper order.

'Yes, I'd say. Do you believe me now?' I asked.

But there was no answer. John was too busy realising I hadn't lied to him about anything. On his face, I could see a replica of his mind, as if his trail of thoughts were clearly displayed to the three of us, as he jumped from the idea of acknowledging Time's existence to the stranger he had brought home. Finally, after a few minutes, he rejoined the conversation Anita, Noah, and I were having about Time's last words.

'Did I put us in danger? Was that man a bad man?'

'You have no idea.' Noah preceded me.

'What happened to him? Where is he now?' John added.

'I think he is gone, John. Time has the power to do that,' I replied.

'Gone, you mean, dead?' Fear mounted back in his heart.

'He wasn't human, John. Whatever that was, it wasn't a man. It was pure wicked evil, come to test us, to hurt us,' I quickly reassured him.

'Still, he was here, even after Una killed him...' Noah objected.

'He did say he can't die,' Anita added, sitting back down at the table. 'Time called him Harpy... He must be one of the Awoken Ones your mum wrote about. Can you bring the journal? We need to get to the bottom of this.'

'These Harpies, they don't die? How long do they live? He said they have been waiting for generations. What did he mean? They have been living all this time? Or have they simply been passing their mission to their next generations?' I asked, sitting beside her, waiting for Noah to come back.

It was like we had suddenly put John aside. We could have easily been back in Runae, leaving our real world behind, fully immersed in our personal, private space. He, on the other hand, wasn't pushing to join the pack. John silently stood right in the same spot he had been for the last thirty minutes, his eyes fixed on us, his ears fully attentive, unable to speak.

'Remember what Noah read to us over the phone? His mother met this individual who told her stuff, stuff she could not believe?' Anita continued.

'You think it's the same one?'

'It might be. But how did she manage to push him away? If it wasn't for Time, we would have fallen into his trap...' Anita had a point.

'Unless Noah's mother was a Praetorian? Like my grandma? If they were meant to protect us, maybe they were able to resist their magic?' My conjecture felt weak, yet it made sense to me.

'She must have been,' Noah said, placing the journal on the table. 'I had nobody else, but her.'

His mother's journal was just as old as I had imagined. The pages were yellowing, with some parts turning brown. A torn leather cover protected the fragile paper, and inside, beautiful handwriting filled every empty space. Since Noah already knew the contents by heart, he opened the journal halfway through. A small white page, different from the rest, marked the spot, and a few notes in Noah's handwriting revealed he had been taking notes.

'Here! That's where she talks about the Snake who came to persuade her to give me away.'

'The Snake, she calls it.' Anita was already in full research mode, her finger rapidly but carefully moving from row to row. 'Time called him the same name. A liar who manipulates? It must have been him.'

'How did he find us?' Noah asked.

'How long has he been looking for us?' I added.

'Why did he come through me?' Suddenly, John rejoined the conversation.

'I don't understand.' Anita talked to herself, out loud. 'How could this Lëogan not influence a Praetorian, and sorry, Noah, I don't want to diminish your mother's strength, but how could he not overpower her and yet overpower the two of you? And Time destroyed him without even moving his fingers. Shouldn't you be like him?'

'Well, Anita, whenever you are going to remember everything, you'll realize we have no such power. It doesn't matter if we are alone or together, neither I nor Noah can do what Time does.'

'For now, perhaps…' she replied, finally looking at us.

'What do you mean?' Noah wasn't following, and neither was I.

'Think about what that man said. "*You won't wake Soul up and neither Love.*" Did he not say something like that?' Anita was digging restlessly through the depths of her mind.

None of us could take the lead on our way out of that conversation. We were stuck with tons of signals but not enough to understand the full picture. Eventually, the three of us ended up sitting back at the table, the journal in between Anita's arms, and Noah and I taking notes on every detail.

'Shall I make you some tea? I feel this is going to take some time,' John asked.

It was like he had switched from one personality to another. His face was calm, and fear had completely left him. I wasn't sure if he wanted to help us or if he just wanted to leave that space with an excuse and be on his own, but his offer was well received, and we all said yes.

In the background, amidst the three of us and John moving around in the kitchen, something was manoeuvring, planning its next steps, preparing for the future we were about to face. In the back of my mind, Anita's words were whispering for attention. There was indeed something strange in the house, something we could barely perceive—a force moving us like unwitting pawns on an invisible chessboard.

Chapter Five
Siobhan's Memories

∞

*I*t is what it is today. The storm is worsening here, and there is nothing else to do but stay inside, taking care of my little Noah by the fire. He will be turning four in a few days, and I don't think we'll have the chance to go out and do something nice. It seems like he doesn't know much about what has happened. It's impressive what a child's mind is capable of— erasing and rewriting its history, leaving no memory of what has happened to it.

I can't help but think about what his life will be as a young man. It feels foolish to consider amidst the current state of the world and the challenges our country is facing. Just a few days ago, another bombing, another dreadful attack shook our faith in a better future. Here, we feel protected. Here, we think the madness is too far to reach our shores, but the truth is, it's happening only one or two counties away. How long before the borders we hold on so dearly break? How long do I have before we get swallowed by all this hate? How can my child become what he is destined to be in a world like this?

-

It's going to be two years very soon since he came to us, and I still can't believe how lucky I am. But I'm also worried that I won't be enough for him, that we won't be enough for him. What are we going to do when the time comes? I can't stop thinking.

-

I had plans to bring Noah to the lake house, to let him enjoy nature, the wilderness, the magic. I haven't been there much since Mum and Dad died, but I always wanted to return. I even considered leaving Noah's Bridge behind, maybe permanently. But here, we must stay. I made a promise; it was the price we had to pay for this blessing. My child has to remain where he was born, even if I don't fully understand why. Something is drawing me towards this place. I can hear it in my heart and sometimes even beyond. There are whispers in the woods, sometimes near the strange tree and the old stones. I could swear I've seen shadows moving at sunset. I know I'm driving myself mad just thinking about it, but if this magic is true, why wouldn't that be true as well? He is such a creative, energetic little boy. He needs to see more than just this small village.

-

Dōron hasn't come back any more. During the first year, she would occasionally visit, even if only briefly, to check if Noah was doing OK. But it has been long since she was here last. Sometimes I question if I imagined everything, but then, how could I explain Noah and everything that happens around him? The other day, I caught him talking to the walls again. He was playing with his toys, but he wasn't talking to them. He was engaged in a full conversation with someone…someone who wasn't there. I don't know whether to be scared by it or by the fact that, at the age of five, he can articulate so well. He's like an adult in a child's body.

-

We say luck never gives; it only lends. Yesterday, I met a strange man outside O'Reilly. Initially, he seemed gentle and sweet, offering to give me a hand with my shopping bags. I had Noah with me, and he showed an unusual interest in him. He shared he had a child who passed away years ago, and somehow, I believed he was just a gentleman with a heart burdened by pain and kindness.

He walked me home, helping me with the heavy load, so when we arrived, I thought it was fitting to offer a cup of tea. Sean was still at work, so I made two hot cups of tea for both of us. However, everything changed suddenly. His tone shifted, and his words turned dark. 'You won't be able to bring this child into the world, just as you were unable to carry a few bags home,' he said.

In that moment, I knew something was wrong with him, with everything. 'Does the name Athymos mean anything to you?' he asked. 'This is your true name. You are one of them, one of the Harpies. The child is not safe with you!' he added. But I understood his intentions. Dõron had warned me about him and his kind! I could see his lies pouring into my ears. I wasn't a Harpy; in fact, I was standing face-to-face with one of them, and I finally realized it!

I sent him away, asserting that I alone could protect my child. I hope he doesn't return!

-

-

'Yes, Noah, you definitely stepped into something when you found this journal!' Anita was in hunt mode, full on. Her eyes moved from page to page, almost anticipating her moving finger across the words. As suggested by Noah, we had skipped a good number of irrelevant pages and quickly got close to the halfway mark.

'If we have to believe Lëogan was real, and none of us can deny it any more, we have to believe this…Dõron? is also real?' I asked, looking at Noah.

'How is it that we are learning this only now?' he replied with another question.

'You mean, about the Harpies? Maybe our trip to Runae has triggered something?' I had no other ideas.

'Not really…' Anita was finally back in the present world, the precious journal left aside. 'Lëogan himself said they have been watching. She said she felt herself being watched. They have been here for generations, waiting, stopping you. I wouldn't be surprised if you have met them before, even without knowing it was them.'

'Hold on a second!' Something popped up in my mind ruthlessly. 'I might be completely wrong, but… If I told you about a time…when we were on a trip, just before meeting Noah… Has anything strange happened that, in a way, could have prevented us from meeting him?'

'Keep going?' Anita wasn't following.

'John's pub? The place that wasn't there? Remember what your man said?' I pushed a little more.

'Oh my… That creepy place! The man who insisted the bridge wasn't there any more… He said we had been there before, and there wasn't much to look forward to?' Anita was rapidly rewinding her memories, her face revealing the truth finally coming to light. 'Oh my God. Are you saying we were deceived?'

'Well, we know that place didn't actually exist. We know we didn't have any food at all. We only didn't know who was behind it. We thought, logically, we were experiencing one of my daydreams. But what if it was… them?'

'The Snake! The Liar!' Anita cursed him at every word, Time's exact disgust showing up in her words. 'Wait a minute…does this mean we were also prevented from going the first time, three years earlier, by him? By them?'

Anita's question left me speechless. It was impossible to think Grandma's sickness had anything to do with them, with me. I was holding on to my belief that the Harpies could not have made her sick, that I wasn't the reason why she had lost her mind. After all, as proved by Siobhan, weren't Praetorians invulnerable to their powers?

John had come back with some tea just before we could continue our dive into all the possible scenarios where Harpies had manipulated our lives in one way or another. His face looked a bit more relaxed, as if the shock had left his body and mind, but his movements still showed signs of fear. His hands shook slightly, causing the tea to spill on the table. Mine instinctively reached for his, trying to help him out, showing him I was still by his side. A shy smile responded to my gesture, and a few moments later, John moved back to his chair, sitting quietly with his hands brought together below his chin, like a prayer that could neither start nor finish, prevented from reaching any God, anywhere. I could tell when he loved me and cared about me, when I had lost his trust, and when he didn't want to be with me any more, but I could not tell how he was feeling now; his mind was unreadable to me.

'So, they have been watching us? For how long?' Noah asked, as if questioning himself out loud. 'I'm confused now. Have I seen them? Were they my three people?'

'I don't know, Noah. I doubt it. It seems like the Harpies' intentions are very wicked. I never felt anything like that in any of my visions. Have you?' He nodded in a confused 'nope'.

'Guys, listen to this!' Anita dove in again, sipping her tea.

I brought Noah to the lake yesterday to celebrate his seventh birthday. We are staying here for two days, but Sean will join us tomorrow. Hopefully, the weekend will be warm and nice. I'd love to have him swimming! This morning, somebody showed up at the house. I was at the back with my boy by the large tree, showing him how to plant a few roses, when a voice reached us from the front, across the porch.

'Ma'am,' he shouted. I left my son at the back and went to see. Then he called again, this time using my name. I couldn't recognize his voice, and once I saw him, I was sure we had never met. 'Siobhan, I'm sorry I'm late. I'm here to give you a hand?' he said. I didn't answer. He asked again, so I told him to go away or I'd call the Gardai. I panicked for a few minutes, but he eventually left. Somehow, I knew he was there for Noah. I can't be sure of it, but I know it in my heart.

-

Whoever is after us, after Noah, can follow us anywhere. Another strange event unfolded just a few hours ago. Thankfully, Sean was already here, but we're not going to face any more risks. It seems like these weird things are happening more often here. Whispers are multiplying at night. Something is happening in the woods by the lake. I'm sure I saw someone walking in the dark. At the back of the house, by the large tree, there is a sort of electrifying feeling that seems to be covering the entire space. I can't tell how many of them are roaming nearby but one seems to stay around all the time. I held myself together this time and went outside. Whoever was there didn't seem to have evil intentions. They were just standing there, by the large rocks and the tree. It seemed as if they were watching over something. My heart tells me it was Dõron but why would she not make herself known to me? I can't risk it. We are packing our things tomorrow morning at sunrise.

-

We are back at Noah's Bridge. We cut our weekend short and left in a hurry. The other night something else happened, someone knocked at our front door. Our house is pretty isolated. We didn't expect anybody to come and bang on the door in the middle of the night. It was like hammering, the sound of knocked wood bouncing everywhere. I had told Sean about the man who had visited earlier, so when the horrible knocking started, he ran right to the hall, only to find the front door wide open. There was nobody anywhere. The lake, the woods, everything was quiet. It's like someone is trying to play tricks on us, to break our will, to make us vulnerable through fear. I know I probably made a mistake, but Dõron is gone, and I just want to raise my child in peace. If no one is coming to help, then I can only do one thing. I'm leaving this 'fate' behind in the woods, buried under a foot of soil. May our mother earth swallow the curse we have upon us, making us free.

-

I'm here, writing in this journal again. I can't believe it's back to torment me. We have had five beautiful years in peace, in love. Even after Sean got sick, things have stayed calm and safe. I've been running the place myself. Noah is a young giant, goofy but beautiful. He is giving me a hand with the family business. He says he wants to become a doctor and leave the shop behind. I wish him to do so. But yesterday, they came back. I'm sure it was them! At the hospital, they showed up in Sean's room, right next to me. I was resting by his bed, tired from the long night. A cold breeze woke me up to a horrible discovery. The same man I had seen years ago at the lake was there! He said something, whispered some horrendous words. He said he had come to finish his work, to take Sean away! Unless I gave him the heart… The heart… I knew what he meant. He was asking me to trade my husband's life for my child's. I shouted, called the nurses. I had to send him away. He was gone before they could come to my rescue, to calm me down, thinking I was just under a severe amount of stress. But I didn't care. All I wanted was for that thing to leave!

\-

'Let's stop for a bit,' Anita said, her mind spinning fast. 'I think it's best if we try to understand what we just read before moving ahead.'

'Why don't we move inside? It's getting dark and cold in here. I'll make some more tea while you move. Leave it. I'll clear the table,' John said before any of us could answer.

John was right. We had lost track of time. The late summer evening was giving way to the chilly night. The outdoor lights were on, but everything around us was getting darker.

'Look at the time!' I said, walking into the sunroom. 'Let's give it another hour, then we might reassess.'

'Sounds good to me,' Noah replied, looking at Anita for a consensus that didn't take too long to arrive.

'Now, I know how it feels…to navigate in this fear and mystery, but I can't imagine how hard it must have been for your mother to go through all of that and stay strong,' Anita started, sitting on the couch between me and Noah. 'Let's think again for a second. What did we read?'

'Someone came and visited them at their house by the lake?' I answered vaguely, unaware that my mind was rewinding to some other, more important detail.

'Yes. And terrified, Siobhan decided to put an end to it, burying it away?' Anita looked at Noah.

'What if she didn't mean metaphorically?' he asked her back.

'Like she literally buried something in the ground?' I joined in with another question.

'Not just something. Something that's connected to you, Noah! She wanted you as a child, she wanted you to be just a free child, without all that fear and magic,' Anita said, getting closer to the truth.

'And she felt she was finally leaving it behind with it.' Noah and Anita shared the exact same thoughts.

'Daniel,' John said, just putting more tea on the coffee table before sitting in an armchair right beside me. 'Doesn't that sound familiar? The way she talks about that banging, that knocking at the door. To then finding it open?'

His question captured what I had been trying to articulate. Anita and Noah fell silent, their thoughts aligning with John's statement. It felt as if we were all aware of this similarity, yet something seemingly more important had taken the spotlight.

'That's exactly what I was trying to figure out—how her story resembles ours,' I said.

'I thought you were visited by, I don't know, someone good?' Anita replied, her expression unconvinced.

'We don't really know who visited, do we?' I looked at John, glad to have him finally part of the conversation.

'But they left you the cloak—the same cloak that protected you from *them*,' Anita said, struggling to piece everything together.

'The cloak was there the morning after. Yes, it's suspicious, but we don't know if they left it or if someone else did to protect us against them,' I continued.

'So, you're saying that the Harpies visited you, and because of that, someone else left you the cloak?' Noah was getting closer to my idea.

'And this someone is the same one Time mentioned earlier. I think there's a good side we don't yet know about. It aligns with what Siobhan said about those whispers and the people she saw at night. She felt they weren't evil, which is the opposite of the man who visited her...' I added, sipping the pleasant hot tea.

'I thought it was just you two and... Time... besides the bad ones?' John asked in response to my theory.

Once again, John's question was met with unexpected silence. It wasn't because he had said something wrong or unimportant compared to the rest, but because his questions forced a wider perspective. As an outsider, he was unbiased and unchallenged. A few moments later, to break the deadlock, we quickly recapped.

'We know the Harpies had been in our lives long before we could even perceive them. We know they wanted to prevent Daniel and me from getting together. We know they have powers and that some episodes look suspiciously similar,' Noah said.

'Do you think he could really hurt him? Hurt your dad, if he wanted to?' I asked him.

'At the hospital? I don't know. They have powers, right?'

'The power to kill us?' Anita asked, almost rejecting the idea.

'The power to make us sick? To make my grandma sick?' I continued, fear reflecting in my eyes.

This time, it was me who stopped the conversation. My emotions burst out without warning. The four of us sat in a room too small to contain all our pain, worries, and fear, but we held our ground, trying to prevent our feelings from taking control. John put his arm on my shoulder, his lips on my wet cheek. He was back in my life, trying to protect me in the only way he could, despite the odds and the clear, loud evidence that we were facing something greater than we could handle.

'To me, if I can give my two cents,' John said, 'it looks like there are two sets of…beings in all of this. The ones who are against you and the ones who are protecting you.'

'Yet Daniel and Noah have no memories of either,' Anita added.

'My mother met both—the good one, who she said stopped visiting, and the one who tried to take me away. The same one we've just met in this very house.'

'Grandma never said a word about them. Even the last time we met, for the few minutes she was back in my world, she never mentioned those *Awoken Ones*,' I let out. 'However, I do recall Carla saying something about a stranger, a man coming to visit, trying to get to my Grandma.'

'You mean Carla might have met them?' John asked, as if hinting at the jokes we had made in the past, laughing about how her appearance might terrify anyone, even the most terrible Harpy.

'Was it a good one or a bad one, I wonder,' Anita replied, looking at the clock again.

'Yes. I wonder too. From what she described him like, I'd say it was the same one we met tonight. So, a bad one! But the night we found our front door open... Was it a good visitor or a bad one?'

'Now,' Anita continued 'Look at this.'

I went back to the house by the lake yesterday. Taking the chance of Noah being in school all day, I had to go back to that place where so much happened. I wanted to walk in the house as if Sean was still walking through that door with me. I needed to feel his presence, instead I felt someone else's. I'm convinced someone is looking after the land, someone who doesn't come to light, does not speak but watches me, watches us every step of the way. I remembered me taking notes in one of the notebooks I left in that very house. Notes about names and things Dõron had told me. I wondered if I could read those names again, maybe use them to call them up, summon them to my presence and have them telling me what I'm supposed to do now that it's just me and my son facing this uncertain future. But I could not find the courage to walk in. I could only hear their voices spreading across the land, blending with the sound of the leaves rustling in the wind. I could not find the strength. I hope I am doing the right thing.

-

'I think we know what to do next...' Anita said, after staying silent for a few moments.

'We need to get that notebook? Find this Dõron?' Noah asked.

'And find out what else is hidden in that place. If she is right, we might find the other artefact in there,' I added.

We found ourselves moving away from Siobhan's journal, trying to connect all the pieces we had together, over and over, then returning to it, hoping to grasp the truth all at once. Exhausted from the encroaching night and with no more words to add, we fell into silence. Our minds spun frantically, but our mouths stayed shut while someone else's whispers multiplied within our home. Though we couldn't see or hear them, we knew we were being watched. Like Siobhan long before us, we were hunted by someone unknown—whether good or evil.

Chapter Six
The Others

∞

By the time the four of us had stopped reading Siobhan's journal and made assumption after assumption, midnight was long gone. We hadn't managed to reach the three-quarters mark, but feeling tired, we decided to postpone the rest of the research until the following morning. A few seconds after Anita and Noah left the house, just as the car disappeared beyond the closing gates, John approached the front door with a look of remorse on his face.

'I know there's a lot I don't know about your family and your past. I never wanted to ask too much. You always made it clear…it was painful to think about it. Was all of this also a secret? Did you push it away along with everything else?' he asked, his eyes fixed on mine.

'What are you asking? If I knew about it and intentionally kept you in the dark?' I didn't know what John was hinting at, but I hadn't forgot how cold he had been to me the day before.

'No, I guess not. I'm not saying you did it on purpose. You know how sometimes we bury our painful memories until they disappear?'

'I'm not in denial, John,' I replied immediately. Somehow, his change of heart hadn't made me forget the way he had treated me in the past few days. 'I can't believe you're throwing my own profession in my face. This was never out in the open in my life, for me to know, for me to understand. I had no idea I was someone else, something else. I had no idea I shared a secret path with somebody else. Yes, there are things we never spoke about, things I never wanted you to be a part of, as if I would infect you with them if I did. As if I would tarnish the beautiful picture you had painted for both of us. But the things I have kept from you have never had an impact on us. They were what they were, in the past, where they belonged.'

My long monologue had rendered John silent. Our roles had completely flipped. I walked into the house, and he followed me around, captivated by the power of my words. I didn't know what it was, but it wasn't the same feeling that had drawn me to him. He was like me, before the madness, but his feelings were different. He wasn't adoring me. He wasn't living in the shadow of my charming personality. Whatever it was, I didn't know. The cracks in our hearts, in our relationship, were at the very core of that difference, but I wasn't ready to see it. I wasn't ready to confront it. Something in the dark corner of a cage where my soul was trapped, I was still holding on to the idea that we were meant to be together, to stay together through those challenging times.

'Where is this leading?' His words were measured.

'You mean me? Us?'

'I mean everything you mean. It's clear I know very little about all this, and it's taking me a lot to even comprehend it. I'm trying to catch up. What's going to happen now?'

'I told you. Noah needs to find his half of the artefact. Once that's done, I guess Time will tell us how to free Soul. After that…I don't know.'

'So, what does that mean? Are you going on a quest now? What happens to your life? The things you've built, the things we've built together?' John's questions started to sound like my own consciousness, in a full-on interrogation.

'I don't know!' I shouted, exasperated. 'I don't know, John! I'm taking it step by step. I have no clue where this is going, and I have very little clue on how I've got this far, to be honest. I understand how you feel. I feel the same. I care about you more than anything else in the world. It's clear that I can't stop this, no matter how much I want to.'

'Tell me you would choose me, us, if we weren't threatened by all of this,' he asked, his hand on my face, his eyes locked with mine. 'Tell me to accept this whole madness because, in the end, you'll come back to me!'

'Who are you asking this question to?' I replied after a few seconds of silence. 'Me? The me you know? The me I know? Because that Daniel is long gone. I don't know who

I am, but I can tell you that whatever this is, it won't let me go back to who I was.'

Once again, my words struck a blow to John's head. His body almost physically recoiled from the impact, and he took a step back. His arms dropped to his sides, and he exhaled a long-held breath. It was as if I had released him from a spell he had enchanted himself with. We didn't speak again until the next morning when we got into the car and drove into town. John had decided he wanted to be part of the conversation. I wasn't sure if he wanted to be there with us to control our next moves — my next moves — or if he genuinely wanted to help and prove his support during those difficult days. Anita, Noah, and I had agreed to meet for Sunday brunch in town, near the bed and breakfast where Noah was staying. And so, John came along to meet them, unsure whether it was out of fear, courage, or simply hunger.

I parked a few blocks away, and we walked to the place. From the far end of the square, I saw Noah sitting outside a bar at one of the small tables. I knew he must have been surprised to see John walking beside me. The sun was unusually strong, and the long summer held its grip on an otherwise rainy, grey country. My spiritual half absorbed the light as if he were made of the same matter. His eyes spoke to me from many steps away.

At my side, the other man followed me like a shadow, silently. His gaze was fixed on the crowd through which Noah pierced and rose above, emanating the strength of his beauty. *If this is what a love triangle is, I don't understand the appeal*, I thought. Just before we reached the middle of the square, Anita's tall figure appeared from the other side, her hand waving at me. Upon closer inspection, her face appeared grey and tired, as if she had had a rough night. After quick greetings, I asked her what was wrong.

'You know what? I don't know! I had the most random nightmares last night. I went to bed, obviously thinking about what happened, but I was fine. Then I woke up, or maybe I dreamt of waking up, I don't know… Long story short, I feel weird. Like my head is buzzing or something.'

'Oh, I'm sorry, Anita.' I didn't know what else to say. *Is this another thing to add to the 'This is my fault' list?* I thought.

'Well, you're the brain of the whole operation…if you don't function, I don't think we're going to get very far,' Noah said, smiling.

Anita briefly looked at him and smiled back. I knew their relationship had changed since that day at the beach. Nobody would have noticed that small, imperceptible change, but I could. They were getting closer.

'Don't worry. My brain will reset after a cup of coffee, and maybe some food?' Anita said.

'Should we order?' John interjected, as if he had just appeared out of nowhere. Neither Anita nor Noah had acknowledged his presence until then.

'Are you OK?' Anita asked him, her face sharply focused on John's. It seemed like she was about to reprimand him.

'Yeah…yes, yes, I'm OK. Why?' John seemed taken aback.

'I don't know…' Anita replied, studying John's face intently. 'You look in pain.'

'What?' John replied, smiling. 'What's wrong with you?' His question echoed my own thoughts. Anita was acting strangely.

'Did I say that? Oh God, I'm losing it!' Anita exclaimed, covering her face with her hands. 'Forget about me, I'm out of my mind.'

'It's OK,' John said, his hand resting on her shoulder, a soft smile on his face. 'I'll go and order. Coffee for you, and everyone else?'

John quickly moved on, his mind preoccupied with trying to process the crazy events he had become entangled in. There was no room for small, silly comments. He went inside with the list of things we wanted, the thoughts rolling in his mind. The place was bustling, and a few people were waiting in line to order. I took the opportunity to ask Anita what had happened before John returned.

'I told you, I had a bad night, that's all. But I think I understand now...' Anita said.

'What do you understand?' I asked.

'I understand how you must have felt, both of you. Having your thoughts all jumbled up, your head spinning,' she replied.

'What do you mean? Did something happen?' Noah sensed that something was wrong, just like me.

'I think all my memories are coming back,' she whispered, as if her voice could be heard over the chatter. 'But I also think that strange man did something to me.'

'The Harpy?' Noah asked.

'Yes! I don't know, he did something to us. To me. My mind has been in turmoil since last night. It's like there's a hole somewhere, and thoughts come and go before I can even grasp them.'

'I thought Time had stopped him from causing us any harm, didn't he?' Noah looked at me, hoping for a positive answer.

'He did. I'm OK, and you're OK?'

'I am. But she obviously isn't.' Noah's hand reached out to Anita, who was frantically searching for something in her purse.

'I don't think he did something to me in that sense. I think he somehow triggered my memory to come back,' Anita explained.

'Wasn't he trying to do the opposite?' I said, watching her closely, my eyes waiting to see what she would find in her bag.

'No. Yes! I mean, maybe the fact that Time had stopped him…maybe that left something open, something broken. Here, look at this!' Anita unfolded a crumpled piece of paper.

As she smoothed out the paper, I caught glimpses of her doodles and scrambled words. Eventually, when she had flattened it completely, something clearer emerged.

To give and protect, to rescue from the fall. Cherish to awaken, the long night is gone. Cherish, Cherish to call. Cherish to be, the long night is gone.

Noah and I kept our faces composed, even though whatever she had written didn't make much more sense than before she had smoothed out the paper on the table. Anita remained silent, her gaze fixed on us, waiting for a clue. She had written those words, but she blamed us for it. We had to come up with a reasonable explanation, and time was ticking.

'You wrote this?' Noah asked.

'Yeah, that's her handwriting. But what does it mean?' I added before Anita could answer.

'Well, I don't know what it means,' she replied.

'But you wrote it,' Noah interjected.

'But I don't know what it means.'

'OK, hold on. We're going in circles here,' I smiled. 'When did you write it?'

'Sometime between last night and this morning. It was on the bed, next to me,' Anita said, visibly upset.

'This is definitely part of everything. We don't need to question that, do we?' I asked, looking at them. 'We know Anita was drawn into this craziness because of us. Whatever she's experiencing now is because of us.'

'Do you remember seeing anybody, anything? Anything specific?' Noah asked her. John had made progress in the queue. We all felt the urgency of going through the recent events quickly.

'I remember arriving in Runae. I remember flying with the Chomps and most of the things that have happened. But I remember them as if I watched them from behind. Like I've been used,' Anita explained, her hands moving to her shoulders and up to her neck. 'Something has attached itself to me, here, in my head. It's like there's someone else in my brain.'

'Another Harpy? Could it be?' Noah asked, concerned.

'We know there are more out there. But why would they go after her when we are both here, just as vulnerable?' I stated, scanning the surroundings as if I could detect any unwanted presence with the power of my mind.

'I don't think it's evil,' Anita continued. 'I didn't feel threatened, just very confused, like now. If it wanted to hurt me, it would have, wouldn't it?'

'Does this presence communicate with you?' Noah inquired, trying to help Anita in any way he could. He hoped that his past experiences might be of some use. Unfortunately, Anita didn't see any spirit or God taking human form. She was gradually coming to a long-awaited understanding. She was reclaiming more than just the memories of the past few weeks. Something was piercing through her unconscious mind. Back then, we had no idea what Time meant when referring to her 'being still in the picture'. Anita wasn't merely an unfortunate guest on our crazy journey. She had a ticket—a ticket purchased long before we had even met.

The sun had shifted across the square, breaking through the small surrounding buildings, and the heat began to intensify above our heads. People engaged in random conversations, and I could hear them commenting on the extraordinary weather we were experiencing. The glasses on the table glistened under the brilliant light, with water droplets forming on their sides, almost like sweat.

'Done! The waitress will take our food order when she brings our coffees,' John announced as he returned, interrupting our conversation. 'Isn't that Shannon?'

Across the square, Shannon emerged from a shoe shop, a few bags in hand. Her long blonde hair swayed as she walked, as if she were deliberately showing off. Her eyes caught John's gaze, prompting him to wave at her before Anita could signal for him to remain unseen. Having her join us, or even just sitting with us, would undermine the purpose of our meeting.

'If it isn't my favourite people!' she exclaimed, a high-pitched tone to her voice. 'Oh, John, did I tell you how stunning you are? We should take some pictures together and have a catchphrase like "Blondies besties".' Anita and I exchanged disapproving glances at her remark.

'How are you? In the mood for shopping, I see,' John quickly responded, concealing a shy smile.

'Yeah, I wasn't properly equipped for such a long summer! I had to go and find something new.' Shannon's eyes scanned the table, ensuring that we all heard her statement.

'Is Mark around?' I asked.

'Oh, no. He's at the pitch, playing football. These boys! Anita, Mark told me the guys were devastated after losing Patrick. The team doesn't feel the same, he says.'

She said it so casually, as if she were talking about a distant friend. Afraid that she was deliberately trying to provoke Anita, I swiftly changed the subject.

'Are you planning to go on holiday when the good weather is gone?'

'Yeah! We're going to Turkey in a few weeks! I forgot to mention it. Actually, I have to run and buy a few more things for our trip, so excuse me if I can't stay…'

And just like that, she glanced at her phone and bade us farewell, leaving behind the sparkle of her numerous flashy bracelets and an intense scent. Without much effort, we had avoided the risk of her joining us for breakfast. However, something didn't feel right. Even though we belonged to two different worlds, we let her go without resistance. The waitress arrived promptly with our coffees, her hands full, and started taking our orders. I reached across the table and quickly read Anita's piece of paper in silence. My ears tuned out their voices, which were now happily placing their food orders, and I could only hear my own thoughts as I read Anita's words.

'The long night is gone', I thought. *What does it mean? The darkness of her memories? Perhaps it means she can now remember. 'To awake', to awake who? Time? Us? 'Awake' like the Awoken Ones? What is this 'Cherish' everywhere? 'Cherish to call'? It doesn't make any sense.*

'Daniel!' John said firmly, bringing me back to the present. 'What do you want to order?'

'Oh, sorry!' I replied, embarrassed. 'Yes, I'll have what you're having.'

'It doesn't make sense, does it?' Anita asked, retrieving her notes. I thought we were keeping this last part from John, but I must have been mistaken.

'I have some ideas, but overall, I don't know what you meant,' I admitted.

'What is it?' John was catching up.

'It's something I wrote...let's say, in a moment of distraction. I wrote a few lines down, but now I don't know what I was thinking.'

'Can I see it?' John asked. After a couple of minutes of pure silence, he said, 'Looks like a nice way to say what has happened to the three of you, at least most of it.'

'What do you mean?' It seemed strange to me that John would find the solution to that rebus before we did.

'To protect, to rescue. Isn't that what you have done? Did you not rescue this...Time?'

'What about the rest? All that cherish...' Anita was glad he could shed some light on the matter.

'Yeah, this part is a bit weird. It does feel like a name more than a verb, don't you think?'

'A name?' Noah and I said, both at the same time. It was unwanted, but we were uncomfortably showing John how close our minds were.

'Yes. Cherish and call...Cherish and be. Two verbs together, twice? Makes more sense if Cherish was a name, right?'

His unexpected ability to navigate the matter had left us in silence long enough for the food to arrive. The meal was met with a renewed will to talk, to talk about the things we wanted to discuss. Putting aside Anita's notes for a while, our conversation returned to the main plan. We had to find

Noah's artefact, understand who these Awoken Ones were and how to avoid them at all costs, and, most importantly, find a clue in Siobhan's journal that would put us on the right track.

'I still believe we need to intend it physically, not metaphorically!' Anita repeated. She was sure Siobhan had literally buried the artefact at the house by the lake, and that was what she meant by saying 'leaving it behind'.

'OK, let's say my mother hid the artefact there. What are the chances it is still there? What are the chances the Harpies haven't found it yet?'

'How would they know?' John asked.

'I think they do. I think they can sense it…' I said, capturing everybody's attention. 'Remember when I told you about my grandma receiving a visit from a strange man? I wasn't there, I hadn't been there for a long time! But they were still after her. What if they were actually after the artefact she had kept hidden away?'

'You are saying they knew it was there and were trying to get it?' Anita asked. 'Why not force her to give it to them?'

'Because they couldn't. The Praetorians are immune to their power, aren't they?' Noah said, repeating the words I had said previously.

'That's what we thought…but we are not completely sure of it…' Anita concluded.

'Why would they be after a thing when they are also after you?' John was asking all the right questions. After biting into a crusty piece of bread, he continued, 'What does this thing…this artefact have that you don't? Either you have the power or it has it, right?'

'From what we know so far, it looks like whatever these two need to do…to be…requires these artefacts.' Anita mimicked John's gesture, putting a large piece of toast in her mouth. Her face showed pure satisfaction from tasting good food.

'Hey…' I exclaimed. 'These two! You're talking about your friends!' And without realizing it, I had legitimized Noah's status in their newly formed relationship.

By the time we had finished lunch, the late morning had given way to a more chilling afternoon. The sun had shifted, hidden behind the square buildings, and a sense of lateness had settled upon us. Being the first to stand up, I had given the hint that we would be better off somewhere else, indoors. Right as we walked out of the coffee shop, Anita said:

'Hold it!' Her hands reached my and John's arms, stopping our walk. 'Look at the very end, down the road. Can you see them?'

'See whom?' I asked. There were a few people walking up and down the street, but nothing unusual.

'There, at the corner. By the McMahon shop. Can you see them?' Her voice went lower, like a whisper.

'What are we supposed to see?' Noah came closer, trying to understand what we were all looking at.

'There are two dark shadows, wobbling. They are right there, can you see?' She was talking without moving her mouth or body, as if we had been detected and were trying to be invisible again.

'The two men over there? What's wrong with them?' John asked. It was like Anita was seeing beyond our natural, usual world.

'Yes!' She continued. 'Just behind them. Move your head slowly. You can see it, like smoke moving from place to place.'

'What the hell!' Noah had finally seen it, while John and I were still trying to grasp that mystery.

'It's almost imperceptible… What is it? Is it them?' I asked, after finally capturing those dark shadows.

'It's not good. We should leave now. Let's go to my place,' Anita said, her feet already turned the other way.

Although imperceptible at first, it had become clear that more than simple humans were walking those busy streets. Like unwanted parasites latched on to people's bodies, something similar to the one who had attacked me and John at the house was now following our steps closely. In the large, safe heart of our town, we were being followed, in plain sight. Our lives were theirs to watch, to stalk as they pleased. It was then we truly realized we hadn't started running for the first time in Runae. We had been running all our lives, and we were still running—wanted criminals looking for a safe spot in a never-ending hunt.

Chapter Seven

The Gifter

∞

In the rush of the moment, and with the two men right in our way to my car, we hopped into Anita's vehicle without even thinking. Her car was too small for four, and it squeaked a little as we settled in. In answer to our prayers, it finally started after several attempts, accompanied by a loud sound bursting from its back.

'What is happening? Who were those people?' John, seemingly the only one who had yet to receive the gift of sight, asked.

'It looked like the thing that came after us in the house, just before it turned violent,' I answered, holding on to the side window as Anita sped through town.

'I didn't see anything. The other night I did, though,' John continued, still puzzled.

'Maybe they can hide themselves from being seen by us when they want?' Anita suggested, persistently looking at the rear-view mirror as if they could magically fly after us.

'That's pretty selective. You just saw them!' Noah replied, sitting in the passenger seat, his head turned towards me and John. 'He did, the other night. Are we sure that's them?'

'We left the house keys in the car!' John exclaimed.

'It's OK; we're going to my place,' Anita reassured us.

'But if they know we are all here, they know nobody is at the house. Weren't they looking for that box you have?' John's words struck us out of nowhere.

'Right! Let's go!' Anita and I replied simultaneously, our eyes meeting in the small mirror.

The recalculation of the fastest route was a quick, loud agreement. We had to go all the way back into town, cross it, and then head home. That wasn't feasible. Cutting through the motorway felt like the obvious choice, so we went as fast as that busy, tired car could go, our fear mounting.

'Are we worrying for nothing? Maybe those beings thought we had it with us. Otherwise, why follow us?' Noah said at some point.

Our fabrications rose and faded like dunes in a stormy desert. One moment we felt we had the answers, the next we doubted the very core of our certainties. But we didn't have to wait any longer. Once we arrived at the house, we left the car on the road and rushed to the far gates, only to be greeted by an evil welcome committee at the front door. The four of us stood still, in shock. The two stalkers had multiplied, with copies of copies moving in unison, their eyes fixed on us, as if they could smell us from far away, their dark hearts tuned to ours.

'Who are these people?' John asked, petrified.

'There are so many! Where did they come from?' Noah added.

Long, grey cloaks danced with their movements, their colour matching their horrifying long faces. Their eyes were too small to be seen, with heavy shadows at their bottom, turning them into large caves, empty of spirit and light. With their arms and hands exposed, their skin had lost its colour, turning from pink to old silver, covered in ashy spots.

'We are too late,' I exclaimed. 'There is no way we can face them all!'

'Look at their faces. It's like staring at death itself!' Anita added.

'They seem normal to me,' John replied, surprising us. 'I mean, they look odd, like they just came out of an old black-and-white movie. But they are human, aren't they?'

It was as if their magic could travel for miles, casting its spell on anyone in its path. John couldn't see their true identity. To him, they were carbon copies of Lëogan, extravagant pawns that could trick him into believing they were just like us.

'What do we do?' Anita asked.

'We have to go in. What else can we do?' Noah replied, his fear succumbing to his strong will.

'No!' Anita exclaimed in a loud whisper.

'I'm afraid there is no other way. Those other two are here. Look beside your car!' I said, defeated.

They had caught up with us quickly. The news of Lëogan's death must have travelled to every corner of the planet, bringing their army to our doorstep. We had no time to run, and Time was not by our side. There wasn't much we could do but face our fear, our enemies, and lay our hands on my artefact. As they moved as one, like puppets manipulated by the same will, we found ourselves surrounded, just a few feet away from our home, our Daisy, my shell. Their voices sounded like an old tale, with words that held no meaning, repeating the same sentence over and over again. Their hands held together in a gesture of praying, their sacrilegious enchanting was turning the space dark, like clouds had come to give them strength. Different in sizes, some very tall, some quite short, they had arms disproportionally long. Then, in the depths of my mind, it came to me.

'The cloak! It came to rescue us before. It might do it again…'

'Are you sure? What is it waiting for, then? Are you supposed to summon it?' Anita asked, panicking.

'Can it protect all of us? We are four, and there's only one cloak,' John added.

'There is only one thing we can try,' I said, looking at Noah. 'Give me your hand!'

Compelled by the great risk we faced, none of us thought about John, who was about to witness how close and powerful Noah and I could be. So we held hands, forming a circle open only to us.

'What are we supposed to do?' Noah whispered, his head close to mine.

'Think about a warm, shiny, protective cloak landing on our shoulders. And now, close your eyes.'

As the wicked group closed in, their monstrous hands reaching out, we could feel the cold, oppressive power closing in on us. It was an anticipation of something greater, something we had already experienced the night before when Time had come to save us.

'It's not working!' Noah shouted while a powerful pressurizing sound hit our ears, and our throats felt like they were stabbed by invisible thorns.

'Cherish to protect, Cherish to call...' Anita whispered behind us, her voice barely reaching our ears. Her eyes had gone dead, a grey shadow falling over her pupils. Whatever magic the wicked army had brought on us, it seemed like it was attacking her first.

'*Hold on!*' a voice shouted out of nowhere.

A bright light appeared in front of us, amidst the evil gathering, flickering. A blurry face shifted from a mysterious plane to ours, going back and forth like a message on repeat from a faraway land. As both warring parties remained still, the face whispered to the thin air:

'Go, get them all! Go fast!'

Before we could even realize it, the white cloak burst out of the house, smashing through the sitting room window and shattering it into pieces. The moment it reached us, a vacuum of light sucked us into nothingness, leaving an empty space amidst tens of angry faces, once again defeated.

''Where are we?' I asked. Around us, there was nothing but darkness and emptiness. My voice echoed back multiple times from invisible walls. We were standing in pure nothingness, unsure if our feet were touching the ground or the skies. As far as we knew, there was no up or down, left or right.

'Is it them? Is this their doing?' John added.

'I'm not sure,' I replied.

The cloak magically appeared from a far end that had no space or direction. It came to us in a blink, carrying the things we cared about the most: Daisy and my grandmother's box. That was a sign that we had been rescued, not attacked. John's eyes shimmered at the sight of his little girl, and a smile filled his face completely.

'I'm sorry,' someone said. 'There was no other way. I'm not strong enough to do much more, but I could not stay put and watch any longer.'

A figure of a woman appeared just beside us. Her body shifted a few inches on each side, as if she wasn't really there, a pure projection from a long distance. Her face was partially covered by a white embroidered veil, her golden eyes clearing the blurry shape, and her skin was as dark as her long hair. A strong, sweet scent wafted through the empty nothingness.

'Who are you?' Noah asked.

'I'm the Gifter,' she replied.

'The Gifter? What does that mean?' Noah asked again.

'I have met you before, haven't I?' I asked before she could answer his question. 'You…feel familiar.'

'I'm the Gift protector. I've been for many…many years. I've been with you all your life, in yours and his. The two of you were one to me, but I had to take form for one or the other. So, every generation, I've chosen one over the other. This last one, it was the both of you, Daniel, Noah.'

Her tone was calm; she spoke as if she were praying after a long, suffering watch—a story she had been telling the worlds before us. Her body wobbled through physical realities, taking form and then losing it quickly.

'You are a Praetorian?' Noah added to his list of questions.

'You were my grandmother…you are…aren't you? Grandma?' I said, almost certain. Her spirit was Grandma's, her voice was different, but her pure essence was hers.

'I was, for a while. When you were given to her, I had to leave Noah to come to you. Your first years were more dangerous. A risk, I'm afraid, that never went away,' she replied.

'What about me? I've seen my mother's journal. She was constantly attacked by those evil people…'

'I was with her, at the beginning, before Daniel was moved away, before the other Gifter, the one who should have protected him, fell in the abyss. Your mother knew me as Dõron. I was with her for a while, and I had been watching you and her even when I had taken place with Daniel's grandma. Don't be upset,' she quickly added, seeing Noah's face turning sad. 'You were both watched closely by me, but Daniel needed more care. He was too close to one of the most powerful Harpies for many years. Your mother, on the other hand, was strong, almost unbeatable.'

'Where are we, right now? How is it that you came out only now?' Noah asked, his words still showing some resentment.

'We are in between here and there. What is left of me is hanging on a memory. I am what is left of my own will. I'm afraid I could only do this much, carry you to your next step. And for that, there is no way in but one place, the Bridge. You know it, you have been there before. You call it by your own name...'

'A way into where?' I knew there was something peculiar about Noah's Bridge, but I didn't know much about it.

'A way to the past. These are not today's words. We cannot discuss it any further...for now.' Her voice was still soft, but a sort of authority had infiltrated her tone.

'Why now?' Noah hadn't forgot his question.

'I wasn't going to...my spirit is almost gone, but another Awoken One was reaching the surface, and she is not ready for it. I had to stop Cherish from revealing herself.'

That name was coming up again. *She was an Awoken One and against us? What Anita dreamt and written was a warning, not a help?* We were all thinking.

'So, she is not on our side!' Anita finally spoke.

'Oh, dear… She is…' And a smile appeared on her insubstantial face.

'But my mother calls the Harpies the Awoken Ones?' Noah immediately interrupted her.

'We all are. We are all Awoken Ones. We come when we are needed. Some of us for the good, many of them for the bad… Many, many generations ago, we were equal in numbers, and our strengths were evenly matched. For one of them, there was one of us. Then the Gods failed to come back, attempt after attempt. Thirty years is too long of a wait, and many thirties have gone by with too many failures. So, some of us have faded away, some have lost the battle, some…have joined them.'

'How many of you…of the good ones are left?' John finally joined the conversation, fully engaged.

'Too few to fail again, I'm afraid. I'm close to my end. Cherish has gone to sleep to save her energy, but she is coming back, you can feel it, can't you? There are a few more, but this is all we have.'

'So, it was you and the others who came to me all those years?' Noah finally put all the pieces together.

'I have been there, but the ones you mention did not come and visit. They simply could not. They were talking to you through your memories, through the shared power you possess, through the same spirit you are made of. Those were the Gods.'

'We freed Time…' I said, seemingly out of nowhere, as good news was strongly needed to counterbalance her statement.

'I know, and I'm sorry I could not come and help in your recent struggles. But I knew I had to come back now. In all the pages of the past, this is the only one that carries the opportunity, and that must mean something, right?' She smiled again. 'Now, I can't keep you in here much longer. You know your way. You must act now! Iris is still watching the spot. She will be there, waiting for you.'

Before we could ask any more questions or hold on to her a bit longer, we were gone. The empty space dissolved quickly, filled with hills, trees, and a familiar, vast, shiny lake. We were back in our reality, far away from home—our home—but closer to someone else's. A place Anita and I had learned to know several weeks prior.

'This place looks familiar…' Anita said, almost immediately.

'It does indeed!' A smile appeared on Noah's face.

'What? Where are we? Where is the house? Where is she?'

We had completely forgot that it was John's first time travelling through space. Although inexplicable and magical, we had become accustomed to it and had left John behind for a solo experience. His arms were still holding Daisy firmly, the cloak on his shoulders—my treasure to protect. Somehow, that gift was doing the work for me, too distracted by our mission, the recent revelation, and the pressing next steps.

As if we had travelled through time and space, we were transported to a place we had visited before. Everything looked like a flashback, with some new added touches. There were no cars parked on the side of the road, and it wasn't just Anita and me any more. But the lake downhill on our right, the many trees multiplying on our left, everything else was exactly like the day we had reached Noah's Bridge.

My eyes gazed in the space around, and the glittering surface of the lake captured my attention. *How close were we the first time?* I thought. *Is this a way of telling us that we failed the first time around? Did we fail to see, touch, and do all the things we were destined to do?* Once again, our conversation about being prevented from going to Connemara three years prior came back to my mind. *Were we pushed to fulfil a destiny we had been fighting against? Or is it the other way around?*

Somehow, I knew we had been held hostage by someone else's will. We were not meant to do all the things we were meant to do before the time was right. Somehow, I felt in my heart the ticking of time. That was the right moment. All of us together, Time on our side, and the ones I loved close to me. There was no other way but to accept this pressing truth: I was not meant to answer that call before my time, and that moment had finally arrived.

Chapter Eight
A Buried Past

∞

So, she was the real Praetorian, taking shape through your mother and your grandmother,' Anita said, still actively working to put everything together.

'She said she could not come and help before now. I don't think she is the one who gave me the cloak, to protect us from them,' I added. 'There is someone else we don't know of, someone who left it there after one of the Harpies had visited the house, that night.'

'So that's what it was?' John chimed in. 'I doubt a chair at the front door would have improved our security system!'

'Why are we back here? I mean, I can't complain about the quick lift home, but why here?' Noah was already walking his way up the hills, where we had met for the first time. For a moment, it felt like years had passed since then.

'How far is the lake house?' Anita asked. 'I'd say we are here to get the heart. I know now we were on the right track!'

'It's ten minutes driving, on the border to Mayo.'

'We lost both cars, how are we getting there?' In the space of a few hours, we had left behind both our vehicles, and I didn't want to think about what else we would need but had left aside.

'Let's go. I can borrow one!' Noah replied.

We had moved across the country in the space of a few minutes, but none of us were thinking about how that was affecting John. He was part of the pack now, and everything that had preceded was, for us, a given fact. On our walk up the hill and down to the other side, John kept his distance, his mind trying to process the events as best he could. Daisy was all he could keep close, in his arms, listening to our conjectures.

'Can we assume they were all in Castlecross? Just to know if we need to watch our backs still,' Anita continued.

'Hard to say. We don't know how many are there,' I said.

'We don't know if they can teleport too,' Noah added, turning right at the down slope where we confessed our troubled thoughts and feelings only a few weeks prior.

'I don't understand how they could find us,' Anita said, following Noah closely, her eyes pointed at me. 'There must be a way for them to trace our steps.'

'It feels incredible how we were here only recently, you and I, in between these trees, before Runae…before all of this,' I let go, almost certain John was too far to hear.

'I'm starting to think this was all meant to happen,' Anita went on, holding her pace. 'I mean, we know you were destined to meet, but I mean *everything!* This place, our plans, you and me, you and John even…perhaps.' It was like she was also trying to keep him in the big picture, forcing a scenario that in John's mind was highly unlikely.

'You mean we are just following a script? A sort of bigger plan?' I asked, looking back at John and Daisy, who had now joined us. Anita's words were echoing my thoughts.

'It feels claustrophobic,' Noah added. His hunger for freedom was being put to the test.

'Think about it!' Anita continued. 'She said they have been trying, you have been trying to come back many times… Every thirty years, she said?'

'What happened to you every time?' John asked. 'I mean, if this is sort of a loop, you have never passed thirty. What happens then? If it just fails, you grow old and that's all?' I wasn't sure if he meant we could take that easy road and get back to our lives or if he was worried about our imminent future.

'Remember those records I dug up about Noah and this place?' Anita replied. 'I'd say it's safe to assume you just…disappeared from history, to then reappear as a child.'

John's face showed obvious worry; although the idea of dying, disappearing, was traumatic for me, I had the time to process that truth at every step, every revelation. The chances of being killed, erased from existence, were mounting since the moment we had stepped in Runae, and a common theme, a strange idea, had started to infiltrate my mind. *If we were meant to be brought back, if we were Love, how can we be two instead of one?*

'How do you just reappear as a child? I mean,' John added as we resumed our walk, 'who gets to find you? How did you end up in your family? Both you and Noah…'

'I had several visions in these past weeks, especially before Runae. In all of them, there is someone who is watching us, someone who passes the burden on to someone else. That's how I got to be in Italy. At least, that's what I got from those blurry pieces.'

'Is there a way you could trigger it again?' Anita asked.

'You mean to know more? I don't really know how it works still. My visions seem to have stopped…'

'Here we are. Let's cross the bridge. I'll ask Niamh if I can borrow her car,' Noah said as we walked to the other side of the river.

Noah disappeared behind a corner, not too far from the inn in which Anita and I had stayed during our visit to Noah's Bridge. Funny enough, I didn't think about the mysterious Elaine whom we never met. Whether she was real or not wasn't important. I had forgot how simple my thinking was before everything. Waiting for him to come back, we moved two blocks away and sat by the bus stop, on the same bench where Noah and I had talked for a while, our hearts beating as one in a discovery path that had ironically brought me and John to the same place. If someone was writing my story, my present and future, they had to have a very sarcastic sense of humour.

'Is it always you?' John asked after several minutes of silence. It was like we had gone on a solo trip, caught up in our own digging.

'What do you mean?'

'Is it always you…you? Or every time you are someone else? Every time you come back…' he added.

'I don't know. From what I can guess, maybe not. If we did come back, if we do come back every time, we might be different people.'

'How do you explain Noah's Bridge then?' Anita left her thoughts behind, hooked by a new hint. 'If this place has his name, it can't be a coincidence. Remember the pictures we saw at the inn? And all those pictures we saw at the festival, with the same man in it? This place and the bridge go back a long way. It's safe to assume Noah comes back always as Noah? And don't forget Noah's name was the one appearing in the old articles and newspapers.'

'This is why Siobhan had to stay here? Because Noah comes back here every time?' I continued, knowing where Anita was going with that.

'It would make sense, right?' Anita stopped talking again, her mind silently processing the consequences of those assumptions, her face pointed at the river, her eyes travelling miles away.

'How are we going back home, after all this?' John asked.

It felt like a throwback when we had gone to Runae and Anita was desperately asking to go back home. It was impossible then, and it felt impossible now. All I could do was look at him right into his beautiful eyes and smile. A smile of defeat and disappointment. My arms instinctively reached him, and I hugged him and Daisy as that was the only way I could answer that difficult question. By the time Noah came back, the sky had darkened a little. Grey clouds were hanging over our heads, speeding up the arrival of the night, and the air smelled wet, like rain was on its way.

'I got us a car! It took me a while as I had to borrow it from someone who doesn't need to have it back immediately. I know where the place is, but I don't know how long we are going to be away for,' Noah said, pointing somewhere to the far left.

We promptly followed him around the block and to the end of a narrow street. An old, long car was parked on the side, in a lonely spot. *Whoever he has borrowed it from must be quite old,* I thought. The doors made a creaking sound like age had turned them stiff, but the inside was pristine, and a mix of naphthalene and lavender scent welcomed us in. From the back seats, large gardening tools popped up from the boot, and two small plants lay in the middle, waiting to be moved out in the open. The back screen was filled with stickers, some saying *Peace, it's a conquest, Our day will come, Beidh an lá linn.*

'We are heading northwest. The place is right before the border with County Mayo. It's getting dark but I'll remember the way.'

Noah settled into his seat and started the car while the rest of us were still wondering who the owner of that strange vehicle could be. Soon enough, we left the spacious roads for a bumpy, narrow one, causing us to shift and shake in sync with the wheels.

'I have to say, it's not very smart doing this at this time of the day,' Anita said, looking out the window by the passenger seat. Very little was visible, with trees blending into the darkness of the evening and a thin layer of fog rising from the ground.

'Don't worry, these country roads don't all look the same to me. I'm used to it,' Noah replied, smiling.

'I think I saw a banner over there saying *Best Music in County Mayo*. Did we pass our turn?' John asked.

'The border goes up and down these places. It's not strange to cross the border and be back in Galway a few times before leaving the county for good. We're nearly there. At the next crossroads, we turn right, then we go on foot,' Noah explained.

'On foot?' Anita and I exclaimed simultaneously.

'Yes. The road is too narrow over there. It's OK. The house is just a five-minute walk from there.'

As promised, we soon reached our destination. We parked the car on the side of a rustic farm road, right at the edge of a slope, which meant we had to exit from the left side. The air was extremely damp, frozen in time, turning the tall, large trees into rigid cardboards. There was complete silence—no passing cars, no nocturnal birds chirping to each other. We could almost hear our breaths echoing in the stillness. In front of us, a smaller road wound its way through the vegetation, its end hidden from sight.

'It's here,' Noah said. 'Just a few minutes that way.'

'This doesn't look very inviting,' I voiced my concerns.

We quickly increased the distance between ourselves and the car we had left behind. In my mind, I strongly considered the idea of going back to retrieve some of the tools from the trunk, just to be safe. As we got closer to our final destination, the soft sound of lapping waves reached our ears, a clear sign that the lake must be nearby. In the darkness of the night, we could have easily walked in any direction, maybe even back and forth, and not noticed the difference. But that sound served as our guiding star. We were heading to the right spot.

'This doesn't look right,' Noah suddenly said.

He stopped at the edge of a large field, with trees and bushes encircling a cluster of large and small stones in disarray, as if someone had hurriedly left them there. Some stones stood tall with pride and ruthless ambition, while others lay broken, collapsed under their own weight. In the centre of the stones, a space remained untouched, where an upside-down tree had been planted into the ground, its trunk protruding several feet above the rusty soil, and its roots wildly breaking the air around it. At the sight of this puzzling gathering of silent monoliths, we instinctively moved closer to each other, a shared sense of danger connecting our bodies. Before anyone could utter a word, Anita spoke up:

'I can't believe it! This is a stone circle! A Druid altar,' she said, carelessly leaving the pack and reaching out to touch the cold stone. 'This is unbelievable. Look at the cup and ring marks,' she added, pointing at circles faintly visible on the surfaces of some stones.

'Where is the bloody house?' Noah asked, ignoring her discovery. His hands were hanging in the air, his eyes enlarged by the shock.

'Anita, I don't think it's wise to get that close,' I said, my worries slipping through my lips.

'What are you talking about? These are…beautiful!' she replied, moving further away and walking around the inner circle.

'Where the hell is the house? It was here!' Noah's voice grew louder. 'It was always here…'

'Look at this tree. It was planted upside down, its top buried in the ground. I've heard of something like that before, but to see it…it's different,' Anita said, fully absorbed by the unusual discovery, as it touched the very core of her soul—her passion for uncovering, excavating, and connecting with the past.

There was nothing else there, nothing we were actually searching for. Noah's home had vanished from sight, leaving the three of us bewildered. As we followed Anita's trail of bravery, moving towards the ruins, whispers began to stir across the site, rustling through the trees and converging at the centre. It was barely perceptible at first; John and I caught the sound before the others, our eyes darting around, searching for clues. As the indistinct voices grew stronger, Anita and Noah turned back, their faces searching for ours, exchanging wordless, unanswered questions. We could easily be immersed into the depths of

Siobhan's stories, as if we had physically entered her journal, her long-gone past merging into our present.

'Who's there?' John shouted, his voice swallowed by the night.

'What's happening?' Noah asked, turning back to Anita, who stood frozen beside the dead tree.

'It's old Irish…very old,' she said, her face turned to the dark sky. 'It's Celtic… No, beyond that… It's like many versions of the same language.'

'You know that? How?' Noah replied, shocked.

'Move away, Anita, now!' I shouted from the far end of the circle.

'It's OK!' Her face appeared serene, almost happy. 'It's a good message. They're talking about a ceremony, a conjunction…between past and future, between death and life… It happened…it's not happening now.'

'What does she mean?' Noah asked, looking at me and John in confusion.

It was as if Anita held the key to the event, translating for those left untold, behind. John's petrified face was suddenly awakened by Daisy, who began barking loudly. In an instant, she jumped out of his arms, her paws planted on the ground, her snout facing Anita. Our little warrior was ready for a fight. Then, as if the air were made of thin, clear plastic, the space between us and Anita wobbled, like the surface of the sea bending against a thrown rock. Someone had joined the ritual of the dead.

'Don't worry… I'm here to lead you to it. I've been waiting for a very long time.'

A woman, covered with too much fabric, appeared out of nowhere, her feet above the ground. Her presence was intangible, but her voice was soft and clear. All other sounds ceased, and the enchanted chorus faded, leaving space for the one who knew.

'I'm Iris, the Messenger. I'm the link between here and there, between now and then. I hold the passage in custody, for the only one who can cross it…and you are finally here.'

'Dõron has told us about you,' I said, finally released from my initial fears. 'We were told to come and find you.'

'Good! Very good,' she replied. Although her face was completely covered by a large dark hood, we could sense her smiling. 'These places are not safe. Nowhere is, ever! But I can keep you here as long as we need you to be. From what I see, there is much you need to know, there is much…' she briefly turned to Anita, '…that hasn't come to light yet.'

'I'm Noah, this is Daniel, Anita, and John…oh, and Daisy,' Noah interjected. 'Where is my house? What happened to this place?'

'Your home is where it has always been, just not here, not now.'

'What does that mean?' I asked.

'Oh, you are in the right place, indeed, just in the wrong time. Come! Come closer to your lady friend. It's time to tell you all there is to know.'

With our worries gone with the thousand voices, we felt it was time to trust her, opening ourselves to another piece of the truth we all craved. As we reached the inner circle, right at the centre, we all took a seat on the broken but solid rocks scattered around the tree. The darkness of the night was challenged by a bright, small flame that appeared in Iris's hands and was placed amidst the myriad of roots of the ancient tree, casting suggestive shadows on the surroundings. The scene was set to take us on an incredible, evocative journey, a story to be revealed with the added drama of light and darkness engaged in a never-ending war.

'This is not your time… You are not in your days here. This is what it was long before you came to be as you are now, but after you became for the first time. This place was much more than it appears now. For a very, very long time, this was the only gateway, the node out of this world. It was also one of the few places where the conjuring ceremony almost took place and one of the many where it never did.'

'Like the island in Runae? The node to where?' Noah fearlessly interrupted.

'To the other protected worlds. And for the other Gods, it was the only way to enter Earth. My spell has hidden this place, almost constantly, since the war against the enemy, even after our protector took the node within himself.'

'The protector? Love?' I asked. 'What do you mean by taking it within himself?'

'It's a long story, and it belongs to a past you don't need to dive into hastily. There are much more important things you need to know first. But, to answer your questions, yes. It was Love who took the node after one of the Harpies managed to pass through it. To this day, I still don't know how it was possible, but, as a precautionary measure, Love took the node away from this place and carried it with him.'

'I have the feeling I know who that Harpy was…' And Noah looked at me and Anita, hoping we had reached the same conclusion.

'What are you?' John inquired.

'I'm an Awoken. A spirit of a dead God. My body has failed, but my soul, my magic, hasn't yet. I was resurrected, evoked, to fulfil a duty, as we all Awokens were. For every battle, there are armies pulled for the good and for the bad. The evil has lost once but has won many, many other times. With each victory, there are fewer of us and too many of them.'

'Who brought you back?' I asked, hoping it was OK to interrupt her once again.

'You did. Your spirit, your being,' she replied, leaving me and Noah in disbelief. 'Even broken, a heart still beats and loves the same. It's a force that cannot be stopped. It's Creation's curse and protection. You cannot die. So, even if you have never returned, your power has managed to generate us, to bring us into existence.'

'Where… *When* are we right now?' Anita asked.

'It's the thirty-first of October, fifty BC…more or less.'

'How did this happen? How is it possible?' John asked, certain that was a lie.

'It's Halloween,' Anita said, almost speaking to herself.

'That's your first thought?' John replied.

'No, think about it. Samhain, known today as Halloween, is the night when the dead and the living come together, the past and the present… Right?' She looked back at our gentle host.

'You're not too far off. That's how the myth came to be, yes. This was the last and only night when the ceremony took place, nearly succeeding…' For a brief moment, her face turned sad.

'How are we going to go back to our time?' I asked.

'You never left. This is the only place that still has a link between then and now, and as the gatekeeper, I can move back and forth.'

'Another gatekeeper! Like the Aqualymph…' Noah said, looking again at me and Anita.

'This is where the heart has been waiting, for many years now. Noah's mother was *pushed* to think that this was the best place to hide it. And indeed, it worked. No others could find it because it wasn't there in their time, but only now, with me. Many Harpies have come and gone, sensing the heart, feeling its presence, but they could not find it.'

'You told my mother to hide it?' Noah was in disbelief.

'I did indeed. Try to understand. You were long gone and just reborn. Our strengths were so low… I could not do much more than manifest through visions and whispers. My focus was to keep this moment frozen in time for eternity. I had to save all my magic for this one duty. But with time, Siobhan understood she had to do it. Night after night, she would come into the woods, at the back of the house, responding to my call. Without her knowing, she was almost stepping in and out of time every time.'

'Oh my God…' John's fears were multiplying. The more he believed in my whole truth, the more he feared it.

'So you tricked her into leaving the artefact behind. Why?' I asked, trying to understand how she could separate the heart from Noah.

'In human eyes, yes, I suppose that is what I did. But for Love's sake, that's what needed to be done. The Harpies were after her, after the little child. The Gifter was gone far away, by Daniel's side. It was the only thing I could do. As I had told my God centuries and centuries before, the key to our victory was to hide. Hide the key, hide the node…'

'Where is it now? Where is my artefact?' Noah asked, looking straight at that strange being.

'It's in the tree, isn't it?' Anita asked.

'You can see it, can't you?' Iris smiled at her.

'It's in the very centre of the foliage, underground, as if the tree was standing up in an upside-down reality,' Anita continued.

'How do you know these things? How can you see it?' I was puzzled. Although we were the rightful owners of the artefact, we were prevented from sensing it, seeing it.

'Because she is the one who sees. The truth seeker, the protector of memory. She has been the most loved one above us all. In return, she has spent millennia and her power to protect him, to safeguard the memory of him. She is the one who can see beyond history, the overlays. It's Cherish's duty, it's Cherish's destiny.'

Chapter Nine
A Failure on Repeat

∞

The silence burst the invisible doors of our imagination wide open. We had learned to be surprised by the unbelievable truth around me and Noah, but knowing that others were secretly, unknowingly dancing our same dance was beyond our reach. My mind was split in two. A part of me could not tolerate any other revelation of secrets that could prove my life, our lives, had been manipulated since the beginning of time. But on the other hand, knowing that Anita was with me in this difficult journey because she was destined to be—and not because of me—filled my heart with relief. We were equal in this search for the truth; we were really in it together.

'This can't be…I'm sorry, this can't be,' Anita said, after collecting her thoughts. Her face switched rapidly from shock to refusal, to an almost funny denial. 'I'm not. I simply am not. This doesn't make any sense. I fell for…that one, what was his name…the Snake! I couldn't see through his lies. I couldn't see that the place we had been together was fake, an illusion,' she added, looking at me.

It was as if she were afraid of hurting me somehow. Her mind was going in every direction. Anita didn't want to think she had the chance to help me, but all that time, she didn't know how. She didn't want to take the spotlight, to become more than she was ready to be: a friend, a support. Her head was moving in a loud, silent 'no', a resounding denial.

'You are still you, my dear,' Iris continued.

Finally, Iris's hood was pulled down, revealing an unexpected appearance. Half of her face was tight, young, and sharp, while the other was almost deformed, wrinkled from too many journeys back in time. Her left eye was dead, almost missing, increasing the shocking discrepancy with the other one, which was golden and bright. Some of us showed horror on our faces, but Iris gently ignored it, continuing her story.

'Cherish went quiet many, many generations ago. Her spirit was weak, like us, victims of too many failed attempts. She is not awake just yet, but I can feel her, I can feel you. You are not too far from awakening again. But let's take some time before getting back to this. What is important here is the full picture. You, Love, have tried to come back many, many times. The only way to bring back the God is through a spell ceremony, a conjuring of powers. Three, to be exact. Three, like the Gods that we know of…'

'Three? If Love needs three…Time, Soul…' I said, remembering Time's story.

'Unfortunately, this is where our story has failed us. We never managed to get any of the others. Now, there is a story around this time, fifty BC. This was actually when both halves of the God were here, standing where you stand. Two beautiful Human creatures were ready to let Love finally manifest. But we had no other Gods on our side. They were never freed. It was only us against the evil. We had not yet learned…it was indispensable to have them, to cast the spell. On the other hand, Nothing's disciples were too powerful to overcome. The dark blade had reached you from the south. Armies of soldiers, under a wicked spell, were moved to these far lands to conquer, to destroy. It wasn't what history told you. It wasn't the great empire. It was *them!* The evil was whispering in their ears, pushing them to eradicate us, the ones who could still protect you, prepare you, start the rite.'

We were completely captivated by her tale. Her words, her tone, were passionate and personal. Her visions were still vivid in her head, nearly projecting from her golden eye to our minds.

'Even with their diabolic attempts to eradicate it from history, few elements of the ceremony have survived in the legends, transformed into vain customs to dissipate the real reason why it happened.'

'Was that the last time you tried?' Noah asked.

'Two thousand years ago, yes. That's the only time we came close to it. In the centuries ahead, Love has never come any closer. Most of the time, the two halves haven't even met, and with the ages, memories started to fade, the truth was watered down. Cherish went to sleep, and so did most of the Awoken Ones. This is the first time, since then, that I've actually seen you together. This means a lot. This means the chance is high, but so is the danger of failing again.'

'So, in all this time, you…all of you have come back over and over to make this happen. To make it possible for us to meet again?' I asked.

'What changed? This time, I mean, how was it possible?' Noah added.

'A few events have differed this time. First of all, the extinguishing of Daniel's long-time protector…Oriohn's energy was exhausted after he was born, allowing Daniel to get lost in the world. One night, as his Praetorian was sealing the sea, he fell ill. Not simply with a Human sickness. His spirit, Oriohn's spirit, had fallen too. A strong, kind man found him lost in the dark waters and rescued him. But it was too late; we could not save them both, Oriohn and Daniel. So Dõron, Noah's true protector, entrusted the old, kind man with Daniel's life. Swearing to protect him, he moved the little child somewhere else. The evil had lost his trace for a good while. However, a sick joke, an unexpected coincidence, happened: an evil Harpy had come to be extremely close to Daniel. Her name is Athymos, the evil Awoken who better represents the opposite of what Daniel truly is. Her inability to feel any feeling for anyone prevented her from realizing what an amazing opportunity she had, right in her hands. Her power to subjugate emotions spread over Daniel's young soul, making him undetectable. Somehow, her power hid his, back then weak, flickering signal. Daniel had been out of the evil's sight until the day he moved away from her. And slowly, it regained strength, especially since the day he came to you, Noah. The day he walked on Noah's Bridge, that's when the Harpies knew. That's when their will became stronger.'

'This means they didn't prevent me from going the first time,' I said out loud, looking at Anita. Our conjectures around that part felt wrong.

'It wasn't them. It was us,' she replied, surprising me. 'It was Rita-Louise's choice. Her mind, her soul, and Dõron's had been together for a long time, so when the time came, when your heart was pulling you close to Noah, they stopped you. It couldn't have happened before the time. It was too early, and you would have been seen by the evil with no power to fight them back. The spell had to be cast after the Gods were liberated.'

'What happened?' I asked, almost predicting her answer.

'Your grandma sacrificed herself to Dõron. She gave herself to her, her body and her mind, to pull you back, to deviate your path for a little while, to give your protector that final spark she needed. Those last three years, Dõron has consumed what is left of her own energy. She is almost gone. If we fail this time, I'm afraid there won't be a Praetorian any more.'

That version of the story was much worse than I had built in my mind. Thinking someone evil had cursed grandma felt different. It was a different kind of pain. Now I had learned she had given herself for me. How strong her love for me must have been? How stronger than I ever knew? John came closer to me, once again to be by my side, understanding how deeply that truth would affect me.

'And then you met me,' he said, nearly whispering in my ear, his arm around me.

I felt his warmth, his attempt to be with me in the moment, but I had wronged him right there, my eyes fixed upon Noah's, my thoughts tethered with his. I wasn't running away from my feelings for John to run with my other half, but my heart was growing duller to what I used to feel, to who I used to be.

'You, John, were our chance to wait. Daniel's love for you was of a different kind. We didn't push for it, we never planned it. If there is something we couldn't do, it was to make Love be any different than what he is. That was Daniel's path only. His will and pure instinct,' Iris said, making me feel instantly worse. Her honest illustration of what John and I had was a strike to my heart.

'Are you all manifestations of Love?' Anita asked, clearly pushing away any connection between them and her.

'Exactly. Love is true. Love is protection. Love doesn't forget, it makes things immortal, creates, pushes, connects.'

'Now that Time is free, Soul is our next move. That's finally clear,' I blurted out, almost as if I hadn't listened to what she had just said.

'So, we are here only to get the heart back. Not to bring back Love, yet,' Noah added.

'What are these artefacts meant to do?' Anita asked. 'I mean, what happens when we get them both?'

'Without them, we can't bring him back. Without them, we can't bring anyone back,' Iris answered. 'Now, you will leave this time to come back to yours. Once there, the house will be back. The heart is buried right by this tree, which, of course, will be right up. I'll keep the pathway open as long as you need, but once you have it, you are alone. You are exposed. Try to understand. The heart will be in your time and their time. They will try to take it away from you, the heart and the shell. Whatever you do next, you must do it quickly!'

'I think we need to get to Time! That should be our next move,' Anita said, almost projecting her feet into our next run.

'Before you go, two things!' Iris interrupted. 'Anita, your journey has just begun. I know it's difficult for you, but believe me, you will understand, in your own terms. Please, don't ever leave them behind! Also, my sincere apologies. This window of ancient time opens with some…side effects. It opens and closes always on the same day.'

'What does that mean? We won't be able to see you for another year?' Noah asked.

'No. As long my spirit lives, this place will always be here, anytime. But once it opens, it opens on October thirty-first, and it closes on the same thirty-first. This is the exact date you will be back, in your time.'

'What?' John exclaimed. 'We just lost more than two months in these last twenty minutes?'

'Precisely. Again, apologies. Now, come close to the tree. You will see this place turned upside down in a blink. Mind your feet!'

We quickly gathered together by the large roots. In the snap of her fingers, Iris disappeared from sight, and the place brightened with a cold, late afternoon light. The lake house appeared behind us, and a large, colourful tree stood right in front of us.

'There is no way they won't fire me this time...' That was the first thing slipping through my lips, almost clinging to the idea that there was going to be a journey back.

'You mean it's for real? It's nearly November... Look at the trees...' John said, his eyes roaming around, looking at the multitude of yellow, red, and brown leaves now dead on the old grass.

'The heart is there. I can see it through the soil...barely buried,' Anita pointed out, gesturing to a gap between the roots of the tree. We were caught by surprise again. Whatever was happening to Anita, it was going fast.

Noah, already with his hands on the ground, moved away the thin layer of soil covering a squared box. Inside, tired from the long wait, the heart was pulsing, eager to meet its owner again. All eyes were fixed on the new discovery, waiting to see what incredible magic it would unleash. My body started to feel strangely drawn to it, my skin moving my muscles and bones as if it had magnetized me, pulling the invisible strings I was entangled with since the day I was born. Noah lifted the small square from the ground, bringing it close to his chest. His quest felt nearly over, accomplished. With his face glowing with a strange light, he turned around to the three of us, looking directly at me.

'We made it,' he said.

'I feel strange,' I replied, exchanging a private look with him, as if he was the only one left around.

'Is it in there? Should you open it?' John asked, the only one among us unable to perceive the presence of the magical artefact.

'It's there, alright,' I said, smiling.

It was as if I had found purpose in life once again. An unnatural joy possessed my body and soul, and Noah, too, walked a few steps towards me, his head down to his hands, ready to unveil our common secret to the world.

'I think it's safe if you keep it in there, for now. I'm afraid its presence has been felt by many, other than us,' Anita promptly said, her right hand on the cover of the box, preventing Noah from opening it. 'Why don't we do it after meeting Time?'

'You might be right,' he replied, his heart still reluctant to follow her suggestion. 'Let's get in the house first. Then we will leave this place at once!'

He walked around the house, heading towards the front door, before we could even ask him to postpone that visit to a more opportune time. After all, Iris had said we were supposed to move fast once the heart was taken from its protected spot. Nevertheless, we followed him to the other side of his old home. The walls were made of grey stone, as if the old times had seeped into the pure soul of that house.

Its roof sagged, tired from too much rain, and all the tiny wooden windows almost pushed the narrow space to its limit, widened by the water they had drunk over the years. The front door was as brown as the soil surrounding the place, with a carved symbol of three circles, one inside the other, adorning the top centre.

'Look at this,' Anita said, pointing at it. 'Not a coincidence. It's the same symbol I saw on the stones.'

'Here, this door doesn't lock,' Noah added, opening it and walking in.

The last time he had been there, when he was still with his family, must have been a long time ago. A strong smell of wet grass welcomed us inside. The weak afternoon light was too dim to guide us, so Noah turned on the lights, exclaiming, 'Oh, I wasn't expecting them to work!'

'Was it then…the time your mother speaks of in her journal, the last time you were here?' Anita asked, her hands skimming across the few pieces of furniture, displacing the old dust from its rightful place.

'I've been here since then, but not since my mother passed away,' he replied, moving to the further end of the large room we had entered, disappearing around a partition wall that stood in our way to a tiny kitchen.

'I have to say, if it wasn't for the situation, this would be a beautiful place to spend the holidays!' John said, his hand on the staircase rail leading up to the second floor.

'I have always wanted to be in a place like this, maybe around Christmas.. Lighting the fire, a book to read, Daisy asleep on an old couch…you know?' I replied to him.

We were in Noah's home, his family home, but I pictured myself in it without him, with John and Daisy by my side. My heart and mind constantly swung between the life I had and wanted, and the life I was destined to live. The pain of feeling wrong in either situation grew little by little, insinuating itself into all the small things I had never thought of.

'The place was hidden, the ground, everywhere, but not this…not this house,' Anita said suddenly, her hand on a picture frame on the east wall. 'Except for today, Iris must have left this house out of her magic. The Harpies were here… They have been here, many times… I can feel it.'

'How does it work?' I asked, finally ready to explore that reality we were thrust into a few minutes prior. 'You see it? Is it a sensation?'

'I can't explain it. It happens randomly. I can feel it in the air, on some things. Things they touched,' Anita replied, moving to the other room, searching for Noah.

'Here it is!' Noah emerged from a small room on the left side of the kitchen. 'I knew I'd seen another journal in here somewhere. This is what my mother was looking for! I wonder if there is anything in here we need to know.' The diary passed from his hands to Anita's, as if she were the one in charge of reading it, decrypting it and uncovering its truth.

'Is there anything else we might need in here?' I asked, hoping that a powerful secret weapon might come in handy, but Noah immediately said no.

Without us even noticing, John had silently gone upstairs through the narrow staircase, Daisy once again in his arms. As we regrouped in the large room, his absence became apparent.

'We have to go,' Anita said.

'Where is John? John?' I shouted, a silent fear of losing him, leaving him behind, lurking within me.

'I'm up here… This place is incredible!' he replied, his voice muffled by the thick, squeaking ceiling. 'What's wrong, girl?' he added, looking at Daisy, who had started growling.

'We really have to go!' Anita repeated.

'John, come down! We need to hurry!' I shouted again, aware that Daisy had already picked something up.

In the blink of an eye, the outside darkened as if the entire world had lost power all at once. A strange wind fiercely moved the front door, which had been left open. Our faces turned to the ceiling, hoping to see John coming out at once; we had moved closer together, our breath held by the feeling of being hunted again.

'You need to go…now! I can't bring you back to my time without letting them see you,' a familiar voice whispered from behind Anita's head, the air wavering slightly. 'They are here!'

'Something is happening!' John rushed downstairs, while Daisy barked loudly.

'They found us already? How?' Noah asked, panicking.

As the four of us gathered together, a massive explosion shook the floor, sending John and Daisy crashing to the ground a few feet away from our horrified faces. A forceful roar blew out all the glass windows, violently unhinging the door, as a ruthless intruder arrived to put an end to our visit. Items fell and scattered around with rage, leaving only the bare walls as defence. As if an evil artillery had been summoned to kill, sharp pieces of glass whizzed through the air, piercing the walls and the defenceless furniture. Then it appeared.

A large, unnatural giant of a man stood between us and the only way out. His arms were long and contorted like branches of an old tree, his hands horribly twisted. His face folded on its own, resembling dark waterfalls of energy, with two small black holes staring at us. His presence obscured the smaller figures behind him, ready to strike in his command.

'This is getting tiring,' he said, his voice a shrill moan that sucked the air, making it whistle high. 'Your destiny is to die by our hands. Give me the key and *die!*'

There was no time to think or hesitate. He wasn't there to engage in conversation. He wasn't Lëogan; he didn't come to convince or trap us in a web of lies. Our time was up, no games were left to play, and no other strategies were available to us. As another explosive blow was triggered, the space turned to dust, and the house crumbled into ruins. It was a definitive, merciless death sentence.

Chapter Ten
A Friend for Life
∞

Through a thousand light-years, we had travelled from death to life, from a death sentence to freedom. The four of us had gone out of sight just before we could be destroyed. Noah and I were holding hands, his crystal heart pulsing between his arms and my shell shining between mine. The protective light that had saved us from a horrible end surrounded our bodies, as well as Anita, John, and Daisy. The walls of the house had given way to a large, familiar sea, and the floor had turned green and soft. In front of us, a large blue expanse greeted us silently. We stood safely on a solitary small island.

'Oh my God! I thought we were dead, finished!' John shouted, looking around in disbelief.

'I know this place! Don't worry, John, we are safe now!' Anita reached him quickly, on the soft shoreline where he had stumbled and fallen to his knees.

Returning from our enchantment, I left the magic of our spell and ran to them, my legs on the ground, my attention focused on John.

'Are you OK? Are you hurt?' I asked, searching his face.

'No, I don't think so...' He turned to look at me, revealing fresh wounds left by piercing, shattered glass on his cheeks. Blood was dripping onto his clothes, clearly contradicting his words.

'Oh no... John, you are bleeding! I'm sorry, I didn't know what to do...' I said, and my hands moved to wipe away his warm, red proof of love for me, as if I could simply erase it from our present.

Daisy sat between his legs, her tail hidden from sight. She was as petrified as the rest of us. She had survived the blow without scars, but her eyes darted around in terror. I pulled her into my arms, and as I turned around, I caught a glimpse of the bright shell moving towards me before it disappeared. Noah's heart had just done the same, leaving its owner worried and disappointed, just as he was before finding it.

'We're back... I thought we weren't going to see this place again,' I said.

'Welcome! I see three, no four too many!' a smiling face said. 'It looks like your group is growing...' And the Aqualymph finally took shape, her watery soul transforming into a more friendly form. The same colour of the grass was covering her legs, brown spots appeared on her chest and arms. John looked at her, enchanted by her magic.

'Aura?' Noah said. 'We're here to see Time…'

'Of course! We were expecting you…again. The protector of Runae is by the Mirrors. I believe you remember the way?' And her soft, delicate hands extended in an invitation we all recognized.

'Come on, John, let's go. I'm going to show you something amazing,' I said, and mimicking the gatekeeper, I reached out my hand to him.

The short journey through the depths of the sea was as incredible as I remembered. We all sprinted through the cold water without touching it. Like waterproof dolphins, we led the way for John, who quickly replaced the pain of the recent event with excitement. As we approached the other side, our group grew larger, with more Aqualymphs joining us in our submerged dance. Aura was no longer alone. Somehow, her kind had returned from the realm of death. Once we reached the dry land and her spell had faded, I asked her:

'You are not alone any more, how?'

'After Time erased the Crimson Queen from these lands, he also erased our past. Instead of leaving them dead, he mercifully reversed the spectres' timeline to a better one, when they were enjoying the beauty of life and the sea.'

'Did he do the same for everyone else?' Noah asked, thinking of the one we had lost in the fight for freedom.

'Why don't you see for yourself? Go now, the road is the one you know. Up the hill, look for your friend. He will be very happy to see you. Say hi to those little wings!'

And with a final smile on her vanishing face, Aura left us there. We knew our way, indeed. The infinite challenges we had once thought insurmountable had turned into happy memories of a better time compared to the present. Waking John from his latest exciting shock, I took his hands and led him up the hill. The sun bathed our shoulders as we had a bit to go, and the anticipation of what else Time had fixed propelled our feet forwards. The vast forest stood in our path, its colours brighter than we remembered, and the scent of leaves rustling in the wind reached our noses swiftly.

'So, this is where you three have been?!' John exclaimed, his head turning restlessly, his feet almost leaving the ground. I turned to him and smiled, happy to show him things he would never have believed otherwise. Our shadows swished rapidly from tree to tree. It was like a memory on repeat. Soon, Trusk's voice would reach us, to save us, just as he had saved us many times before.

'Look, the hills!' Anita pointed out as we walked out of the woods.

'It looks the same, but it feels different, doesn't it?' Noah added, smiling.

The tiny road appeared, its signs standing firmly by the river, twisting with the landscape. The old age of that place had been made young again, with more signboards sticking up from the ground, showing the many places we could have reached if we wanted to. Some signs stood just about our waist, a clear sign that the Chomps had been helping to rebuild the beauty of their world. Time's magic was visible everywhere, as if the pure power of life had been injected again into a once-dying world. As we walked slower, the steepness of the road opened up to tons of tiny, smoky houses.

The Chomps' village was growing larger right before our eyes. Before we could warn John about what he was about to witness, a group of short residents spotted us from afar, their wings flapping as fast as their joy was rising. In the space of a few seconds, we were surrounded, overwhelmed by the sound of happy voices. In sharp contrast to our first visit, we were no longer unwanted, suspicious guests. We had become celebrities of a different kind of show. Their rounded faces smiled at us; their hairy feet resembling Daisy's paws had taken John by surprise.

'You're back!' one said.

'Are you here to stay, yes?' another one asked.

'Chomps! Chomps!' A voice interrupted the noise from a distance. 'Let them pass. They are here for an even more important cause this time!'

We knew that voice. We had learned to recognize it instantly. All the stories he had told us, the endless journeys he had taken us on through the Mirrors, just with the power of his words. I could still recall how resolute he sounded when he had told me to act, to trade his life for ours, in the presence of the same evil we had managed to defeat. It seemed impossible, but it was real. He was back.

Treekan stood by the edge of a walkway, a bridge connecting the two parts of the village. His arms were open, his face filled with gratitude and happiness. We crashed on top of him, dragging him down to the ground as tears flowed down his puffy cheeks. John, left behind, was astonished by his new discoveries, with the Chomps bombarding him with questions. They didn't know him, but he was as welcome as we were, having arrived with a free pass granted by the gift we had all given them when we released Time.

'How? Was it Time?' I asked Treekan.

'Yes. Everything! Me, them, Runae. It's like it was before…but better!' the old Chomp replied, winking.

'Everything, you mean everything?' Noah asked, hinting at the possibility that other less-peaceful beings might have returned as well.

'But better!' he repeated.

'Where is Trusk? I really want to see him!' I said, pulling the old Chomp up from the ground.

'And Revelia…' Noah added.

'Revelia is at the temple. She is working hard to finish the work Time has started. Trusk is by the Ancient Mirrors with Time. I suggest we go and see them. Oh, and we must pay a visit to my fearcel. She won't forgive me if I don't bring you to her. Come on, let's rescue your friend from those noisy old Chomps.'

Led by Treekan through a familiar road, we soon reached his home. The old roof, the tiny chair by the tired porch, everything looked exactly the same. Whatever spell Time had released upon them, it had shamelessly missed that spot. Reela was already coming towards us, her smile as big as the star above our heads.

'You know? It hasn't rained since the day you left?' That was the first thing she said after squeezing us tightly.

'Really? Did we do that?' I asked as we moved inside the house.

'No, no. It will rain. Time has frozen the space for a little bit, just to give us the chance to recover and rebuild before he leaves us again,' Treekan replied.

'Is rain a problem?' John asked out of nowhere. It was like we had forgot he wasn't there with us the first time around.

'Yes, young man. There is a lot you need to catch up with these three! I see you are still too busy running to explain...' There, we were scolded, and honestly, rightfully so.

'Reela, this is my fearcel...' I said, remembering the conversation we had in that very same house.

'And he looks exactly like one!' she said, taking John's hand, her eyes glancing a little.

'Fearcel?' John asked, looking at me.

'It means "the one who you can't be otherwise",' Treekan replied.

'Soulmate...' Anita added, smiling at the two of us.

As sweet, embarrassing, and confusing as it was, considering the circumstances, a brief silence fell upon us. *It's funny how even the most joyful moments can be watered down by a reality that was never addressed. Like a poison that infects even the healthiest, most powerful moments*, I thought.

'Alright, let's go. We'll be back in a bit, Reela,' Treekan said, and we followed him outside at once.

With their home behind us, we took the old road to the Ancient Mirrors. Expecting to see a familiar landscape, we were surprised to find the large square empty. The warm Flare that used to flicker at its centre had disappeared.

'The Flares are really gone…' I said, walking beside the small Chomp.

'They are. We've regained too much good to be sad about it, really. Time might bring them back, you know, if we need to protect our world once again. To be honest, the Flares might have done more bad than good to our world. Oh, the things Una did…and the things Queen Eah did before her! Not to mention what the Humans did with their evil machine… But with the past gone, I guess we won't face that threat again.'

'I wish it was that easy…' I let go.

'So not everything is back…' Anita said.

I knew the wicked Leonty wasn't the source of all the evil we were fighting against. She was a pawn, a marionette moved by something greater than her, greater than all of us. How much Treekan knew, I wasn't sure. He knew as much as the Ancient Mirrors had told him and he had shared with us what he had learned years prior. But since the dark magic was gone, we had moved ahead without him. After all, he was gone. We were gone.

'What else is there?' Treekan asked.

'We found another mirror in Una's tower…' Anita replied. 'All the kinds in Runae had their sets of Mirrors, telling the story since the Great Dawn. She had destroyed all the ones that Leonty had, and maybe more, but she kept one.'

'The one that could reveal the truth about how she gained power…' Noah continued.

'And how she turned evil,' I said, as Treekan looked at us, speechless. 'We know who the real enemy is…but we don't know if we can defeat it. We found the other God, Soul.'

'So, there are now three Gods standing up! Good! This is really good…'

'Not really, not yet,' Noah continued. 'Right now, there is only Time. We don't know how to bring Love back just yet, and we know Soul is alive, but where…we do not know.'

'Which is much more than we had before. This is really good!' Treekan insisted. It was like a positive mindset was taking over any risk. He was brought back to life, and so was the hope of a better future.

'Where are we?' John asked, looking around as we got closer to the crooked building. Its top side was still missing.

'This is the old part of our village. We have arrived…' And Treekan pushed the large doors just enough to allow us to enter. 'What is that creature you're carrying? I've never seen one!'

'She is Daisy,' John replied, almost offended by Treekan's ignorance.

'Does a daisy talk?' he asked, bringing broad smiles to our faces.

'No, Treekan. Daisy is her name. She is a dog. In our world, a dog is a creature that keeps humans company. They don't talk, but they can communicate...' Anita replied.

'Fascinating! Hello, dog...' And Treekan moved his tiny hand close to Daisy, who started growling, scaring him away. 'Mmm...this one looks like a warrior! OK, come on, let's go see Time.'

Although still in ruins, the inside of the huge building looked different than before. Large tables had been moved in, randomly placed everywhere in the vast room. Books of every size were piled high on most of them, and lit candelabras cast a bright light in every corner. In the centre, right in front of the Mirrors, Time stood, his hood covering his form, his tall, broad back hiding a small creature from sight.

'And as I expected...you succeeded,' he said as we were getting close, his body still turned away.

'With some risk, yes, but we made it!' I said.

'Daniel?' Trusk's head had popped up from behind Time, his face showing renewed joy. 'You are back! All of you!' Trusk's arms were around my shoulders in a flap of his wings, his eyes on Noah and Anita as if he could not contain the size of his happiness. Caught by surprise, he then said, 'And fell me, who are you?' Trusk jumped down and walked right in front of John, his hands on his sides, a challenging expression appearing on his cheeks.

'Let him be, Trusk.' Time finally turned around to greet us.

'You have been busy…' I said. 'You brought back life to this place!'

'I wish I did. All I could do was bring back…well…time. I could undo what needed to be undone, but no, I can't create. We are Creation's work, not the other way around, I'm afraid.' He was speaking in riddles once again.

'What are all these books? Where do they come from?' To Anita, the old, large tomes were magnetising. Her hands already on some dusty ones, she lift the cover of the biggest one, ready to inspect it.

'These come from the Radhal Daíuh, in the Crown city. They belonged to the Humans. I've been using more than my power to rewind and scan the past, my friend. As I brought most of the people of this planet back, I wanted to see and learn the many things that happened while I was, well, preoccupied with other things. I learned a great deal.'

'The Flares are gone…' Noah said, almost asking why Time hadn't brought back that power.

'They are, for now. The Flares were just a manifestation of Mother's power and my own power embedded in these lands. As soon as I walked out of my slavery, their power came to me allowing me to undo what had been done to this planet.'

'You brought back all the beings that we never got to meet?' Anita asked, her eyes projecting the excitement of meeting all of them.

'The Garughals, the Aqualymphs and the Valahans, yes. I haven't reverted the Humans back to their time. There is a lot of evil in their history.' And Time pointed his fingers to the books Anita was still browsing. 'I need to think this through.' That last sentence got me by surprise. *Why being so selective?* I thought.

'We have it. We found the heart...' Noah interrupted him. He knew he was counting on it, as we all knew that was all that mattered.

'I know. I sense it. Your presence is stronger now. I felt you as you walked through the node. And I'm afraid I'm not the only one. We need to act fast now.' He fell silent for a few seconds. 'These books Anita is so interested in tell a lot about how some kinds abused the power I had gifted them with. It's true the Flares' magic could protect them while I'm gone, but the risk is high. I don't want history to repeat itself.'

'You are not giving them back some of their power?' Noah asked.

'I have to. We don't know who might strike while we are gone. Treekan is organizing the resistance together with the Aqualymphs and the Leonty.'

'What about the others? What about the Valahan Mogs?' I asked, their bones and metals buried under hundreds of stones still impressed in my mind.

'They are involved too. They are using their expertise to rebuild this world. But not digging, this time.' A brief smile appeared on Treekan's face.

'When you say you don't know who might strike... I thought nobody could get in without a key...and we know someone did,' Anita said, looking back, as she could still see the far island we had come from.

'The key is a powerful spell, but that's all it is, just a spell. Unbreakable for many. But there is someone who can. And if he is not after us, he could be after them, again. After all, as you remember, it has happened before…'

'What are we going to do?' I asked, picking up on Time's sense of urgency.

'I found Soul. I know where he is, but we can't enter that world any more; its node is gone. I've spent some time trying to find a way in, but the only thing we can do is go back to when it was still possible.'

'You mean travel back in time?' Noah said, thinking how the idea of rolling back the wheel of time could actually be the solution to everything. If we had gone back, we could have gone right to the time when the evil came to be.

'I can't go too far back. The wider my power spreads, the easier the evil would find me. But I can rewind parts of all the things that have been. Here, look at this…' And Time raised his hands above his head, his face still partially obscured by his hood. His eyes glared a little, a tiny spark giving life to something bigger, something that fluctuated in the ceiling above our stunned faces. It was like the visions we had seen long before in the Ancient Mirrors had expanded, enveloping the space and time around us. We had become witnesses to a new magic.

Heavy, dark skies turned grey in a wicked dance of lightning, mirroring the war raging below on the ground. Hundreds of thousands of beings mixed their blades in a vain attempt to overcome a merciless destiny. Above the two warring factions, a large, intangible figure held the space between the ground and the sky, an unbearable pressure building on its shoulders, the crash imminent. As the clouds darkened, a black shadow took shape. Two large hands pushed it down to annihilate its resistance, almost unmatched, unchallenged. With no power left to withstand, the proud warrior collapsed in a massive implosion, dragging the pure elements of the ground with it, pulling its foundation to the centre of its energy. Where it stood, a giant mountain suddenly formed, a burial monument, an impenetrable prison that would keep him away for eternity.

'This is where Soul is. Dormant, but alive,' Time said. 'His true nature has been preserved somehow. I thought Creation's spell had made only me and you immortal, but he was not destroyed, just silenced, as Nothing had buried him alive, forever. There is nothing left on Varayal, no being left alive. Nobody is watching over his prison, but also…there is no node to be reached.'

'So how…I mean, when do we reach him?' I asked.

'Between what you have seen and the moment the node was destroyed… Here…' Time moved his hands further, creating another vision. The lands were left empty. There was no war left to be fought. Nobody was left standing. The planet had turned red, fire raging wildly, and grey smoke twining on the ground. From nowhere, the smoke turned into fog, and the fog shaped into something more sinister. Its steps led to a collapsed building. The only piece left untouched was two large golden doors, closed shut. They stood as a walkway to other worlds, unaware of the events they had witnessed, without scratches or dirt. Their surface was clean and shining, but they were not meant to last in the face of this new wicked threat. As the fog approached, its hands on their round handles, they turned into dust, into the nothing that surrounded them, as if they had never existed. Thus, the node was gone, just like that world.

'We need to get there before this very moment…' Time continued. 'I can bring back the path for a little while, but with it, I'll also bring the time they lived in. Just that bit for our mission to succeed…'

'Don't get me wrong, I understand this is the only way…' Anita said, visibly worried. 'But how are we going to make it work? That place is…dead.'

'Not to mention this will bring us right into his hands!' I added.

'It is the only way. We will need to move fast, stay sharp,' Time replied, looking at John. 'I'm afraid this is not a journey for you. But you can stay here, protected by Runae's magic.'

'Hold on…' John finally stepped in. 'I know nothing about anyone here, nothing about this place. Shouldn't I just go home?' His eyes pleaded for help, fixed on mine.

'John, I know this is worrying, but it's safer here. There is nobody that can protect you back home. They know where we live, they know who you are. Here you will be unreachable and, believe me, in great company!' But the line between acceptance and disbelief grew wider.

John had spent too much time discovering and doubting everything and everyone. All he knew was how he felt, and he felt alone, in danger. He instinctively moved away from us, as if he could protect Daisy from harm, as if we were the enemy, as if I had walked to the other side, leaving him alone. Knowing there was no other way, I briefly looked at Time and approached John. In my heart, I knew I needed to take care of him, of her, of my family, before anything else.

'You are not alone. I promise you. Let's walk outside; this madness can wait.' With my hand on his face, I opened the way back to the Chomps village. I wanted to ensure that John knew where our lives were heading. If we were to leave him behind, he had to feel safe, he had to be with someone who could make him feel at home. My immediate need was to have him under Reela's care.

Chapter Eleven
The Parting Ways

∞

John and I walked outside, leaving everybody else behind. The group and our conversations carried the weight of a reality we had learned to accept. John rightfully felt left alone, estranged by the destiny taking shape around our lives. With the large star on our heads and the heat growing stronger, we went downhill on our way back to the Chomps' village.

'I know how you feel, John,' I started.

'Do you? Do you really?' His tone was cold.

'Of course I do. Although it's clearly something that brings a huge amount of weight on my shoulders, I haven't changed my feelings or my mind. You and Daisy remain in my heart!' I reassured him.

'So, let's leave! Let's go back to our lives as they were,' he said, stopping beside a large, lonely tree standing at the side of the paved road.

'We can't, John. Since everything started, I've been spending all my energy trying to put it away, ignoring it. But it won't go away. No matter what I want, no matter what you want, it's going to happen anyway. You know everything I know by now. I understand you were not with me the first time we came to this place, so you don't know how safe it has become, how safe you can be here. But you should look back at all the things that have happened in just the last few hours,' I explained.

'So, no matter what I want, what I believe, I'm a victim of all this? I don't own my own future any more. Is that what you're telling me?' His face showed even more sorrow than before.

'You know the answer, and it's as painful for me as it is for you. You have to understand that this is happening. All we can do is try to come out the other side alive, unharmed. If I could spare you from all this, I would. Why do you think I lied to you before? I was trying to save you from something you would have never hoped for yourself, for us! I'd do anything for you, John. But this is not in my hands any more.'

'You're leaving me here? With them?' He pointed back to the village.

'I don't know where we're going. If Time says it's risky for you, I prefer having you here. Chomps are incredibly kind…and funny if you give them a chance.'

'How long is this going to be? Well…considering how time is going at the moment, I can answer my own question…' He started walking again, his will surrendering to the horrible idea of staying.

'Reela is great. She reminds me of your mom, somehow. She is sweet, sharp, and also hilarious… She will take care of you while I'm gone. Also, you haven't met Revelia yet. She is a Leonty, a different being. She is very smart!'

'Am I? Thank you!' a voice exclaimed from nowhere.

At the crossroad right before the Chomps' village, the Leonty appeared on our left side, wearing a welcoming smile. The black marks inked in her face stretched around her cheekbones; her green skin looked like rich velvet clashing against the red ribbons tying her long hair. John froze suddenly, shocked by seeing her strange look for the first time. Revelia, on the other hand, showed no surprise at seeing him with me, almost ignoring his presence. If he felt she was being rude, I knew what magic she had just used.

'I thought you could not see the future any more,' I hinted at the obvious.

'Time has given me back my gift. It could be handy for whatever is coming,' she replied, doubling down on my bet.

'You saw us coming…you know John then. John, this is Revelia. She could be handy to have around when it's gambling time,' I introduced them, smiling at him, knowing she wouldn't understand.

The two exchanged a short greeting before we resumed our walk downhill. The list of things and people John had to remember was growing fast. In his heart, it didn't matter who was who and what they were capable of. The only thing running in his mind was the idea of seeing the one he loved and trusted moving away, leaving him in strangers' hands.

Revelia started sharing how her kind was brought back in time, all her sisters but one, the same one who had no chance to be redeemed. I still couldn't understand how Time could be so selective. After all, I had seen how the Crimson Queen had come to be. She was evil, but an evil made by others' hands. Una was a victim of a fate we all shared, although she had chosen the wrong side of the eternal dichotomy.

'Do your sisters know?' I asked.

'What it was before? Yes. They were brought back as they were and given the chance to change our present and our future,' she replied.

'I wonder if she would have chosen differently if given the opportunity…'

'Una was born to be evil, an evil you can't forget or forgive, no matter how much I hoped not,' Revelia responded, sharp.

'But you don't know, do you?' I challenged her. 'I know it sounds strange coming from me, all things considered, but I can't accept the idea that someone is just born one way or another. We become who we are. Our future is not written anywhere, not in Mirrors, not in ancient prophecies. We are who we are as a collection of events. You change one, and you could easily become someone else!'

'You would know if you could see the many futures she would have been in. I can. She would have chosen the same side, over and over again. I know, Time knows it, and *he* knows it. That's why *he* chose her. It's for the same reason why Time didn't bring back the Queen of the Aqualymphs. Given the chance, Queen Eah would once again steal the Flares for herself.' Revelia's power was bolstering her confidence. In my eyes, all I saw was her rejection of what I'd said. Whether it was because that concept contradicted my beliefs or because it implied that I too was destined to be who I was told to be, it didn't matter. I wasn't content with the idea as a whole.

'Who is *he*?' John asked as we approached Reela's home.

'The one behind. The one who caused everything that Time has recently unmade,' Revelia replied without giving too many details.

'He is called Nothing. We don't know what he is, we only know he is the reason for all this. Time talks about him as the vast matter that existed before anything came to be…before anything was created,' I added, knocking at the front door.

'Like an antimatter evil entity?' John was trying to put some sense into my words. Before I could answer, the house's owner showed up.

Reela was surprised to see us back so soon, just the three of us. After some explaining, she took John's hand and smiled at him, exchanging unspoken words hidden in that small gesture. She wanted him to feel at home, and he felt so as he smiled back at me.

'I imagine Treekan will go with you?' Reela asked.

'I'm not sure, Reela,' I said, turning to the Leonty. 'Revelia?'

'No, I don't see him with us. Just Trusk,' Revelia responded.

'Us? You are coming with us?' I asked, surprised.

'We will have to move fast and swiftly. I think Time wants me to help you choose wisely.'

I wasn't sure why we needed Revelia when we had the very source of her power, Time. *If we need help, why is he relying on her?* I thought. Visibly tired from the long journey and with the powerful star increasing the heat radiating from our bodies, I led John to the porch, under the relieving shadow of its roof. Reela served us a strange, green juice. The smell was incredible, but it was tasteless, so John asked what it was.

'It's made with Gochi water! It helps with the changing weather. We haven't made any of it for years… But I still remembered how to do it. It's very strange not having rain for days and days. I hope it comes, eventually.'

'We should bring you home then!' John said, smiling again. Whatever was in that juice, it was improving his mood.

'You better be prepared in case that happens. Chomps are very peculiar in the rain,' I warned, glancing at Reela, who was keen on learning more about our world.

'Don't you go away and sleep when it rains either?' she asked, looking at John. 'I remember last time they were here, but I can't tell if you are like them. Do you have this weather all the time?'

'No, we don't…actually, we hope to have it, but we don't,' John replied.

'John, Chomps have a strange connection with the rain. When it does rain, they fall asleep,' I explained.

'Just like that?' he asked.

'Just…like…that,' Revelia replied, lying down on the patio floor. 'Let's rest a little. They will be here soon.'

As we found a moment to rest outside in the warm air, Chomps were bustling around every corner, busy with their work of building, fixing, and chatting. Occasionally one of them would approach out of curiosity, offer greetings, exchange a few words with Reela, and then leave. Their wings would flutter frantically, reflecting their emotions as they drew near. Despite the fact that we were heroes in their eyes, they still knew so little about us.

'Revelia,' I asked before I dozed off. 'We never met this Queen Eah. When we came here, Aura was the only Aqualymph left. Who was she? What happened to her? And why wasn't she brought back with the rest of her kind?' John moved beside me, sitting on the floor with his back against the low windowsill and his head on my shoulder. For a moment, when his hand took mine, I felt like we had gone back to the way we were, close and fond of one another.

'What I know is what I just learned. I was born way after she was gone, after the Great Dawn. It's said Queen Eah was the most powerful being in Runae; this, of course, was before the war. Then the Flares came, and everything changed. The Humans asked the queen to move against us Leonty, and she did, despite the fact that they were not meant to leave the waters. I don't know why. They were meant to protect Runae, protect the node.'

'I know why,' I interjected, interrupting her story. 'It was a Harpy, an evil that came from our world to yours through the node. He is, well…he was able to manipulate minds as he pleased. After getting here, he was brought by Aura to her queen. I can only imagine what he did to her.'

'The Snake?' John whispered in my ear, and I nodded in agreement. He was catching up fast.

'I see…' Revelia replied. 'Anyway, once she reached our lands, although she didn't harm my kind, the queen took our Flare from us and climbed the Cloudy Mountains, where it was said the evil resided. I don't know what happened there, but I can tell you that's how everything started—the Garughals dying, the steppes turning into a desert, the Aqualymphs turning into spectres.'

'And you said Time didn't bring the queen back because, like Una, she would do that again?' I asked. Time's and Revelia's trust in their own omniscience made me uncomfortable. Apparently, the queen and Una's malevolent actions shared the same origins: Nothing and his Awoken Ones.

'Precisely,' Revelia concluded. 'Now, let's rest a little.'

'I really don't understand,' I whispered, turning towards John. His eyes met mine, but he was about to fall asleep. 'Why couldn't they be saved?'

As the star moved across the purple sky, the heat gave way to a pleasant, fresh breeze. I dozed off briefly, feeling like it lasted only a minute or two. Last thought rumbling in my fizzy mind was the one of Noah leaving Anita and me behind, running in the search for his destiny, ending up in the Crimson Queen's hands. Eventually, John's smile woke me up, and he presented a strange dish filled with various ingredients, awakening a hunger I didn't know I had.

'This food is delicious! Come inside, everybody else is back, there's more food indoors. You need to eat before you go!' he exclaimed.

As the magic juice had strengthened its influence, John underwent a complete transformation. He appeared excited, almost happy. I knew he would love the place, but the change had come sooner than I had hoped. Inside, in the main room, the side wall had been moved again, opening up space for all of us. Anita, Noah, and Revelia were seated at a table with short legs, struggling to fit their limbs comfortably on the floor. As John entered, bending slightly, I noticed Time's absence. Reela stood in a corner with Trusk, near the tiny narrow staircase. She seemed anxious, ensuring her son would be careful on his upcoming journey.

'Treekan?' I asked, moving closer to him and taking a seat at the dinner table. 'Where is he?'

'Time has gone to speak with the Aqualymphs. When you're gone, Runae will need extra protection, especially there,' Treekan replied.

'Can anyone come in this time? Through there, I mean,' Anita joined our conversation from the other side of the table. John had just sat beside her.

'Everything is different now. If you'd asked me a yac ago, I would have given you a different answer. I think not, but Time knows better,' Treekan responded.

'What do you see?' Noah asked Revelia.

'I see nothing, which is strange. Really nothing. I see the last thing I saw before everything ended, when Una left. I don't see my sisters; I don't see much of anything. It's like I skipped this new life and am stuck in that last moment. But I did see you coming...' Revelia explained, her eyes turning a shining red, capturing John's attention.

'Is that normal?' he whispered to Anita.

'Yes, whenever she explores the future with her mind,' Anita replied.

'This place defies all the laws of physics,' John blurted out.

'Welcome, John, to our group! We gather here every Wednesday. I'll give you your badge at the end of this session,' Anita responded, making us Humans laugh and leaving the rest perplexed by the inexplicable joke.

'Who is this Wednesday, a friend of yours?' Treekan asked, causing us to laugh even harder.

It felt like we weren't embarking on a perilous mission soon. Our mood was good, and we felt strong and relaxed. The rush, panic, and fear had vanished. The Chomps had worked their magic once again, just as they had the first time. Flying wasn't their only magic; they had another set of invisible wings, giving them the ability to lift our spirits. Soon, our dinner was finished; Trusk helped his mother clean up the remaining dishes, and the rest of us sat by the side of the house where the large wall had been moved, providing an incredible view of the large star setting behind the towering mountains. Daisy, asleep beside Anita, was the only being unaware and untouched by our impending journey.

'Time will be here soon, Humans. Make sure to keep an eye on my son while you're gone,' Treekan stated.

'He'll be fine. We'll be fine. You, on the other hand...' Revelia stood by a large wooden pillar under the crooked roof, a similar weight on her heart, her gaze locked with the old Chomp's eyes. 'You need to ensure the spells will hold. I can't see beyond a certain point; no matter how hard I try, I see absolutely nothing.'

'I know this sounds crazy, but...' Anita began. 'Maybe the three of us should go and leave Time behind to protect you, to protect this place?'

'Unfortunately, we aren't powerful enough to face what lies ahead,' Revelia replied, and the Leonty moved further away, gazing at the mountains as if she could see through them, right at the temples where her sisters were still recovering.

A few moments later John stood up too and left the room to reach the front porch. It was as if the group had suddenly started to fall apart. We were together, but each of us had our own worries and wishes. After a brief exchange of silent words with Anita, I also left, following him outside. His face was pointed south towards the node, his mind travelling millions of miles back home where we belonged.

'You said it's safe for me to stay here…' he started, as I moved beside him, looking into the far distance, searching for his same illusions.

'It's safer,' I whispered.

'Being with you, and you with me, that should be safe. Doesn't it usually work that way?' he asked.

'It does. But there isn't much usual left in our lives,' I replied.

'What if you won't make it back? What's going to happen to you? To me, to Daisy, to them?' he asked, his voice filled with concern.

'Once again'—I let out a deep breath—'I do not know. This time you are with me, fully with me in the unknown. I did this right, eventually. I brought you with me, into my deepest secrets, my true self. Isn't this also the usual in a relationship? Hasn't it paid off, has it?'

'I won't be with you much longer, though.' He finally turned his eyes to mine.

'There is a limit to the risk you can take, that I can take. We need to draw a line between being together and suffering together, dying together. Once we pass that line, what kind of love is that?' I asked, almost as if I was asking myself.

'Isn't it the vow we were going to make to each other, eventually? In sickness and in health, until death takes us apart? I truly believed this is what we were going to have, soon. Getting married, build a life with hundreds of thousands of moments…' he said.

'We were. Yes. Before all this,' I replied, reflecting on our past.

'So, what's going to happen if you do come back? Will it be you, my Daniel? Or is that gone already?' he asked, his voice filled with emotion.

'A piece of me is gone, John. There is no way to deny it. I think a part of you is gone too. You have seen too much to simply rewind time and pretend this has never happened. We have changed, we are changing. In different ways and at different speeds, but we still love each other. That's why we are resisting, why we are holding our ground,' I explained.

'I can't let it go… I can't let you go.' He turned his face away to hide his tears.

'I don't think we can be tested more than we have already. In the last two months we have moved years ahead. There is something holding us close despite everything. Forget about all this magic future, this is our magic! Yours and mine alone! Our love has faced so much and grown so much that it reaches the stars above our heads. I'll miss you while I'm gone, but you won't be really far from me, ever,' I reassured him.

And then, his arms were suddenly around my shoulders, his neck touching mine, as if he was trying to merge his soul with mine. I could hear his heartbeat, his thoughts, his dreams shattering under the weight of reality. In that moment, Noah had completely disappeared from my mind. The connection we had, the soul of the unknown God we shared, was a tiny memory lost among the many screaming in my head. Whatever I felt for him wasn't what

I was feeling for John. Once again, I had two minds, two hearts inside my own body. Two wills moving apart, reaching for the distant purposes of my life. I was alive to fulfil someone's destiny, and I was alive to fulfil mine.

'How is it that she can come with you, and I can't?' he said, sobbing.

'Don't ask me that. You wouldn't like the answer, and neither would I,' I replied, knowing deep in my heart that he was the only one I couldn't sacrifice, the only one I couldn't exchange for the truth we were hunting for.

Before we could let go, Time appeared a few steps away, staying silent for a few moments. He pulled his hood down for the very first time, revealing his incredible form to the two of us. His eyes were like galaxies, moving fast and torn apart, his skin was pale, almost green, and white, almost liquid gold, wobbled on his head, as if his hair were made of fused metal.

'If this call is hard for anyone, it would be far more for you.' Time spoke. 'You are the pure essence of Love, with its pride and glory, but also its pain and suffering. You can't let go, but you can't stand the consequences either. Believe me, I know how it feels. As the power of time makes me a giver, it makes me a taker too. It's our destiny to carry both sides within ourselves. There is no escape, and I'm sorry for that.'

'Thank you,' I replied, releasing John from our hug.

'We need to go. The journey is set. Let's call the others,' Time said, his body flickering as he moved inside the house.

'I'll do anything to come back. I don't know what is going to happen, who I am going to be, but I'll be back. I'm not leaving you!'

Those were my last words to John. Soon, we left him with Reela and Treekan by their house. His face, carrying the sadness of our goodbye, was the last thing I saw before turning the corner of the village, entering the quiet forest, and starting a new chapter of my life. Something in the back of my head told me to hold on, to hang on to that moment a little longer, as if I could absorb it all through my skin. An unnatural essence was stretching its limits from my heart to John's, keeping them connected at all costs. As if I could leave behind the part of me attached to John, I counted the infinite number of steps between us and Treekan's home, where I had left him, with the hope of finding him again and staying beside him forever.

I wasn't leaving just John behind. I was leaving my life, my dreams and my heart in the very same place we hugged. Without me knowing, I had sealed that spot with a magic of superior making. With a part of me, a part of Love was secretly left behind.

Chapter Twelve
Varayal

∞

Aura was already standing on the other side of the large lake. Her transparent figure fluctuated just above the warm water, waiting for us to arrive. We had left the Chomps' village on foot and, on the edge of the forest, we had become invisible, shifting from one place to another near our destination. It was as if Time had granted us and them the dignity of a long goodbye, drawn out by our slow walk into the unknown. Once out of sight, the urgency returned, and we arrived in the blink of an eye. Aura held her arms up, clutching five small jewels in her hands. The pendants were familiar in shape, resembling five miniature versions of Time's clepsydra, attached to a thin golden chain.

'These are for the five of you,' she said. 'We will watch this spot and stop anyone who doesn't possess one, no matter what they look like, no matter what they say. The only way to return here is with Time or with these.'

'Will our key not work?' Noah asked, referring to his heart and my shell.

'You can't use it. I have a growing fear in my mind about our artefacts. Something tells me they no longer contain only our mother's will. Somehow, the enemy can trace them! If you use yours, you will be seen,' Time replied.

For some reason, he looked troubled. In the depths of his mind the God of Time was lurking towards the many possibilities when the impossible was made. Somehow the evil had found a way to connect with him, with the Gods and their artefacts. Whatever spell was cast on them during their fall, it held its grip firmly. Wherever we went, we were followed.

'Is this how they found us in Castlecross?' Anita exclaimed, her mind piecing together all the clues.

'What about you? Won't you be seen as well?' I asked.

'I will, but I'll use my artefact only if necessary. And if I am, I hope I won't become a priority. After all, I'm a side risk, not the main one. You are, to *him*. So, you need to go unnoticed for as long as we need to. If I fall behind, take Soul away and use those amulets.'

'What's the point of freeing Soul if we lose you? We need to be together to make it work, right?' Noah questioned, not understanding Time's plan.

'You won't lose me. Trust me. But we need to protect you more than anything else. Once in Varayal, you must promise me, *all of you*, that you will do as I say. Promise me!' Time urged.

After a brief hesitation, we all said yes. Following Time's instructions, we took each other's hands, forming a sort of magic circle with him at the centre, the core of the spell.

'I will turn the wheel back, to just before the node was destroyed. Everything else will be as it was then. Do not lose or remove your amulets. They will keep you within the time space I will create. If you do, you will be trapped in that timeline and If you attempt to come back here, you will be here in that same timeline! Human girl,' Time added, looking directly at Anita. 'It's time for you to let her drive you. Do not resist! Let's go!'

Before we could ask any questions, the air began to spin around us, faster and faster, lifting the yellow sand and grey soil in a greenish twister. Our feet lost contact with the ground, and in an instant, we were gone.

The other side couldn't have been more different from what we had left behind. The harsh landscape was foggy and violently red, the colour of war, the colour of death. The wind from Time's spell had given way to a brownish storm, angrily swirling from all directions. We appeared suddenly, immediately buffeted by the fury of the elements, our hands barely holding on together. The air was dry in our mouths, tasting of metal, stinging our tongues. If this was the hell as we had imagined, we had stepped right into it.

In the far east, just above the horizon, a bewildering, large spot rose from the ashes. Something in the distant skies convulsed, dragging the lights and colours towards its invisible centre. Like a hole punched into the fabric of all matter, an impossible monster awakened before our eyes. The aftermath of Nothing's delivery stood there, ready to fulfil its wicked plans of eternal destruction. Like an unmerciful slave to an even darker master, a black hole became its means to erase every trace of Creation's making.

'Let's go. Soul is to the north from here!' Time shouted, trying to be heard over the roaring wind.

'If that's what I think it is, we are surely doomed!' Noah added, pointing his hands towards the giant omen.

'What is that?' Revelia asked.

'That's a black hole!' Anita replied, shielding her eyes from the raging red dust. 'It's as if Erion had imploded, creating this gravitational force that draws everything into itself!'

'Time! If that thing is already this close, we might already be too late and trapped here forever!' Noah exclaimed, his voice filled with worry.

'We are not! My own power can sense there still a chance. Though slightly affected, time is still running, for now. We have to hurry!'

Time pointed out the worst part of an already horrific landscape. A large mountain spewed fire and smoke as if a volcano had split in two, pouring its deadly lava onto the ground. Soul lay trapped at the mountain's feet, his rocky prison towering above a melting red river.

'Is that where we are supposed to go?' Noah asked, his voice drowned out by the surroundings.

'God, it's hot! How are we going to get there?' Anita added.

'This is worse than what the Valahan left behind by the Mogs mountain!' Revelia said, her hair whipping in the hot wind.

'We need to walk! We can't risk being detected. We must refrain from using any powers unless necessary!' Time shouted.

'It seems necessary to me… I feel like my face is going to melt soon!'

My fear wasn't solely triggered by the elements. If we were not supposed to use any magic, how would we defend ourselves against any attack? *How would we know if something or someone is already pursuing us*, I wondered. I was carrying the weight of the little Chomp on my shoulders; Trusk was clinging to my neck with his tiny hands, resisting the stormy pull of the wind. Behind us, the sky appeared torn by an invisible force slowly tearing the desolate planet apart.

'Someone is coming! Approaching soon!' Revelia said, capturing Time's attention.

'Where?' he asked promptly.

'Just over there, at the rocky hills, further away. There is an overwhelming sense of death emanating from them. They are scavengers searching for something,' she replied.

'They are looking for the Tiara of Souls! Can you see beyond that?' Time pressed, quickening his pace as we reached the bottom of an immense red canyon.

'We are hiding, waiting. There is blood everywhere,' Revelia answered.

'Can you see beyond that?' Time grew impatient.

'I don't see anything but red, red all around!' Revelia shouted, almost in tears, her eyes hurt by the raging dust.

'Are we all together?' Anita asked, more concerned about the group's safety than anything else.

'Yes, we are!' Revelia replied, relieved.

'Good. Then let's go!' Time added.

Thus, we attempted to quicken our pace against all odds, rushing into the depths of the towering walls. As we ventured further into the canyon, the wind subsided momentarily, only to return with even greater force at each turn. Tall, brownish walls stood on both sides of the rocky pathway, their faces seemingly fixated on us. In the red fog stirred by the storm, something was counting our steps.

'I feel someone wafching...' Trusk whispered in my ear. 'Look af fhe rocky walls...'

'I see nothing, Trusk. Where?' I asked.

'Fhere! Look! Fhe walls have eyes!' His voice grew louder, capturing everyone's attention.

The walls were moving, wobbling like countless snakes, slowly squirming against the surface. Here and there, sets of eyes formed, mouths popping up only to disappear again. If something was trying to emerge from the rock, it was being held back.

'What magic is this?' Revelia asked, looking around.

'Are they alive?' Noah added.

'It's Soul! His power is seeping into the very roots of this planet. Things that should be dead are gaining a life of their own,' Time explained.

'Why didn't I see that?' Revelia questioned, puzzled.

'Because they have no mind, no will of their own. They are simply dead matter filled with the spark of a soul. They are emotions, nothing more,' Time continued.

'It's like Runae before we freed you, but this time the place is filled with its master's different power,' I said.

'Why are they not leaving this place?' Anita asked, almost as if they could wish for some kind of paradise. Instead, they were trapped in a living purgatory.

'Soul's power requires a real host, someone capable of containing the magic he possesses. I'm afraid there are no living bodies left to accommodate this spell any more,' Time replied.

'I swear I thought I saw a face form, mouth the word 'help' and promptly disappear. 'Did anyone see that?' I interjected, but my question went unnoticed amidst the rush of our mission.

Walking through that narrow pit felt like being baked in an enormous oven. The heat grew stronger, making it difficult to breathe. In an attempt to escape the searing of our skins, we hurriedly left that place, forgetting about the beings watching us, crying out to be set free. Eventually, the canyon opened up to a large area filled with scattered rocks. Some larger ones stood silent, bearing witness to a long-fought battle that had left the ground littered with hundreds of dead bodies. They had become nameless gravestones. As for their owners, every memory had been erased by fire and storm. We had reached a graveyard of forgot beings.

'Oh my God…' Anita exclaimed, shocked.

'This is where I saw them. It's here!' Revelia added.

The place was horrifying. We had stepped into the aftermath of a raging war. There was nothing alive left, only the unbearable truth of an enemy too powerful to be defeated. Everywhere, the blood had already dried, parched by the scorching air. We were too late to make any difference, but we were just in time to take advantage of their misery. In the silence of that deadly place, we could sneak in, release Soul, and leave everything else behind. Like cowards, we became the scavengers, picking up the bones left behind and taking only what we needed.

'Why didn't we come back before all this? Could we have saved them?' I said, desperation consuming me.

'This was done by a hand we cannot overcome. Neither me, nor you, nor Soul,' Time replied, dismissing my words with a cold, bitter reality.

Whoever had brought such destruction would have done the same with or without us in the midst of the fight. All we had managed to do bravely was release Time and allow him to defeat the Crimson Queen. We were not warriors, and we had no magic tricks up our sleeves. But I couldn't help but think we should have tried anyway.

'I fhink we made a misfake coming here,' Trusk whispered, gripping my neck in terror, making it even more difficult for me to breathe.

'No! We are exactly where we are supposed to be. This is the only option we have,' Time replied firmly.

'They are close,' Revelia said, her eyes turning red. 'We can hide among those rocks. There is a small cave…'

Without hesitation, we all moved in the direction indicated by the Leonty. We had learned to trust her power, and once again, she had not failed us. A few moments after we hid, we heard the sound of running beings approaching from the north. Heads down, our bodies shrinking behind the large rocks, we became black dots in the dark shadow of a tiny cave. Time covered his face completely, as his shining features posed a risk for all of us.

Initially out of sight, some of the creatures moved closer, digging and shifting bodies in their way, pulling their flesh out of their bones. They were searching for something, coming closer to our hidden spot. All we could hear was a rattling sound in their voices as they spoke to each other in an unknown, frenzied, and aggressive language. Within the crowd, a fight broke out. Three or more individuals pushed and shoved, their voices raised high, punches and blows landing. Metal clashed against metal as they fought over something we couldn't understand.

Eventually, one of them turned the rock standing between us and them, revealing a shocking and almost repulsive figure. It had two pairs of arms, one on its shoulders and one on its sides, wearing rags held together by clinging metal. Its face was deformed, skinny, and egg-shaped, topped with a helmet and featuring a large cavity at the bottom. No eyes were visible, no ears discernible, but it moved as if it had many, hidden somewhere. We remained completely silent, holding together. My arms were around Trusk, his face buried in my chest, as I tried to prevent him from seeing that thing and screaming in terror. Then, suddenly, it moved away, called back by an awful, squeaky scream from a distant land, allowing us to breathe again and release the fear that had gripped our contracted muscles.

'We were so close,' Noah whispered, panting, his heartbeat growing louder.

'What was that?' Anita asked.

'I don't know the creatures of this world well. This was Soul's protected planet. However, even if I did know, they are no longer what they once were. Nothing has turned them into war machines. That creature was searching for Soul's artefact. That's the only reason why the evil kept them alive, so he could focus on chasing the rest of us,' Time explained.

'Do we know how long until they find it?' I inquired.

'Hold on...' Revelia said, extending her arms and placing her hands on the scorching rocks. 'It's not too far, but it's not imminent. They have found it, and the node hasn't been destroyed yet, but...something strange is happening in these lands. There is a power much greater than them. The same power is taking the artefact they seek. And it's not alone?' Revelia strained to decipher a very puzzling vision of the twisted future. 'I can't see clearly. It's like a loop of memories. I catch glimpses of the master of this world wearing a tiara on his head, but this is the past, not the future.'

'That might explain why they haven't found it,' Anita suggested.

'Come on, there is still a long way to go, and we need to move quickly,' Time urged, as if he wanted us to stop asking questions.

Emerging from our safe hiding spot, we became shadows moving silently across the red land. Conversation ceased as our minds focused on the towering mountain that held the reason for our rescue mission. Amidst the large flows of liquid fire and the intensifying heat, dark clouds rose from the destroyed buildings, remnants of a war where resistance must have been minimal, and the unleashed power was too great to leave anything behind. A strange, melancholic cry echoed in our ears from all directions. The place was speaking to us, begging for attention. It felt as if those who had perished there were still alive, their souls transformed into a sorrowful whisper.

'This feels too familiar… It's like the dead who were trapped in Runae, remember?' Anita said, looking at me.

'Those Humans were trapped in a time between death and life. These ones are long gone. You were right asking why they are still here. What is it keeping them trapped?' Revelia asked.

'Their bodies are gone beyond, but Soul is keeping them here. This is his magic!' Time replied, turning fast around a large rock. 'Here, we are getting close!'

What it had opened in front of our eyes was beyond incredible. A large, long stone bridge was running in between two high hills. Broken in parts, it had a large hole in the middle, its intricate, white marble decorations gone interrupted, defied. To the other side, three dusty white towers were holding close together. Like solitary siblings left orphan of their mother, two were left standing in the very centre of a large destruction. One, almost completely destroyed, was left in ruin, its sides still crumbling to the far ground. Behind them, the large rocky mountain was watching over them.

'Soul is buried in there! The mountain behind those towers is keeping him enslaved,' Time exclaimed.

'Somewhere in there, two large doors are guarding the passage. We need to break the seal to get in!' Revelia added.

'How are we going fo break if? Is if like fhe key we used fo free Fime?' Trusk said, jumping off my shoulder and flying closer to the bridge.

'We don't even know where it is!' Anita added.

'It's buried somewhere, among rotting corpses. I can see them pulling it from the remains, amidst dust and blood… No, hold on, something is not right,' Revelia replied.

'Yes, but where?' Time asked again, his tone sharp.

'I don't know. I don't know this place. Everything looks the same. Desolation and horror! How am I going to know which is which?' she retorted.

'Just tell me what you see!' Time's tone was demanding, almost rude. If he had a plan of his own in his mind, we did not know.

'I don't know what I'm seeing!' The Leonty pushed back once more. 'What I see is supposed to be the future, but it's actually the past! Something is changing, and I don't know why…'

But before we could move further, before we could find a way to our next steps, fate had already chosen for us. A large explosion erupted from our right side, shaking the ground so wildly that we fell on our backs. Cracks ran fast through the fragile soil, breaking the foundations we stood on. Afraid, we moved forwards, pushed by a threat we could not see. Our feet ran onto the bridge, oblivious to the impossible jump we had to make to escape.

'Move, move, move!' Time shouted.

Tons of horrifying scavengers were chasing us from behind, following the scent we didn't know we had left. Like following the trail to their prey, they craved fresh blood, holding exploding devices in their hands, screaming rattling, incomprehensible words. The steam and smoke coming from the pit we stood over made our way ahead difficult and unpredictable. We could barely see the white adorned rails on both sides of the walkway; the end of our path was hidden from us.

'Slow down, no, no, no!' Trusk shouted, many steps ahead, turning around, his tiny hands stretched into the air.

But we could not stop; our backs could almost feel the enemy's metallic hands coming from behind. So, we went ahead, speed on our feet, a large hole waiting for us. Trusk grasped Noah, Anita, and me, pulling and helping us make the impossible jump to the other side. We flew for a few seconds, just long enough to escape certain death, just as much as Trusk could bear with his little powerful wings. On the other side of the cracked opening, Revelia and Time were left behind, their bodies standing at the edge. All we could see was their still forms amidst the loud, evil choir singing a song of killings. For a quick second, a bang took us by surprise, making our hearts jump to our throats. Then silence fell, no more sound, no fight. All we could hear was the rumbling of the volcano in the far distance.

'Where are they?' I let out desperately.

'Revelia! Time!' Noah shouted into the red fog.

But no answer came. There was nothing but the four of us, left alone in horror. It was as if both of them had disappeared into thin air, taking the raging flock with them. No enemies, no friends, just desperation in our minds.

'It's like they are all gone? I can't see anything,' Anita said.

'I'll fly fo fhe ofher side and check!' Trusk replied.

'No! We don't know what is in there! Please don't!' And I pulled Trusk by his arm, afraid of losing him too.

'We can't lose them…please tell me they teleported somewhere,' Anita leaned forwards, stretching the balance to its limit, trying to see the other side.

'I'm not sure if he used his magic, Anita. He said he wouldn't,' Noah replied, pulling her back and holding her in his arms.

'Let's move back and wait. We can't stay here in the open. They know we are here; they all know. Time and Revelia might be waiting at the end of the bridge?'

I knew I was lying to myself and to them, but I couldn't let my hope go, not in that moment. We had lost the two most powerful allies we had. *This must be a mere hiccup, it will all be fine*, I thought. So, we moved from that spot, our hearts full of sadness and fear, and walked all the way to the end, at the feet of the towers. Our rush had left us; we dragged our legs, hoping to hear them coming back from behind. But that moment didn't come; the quest to rescue Soul had come with a nasty trade. One God in exchange for another.

Chapter Thirteen
The Towers of Light and Darkness

∞

We soon reached the first of the three towers. It was immediately clear something else was playing its game in that harsh land. The unbearable heat came and went randomly as if we walked in and out of bubbles of freezing cold. One spot felt like a world on fire while another was suspended in glacial emptiness. There were no boundaries, no warnings. It was like roaming blind from one to the next. To the side of the tower, a large, unhinged door hung on its side, while its twin stood strong and shut. Carvings covered the door from top to bottom; an unknown script spoke of an ancient magic we had no knowledge of. A stone-cold air breathed through the opening. As if an arctic world was waiting at the other side, the broken doors kept that magic separated from the rest.

'It's like something happened in here. It feels like some kind of bomb exploded, and now the space is all torn apart,' Anita said, putting her hand on the door left standing.

'Whatever it was, it must have been pure energy. It's like walking out in space, if I could ever imagine that,' Noah added, still looking behind, hoping to see our friends coming out of the smoke.

'Remember how it felt in Runae? When Time was still a prisoner and his magic was spilling into the planet? Stuck dead in between past and present, the Ancient Mirrors… I wonder if this is the aftermath of Soul fighting,' I asked, taking a peek inside the tower.

'Is there any point in moving forwards? Even if we made it to Soul, can we release him?' Anita added, sitting on the ground, her shoulder against the cold stone of the tall building.

'We lost the ones who were supposed to lead us,' Noah said, taking a seat beside her.

'Why bring her, though? I wonder… We made it here because of Trusk. By the way, buddy, thank you!' I said, moving my hand on his head. 'What if Time knew about this very moment? We needed the Chomp's magic. Maybe he needs Revelia's?'

'If that's true, why didn't he tell us?' Anita objected.

'Because if we knew, it might not have happened,' Noah added, connecting his thoughts with mine once again.

'Let's wait here for a little bit. If we can't think of anything else, I'd say we stick to the plan and move forwards,' I suggested.

'Without the key,' Anita said.

'Without the key,' we all agreed.

We let time pass for a little while. We could hear the restless world moving around us as it had found its balance after the long fight, oscillating between light and dark, cold and burning fire. The frightening metallic sound of death was long gone, and our fear was finally subsiding. Noah had pulled out the second journal he had taken from the house in the woods, before it shattered. Without realizing it, he had immersed himself in a deep dive into his mother's words. Anita looked at me and Trusk as he sat behind the broken side of the large door.

'What if Time brought Revelia with us because he can't use his power? She might be able to do his work without the risk,' Anita pondered.

'That's a good one,' I replied.

'Also…there could be another reason. He said he was going to give his power back to the Chomps and the other people of Runae to protect them while we were gone,' Noah explained.

'You mean he has no power at all now?' I asked, petrified by the idea.

'Maybe just as much as he needs to get us through this,' Noah replied, then added after seeing me lost in my thoughts, 'What's wrong?'

'I know we've only been gone a few hours, but I hope John and Daisy are OK,' I expressed my concern.

'Mofher is making him work a lof by now...' Trusk said, looking up. 'I can already see if: "John, do fhis. John, do fhaf."'

'Well, that will keep him busy,' I replied, smiling.

'Guys, read this,' Noah suddenly said, holding up the journal. *'I'm pulling memories out of my head and transferring them here, trying to remember what was said. There are only a few good ones left, but how can I find them? If Noah needs them eventually, how can I make his future possible?'*

'Is that your mother's journal?' Anita asked, her ears fully tuned to its secret content.

'Yes. This one seems to have been written before the other one. Only a few pages were used, though. Not much after the first ten or so,' he said, quickly skimming through it. 'Here, look. *The further the waiting goes, the more they fade. Like plants too long away from the sun, they have lost strength and are dying one by one. Only a few stand still. Dõron the gifter, Cherish the protector of memory, past, and future, Iris the messenger. Mnemosy to forget and Eleoen to forgive...'*

'Cherish is mentioned again...we know Dõron, and we have met Iris,' I interjected.

'Who are these...what did she call them? Mnemosy...which literally means forgetting...and Eleoen to forgive? They sound...Greek? The goddess of mercy?' Anita replied, almost dismissing the fact that Cherish had been mentioned and that we all knew how close we were to her.

'To protect past and future?' I returned to that thought. After all, we had been receiving hints about Cherish's impending arrival. 'What is she supposed to do?'

'Don't look at me,' Anita shrugged, smiling with a hint of embarrassment. 'Changing the topic, I've been thinking…'

'Of course, you have,' I chuckled, causing her to look disappointed.

'If we do succeed… If we free Soul as we did with Time, that makes three of you, not four,' Anita said.

'What are you saying?' Noah asked.

'Remember what Iris said? We need three to bring Love back. Three. Not two. Time, Soul, and…?' I trailed off, then continued. 'Time has talked before about Health.'

'But he also said Health was destroyed… I don't understand,' she said, her mind making the most impossible conjectures.

'Maybe Iris didn't know…that Health is gone, I mean,' Noah added.

'Then the whole conjuring would not work, would it?'

Once again, Anita's pragmatic approach to the most mystic events was highlighting the dark spots in our knowledge. We had gone quiet for a good while, our minds spinning, our brains trying to come up with something that would help our current situation. Suddenly, Anita resumed.

'We were worried about the three weeks we spent in Runae… Imagine when—if—we come back home, this time.'

'For all we know,' I said, 'my house is their house now. The Harpies must still be there, watching.'

'Exactly. Maybe it's a good thing that Patrick left.' She suddenly changed the topic. I could not let the opportunity go missed.

'Do you say it because you think Patrick was also…well, destined to leave and let us do all this… Or do you mean it's good he doesn't get to be involved in this madness?'

'Maybe both? But think about it. John cannot leave your side. Despite the latest problems between the two of you, he still could not leave your side. Neither can you. I've seen you in these last few moments. You really are fearcel one to another…' Noah suddenly stopped reading his mother's journal. The mere mention of John's name must have hurt him.

'So, you're saying that Patrick had no part in this because he chose to leave you?' I asked, but Anita didn't answer. Instead, she briefly moved her shoulder in a sign of doubt. 'But what about the others? Take Harry, for example. He is in my life, in our lives. He was even mad he wasn't with me when…well, when we were gone.'

'Yeah, but Harry is not a great example.' She dismissed my whole argument just like that.

'Do you miss him?' I asked, boldly.

'Harry?'

'Patrick!' I smiled. But once again, she wasn't ready to answer that question.

'Maybe this is part of our journey?' Noah chimed in. 'Not just physical, but emotional? I can't help feeling how we are losing more and more connection with who we are, with the people we are close to. I literally have nobody but you guys.' And those words hurt my stomach. I kept forgetting how important I had become, how important we had become for Noah. 'And you, your friends, your lives are taking the same unpleasant turn…'

'He's not wrong,' Anita said, looking at me as if I needed to be convinced in believing that.

'I know,' I replied, sighing. 'It doesn't feel right. Like those souls trapped in this world, it doesn't feel right…'

'He's not wrong either,' Noah said, looking at Anita, mimicking her expression. 'Whatever happens, I don't want to lose any of you.'

Silence fell upon us once more. A few times, I caught Noah's gaze, as if he wanted to say something. But the persistent waiting for Time and Revelia to come back choked off any other word. We were only allowed to listen.

'Daniel?' An hour later, Trusk reignited the conversation. 'Should we move? I don'f feel we should waif so long.'

'Yes, let's move!' Anita clearly used that as an opportunity to avoid bringing the conversation back to any of the previous topics—her and Patrick, her and Cherish.

Pulling ourselves back together, we waited a few more seconds at the large door. We had no idea what awaited us on the other side, and we were still not sure if it was the best way forwards. Nevertheless, ahead we went. Passing through the narrow space between the two doors, we stepped into an incredible cluster of ruins. The wall of the round tower ran around us, marked by pitch-black spots interrupted by bright bubbles of light. Something stirred inside, a silver, brilliant fluid dancing in a rotating motion. Some spheres were small dots fluctuating in thin air, while others were large enough to swallow Anita's kitchen with all her books.

'What are these things?' she asked as we moved forwards. Her voice bounced back and forth, like an echo lost in too much space.

'Again, that feeling…like something is pulling me by my skin,' Noah added.

'It's not just pulling,' I said, moving closer to a large one floating beside a white staircase on the far right. 'There is something else… This…crying? I don't know. It's like sadness, desperation.'

'I don't feel anything,' Anita said, with Trusk agreeing with her.

'No, it's true. Something is alive in here,' Noah replied, near a smaller one beside the front doors.

'Look! A way out, right there!' Anita moved to the other end of the circle, pointing at a wide crack between the bricks—a painful rip between in and out.

Before I could turn around and look, my right hand moved on its own, close to the bright surface of that shiny object. As my finger barely touched it, a warm wave took me in, sucking me with pure energy. My body disappeared from sight. A large, broken pavement ran all the way to a shrinking upper end, right in front of my eyes. Here and there, the walkway was torn apart, with pieces floating into nothingness, turning around on their spot. I was standing on the ground, but gravity felt minimal, as if I would fly if I attempted a jump. The others were left behind, and I found myself alone in a sea of darkness, the silence proudly sitting in a chair of final conquest.

'Let me go…' a soft voice cried from behind me.

'Who are you? What am I?' another added.

Deformed figures emerged out of nowhere, multiplying rapidly and moving towards me, their bodies contorted. They were horrifying, yet strangely, I wasn't afraid of them. It was as if a pure manifestation of sorrow had come to greet me. Soon they reached me, their hands forming quickly from their bodies, and they began touching me, begging for help. The cries we had heard materialized before my eyes. They were the dead, seeking rescue, hoping I could show them mercy and set them free. Whatever they had felt, they had mistaken me for a God. I wasn't Soul, and I wasn't meant to answer their prayers. I didn't know how I did it, but I understood their emotions. Their feelings were strong, piercing through my heart, bringing tears to my eyes.

'We came from nothing, but nothing won't let us go back.'

'It took our lives and imprisoned our way further…' another one said, its voice dragging each word.

'I came into being just now, but I don't have a body to give myself to…my purpose is gone. What am I now?'

'Who are you? What are you?' I asked gently.

'We don't know any more. We only know the present and nothing more…'

It seemed like their memories had been wiped out, and I couldn't determine if they had existed and were trapped in bodiless form or if they were meant to become beings but had been prevented from doing so. *Were they ever, or were they never?* I asked myself.

'Do you know where Soul is?' I asked as they moved around me, inspecting me.

'We only know the present and nothing more,' someone repeated.

'You bring with you the same sorrow he brought upon us,' another voice said, their body shifting in front of my eyes. 'There is something inside you…carrying the look of the enemy. He sees you and sees us through you… *Go away!*'

'Daniel? Daniel!' Anita's voice reached me from behind, from a dark wall of nothingness.

On the other side, a white, shining staircase had formed. It curved to the right, slowly ascending to the top. Whatever that vision was, it showed me how the tower must have appeared in ancient times. A bright dot appeared at the top, floating calmly. It wanted to be seen, it wanted me to follow it. Ignoring Anita's worried voice, I responded to a different kind of call. A few steps ahead, I encountered another glimpse of that strange magic.

'The evil is going to turn his eyes on me and all of you soon,' a tall being spoke softly. His head was covered by a bright light emanating from his hair, and his hands were like crystal, reflecting the space around. 'We must prepare to engage in battle!'

'How? He is pure energy. The people of these lands are made of flesh and bones. They will not stand a chance!' someone replied, made of the same magic.

'It's up to us to protect them. At this stage, all we can do is resist him…'

Anita's voice grew louder and louder. As I turned around, following her voice, I crossed the dark matter, returning to the real world as if I had moved from one plane to another with no trace in between. I was back where I belonged.

'Where the hell did you go?' Anita shouted, worried.

'I…I don't know. I touched that thing, and I was transported to this dark, very dark place, filled with…souls.'

'You did what?' Noah asked, surprised that I had embarked on a brief solo journey without his help, without our special connection.

'I just touched it, and I was gone. There is nothing in there,' I explained before Noah could test it for himself. 'Just loads of…people who wanted to move forwards. They are dead! They are all dead, trapped in this dying world.'

'Did they say anything?' Anita asked.

'Yes. They said they know nothing. It's as if they have no idea what's happened to this place. I asked about Soul. Nothing, they know nothing.'

'Alright, stop touching! All of you!' she exclaimed, pointing her finger at me and Noah. 'No touching! There is a way out over there.'

The opening Anita had pointed out led to another bridge, smaller this time, floating above the red vacuum below. Connected to it, a second tower patiently awaited us. The doors had been torn away, revealing a wide entrance. Afraid that the walkway would collapse beneath our feet like the previous one had, we ran across the bridge without hesitation, our feet stepping into the next abandoned structure. It felt as if we hadn't moved at all. The interior was exactly the same, but mirrored. Stairs descended and ascended to the left, and the orbs were scattered about, multiplying in number. Unfortunately, there was no way out. The tower's original opening had been concealed by numerous giant rocks that had collapsed to the ground from the top of the structure.

'I fhink fhe way was fhere,' Trusk said, pointing out the blocked, ancient path.

'Where do we go now? Oh my God, this crying is getting louder and louder!' Noah exclaimed, putting his hands on his ears, trying to make it stop.

'There is a way up and a way down, through the stairs. Which one?' Anita shouted, running towards it.

'No going up. Lef me check firsf, quickly!' Trusk flapped his wings and flew up to the far ceiling.

From the very top, Trusk flew through a small, square opening to the outside and came back after a few minutes. Rushing down, he brought unhappy news.

'Fhe ofher fower is crushed! If's up, buf fhere's no way in. Fhe bridge in befween is also gone!'

'Crap,' I said. 'So, we go down, I suppose?'

'Let's take the stairs below. It might lead us somewhere,' Anita added.

With no other options, we started our descent down the crooked stairs, silently hoping they would hold our weight. We were relieved that the way down was still standing, allowing us to proceed. As we descended, the cold pull grew weaker, along with the troubled emotions that came with it. A few ramps below, the white wall bricks turned grey and brown, giving way to rusty, earthy rock. Eventually, a small hole led us outside, many feet deep, in the open. The ground was filled with rocky stones, forming a dirt road between the towers. Here and there, puddles of red fire were puffing dark smoke, increasing in number on both sides of the strange riverbed. It was as if fresh water of a long-gone river had turned into nothing, leaving the surface exposed and burned.

'Which way?' Trusk asked, turning his head left and right.

'That way opens up, the left one closes up in between the towers...the mountain was right behind them, right?' Anita asked.

'Let's go!' Noah said, moving without hesitation.

I wasn't sure if we were heading in the right direction. After stalling for a few seconds, I followed the group, hoping we had chosen wisely. As we walked through the narrow space between the towers' feet, the ground became filled with hot, dark lava slowly flowing in its path, leaving us with little choice on where to safely put our feet.

'It looks like we're heading the right way!' Noah shouted, several steps ahead. 'The mountain had lava flowing on both sides, remember?'

'Even so, are we sure we'll find a way in?' I replied.

But before I could doubt any longer, the landscape opened up to an exact replica of Time's vision. The path upwards widened, leading into the large mountain where Soul was buried. Everything around us was long dead, and silence was broken only by the rumblings of the tall guard watching over the God's prison. At the centre of its feet, a small, grey stone-like dot stood shut. We could barely make out the heavy doors taking shape. As we moved closer, the ground grew more filled with piping-hot, red lava, leaving a very narrow path to our goal. The heat became unbearable, cutting off our breath, and we suddenly felt as if we had been walking for days.

'That's the place, alright,' Anita said.

'How do we get there? There isn't much to walk on, and, to be honest, it's getting very hot here,' Noah added.

'Trusk, can you pull us all the way up?' I asked.

'I can fry…buf I feel very fired. If's like I wanf to shake my skin off!'

'Let's try and go as far as we can on foot,' I suggested.

The path ahead, before we could reach the doors, was still very long. As we ascended, the surroundings grew harsher and more toxic. Stripped of almost everything we were wearing, we placed our clothes over our mouths, trying to filter the smoky air as best we could. Nonetheless, we stretched our energies to their limits, and when we closed most of the gap, Trusk pulled us over the last mile, consuming the little power he had left in his wings. Almost crashing upon landing, we abruptly arrived right by the large doors, tired and burned by the growing fire. Our lungs were failing, our minds starting to fade into the scorching field, and we were draining our very essence. So, we fell, and we fell hard, in a long, boiling silence.

'It's going to be alright… It will only take a moment,' a soft, gentle voice said. She was pure light, her face reflecting the colours of the entire universe. She embodied light and colours, a vast range of emotions, the full spectrum of what was, what is, and what was going to be.

'I…I am…what am I?' I managed to say. It was as if I was hearing my voice for the first time. I was pure realization of being, in contact with the reality I was made of, and I was lost.

'You are the reason why everything exists. It all came to be because I wanted to love the things I have created, and I love them even more now that they are… You are Love,' she replied, her glow diminishing as she revealed her true face. Her eyes were like vortexes of gravitational waves, her skin ethereal and almost transparent.

'There is…so much…I…' But I couldn't speak. I was overwhelmed by my consciousness taking form.

'It's going to be alright… I'm Creation. The pure will of making. Anything you see, hear, feel, touch—it's me making it. I came to exist alone, from dark matter. I slowly came to understand that I was, a long time ago. Once I had a mind of my own, I decided to be even more, to create, to make more matter exist. And I wanted to, and I loved it too. And when the first world manifested out of my will, I felt compelled to make more, to be with it, to protect, to keep it safe. So much did I feel that I abandoned my own home to become another entity: you.'

My body lay on the ground, but my mind soared through eternity and beyond. At the edge of a dying world, I made contact with the beginning of my history, the very first time I existed. I could feel my hands forming, my heart beating. I was becoming, carried by the magic of my creator. I was Love for the very first time.

Chapter Fourteen
The Tiara of Souls

∞

Against his will and against his own warning, Time had brought Revelia and the evil army far away from us. Rewinding the wheel once more, he had dropped them to a time before they had found us and pulled Revelia again through the pages of history, away from the growing threat.

'When are we?' Revelia asked, right after reappearing in a desolate land.

'I didn't want to, but I had to. Our fate was hanging by a very thin thread. I brought the enemy back a few rhocs ago, then brought us forwards.'

'Where are the others? We left them alone!' she said, worried, her eyes already turning red, scanning the time passed and the time ahead.

'Hopefully, they are sticking to the plan...'

'They are! They did. They are at the mountain doors... I can't see beyond that. I see no future after that!' she exclaimed.

'We need to hurry. You need to tell me where the evil is finding the key before it gets too late,' Time said, moving closer to Revelia, who was growing smaller just standing by Time's large figure.

'It looks like before,' Revelia said, after getting on her knees, her hands touching the shaking ground, connecting to the very past and future of that land. 'Corpses are everywhere, rotted by time and fire. It's where the final blow landed. Soul has his key on his head, among the people he swore to protect... I can't see anything else. The mountain is gone? Is Soul still alive?'

'Look wider! Do you see any other details? Look at the landscape around,' Time urged.

'I see *him*. He is very powerful. He is as large as the vastness of his dark will... I can't... I can't look,' Revelia replied, and tears started to stream down her face. Her light, pale green skin turned dark as if the evil entity consumed her from within.

'You have to!' Time shouted, putting his hands on Revelia's shoulders, keeping her energies up, making her stronger.

'I see only Soul and someone who looks very much like him...and me? Between two large hills...there is a river where the dead are drifting as they pass away... He sees me. *He sees me!*'

And the Leonty instantly turned off her magic, petrified by the unusual event. That was the first time she had seen someone from the past connecting with her, navigating the flow of time backwards, reaching her instead of her reaching them. Nothing had discovered Time's magic running through her veins. He knew they had come, tricking the wheel of history, briefly fooling him. Before the magical connection could destroy her, she had to let it go and come back to the present. Revelia and Time had to run again, smoothing out the wrinkles of past days, quickly joining the fight, seizing the artefact, and leaving.

'We have to go and get it! Hold on to me. Whatever you see, whatever is happening around us, do not interfere! Let the past take its course. We only need one thing and one thing only!' Time said, pulling her up.

The bright green clepsydra showed up out of nowhere, pulsing with a strong light. The enveloping energy instantly whisked them away, transporting them back into the middle of the raging war. A trembling, loud sound welcomed them back, the ground shaking under Nothing's will, amidst hundreds of thousands of beings at war. Two sides faced each other in battle, the evil army smaller and weaker, indicating an outcome that was not what we had learned to expect. It seemed they had diminished in numbers, nearing their defeat. In the midst of the raging day, the sky turned dark, a swirling energy releasing its force from both sides of the horizon.

The large mountain was gone, replaced by two hills on fire. In between, a long river flowed with corpses that once belonged to both factions, now on their way to the far sea. The resistance took the shape of Humans, their flesh resembling those known to Revelia in her world. Some were large in size, while others looked like tall, hairy beasts fighting alongside the innocents who were pushing the evil away. Their will was strong, men and women alike, all fighting for their lives. The horrifying sound of clashing blades reverberated throughout the battlefield. Varayal inhabitants had gathered to fight the battle of their lives, pushing against the enemy with no mercy.

At the centre of the field, someone resembling Time stood, hands outstretched from his sides, reflecting light and colours like a precious diamond, holding in place as many souls as he could. If the allies fell, he pulled their ghosts right back up, resurrecting them with the same strong will. Hundreds of thousands of hands surged from the hot ground, their owners returning from the land of death, connected to the very power Soul had unleashed. They dragged their enemies down, holding their feet and slowing their wicked advances. Every element of the land was transforming into living beings, fighters called to a never-ending war for their freedom.

Trees were snatching their roots from the roasting soil, joining the battle, swinging their branches, twirling their enemies in the hot air. Amidst the chaos, large animals were pushing Nothing's army line towards the deadly river. With enormous, sharp teeth leading their charge and coats shining in grey, they moved with lightning-like speed across the lands. Their bones and flesh possessed by the souls of dead Humans, they shared one will and one goal: victory against the invader. A long, silver vest was fluttering in the hot wind, Soul's hood down, his head adorned with a bright, pulsating crown. Like almost invisible, glittering wires, hundreds of strings flowed from his head to the world surrounding him. His magic connected with the planet he swore to protect, Revelia and Time bore witness to the very origin of Soul's power. That was the tiara we had all been searching for.

'There! He is there!' Time shouted, his voice overwhelmed by the metallic sound of war. 'We need to be fast; any moment now!'

'Hold on!' Revelia shouted. 'Someone else has just entered this world and this lost timeline!' But Time had already moved away, his mind and eyes focused on the shining artefact.

And so, the time came when a large, dark shadow enveloped the skies, pushing his will down onto the lands. Soul raised his arms, shielding the people he had sworn to protect, his knees crushed against the ground. But there was no way out any more. Just when they were close to victory, their fate suddenly changed. People stopped fighting, horrified by the support that had come for the evil side, and started to flee, scattering around like prey in imminent peril. Nothing was pure, black energy. He was invisible to the eyes, and yet he encompassed everything that existed. His shadow turned day into night, dismantling the world into its raw elements. He turned proud warriors into dust, shattering their existence in the vastness of the universe. As he pushed his will down on the standing God, Time moved across the space, a mere flicker into Nothing's sight.

'It's going to be alright... I promise you!' Time whispered into Soul's ears as he quickly removed the tiara from his head.

'Time? What are you doing here? What are you doing?! Noo!' Soul shouted.

But just as Time had come, he disappeared. With the power removed from its host, Soul collapsed into the depths of the earth, the soil reshaping itself into a giant mountain burying him underneath. In shock, Revelia was immediately moved away from her spot, as Time returned, turning the future ahead, briefly seen by the source of every evil. In the consciousness of a long-gone past, Nothing had just learned that the book of time had been rewritten. The enemy had come from a distant future in the attempt to change the outcome of his war. His rightful, inevitable victory was being challenged once more.

Revelia's mind raced fast as they moved through time. She had witnessed Soul's fate and the deaths of thousands in just a few seconds. She couldn't stop thinking about how Time could have done that, taking away the only power capable of fighting back. With her mastery of past and future sight, she couldn't ignore the thought that they might have caused it all. Was it destined to happen that way? Was their intervention the reason for Soul's defeat? By the time they reached the mountain, the four of us had fainted from exhaustion and the heat. As I was awakened by Revelia, the first thing my eyes managed to focus on was her troubled face attempting a comforting smile.

'We are here…wake up!' she said.

'Trusk, come on, we got the key,' Time added, helping Trusk to his feet. 'Not long before he comes to turn this place into dust.'

'Can we use the key to get in?' I asked, shaking off the dust from my clothes, my head still spinning.

'No. The cage and its spell are further below. This way,' Time replied, swinging his right arm to crack open the heavy doors.

Darkness ruled that solitary place. We couldn't see anything around us, neither above nor below. Time pulled out his clepsydra, casting a green light into the descent. There was no clear path, only a series of caves running one after another.

'He is after the gateway! He saw you!' Revelia said as we teleported from one claustrophobic space to the next.

'I was afraid he might have. We really have very little time,' the God replied.

'Who saw you?' Noah asked, squeezing through narrow cracks between the rocks.

'Nothing. I took the key right before the moment Soul was cast away. He must have seen me taking it!'

'How do we know this wasn't his plan all along?' Revelia asked, finally voicing her thoughts. 'It feels like we are the ones making all of this happen.'

'What do you mean?' Anita asked, worried that we had missed important details of our short-lived mission.

'I took the key from Soul right before his end. But there was no other outcome. He would have been imprisoned anyway, and his artefact with him… I had to take it then and there,' Time said, sounding somewhat annoyed by Revelia's questioning of his actions.

'How is it possible?' Anita continued. 'After doing something so radical like taking away Soul's artefact, the future, well our past now…this is so confusing…' she added, sighing. 'How is that the future remained exactly the same?'

'This is my point!' Revelia was pushing her idea with no regard for Time's reaction. 'The only way it would remain unchanged is if it was meant to be this way.'

'As if we were meant to be here, taking it from Soul and then making it happen?' I questioned, looking at Time. After all, we were at the presence of the one who owned the ticking of every second in every world of the universe.

'This way, hurry your steps!' Time let out, ignoring our questions.

A few moments later, the last suffocating cave gave way to a large hole. In the middle, a grey, rocky square box lay silent. There was no sound, no magic flowing through that space. It was as if a silent, ceremonial duty was being observed by the many souls we had seen wandering in the desolated lands. As if the ground had contracted under the weight of a deceased God, the centre of the cold room had sunk several feet into the rocky terrain. A few large stones were lifting the burial box from the dark bottom, bringing it into an unnatural light that reflected from the glittering surface running across the walls.

'We found him,' Time exclaimed, his voice resonating in the large empty cave.

'It looks like a sarcophagus,' Anita said, moving closer.

'And look, here is the mark, the shape of a crown. That's the keyhole!' Noah exclaimed. Our voices reverberated back and forth, echoing within the lost chamber. It felt like we were violating that sacred space with our questionable intentions.

'Are we sure this is what we are supposed to do?' I asked. 'What will happen when we set him free?'

'It's the only way. Put your trust in me!' Time replied.

And we had no choice but to trust him. He had proven to be our strongest ally. When we had lost him, it felt like we had lost our own faith. He had come and rescued us from the Harpies. He had provided the answers we were seeking. If he said it was the only way, then we should not question it. It was the only way.

'If he saw me, he knows what we are about to do. The moment I release Soul, I'll bring us back as much as we need to anticipate his move. I don't know if it will work, and I don't know how long I can keep him restrained. Please, remember your promise to me. If I fall behind, please use your amulets to reach Runae!'

Our unusual silence conveyed worry on our part but approval for Time. We lacked the strength to ask or challenge him any longer, so we let our quiet thoughts be mistaken for a silent agreement of 'yes, we will'. As Time brought the tiara close to the lid of the stony cage, the walls around us started shaking violently. After a moment of hesitation, driven by an unbreakable will, Time placed the tiara in its rightful place, carved by a forgot spell from a past battle.

Warm, bright energy radiated from the artefact, filling the space around us. Cracks appeared on every side of the large box, casting rays of blue light into the depths of the cave. An incredible constellation of dots and lines projected onto the walls, with our shadows climbing behind us. Drawn by pure power, the raw elements of the rocky cave emerged from the walls. Particles of metal rose from the ground, broken crystal pieces came together from the ceiling, converging at the centre.

In a magic that reminded us of the way Aura had taken shape by the node in Runae, it looked like the resurrecting God was absorbing the very core of Varayal into his veins, bones, and skin. Slowly, Soul's form took shape before our stunned eyes. His glass-like skin was glittering like wet sand under the kiss of the warm sun. His large shoulders were squaring the silvery cloak that had just formed around his neck and over his back. A shining, bright blue set of eyes revealed the presence of another God, another supreme being.

'Soul...' Time said, moving closer to the reborn God. 'This was the only way. I'll explain later, but we need to leave this place immediately!'

'Time? What have you done?'

'Brother, it was the only way, trust me!'

'Who are these people?' Soul asked, ignoring Time's statement.

'I'll tell you more later. We need to go!'

'I can't abandon this planet. Its life depends on me,' the God replied, still trying to mentally grasp his new reality.

'I know, but a lot has happened while you were gone...' Time insisted.

'Gone because of you!' The God quickly realized what had truly happened. 'And coming from you… Weren't you the one who said we should not leave our protected worlds? Weren't you the one who said you would not leave Runae to help your brothers?'

His face grey, almost shimmering with a silvery light, Soul appeared upset. Memories of recent events flooded his mind, right before his eyes. The veil-like fabric surrounding his body was made of thin, soft silk, acting as a delicate covering for his fragile skin. His head, neck, and arms reflected the light from the tiara he held in his hands. Like a crystal mosaic, Soul was composed of a unique nature, a diamond with hundreds of thousands of facets.

'There is nothing left here to protect.' Revelia stepped forwards, the only one among us who wasn't afraid to speak in the presence of such a powerful being.

'What I protect is not of your nature. Invisible to the eyes, even the most powerful like yours, there is much more that needs protection,' he replied.

'Soul, you can see beyond. Look right there…' Time pointed his finger at us. 'For the first time in many lifetimes, we have each other again!'

'Love?' Soul questioned, after a moment of scrutiny. 'In Human bodies? How is this possible? What sorcery is this?'

The God moved closer to Noah and me, placing his cold hands on our faces. He sent warm waves of pure magic through our bodies, delving into our hearts and minds in a fleeting moment. As if his mind had ensnared ours in a resonating spell, his thoughts became our own, his feelings intertwined with ours, and his memories of a distant past surged forwards, reaching the surface of our present. In the blink of an eye, Noah and I were plunged into something lost in ancient times. We were transformed into one entity, a single God standing in the presence of three others.

'I understand Talush is situated close to the enemy, but we cannot leave our worlds unprotected,' Time stated, gazing from a large opening in an enormous room. In front of him the distant horizon opened up wide, his gaze directed to the sun as it gently caressed the sea's soft skin. His radiant figure challenged the grandeur of the celestial star, casting a trail of sparkling lights upon the tranquil waters. 'You have your own evil growing within your very homes!'

'If we remain divided, we will surely lose!' Soul retorted.

'We must unite once and for all. Together!' Health asserted, pushing against her brother's resistance. 'One by one, he will claim us all!'

'And what will happen when we mobilize together while his armies of scavengers raid our worlds? We may be challenging him, but he already has his pawns in place everywhere! Runae is currently holding its ground against the forces of evil, and it will continue to do so as long as I remain vigilant by its side!' Time refused to yield.

'I must agree,' Love chimed in unexpectedly, taking the others by surprise. They were gathered within his own house, his planet, as guests in his own home. Love gazed down from the towering heights of the secret meeting place, his eyes fixed on the Humans far below. 'This world is falling under the tightening grip of the one we dare not speak of. I cannot see him, but I can witness his influence more frequently now. I have come to realize that I cannot control it as a singular being. I need to do more. I need to be more.'

'What do you mean?' Soul drew nearer, placing his hands on Love's shoulders, sensing a burgeoning power.

'I believe I have discovered a way to be present in all places at once, to be everywhere that matters. I can manifest myself from my own essence, much like our own mother. I can generate new embodiments of myself,' Love explained, turning around to meet Health's gaze.

'This is incredible! You can actually give birth to new lives within yourself?' Health marvelled at the possibility.

'This is madness!' Soul thundered. 'This is too great a risk. If you are truly considering dividing your essence among others, you are not creating, you are unmaking!'

'I don't fully understand what all of you are discussing,' Time interjected as he joined his siblings in the open space. The brilliance of their light far surpassed that of the sun.

'Love is attempting to forge more Gods by partitioning his power among many.' Soul expressed deep concern. 'This is not the power of Creation; it is the antithesis. You are diminishing yourself into smaller replicas, each possessing less power.'

'If Love believes this is necessary to protect this world, so be it!' Time proclaimed, finding a way to justify his stance. If Love chose to remain and defend Earth, it aligned perfectly with Time's desired outcome. Secretly, he too had embraced the idea of bestowing his power upon those who would aid him in his quest. Somewhere within Runae, a spark of Creation's power awaited discovery, waiting to be unearthed, brought into the light, and transformed it into Flares. If he succeeded, his people would possess the power of their own God.

In an instant, Noah and I were brought to the cold reality of that caging cave. Time's hand on Soul's wrist, he had moved him away from us, detaching his enchanting power from our suggestible minds. In Soul's face an expression of judgement had fallen like a dark veil.

'I see you haven't changed… Like the power you withhold, you are immutable!', Soul whispered, moving a few steps away.

'This is not about me, brother. We are here for a far more important achievement. You have to trust me! As you were the second one to fall, there is much more history you are not aware of. Trust me! Our victory depends on how quick we act. We need to leave this place immediately. He is after us.' Time's words magnetized Soul's gaze, moving it away from us, pulling his attention to his words, as if diverting him on his thoughts, like a radio suddenly changing frequency.

'Yes, you haven't changed at all. Your deepest pits are almost soulless. It's always the ticking of what comes next, no space for what is truly within…'

'Dig deeper if you wish…but do it later!' And Time had looked at us, making clear we had to be ready. We were leaving.

That last exchange, that short, sharp conversation, had brought up something we hadn't seen before. As Time was the only God we knew, we had no idea what it was like before our time came. We didn't know how it was to live among powerful beings, being one of them. Their natures were different, their purposes were different. *If Soul cannot see feelings in Time's heart… What is Time seeing in Soul's? In ours?* I thought. Whatever we had put ourselves into, digging for the truth right from the start, it was clearly bigger than we expected. Somehow our truth was not our own to possess. There was more beyond the reach of our minds.

We were silly young adults trying to solve the twisted path of adulthood without anybody telling us what, in the end, we would become. *Take away the magic, the incredible things we have witnessed, the secrets lurking in the shadows of our dreams and fears, what do we have left?* I thought. *No matter what is in store for me, for us, is this not just…life? How really different are we from every other human being trying to leave their teenager years behind, becoming who they are expected to be? Why are we not in control of our own future?*

'What's wrong?' Noah came close, touching my hand. I knew he had a special access to my mind, my thoughts. A few steps away, Anita was looking at us, at me, then at Noah. She was trying to tell us something, tell me words that could not come in the open, freely. Before I could step by her side and ask her, Time had resumed his push on our quest. We had to move and be fast. His hands moved to his artefact, the clepsydra had come out in a snap. A bright green light enveloped the silent cave, making it shake, its walls shedding tears made of dust and stones. The cave's only child was leaving it behind for good. The ancient bond between the captor and its hostage was being broken, for good.

In the blink of an eye, we had come out of the deep cave, right into the open. As Trusk could almost read the Gods' minds, he had flown away as we appeared. For a moment, the fear that he was merely running away came up in my mind. *Am I projecting myself onto him? I would run too.* But like a scout called on duty, he was scanning the road ahead fearlessly.

'He is not going to find it! The gateway is already gone. He has reduced the rings and their doors to ashes already!' Revelia said, screening just a few minutes forwards. And then the space and moments repeated themselves, as if we had been rewound. Trusk was brought back a few seconds before he could leave us. Time had put his hand on his tiny head, preventing him from flying.

'It's too late, my friend. Hold on. We will need to go back just once more before he destroys our way out…' the God said, his mind puzzled as he went silent.

We hadn't moved an inch; our minds had not detected any spinning of time. Whatever magic Time was executing, it was of a different kind. After a few seconds of absolute silence, breaking the hold, Trusk said, 'Whaf's happening? Whaf are we waifing for?'

'Time?' Revelia looked at the large God, who was looking around us with a visible worried look.

'How far back are we going?' Noah asked, believing that was the reason why his magic was taking so long.

'We are not. We are exactly when we were. Time?' Revelia pushed her question once more, right in the God's face. Something was terrifying her.

'His power is growing; he won't let me! In his core, in his pure power, time is irrelevant. He is so close now…' Time said, his voice showing an unusual struggle. 'He doesn't let me go back!'

'Where is he? We can't see him!' I blurted out.

'He is coming…' Soul whispered, his crystal face turning grey, a shadow dulling his bright look.

'Daniel, Noah! You need to use it now!' Anita suddenly shouted, taking us by surprise. Her voice was deeper, her tone strangely demanding.

'No!' the God replied.

But the shadow of darkness and emptiness fell on our heads rapidly. A fast-growing gloom spread into the surroundings, the ground turning black, the sky losing its brightness. We became the same shadows we were surrounded by. Whatever force was at play in the lands, it had the power of a never-ending, timeless nothing. Something was holding its grip on us, squeezing our hearts and mind, pulling the string of pain right across our bodies. The standing Gods had no way to overcome it. We had faced threats before, and we had defeated evil before, but this time we were no match. As the universe opened its devouring mouth, the skies began to wobble, sucking the very essence of creation.

'Why do you keep trying?' A thundering, deep voice travelled through the space around us. 'My order is the only order that can be. You and all of this were never meant to be. Go and be a part of me as you were before.'

'We are not letting go! We are Creation's children, and we will never be gone! No matter how many times you try!' Time shouted into the foggy air.

'You don't have more tricks to play…God…' And that last word sounded so slow that we could picture its invisible disgust in our heads. 'There is no time in me. I'm eternal. You are a mere deviation of what it is supposed to be. Be gone now, with the rest of the beings you thought you could protect!'

We could have easily been back in one of my dreams. There were no stairs, no ceremony, no people rejoicing. But there we were, about to cast the spell to conjure Love back to life, before the dark blade struck us dead once more. There was no way out. Perhaps there never was. We were fools, playing with the lucky circumstances we had. If we had failed so many times before, why would now be any different?

Chapter Fifteen
The Turning Point

∞

Like pawns under an imminent checkmate, we squeezed close to one another, afraid of something we could not see. In a futile attempt to hide Trusk from an evil that could see around and through us, I stood in front of him. His little wings drooped, his tiny arms holding on to my legs.

'Should we fly away, Daniel?' he whispered. His rounded, dark eyes staring at me, he was praying to be moved away at once. But I had no reassuring words that would come out of my mouth.

'Our only way out is back in time; we need the gateway to leave this world,' I said.

'He's holding the wheel; his force is on it!' Time repeated.

'Daniel,' Anita said, pulling my arm. 'You need to use it now!' Her face was shifting as something else was coming out of her body, sending me into a frenzy. Her entire presence, her bones and flesh were there with me, she seemed the Anita I knew, but something else was speaking through her, surfacing to a terrifying reality. 'We need just a tiny moment, a flickering in his power. Time, you will need to act fast. As soon as his attention is on them, turn this present back and set us free!'

'I don't like this idea at all,' Time replied, resisting. 'But I suppose we have no other way.'

'Alright then, act fast!'

Those were Anita's last words before the events started to spin frenetically. Noah and I had taken the risk, betting our lives and the lives of the ones there with us. Our eyes shut, our hands brought together, our hope was hanging on a simple touch. We would come to evoke a magic we had not yet learned to master. We were attempting to repeat the past, when we had discovered our very own connection, on the tiny island in Noah's Bridge. There was no music, no dancing this time, just the ticking fingers of death playing in our hearts. So, our artefacts emerged from our bodies, leaving their secret place inside our souls, shining with a powerful light into the enemy's shocking reality.

As he had warned, the evil was expecting Time's magic, Soul's tricks, to attempt a well-known strategy, but we had come into the open instead, taking him by surprise. Anita's plan had worked once again, at least for the first part.

'I have it!' Time shouted.

'Let's go. Hold on to your clepsydras!' Revelia added, putting her hand on her chest, the amulet squeezed in between her fingers.

In the contorting space between now and then, future and past, our bodies wouldn't move. As if we could attempt the rewinding of our lives only for a few seconds, our faces were deforming and reforming convulsively. Although Anita's plan was the best we could come up with in the rush of the hour, it had a flaw. The way out was open indeed, but the way in wasn't letting us through. Time tried again and again, but our feet were holding the same dangerous ground, preventing us from take-off.

'What's wrong? Can't you bring us back?' Revelia asked as Noah and I were moving closer, dragged by a new, stranger force emanating from our artefacts. Our power was growing wildly.

'I have it! I have the node back in place, but I can't reach Runae!'

'Something else has happened in this past.' Revelia caught a glimpse of an intangible presence. 'There is another God walking through this node! She is so…weak. What am I seeing? There is something else happening in this very spot. Not now, before!

'This won't last long! Let's go to our protected planet!' Anita said. Her voice had changed completely. Whatever had her in hand, it had come forwards. 'Iris will protect us. Let's go to the night of the Great Failure, by the ritual stones!'

Our plan was halted, but the outcome had to be the same. We had to leave at once, but our destination had been changed, forced by an evil impediment. We didn't know back then, but something awful had happened. There was no way back we could use any more. Our amulets, as our hopes, were hanging by a very thin line. In fear of losing the moment, the only opening into Nothing's will, Time had welcomed Anita's idea and made us disappear, once again escaping our fate, delaying our end a little longer.

'Where are we?' I asked, once I opened my eyes. The shell moved away from Noah's heart, waking me up to consciousness.

'I know this place. This is...home,' Noah replied, perplexed.

'What happened? We were supposed to go back to Runae!'

'Daniel, Noah...there was no other way. We could not get in, and we could not hesitate any longer!' Anita took my hands, a weak smile appearing on her cheeks.

'Why, how?' My eyes turned to Time.

'Something has happened...in Runae,' Revelia said, taking over before Time could speak. 'I could not see the future, anyone's future, before we left... And now we can't get back in. Something terrible has happened!'

'We don't know that yet! Let's not jump to any conclusions,' Time said, moving towards a destroyed house, touching its foundation where the walls had been stripped out by a massive blow.

'John!' I cried out, desperate.

'Whaf are you falking abouf?' Trusk finally realized what we all were thinking, his heart following our own sinking path.

'I don't understand...' I continued. 'He was there, in Varayal, in its past time. How was he able to go after Runae if he was there with us?'

'Daniel,' Time replied. 'He is everything and everywhere. He can move across space and time as he pleases. He does not respond to anything we could possibly imagine...'

The silence that fell between us brought the heavy burden of fear. Except for the newly freed God, we all pictured the most horrifying ending for Runae and whoever was in it. Trusk's eyes were fixed on me, desperately waiting for a comforting answer. Anita had followed Time, away from the group, looking for help. It wasn't long before it came.

'Iris, it's me! Open the passage, hurry!' Anita spoke, her voice completely changed. Whoever she was, it wasn't our friend talking.

'Cherish, is it you?' A voice came out from the dark woods surrounding the house. It was as if the giant tree where Noah's heart was buried was talking to us. 'You made it. You brought the missing Gods!'

And the place around us faded away, folding on its own, rolling reality upside down. We were brought back to a frozen point in time, to too many centuries before. It all looked like a wrong déjà vu. John was gone and replaced by a more powerful being that meant very little to me compared to him.

'We have the three Gods. We made it, but at great risk. He knows. He knows we brought back Time and Soul, but more importantly, he knows they are back,' Anita said, pointing her finger at me and Noah.

'It won't be long before he strikes again, then,' Iris replied.

'Will this place hold?' Noah asked.

'As long as he doesn't know about it,' Time replied.

'Or as long as this world exists anyway. If he turns it to dust, then everything will go with it,' Soul added.

'Can we try Runae again?' I asked, shifting to a completely different topic, my hands still holding on to Trusk's shoulders, my eyes on Revelia's. We had left our loved ones behind, and as far as we knew, they could all be gone.

'I've tried again, just a few moments ago. I can't reach it,' Time said coldly, almost dismissing me.

I wasn't sure if it was just me who was reading through Time's words as if he had no real interest in the matter. After all, my emotions were different. I was different. Soul's words to him were repeating in my head. *Is Time soulless? He must feel something for the people in Runae. He made sure they could protect themselves. He brought them back. Was it for a pure sense of duty? Is his commitment now turned to something else?*

'We need to get back; we have to,' I insisted.

'I've tried, Daniel. It looks like the gate is closed,' Time responded.

'Well, Noah and I can try then,' I said, looking at Noah, hoping for support. Unfortunately, his mind was already projected to our next step. His will was the Gods' one; he was ready to release Love.

'I think it's safer if we stick to our plan. Once done, we might really have a shot!' he replied.

'You don't understand, I want to go back to Runae!'

'Yes, me foo!' Trusk stood by my side.

When did we part ways? I thought. *Both my friends don't understand how important John is to me? How vital it is to know that Reela and the other Chomps are OK. How can these Gods be my real family, my own brothers, if we don't share the same values?* We had suddenly broken up into factions. On my side, Trusk and Revelia, who shared my same worries and feelings. On Noah's side, Time and Soul, who needed to move further. Anita stood in the middle, unable to make a decision. Her mind had been taken over by something ancient, and her body was hosting two wills at once. Eventually, she said, 'Quiet! Hold your words, we are not alone any more!' And her eyes darted around, her arms reaching for the walls of that invisible dome between now and then.

Something was moving in the space around us. Like water boiling, bubbling figures were appearing randomly. Some were very large; we could see their shapes but not their true identities. Our breath suddenly held to a pause, my arguing against the others was abruptly muted. Petrified by the enemy presence, we stood still; sweat on our foreheads, wax statues melting under the burning fear.

'It's them again,' Anita whispered. 'They are back, perhaps they never left.'

'Do they know we are standing in here?' Noah asked.

'They don't,' Iris replied. 'But they know something is happening in this very spot. They can sense it.'

'Can they break in?' I asked.

'This is a time bubble. They can walk in but can't be here with us. They are while we have been, if you know what I mean,' Time explained.

I was listening to Time's riddles, but I wasn't really paying attention. Almost annoyed by that other delay, I only cared about John, Daisy, and the Chomps we had left behind. Eventually, some of those figures walked in, right in between us, slowly. Two were very large; one was wearing a dark coat, so long it trailed on the ground, with strange marks on its sides, resembling an ornate, abnormal tail. The other one, walking beside the first, was dragging itself on its skinny, bare feet. It had no shoes but was wearing long, wrinkled trousers. Its arms were exposed, covered in scars. Its face looked horribly deformed, with tiny eyes lost in large, dark cavities. It was the pure expression of desolation.

'These are Algos and Desolos. Pain and Despair,' Iris whispered. 'He has sent the pure strength of his army on us.'

'It would be much worse if we shared the present with them. If you listen closely, you can still feel their presence in your heart,' Anita said.

'Just by looking at them, I feel sick!' And Noah turned his face to the other side, his gaze on me. His eyes showed disgust, mine anger and disappointment. He knew what I was silently telling him, he knew I felt betrayed, and so, a few seconds later, his look went to the ground, staring his own feet. A sudden cold breeze came from the east, its invisible claws marking the hard soil, making the dead brown leaves fly around.

In the silence of the woods, we could feel the weight of their power, their pure essence. Our thoughts were almost threatened by the desperation and pain they were spreading along their path. But that was very little compared to what would come next. A third being, larger than the previous ones and twice the size of Time, moved in, preceded by a shocking, deathly power. The grass under his adorned feet turned instantly dead, trees went grey, and their leaves crumbled into dust. Golden sandals adorned his feet and long, yellow threads wrapped around his knees, leaving his legs covered with a black veil halfway through. His hips were bound by a golden belt, like a shiny break between the bottom and top, and his chest had a large, metallic circle with an X bent on its side. His face was covered by long dark hair, moving and wobbling as if it had its own will, like a thousand snakes looking for their prey. His chin and a portion of a horrifying mouth were the only things we could see. There were no teeth, no lips, only a hole spinning on its own.

'They are not here, my master...' Algos said.

'But they are...they were...' the large one replied, his voice like the whistle of a cold wind. His words were coming out as part of a horrifying hiss, as if he was dragging the space around, as if he could swallow the surroundings with the mere power of his mouth.

As we listened, terrified by their hollow, dark presence, some others started to walk close to us. Whatever they were, it was an army with one purpose only: destruction.

'They are all back to haunt us. Even Death is on your trail.' Iris said.

'Are they the evil of your world?' Revelia asked.

'They are…' Anita moved closer to Algos, her face almost touching his. Whoever had her in hand, it wasn't afraid. 'We won't be able to leave this time and space as long as they stay here. We are trapped!'

'These beings are pure nothing,' Soul interjected. 'They have no core, no soul. It's like pure emptiness. They are Nothing's army.'

'But we have you…and Time! We should be able to overcome them, right?' Noah asked.

'You don't understand. Our power can only do what it can do. Nothing more. Time can spin the wheel of days if needed, and I can give a soul to empty vessels, but we have no fighting power.'

'What about Love? What if we bring him back, right now? Will he be able to fight them off?'

'Even if he did, we can't bring him back,' Time added.

'What?' I exclaimed, surprised.

'Remember what you said, by the towers?' Anita took over, letting Pain pass her by. 'We knew there was someone else missing…' Her voice had changed again. Anita was clearly back with us.

'Is that you again?' I asked, and a spontaneous smile popped up on my face.

'I am… I think… The Gods are supposed to be three…it was always meant this way. Three to bring Love back. Three without counting you.'

'So, I was right! We are not done…we are not done hunting, finding… All this time we were ignoring this crucial piece, thinking we had it in our hands, thinking we were close to our turning point…'

'But we are, Daniel…' Time said, moving close to me. 'Not in the way you have imagined. This is much further than we have ever gone. There is no memory of any other time we managed to go this far. I'm back, Soul is back. This has never happened since the ancient times.'

'There is a way to get that memory back… There is a way to see through the past and bring it back to us,' Iris chimed in. 'Cherish is finally here. With time and in full strength, she will have access to the thousand years in which Love existed.'

'But there is no time,' Revelia whispered, moving away from one of the deadly Awoken Ones that were screening the spot.

Under the impression we were safe in that time bubble, we had dismissed their presence amongst us. Although they were large and terrifying, our thoughts and goals were pushing forwards in our minds, almost removing everything else from our sight.

'We do have two problems to solve then,' I said. 'We need to find the missing God, wherever it is...and we need to get back to Runae as soon as possible!'

But before anyone else could share their thoughts, a large number of evil beings had started to flow in between the eight of us. They were moving slowly, randomly, following our scent lost in time. Eventually, one of them spoke above the wicked whispers.

'There is an upcoming surge...something is waking them up...can't you feel it? Right there, it's coming from right here!' it said. Its face resembled that of a man, but contorted in anger. His eyes were on fire, his mouth curved into madness.

'Strife!' the large one shouted. 'Which ones do you sense?'

'Many...even my own sister is back!'

'Where? Where is she? Where is the rest?' Death shouted, his metal chest brightening up, his mouth spinning like a stormy black hole.

'If Harmonia is here, it means he is back!' Desolos replied from further away. She was showing interest in the large tree that was once overlooking Noah's artefact.

'If that's true, that will be as far as they will get! Go now! Search every corner, find them all!'

'Is it not better to call him? Erase everything, for good?' Desolos asked, her worried look showing more than her pure power of sorrow. If there was a hierarchy among them, it was manifesting right there and then, in front of us.

'He cannot fully act! You know he can't! Go now!'

And Death walked away, his shoulders and body disappearing in smoke as he turned into pure air. His large figure had gone to nothing, leaving a trace of dying earth just where he stood a few seconds earlier.

One by one, the number of those wicked beings had grown smaller. Those that remained loomed around us for a few more minutes before eventually leaving our spot. With the fear finally releasing its grip on our hearts, we breathed normally again. Iris had moved away, into the depths of the forest, accompanied by Soul who had left Time in the centre of that invisible dome. His eyes were fixed on the darkness, his ears tuned to the surroundings. Anita walked close to me, sitting down by a large rock, her face showing a compassion that I couldn't bring myself to understand. It was like she had given up the idea of returning to Runae, and I wasn't willing to accept it.

'I know…' she whispered.

'You seem to know a lot lately…' I replied without thinking.

'Daniel, please stop it. This is bigger than us, bigger than our loved ones…' Noah said, surprising me. His words were stern, and rudeness didn't become him.

'Easy to say. You have no loved ones. Do you?' I blurted out. My words shocked even me, and I found myself regretting them instantly.

'I've tried, I told you. Runae is not accessible…' Time added from a few feet away.

'Did you? Did you really? How can you be so calm with the possibility that we might have lost them?' Revelia shared my frustration.

'Well, considering what Soul said about him, I don't know how hard he really tried…' I continued.

'I came here fo help, nof fo lose my family!' Trusk added, standing beside me. His hands clenched, as if he was ready to throw invisible punches.

Something was widening the gap between our minds. We were no longer connected; we were not pursuing the same goal. I wasn't sure if I had turned away or betrayed them, but I wasn't going to continue with our agenda if it meant losing John, Treekan, or anyone else who mattered. We were indeed at a turning point. We weren't on the brink of achieving anything close to what we had hoped for. Instead, we were losing, and losing badly.

The one I loved was a lifetime away, possibly gone for good. Anita had surrendered herself to someone I didn't know, and was clearly not on my side. All I had were answers to my questions that had turned into a nightmare. *I shouldn't have questioned my visions. I should never have gone to Noah's Bridge. Grandma was right in pulling me away the first time,* I thought. *What if she knew? What if she tried but was defeated by all of this?*

Chapter Sixteen
Love's Ones

∞

Argument after argument had pushed our conversation for a good while. Soul and Iris were still absent, and the six of us held our positions in disagreement. We couldn't move forwards; we didn't know where to go. We knew only what had been, and our hearts were trying to blame each other for the status quo. Noah was placing all of that on me. If I hadn't resisted it, if I hadn't been so cautious every step of the way, we could have already achieved our goals. Anita was playing a strange game. She was arguing with my feelings and also with his.

'Daniel is just naturally worried. The more you push, the less he'll understand!'

'There is nothing to understand. It's all plain and simple. What side are you standing on?' I asked.

'There is only one side here. Our side, against theirs!' Time declared.

'Our side included my sisters, the Chomps, Daniel's fearcel…didn't it? Or is it all forgot now?' Revelia retorted, confronting Time.

We were consumed by unexpected hatred towards each other. Words that would never surface flowed like stormy rivers breaking their banks. Trusk was the only one who wasn't saying much. His small round eyes were fixed on me, searching for a sign, hoping we were going back home somehow. The more he stared at me, the more I felt guilt, sorrow, and anger. Then, eventually, it struck me. That wasn't us. We were tired, worried, but we didn't hate each other. I didn't hate any of them. Our words were driven by something else. Yes, we held our feelings and true nature in our hearts, but they were all good hearts.

'Hold on a second, everybody!' I said, lowering my voice to a sudden, loud whisper. 'I think we've been played for fools!'

'What do you mean?' Anita asked, looking towards the spot I was staring at.

'This isn't us! We aren't like this, ever. There's some trickery going on here, I can feel it now. I can see it!'

As my sudden realization began to manifest its own will, my feelings transformed into a shimmering light, moving away from my body and expanding between us. Much to our disbelief, someone emerged out of nowhere — a woman stood where there was nothing before. Her eyes were bright and green, and short golden hair pointed in the air. She appeared young and strong, her smile welcoming us as a much-needed guest in our time of struggle.

'Allow me to clear the air for you, will you?' she said, gracefully moving her arms around her.

Whatever magic she had just performed, it felt invigorating. It was akin to when Time had come to rescue us from Lëogan. An immediate sense of relief penetrated our hearts.

'Don't be upset,' she continued. 'This place was quite heavy, wasn't it? Strife is particularly good at that. I know because he's my brother. Well, he was, before he joined them…'

'Who are you?' I asked, still adjusting to the refreshing aura she had brought.

'I'm Harmonia, of course! Don't any of you recognize me? None of you?' she asked, surprised, looking at us.

We exchanged blank glances, a clear sign none of us had any recollection of who she was, what her power was like or what she looked like. Her figure was so pale that it was almost transparent, as if we could see through her, floating in the dark space.

'Luckily, you summoned me here! They are everywhere,' she continued.

'We summoned you?' Noah asked.

'Yes, well, he did!' she replied, smiling and pointing her finger at me. 'They've gone, searching for you, but my brother is still here somewhere, observing this space. I can sense his power moving across these lands. Oh, he's good, incredibly strong!'

'What power? Who is he?' I inquired, drawing closer and quickly placing my trust in her.

'Strife, of course! Your questions come as a strange surprise to my ears.' Her eyes had got suddenly bigger and brighter. 'How is it that you don't remember? Anyway, he was the Awoken of Divide—my twin, born of Love. But over the centuries, without me to balance his power, he has grown mad, evil. That's why he joined them. He's no longer an extension of Love…'

'You talk as if you both originated from the same place. How is that possible?' I asked.

'Love's power manifests in many, many ways. Sometimes it becomes so potent that new aspects come to life—parts of his being, parts of what he is. In our case, Love brings things together, yet he can also feel torn apart from being unable to let go. And so, my brother and I came into existence. I faded away long ago…but he didn't. He couldn't. His very nature, his inability to let go—your inability to let go—turned against him.'

Harmonia's words were flowing naturally, no harm was passing through, but I felt somehow judged. She was saying in different words the things Noah had told me before, right from the start. The same words he was saying to me just a few minutes before when we were all victims of Strife's magic. If the two of them were really siblings, the proof was right there in front of my eyes and ears. Both of them were pushing my inability to let go right into the open, where everybody could see it, disagree with it, condemn it.

'The more time he spent without me, the stronger his divisive power grew. I'm not surprised he has joined him. I'm not surprised he's still alive. He's nourishing himself with this misery.'

'So, if I understand,' I resumed, looking at Anita, 'you, him, Iris, Cherish, Dõron—all of you are parts of Love?'

'Yes, we are… We are all facets of the same power. Love can take on many forms. And with his blessing, we all play a small role in this story.' Iris reappeared, followed by Soul. 'We've explored the other side of the dome. I'm not sure if it's because three Gods are present here, or because Love is drawing near, but there are Awokens walking free in your present—good Awokens, now finally reborn.'

'And this is a positive development, right?' Noah asked, his face displaying an unexpected sense of joy.

'It is, as long as we don't lose them. They are out there, exposed, while we are here, unable to welcome them back, guide them, or warn them.'

Time distanced himself from the group, my gaze following him. The enchanted, unshaken trust had slightly wavered over the last few hours. The idea that he might not fully comprehend my emotions was unsettling. Then, as if he was reading my mind, as if he aimed to address my unspoken queries, a mournful voice emerged from his lips.

'Over the aeons, we drifted apart. We Gods upheld the worlds we vowed to protect, our power seeping into the essence of the lands and the hearts of the inhabitants. I didn't know how Soul's power had transformed. I was unaware of Love's evolution. I do remember my brother's intention to split his power into many, but I never imagined his magic could splinter in this manner. I knew of the Awoken Ones, but I had always thought they were Humans transformed by power...'

'With Love, it's the other way around. That's why he was Creation's first God. That's why he is the centre of the rite. He is the only God that can...create,' Soul added, attempting to comfort Time, whose face now appeared upset. We had relied on their vast knowledge, believing they knew everything necessary to move forwards. Seeing Time question his wisdom struck a blow to my heart. I didn't know whether it was empathy, fear, or both.

'Do we know how many are there? How many have returned? Who else?' Soul asked, directing his question to Harmonia.

'And where are they? We need to know their whereabouts,' Iris added.

However, Harmonia didn't have the answers. Having just returned from an unknown space and time herself, she was clueless about how many others had done the same. As our quest broadened and more matters needed addressing, the challenges increased, burdening our shoulders. It seemed that as we approached our goal, more difficulties arose. Fearing we were still being watched, we decided to wait a little longer, trapped in a timeless state. Scattered amidst the rubble of Noah's old cottage, we split into groups. I leaned against a dead trunk, my legs resting on the ground. Trusk lay beside me, an ever-present shadow. Anita sat on the other side, her back nearly touching mine, her eyes closed. I couldn't discern whether

I had regained my best friend or if Cherish was still holding the reins of her restless mind. In between us, Revelia was sitting impatiently, closely watching Soul and Time, who were monitoring the edges of the dome. Towards the far right, where the cottage's front door once stood, Noah and Harmonia were exchanging a few words. His words were counted, slow; Noah was on the brink of falling asleep. Despite my efforts, I couldn't find rest. My thoughts constantly returned to John. Revelia's thoughts intruded into my mind, conveying her worries and fears. Whatever decision I was about to make, she was scanning my future closely. I felt as if she relied on me and me only to drive her own agenda further. She wanted what I wanted and so my hours and days ahead was the only future that mattered. Then, it struck me.

'Anita!' I whispered. 'This place…when we leave this place…we'll be back in time, won't we?'

'You mean we would technically be back in time?'

'Yes! Shouldn't we? And we would see ourselves leaving, finding the heart and everything?' I felt excitement at the thought of reuniting with John, rescuing him before he entered Runae, perhaps.

'No, Daniel. It won't work. I know what you're thinking,' she swiftly responded, dashing my hope. 'Time would still flow. So, when we first walked in, we left several weeks ahead, on the thirty-first of October. When we leave now, we'll emerge on the same day but one year ahead, I think.'

'What?' I exclaimed, catching the attention of Noah and Harmonia. 'We can't have lost another year!'

'I'm afraid so,' Iris interjected. 'Upon stepping out, it will already be the next October thirty-first.'

'While the rest of the world, all other worlds, moved ahead?' The idea that John had been abandoned in Runae for so long horrified me.

'Can't Time do something about it?' Noah joined us, finally in sync with my thoughts.

'He might undo what's been done, maybe,' Anita suggested.

'Whatever happens next, I promise we won't step foot in this bubble ever again,' I declared.

'I've been thinking,' Anita continued. 'The last attempt was, well, around this time—back when the Roman Empire expanded northward into the island… Something tells me you've got closer before then.' Her voice trembled, doubling its sound. 'If Love was the protector of Earth, there are many instances where significant events happened. Occurrences that still appear peculiar today. You know what I mean?'

'Not really, no. Keep going,' I encouraged.

'Well, consider…I don't know…the rise of civilization. We know Humans existed well before that, and now we're aware of even more ancient Gods and evil. But history only reaches so far back in time. Why? Who erased it? Even before that, studies suggest that something massive happened to this planet, something that may have wiped out civilizations larger than ours… What was it? Or better yet, who did it?'

'Like the extinction of the dinosaurs?' Noah's smile was adding a silent comment to his words: The idea was somehow ridiculous.

'Or the biblical flood?' I added. Regardless of how far I had come, my mother's religion still influenced my thoughts.

'What are these "dinnosors"?' Revelia asked, snatching a smile from us. We repeatedly forgot that our group wasn't largely Human. Our ideas and deep thoughts were way different. Nevertheless, our hopes were remarkably similar. Despite originating from different worlds and times, we shared the same dream. *Was it merely a dream?*

'Take Runae for example,' Anita continued, foolishly ignoring how that word was still hurting us. 'Let's say a thousand years from now. What will they remember? What will be left to show that the Crimson Queen even existed? How will they know what we have done?'

'The liberation from evil will always be remembered,' Revelia stated firmly.

'True, yes, of course. But what about the details, the names, places? The idea of the evil and how it was eradicated from your world might endure, but the rest will likely fade, transformed into myth.'

'Only a few remember before fhe Greaf Dawn…when Erion moved, like if does now again,' Trusk unexpectedly chimed in.

'How is this going to help us? Knowing how many times we've failed and when…will this tell us what to do?' Noah asked.

But for a master of history like Anita, that was a silly question. History was vital for the future. Knowing the what, the when, and the how would always assist those wise enough to ask the right questions. I knew this as well as I knew Anita was about to say those exact words.

A few minutes later, a long, quiet silence fell among us. Revelia had drifted away, her mind reaching towards the other side of the universe. Harmonia had gone with Iris, and Noah had fallen asleep beside the large tree, its roots in the air above his head, his mother's journal half open on his legs. Before closing my eyes and letting go, I gazed at the distant sky and its stars, desperately hoping John was still alive. If he was, he would be angry at me for leaving him behind. Perhaps he had even let go of the anger in a year-long, oppressive defeat. Then the space turned dark, and my tired spirit departed our world to find its rest.

'I know, my child. I wanted you to stay close to me, but she is your mother. If she wants to build a future for herself and for you, perhaps it's best this way,' Grandma said, her voice lacking conviction. Somehow, I knew she wasn't fond of any of it.

'I know nothing about this man. All I know is that he is an elder…a priest, as you would call it. I can only imagine how he manages things… Rule after rule…'

'And you've never been good at it, have you?' But that was a question that didn't need an answer. 'Even in odd circumstances, there is always something one can learn, don't you think? You've always been a kind of free spirit. Maybe this is what you need right now.'

She might have been right, but I didn't like the sound of those words. So I moved away, leaving my chair beside hers empty. We were resting after a long gardening session; Grandma had shown me how to relocate a plant without harming it. The similarity to my life, both past and future, was uncanny. Back then, I didn't know my roots belonged elsewhere, in a different time even. But I knew I would be moved again soon. I was already in the midst of my teenage crisis, fourteen years old and so uncertain about who I was and who I was meant to be.

'It can only go one way. Either she'll stop hitting me, or she'll feel even more entitled to do so, with her future husband supporting this medieval way of running a family,' I muttered, loud enough for her to hear my anger.

It hadn't started as anger. It was fear at first, turned into pain soon after. Then something inside me had come to life; a forceful resistance in my heart was opposing my own feelings. It wasn't right; she wasn't right. I should have hated her for what she did to me, but I couldn't. *Why?* I asked myself countless times. And that inability to detach from her, to eradicate my unhealthy love for my warder, birthed a burning rage. I had scars on my body and in my mind, evidence that she wasn't fit to be a mother, wounds that would never fade. My left hand moved on its own, finding the largest of the marks she'd left on my right shoulder. But I couldn't look at it, just as I couldn't face my own thoughts about it.

'Something has always been missing in your mother's heart. I've never wanted you to be in this situation. You know how many times I've fought her. I can tell you this.

It won't last forever. Stay strong just a little bit longer,' she consoled me.

Her words were like the weather we faced. Unbearable, not warm. Her point of view was as real as the world I was living in and it wasn't pleasant. She stood up, sweat on her forehead, her long, messy hair sticking to her face. She was fighting her own will from within but couldn't come and save me. *Why? Why is she failing me when I need her most?*

'Look at it this way. You're getting a sister.' She smiled at me.

'I don't need a sister. And she won't be one anyway,' I replied.

'My child, you know I love you more than anything in this world. But you have to realize one thing…'

'What is it?' I interrupted her. Whatever wisdom she had to offer, it wasn't good enough for me.

'Sometimes, we find a true friend, an ally perhaps, in the most difficult circumstances. Remember this, my boy. It's when we feel there's no way out that we need someone from the inside. She could be your way out, you know? She might be searching for someone who understands how…mad…that world is. You could be each other's strength.'

'I understand. But you're assuming many things here. If things don't go the right way, there might not be a way out for me, ever,' I said and retreated to the house, seeking shelter.

'My child, listen to me once more.' And she followed me inside, like her love for me was pulling her at once. 'It's important you leave this house. You need to see what life is outside these walls. I know, I know,' she added before I could interrupt her again. 'Your mother... You and she need to move away. For your sake and her sake. She can't stay here any longer and neither can you. The house doesn't want her. These walls and my roof are not turning things well for her. She must go and where she goes, you go. You understand me?' Her hands pulled my chin, turning my face towards her. Her dark eyes were like darting blades to my heart. *Why is she pushing me away?* I could not understand.

'I wish you were my mother,' I let out. My eyes in tears met hers. Her feeble smile was revealing the weakness of our hearts. Comfort was struggling to surface in an ocean of pain and sorrow.

'In a way, I am.' And her smile grew bigger. 'There is much more in you than you realize, Daniel. You'll see eventually. I promise you,' Grandma assured me before walking away, disappearing from sight and from my tormented dream.

I wasn't certain of it once I woke up. *Was it real? A vision? Did it happen? Yes, this was a fragment of my distant past returning to haunt me, reminding me of the pain I endured.* Grandma had visited me many times, in various forms. But this wasn't her doing; it was my memories resurfacing. But the reason for this subtle recollection wasn't clear. I didn't know if it had returned due to recent events or if my mind was simply seeking a safe place to rest. She was, as always, my fortress, my strength. What did she say again? I thought.

'You and she need to move away. For your sake and her sake. She can't stay here any longer and neither can you. The house doesn't want her. These walls and my roof are not turning things well for her. She must go and where she goes, you go.'

Chapter Seventeen
Looking for Allies

∞

The time bubble we were trapped in felt like being prisoners in a warm, secure greenhouse, with windows through which we could observe the tumultuous outside weather. A storm had swept in from the west, bringing heavy rain. I woke up to a loud thunder, shaken by it, as if something worse was accompanying it. The others were still in their spots, asleep, except for Trusk, who was clearing away dead leaves from their burial ground near Revelia. The Leonty was gazing out at the dome's edge, her mind seemingly far away from our current location.

'I'm worried,' she said as I approached her.

'I'm worried too,' I replied.

'I was worried about them, but now I'm worried about us. I fear we won't be able to return home, ever again.'

'We will find a way in or out. Well, it depends from where you are looking at it.' And I added a quick smile. 'But we have to leave this place and go back to Runae, and we will! There's too much at stake to just turn our backs and leave them behind.'

'I can still see further ahead, you know?' Revelia looked at me, her eyes blazing like a raging fire, their red colour resembling blood spilled from her irises. 'We won't be together much longer. I see you somewhere, in a place I've never seen before. A place full of resentment and anger.'

'Tell me more. Is there more you see?' I whispered, hoping no one else would hear those unsettling words.

'You're not alone. Your other half is with you, and I think the girl is there too. I see you, but I can't feel what I feel now. Your spirit is gone, hidden from me. I can't explain it, but it's as if your magic is eclipsed by this…emptiness. It's like if someone is covering your magic with theirs… I don't know this world, but I'd say it's here, somewhere.'

'What about you? What about Trusk and the others?' I intentionally avoided thinking about what she had just revealed. In my mind, an idea, a hint was pressing to come to surface.

'We're OK, we will be. Daniel?' she added after a lengthy pause. 'While in Varayal, I sensed the presence of another magic being, a very weak signal of power amidst the pages of time. I felt it when Time took the tiara and again when we left through the node, just before the evil showed itself to us. It felt like the magic of our own God and protector.'

'You mean another God beside Time and Soul?' I was perplexed.

'Yes, but it was like a dying voice lost in space. I'm not sure if it is still alive, wherever and whenever it was. It was like an echo from a very remote past.'

Trusk turned his attention to the two of us. His wings were still down, reflecting the sadness in his thoughts. His right, tiny hand reached my side, pulling me down as if he was about to share a secret with us.

'I wanf fo go home, Daniel. Mofher musf be very worried by now.' His words were like shards of glass cutting through my skin.

'Reela knows you're with us. She knows you're safe as long as we're together. Don't worry. It might take a little longer, but we will go back home eventually,' I reassured him. My gaze shifted to Revelia, who, unable to lie, turned her face away.

Something was trying to come to mind, like a hidden trail of clues bridging what I had seen in my dream and what Revelia had just said. An idea on how we could escape the time trap began forming, but I couldn't think, couldn't put my thoughts into fruition. Then, in the silence of our secure spot, it struck me. It was like pure madness falling into the right place, a dramatic solution to a dire situation. I acted immediately, heading towards Anita, who knew enough to provide me with an honest opinion. If we were to follow through with my idea, I needed certainty.

'Anita, wake up. I have an idea.'

'I'm already awake, Daniel. Did you think I could sleep like that?' She shifted slightly, revealing a few rocks that had been pressing against her back moments earlier.

'Listen, I've thought of something. Something my Grandma mentioned ages ago. It's a bit of a leap, so hear me out.'

'Did you have one of your visions? Was it Dõron?' Her face quickly shed its tiredness and pain.

'No, no, nothing like that. I remembered something, and…it's a bit of a stretch. But I could be onto something,' I said, settling beside her. Suddenly, she seemed very uncomfortable again, her hands touching her back. 'Think about my mother for a moment. We know Dõron moved beside me, beside my grandma because I had come to be too close to a powerful Harpy. I'm pretty sure she was hinting at Victoria. She wasn't just my mother; she was the one called Athymos, right?'

'The Awoken One who represents your opposite. Who told us that?' She immediately delved into her own mental excavation.

'Forget about who told us, just for a second. For the years I was with her, her power hid me from being seen, from being noticed. I think Grandma did it deliberately, allowing me to go with her. Departing from my Praetorian and being overshadowed by Athymos was the only way to keep me concealed from them. Why else would she have allowed that to happen?' I asked, watching Anita doubting my statement. 'What if I were under the influence of her power again? What if I were close enough to be undetectable once more?'

'Let me get this straight, for a moment.' Her hand rose between our faces. 'Are you saying what I think you're saying? Are you suggesting we go to your mother, now?'

'Oh, believe me, I know it's crazy. But we need to leave this place quickly. They'll find us, unless…'

'Unless someone is able to cover your tracks,' she finished my sentence. 'This is very risky, Daniel. Firstly, we don't know if she can still hide you from them. We don't even know if she is still Athymos… Secondly, if she is, she's still one of the *them*. Are you planning to walk right into their hands?'

'But I won't be alone.'

'You want to bring a Chomp and a Leonty into the real world?' She smiled at the audacity of that idea.

'No. Just you and Noah. We have to bring Noah. He is Love too. And, well…we wouldn't last long without you, anyway.' And this time, I smiled.

'I don't like it, but I have to admit it has some sense…'

'I think we will go…oh no, I'm not imposing. Revelia told me we are going to part ways. This is how I finally realized what I had remembered in my dream.'

'Assuming your Grandma let you go because of it…'

'Yes, correct.'

And there was no need to add anything else. As always, Anita's mind had started to spin fast, thinking, screening all the possible scenarios. I was waiting for her to say something, but all she could do was make faces; thoughts after thoughts, I could almost read through her thinking process. She shared and trusted my intuition, but the odds were too high for us to take that step easily.

'Why didn't I think of that?' she said, then went quiet again.

'Think what?' Noah asked, finally awake.

His hair was all over the place, his face showing the same pain Anita had shown me a few minutes earlier. His beauty was still there, but his eyes had large, dark shadows pushing through his freckles. I shared my idea with him, repeating my plan once more. As expected, Noah's desire to move forwards hadn't failed to show. However, he had agreed to the risks Anita had listed right after my explanation. We were going to leave the Gods behind with Revelia and Trusk and set off on our own, hiding underground, waiting for the right moment to act.

'What then? Let's say you are right and we can stay under the radar for a little longer, out of here. What do we do then?'

'Well, first of all, we can give them time to find Health, find out what happened to her. And that's already something, right?'

'You are saying it like you have other items on your list… What else is next? Don't tell me…that's it?' Anita asked, looking right at me.

'Well, we might find beings like Harmonia…' I added, doubting it as soon as I said it.

'As if we are going to find them here and there, just casually…' Anita replied.

'She came right to us…' And I pointed my finger into the nothing Harmonia had disappeared into, with Iris.

'And she left too… Where are they?' Noah asked. 'And also, why only now? Why are they showing up only now?'

'Because you are getting stronger,' Anita said, almost as if she was reading inside her own mind, looking deep for Cherish's thoughts, perhaps. 'Think about it. They all faded away as Love was gone. Now you showed your presence in the world. Something is rising, pulled by it. I know it; it's what I heard inside me as Cherish was…driving…'

'Do we do it then? Are you OK to try?' I asked.

'What else can we do? I say we try!' And Noah took my hand. It was strangely impersonal. I could not feel the way I had felt before as we were touching. His intention was to move forwards, not to connect with my mind, with what that was going to mean for me.

Nevertheless, I genuinely thought that was the only shot we had. If that idea had come to me, it was for a reason. Once again, it was like Grandma had planned it all along. So, we stood up and went looking for Time and Soul. Deep in the woods, they were standing by the large trees at the back of where Noah's cottage once stood. *If only that dome was large enough, we could have spent the night inside a home, instead of on hard, wet soil*, I thought.

'Time, Soul, we need to talk…' I said, starting a rerun of what I had said already twice in the space of an hour.

'It's a big risk; you have to admit that,' Time repeated, more than once.

'We can protect your friends to the best of our abilities. Would you not go just the two of you?' Soul added.

'I'm going with them. I must,' Anita firmly replied.

'She has to,' Time said to Soul. 'Have you talked about it with the others?'

'I'm planning to. It won't be easy, especially for Trusk. Please, tell me you will keep him safe!' I let out.

'We will. We can keep them with us, but we can't keep the others too. Iris is bound to this place, but Harmonia…and whoever else is there, they are attached to your essence. Eventually, they will be with you wherever you go; you know that?'

'We do. How do we leave this place? How do we get there?' Noah asked.

'In the same way you have been travelling with your mind. You need to want it. Picture it, then go. As you reached Runae, to the far space, you can do the same in this tiny world.' And Time turned away, back where we had left the others. 'Let's go. We need to tell them.'

So, the group got back together. Iris and Harmonia were nowhere to be found, so we decided to start the conversation between the seven of us. If Revelia was already aware of what the future was becoming, Trusk resisted a little. The idea of being left behind, of not being by my side, was too much to accept. Eventually, the idea that we would meet again and that the Leonty was going to stay with him worked its charm. She was, for him, the pure representation of home, and that did the trick.

'How will we find her?' Noah asked.

'Let Daniel drive you. Close your eyes, let your artefacts lead you. You might not get to her directly, but you should appear close by,' Time replied.

'Can you please keep trying…while we are gone?' I asked, knowing Time knew exactly what I meant.

'I'll never stop,' he said, and his eyes blinked a little as his magic kept seeking a way through, attempting to access Runae repeatedly.

No goodbyes were exchanged, no tears were shed. We would be together again soon. Our departure was to be brief; we were certain of it. We stood amidst the crowd, Noah's hand and mine clasped together. As we closed our eyes, the shiny heart and white shell appeared between our arms. Anita held on to our shoulders firmly, ready to leap. And so, we went; in a silent pop, we were gone, away from the ones we had come to consider friends. Once more, the three of us were all we had, as it had been on Noah's Bridge, as it had been by the towers of light and darkness.

From a stormy, cloudy forest to a bustling, noisy, warm city, the journey was instantaneous. I had no idea where we had ended up, but we had certainly left Ireland for another place I once called home. I hadn't seen my mother for years; she could have moved anywhere in the country. But the surroundings couldn't be clearer. Colossal, ancient buildings stood everywhere we looked. A wide, chaotic road ran from one end to another, and at one end, a partially destroyed ruin unmistakably claimed the name of that city. The silent colosseum declared it to be Italy's capital, the busiest city—or so it seemed.

'Holy moly, we are in Rome!' Anita exclaimed, her eyes widening.

'Are we in the right place?' Noah asked, as we quickly moved away from the edge of the road where we had teleported to. Fortunately, the chaos was so intense that our sudden appearance went unnoticed.

'I believe so. She must be living in here now,' I said, as we turned the corner of a baroque building, entering a quieter, narrower street.

The place was bustling with people wandering around; small stands were scattered on every side of the road, making it seem even narrower than it actually was. A pharmacy sign blinked words and numbers across the walkway. It was still warm, even warmer than our clothing was suitable for. Some shops displayed pumpkins and spooky costumes, mixed in with early Christmas items that seemed to be pushing the dates ahead. As we feared, time had advanced another year. Halloween was everywhere around us, in a country that had embraced foreign traditions for the sake of profit.

'This won't be as easy as I thought. How are we going to find her in this madness?' Anita said, moving along the sidewalk, her hand brushing against bags and jackets hanging on a stall.

'I don't know a word of Italian! I should have picked something besides French. For your information, I remember very little of it.' Noah said.

'She must be somewhere around here, right? I tried my best to put all my thoughts into reaching her. I wouldn't be surprised if my silent refusal to see her pulled us in the opposite direction…'

'Do you think they know we're here? I'm just wondering if we got detected somehow…' Anita put on a hat taken from a stand, as if it could prevent her from being recognized.

'I doubt that would work. Keep your hands off their stuff. They can be very bothersome if they catch you showing interest in their merchandise!'

'Ciao bella!' A man appeared out of nowhere. 'You buy? Ten euros!' he shouted in broken English, holding up ten fingers in front of Anita's face.

'No grazie!' I said, pulling her away.

'Fake Gucci bags! If I hadn't figured out where we were yet, I definitely would now…' Her expression displayed some disappointment.

Trying to move around unnoticed and ensuring we didn't stray far from where we had landed, I scanned the surroundings, hoping we had teleported to the right place. If she still looked the same, I couldn't know. *How much can someone change in so many years?* I wondered. A phone, nearly forgot, suddenly beeped, bringing us back to the reality of time and reminding us to watch out for roaming charges.

'Great, my battery is almost dead…' Anita said.

'My phone has been dead since we got to Runae. What kind of nuclear device are you carrying?' Noah asked, chuckling.

'I've been turning it off and on…and still, that wasn't enough. Damn technology!'

'Do you still have enough battery to search for something? I have an idea…' I said.

If my mother was around, she might be in a church, hidden within one of those old buildings. She could be attending one of their gatherings. After all, what day was it? Was the thirty-first on a Sunday that year? That could be a good place to start. But Google Maps wasn't particularly helpful. We had no leads to follow, only hunger and fatigue. So, we decided to give up, hoping that spot was one of my mother's frequent haunts. We managed to find a place to stay for the night and checked in quickly before Anita's magical device died completely. We needed a shower, food, and a good night's sleep before we could continue our search. As we had left my house with only Daisy and my cloak, I had to stop somewhere and buy a cheap charger. Fortunately, the right merchandise was available on every corner of our street.

'Buy just one, we don't have enough money with us. This junk wouldn't last anyway!' Anita said as I picked up a few in my hands, eliciting a greedy smile from the seller.

'We should have taken one as a backup!' Noah said, as we walked into our twin room, which felt rather claustrophobic.

'We can take turns using it. I'll charge mine, leave yours here so I can plug it in right away,' Anita suggested.

'OK. We're in the room right beside. Once you're ready, come over and we'll find a place to get some food,' I replied.

'Speaking of food… I'd say we also need to get as much cash as possible,' Anita let out, stopping in front of her door. 'When the lady at the desk asked for my bank card I panicked! We moved ahead another year. A year with no job, no salary, nothing. I'm glad the bank hasn't closed my account yet.'

'I hope they closed mine, to be honest. I was broke even before we disappeared from the world.' And Noah smiled, embarrassed.

'That's a good thinking, Anita. We'll do that on your way to get food. What time is it?' I asked.

'It's 4 p.m. It'll get dark soon. Let's hurry; I don't really think we should be out and about for too long, to be honest.'

The bed and breakfast we found was squeezed between shops and apartments, suffocating amid bricks and stones, but we couldn't be choosy. It was where we were supposed to be, and that was enough to make it right. Our bathroom was so tiny that only one person could barely fit in and out of the miniature shower, so I told Noah to go first as I quickly stepped outside to buy some inexpensive, fresh clothes for us to wear.

'Am I going to get a rash or something, wearing those clothes? I mean, they smell of plastic!' he said, his bare chest right in front of me and a large white towel hanging on his hips.

'We can find somewhere to wash ours later. For now, that's what we have. And stop walking around half naked...' I let out, trying to push away that unpleasant attraction I suddenly felt.

Half an hour later, we were ready to go. Anita hadn't shown up yet, so we hopped onto our beds, waiting. We hadn't exchanged any words since I had gone to take a shower. It was like we were unable to talk to one another or, maybe, it was the other way around. I could not tell if we shared thoughts and minds in a way that talking was pointless or if we had really moved away from the initial bond we had. Then someone knocked at the door.

'And where did you get those now?' Anita asked as soon as I opened the door.

'I ran outside, got us something to wear.'

'I thought you said hands off from the merchandise! Never mind, let's go. There is a nice place where we can get some food just two blocks away. Here are your phones. There is not much charge in them, but that should do for now. If your SIM card has no credit like mine, use the wifi before we get out.'

We left the place at once, our bellies begging for food. If time moved ahead, so had our hunger. We had a year's worth of food we had missed, but fortunately, we were in the right country to enjoy the payback. In a city that never sleeps, even in the darkness of the evening, people were still filling the streets.

Tourists were smiling, laughing, taking pictures of every corner, flooding places looking for a good meal. The restaurant Anita led us to was no different. It was busy, shiny, and the food looked incredible.

'What? Just because we are running it doesn't mean we cannot find a good place to eat, right?' Anita said, after I had looked at her, surprised.

'True! It almost feels like a holiday...if it weren't for...well, you know...' And Noah walked in, following Anita who was already inside, raising her hand to get a waitress's attention.

'So, I have been searching for those, what did you call them? Congregations?' she said, putting away the menu after picking her meal. 'There are none in this neighbourhood; the nearest is a few miles away. Are you sure she was here?'

'She could have been here for other reasons. Maybe she was going door-to-door? I'm sure she still does that.'

'Do those...churches show up? I mean, all of them?' Noah asked.

'Probably not the small ones. But the point is, we need to find her soon. If our plan is to be under my mother's influence, we can't spend too much time on our own.'

'Which is why we will go straight back as soon as we finish this,' Anita concluded.

Partly because of fear and partly due to our long-standing hunger, we ate as quickly as we could. In less than an hour, we were leaving the restaurant, walking back to the bed and breakfast. As our feet were longing for the safety of our small rooms, something strange appeared right across the road. A floating, almost invisible white shadow captured our attention, leading our gaze to a large wooden door popping up between two shops that were now closed for the night.

'Oh, that can't be good…' I said, holding Noah's arm, making him stop walking.

'Is it them?' he asked.

'It looks different. Maybe not?' and Anita was looking at it, inspecting it from afar, searching for signals.

Before we could ponder any longer, before we could decide whether to approach it or run from it, the bright shadow dissipated, leaving nothing but a small golden plate hanging on the door. Something was there to be seen, to be found. So, we moved together, crossing the road. To our surprise, the metal tag said:

Congregation of Jehovah's Witnesses
'The Truth will set you free.'
—John 8:32—

'Well, someone knows we are here. This can't be a coincidence, can it?' I asked, looking at Noah and Anita.

'Is it someone good, though? It felt familiar, didn't it?' he asked.

'*The Truth will set you free*. Well, if this isn't exactly what we are trying to get to, I don't know what else can be. Is it open? Can we get in?' Anita asked, her hand already on the large, round handle.

And it was. The door opened, showing a long corridor, pavemented with square tiles. A few narrow tables were standing at its sides, boxes on top of them, hungry for volunteers' money. After hesitating a moment, feeling the strong familiarity with that place, I walked in, taking the other two by surprise. At the far end, a large room was waiting, filled with people sitting on chairs all across the place. At its far wall in the centre, a stage was projecting its pressure on the audience. Someone was standing on it, preaching, shaping, taking over the many minds in there.

'This is it, guys. She might be in here, right now,' I whispered, trying not to get the attention of a standing guard at the entrance of the main room.

'Why the guards?' Noah asked.

'These are Attendant Servants. They greet people walking in, but also guard the place in case something strange happens.'

'Strange, strange? Or magic-like, strange?' Anita asked.

'No, just strange. I don't know, someone tries to interrupt their ceremony, or if a fight breaks out.'

'I feel weird just standing here. This place gives me the creeps...' Anita whispered.

As expected, we got noticed. One of the servants came by to greet us with a soft, sharp smile. His hand halfway up, he asked if we wanted to get in and sit at the very back of the room, right at the edge of the corridor. Thinking that might give us the chance to check the people in there, we agreed to his welcome and sat one beside the other, under the many serious looks we received as we walked in.

'...because Jehovah reads our hearts and our minds! As Jesus said many times, it's not acting on sin that makes us sinners! If you even think of doing something against our God's true will, you have already sinned in the eyes of our beloved creator!' someone on stage said, as I was translating directly to Anita and Noah.

'Well…I'm completely screwed, then…' Noah whispered to Anita, laughing.

'Shush. These people take this very seriously!' I replied, smiling. 'But yeah, imagine how bad the final judgement is going to be for me!'

'The world tells us you need to be happy with yourself! That what you feel matters the most. The world tells us every day that you come first. But let's not be fooled by their blind sight! Today…my brothers and sisters…today they praise diversity like a medal to a rightful pride! You are right in being whoever you want to be. You are right in pursuing rich careers, money, fame. You are right if you are entangled with politicians, political agendas. But remember how the Holy Bible calls them: Babylon, the Whore!'

'Wow that's a bit extreme, isn't it?' Anita said, as Noah was looking back at us, his mouth open, his eyes in shock.

'Two minutes! Two minutes in here and they already reminded me I'm a whore!' I replied.

But Anita and Noah were the only ones shocked by the speech. The rest of the audience, the people around us, were greeting those words as the rightful ones. Their faces were showing agreement, almost joy, in remembering how they were different from that sick, mad world they had parted ways from. Used to those topics, I immediately tuned out, focused on the reason why we had walked in there in the first place.

'What's the story with their clothes? Why the ties and jackets?' Noah asked.

'And the long skirts. Look at them. None of the women in this room is wearing pants. I feel completely out of place.'

'They have to. Pants are only for men. In the church women have to show respect to men as they are their masters, their superiors,' I explained, my eyes zipping to the Attendant Servant who was looking at me, annoyed.

'What a disgusting practice!' Anita replied. 'I wonder what these books they are holding on to are. They don't look like Bibles…' Anita's resentment had quickly left the spot to curiosity.

Smiling at their continued shock after shock, my eyes started rolling from row to row. I was looking for her, I was looking for her face as I could remember it, hoping the difference time had brought wouldn't be too drastic. Eventually, in a sudden gulp that sank my heart to my feet, I found her. She was sitting in the second row, far to our right. I could see her profile, her face. She was the same and she wasn't. Her hair, long, rusty, almost ginger, was covering her green eyes and her pale skin. But it was her. I knew it as I felt my wounds screaming into reality, brought back my pain as salt water penetrated my fresh scars. Without even thinking, my hand reached Noah's, holding a firm grip on his wrist; he knew I had found her.

'What's wrong. Did you see her?'

'Yes, she is here…'

Chapter Eighteen
Athymos

∞

We had walked in towards the very end of the final Thursday speech. As the audience had been there for more than two hours, a few minutes after we sat, the session was over. All of them stood up, a new book in their hands, a final hymn filled the room, their voices singing a song I barely remembered. At the last note, someone else walked up to the stage and said a final prayer as the audience bent their heads down. Even the kids, though trying to look around, their heads were pushed down by the heavy parents' hands. At the final Amen, the crowd moved around, some of them rushing out of the building, some starting loud conversations. Two ladies moved towards us, Noah and Anita still lost in realizing what they just witnessed.

'Benvenuti!' one said. 'Immagino voi siate studenti!' And one of the two, an old lady with pompous, blonde hair looked at our clothes, up and down to our very shoes, leaving Noah and Anita perplexed. They had no idea what they had just been asked.

'She just asked if we are students. As our clothes are not…well…matching with the drapes, if you know what I mean.'

'Je ne sais pas!' Noah replied, bringing his hands up.

'Noah, that's French and it doesn't mean what you think it means…' Anita said, almost embarrassed.

'Tell them you bought these clothes. I don't want to be escorted out by that man over there because of it,' Noah replied, looking at me, smiling.

'Don't talk to him, Maria!' a woman said, in Italian. 'He is shunned. What are you doing here? This is the last place you should be, and to be fair, the last place where I was expecting to see you.' That was definitely my mother's welcome.

'I was looking for you…' I replied, after hesitating for a moment. A few simple words, but they almost froze in my throat.

'Get out of here. You can't be here, you know better!'

'I know. But we need to talk. It's very important.' I knew she wasn't going to sin by being seen with me, a disfellowshipped one, but I had to try anyway.

'Please leave. I'll be out in a few minutes.' And she walked away, leaving the three of us under the silent judgement of the people who just happened to hear her words.

To avoid any direct confrontation, in the messy crowd of believers, we took her words seriously. So, we walked out, pushed by the eyes of the many who had the chance to exchange their looks with ours.

'What happened? What did she say?' Anita asked.

'She reminded me I can't be seen mingling with any of them as I am unrepentant. She said to wait for her outside. Let's go, we can wait on the other side of the street. Better to avoid any other close contact.'

'What is this practice?' Noah asked, while we were waiting for Victoria to come out.

'If you are a sinner, and much more if you are impenitent, you get shunned, banned from the cult, from being seen with them. Family members, friends, colleagues, have to cut any tie they had with you. You are pretty much dead to them. Till the moment you repent and come back, of course.'

'What sin did you do?' Noah asked, as in his eyes, I could have never committed any crime justifying that practice.

'One that cannot be erased. One that I can't ask forgiveness for… Because I'm gay, that's pretty much it.'

'This is insane! Madness! How did you put up with it?' Anita asked, fuming.

'It's long gone, don't worry about it.' And I dismissed her rage as too familiar to my own.

'All those books in their hands, and still their ignorance slips right off their brains! How is it possible?' Anita continued. Once again, the fact that knowledge and books weren't producing an open-mind effect seemed impossible to her.

'It all depends on what those books say, Anita...' I let out.

'Is not the Bible the same for everybody?' Noah asked, puzzled.

'Apparently not...'

A few minutes later, as most of the people had gone and left, Victoria walked out the front door. After looking left and right, she saw us, right in front of her, on the other side of the road, beside one of the many cars parked randomly by the sidewalk. She looked strangely young, as if most of the years hadn't passed. Her skin showed only a few wrinkles, but nothing compared to what I would expect. Her face was sharp, her mouth shut; she crossed the road and reached us at our spot, visibly unhappy.

'Mother, these are Anita and Noah. They don't speak Italian at all, but it doesn't really matter. They are my friends, and they are here because I'm working on something very important,' I started, secretly thinking of what excuse I could quickly come up with, an explanation that would sound reasonable to her.

'How did you find me?' she said, without even looking at the other two.

'It doesn't matter. It matters that I did.'

'Is this your...' But she could not even say it, in disgust.

'No, Mother. Just a very close friend of mine.' And Noah was looking at me, confused, understanding he had become the subject of our conversation.

'Is there a place we can go and talk?' I asked.

'You know I can't be seen with you. Thankfully they have no idea who you are, but still, Jehovah sees it, and that's bad enough.'

'We are staying somewhere close by for the night. We don't have to be together for too long, but still, I need to talk to you.' And in my mind, I was thinking of how I could convince her to stay close to us long enough to keep the Harpies away.

'I can't now. I have things to do. Tomorrow morning. There is a coffee shop at the corner. I'm supposed to meet a sister for door-to-door ministry at 10 a.m. Meet me at 9:30. I have to go.' And before I could even say bye, she was already gone, without hesitation.

'Well, that was quick!' Anita said, worried. 'What did she say? What did you say?'

As we started to walk back to the bed and breakfast, I translated everything that was said, though it wasn't much. They both agreed she sounded and looked cold, too cold for a mother, but little they knew she had always been like that. Trying to be close to me, Anita expressed her sorrow in seeing her acting in that way towards me and, before going back to her room, she hugged me, as if she needed to make me feel better, protected, loved. For a few brief moments, she forgot how big the picture we found ourselves in was, struggling to fit into the greater scheme of things. She could only see a human reality, a reality of sorrow and pain. In my mind, I was pushing myself to be strong, to be someone else. Somehow Victoria's behaviour was predictable, surgically methodical. I wasn't surprised, and I wasn't hurt. Or maybe, I was simply not surprised to be hurt. Whatever the truth was, it did not matter, and it didn't need to be addressed. Back in our room, Noah and I collapsed on our beds, clothes and shoes off. We were both staring at the ceiling, our minds travelling to different places but both sharing the pain and suffering of thinking about our mothers.

'I can't imagine what it must have been for you…all those years,' he said. 'My mother was nothing like that. She was quite the opposite. You deserved much better, Daniel.'

'Don't worry, my grandma was like that for me. But yeah, you are right, it would have been nice to have a real mother looking after me.'

'Do you think she knows? That she is Athymos? Or maybe she doesn't know, and everything she does is because of it?'

'I don't know, Noah. It feels a bit like an easy way out, don't you think? She was a bad mother, but it's not her fault?' I let out, resentment lurking in the shadow of my words. I was ready to accept it, but not ready to justify her actions because of it.

'And all that preaching and the religion she is in… How could she feel that was a good idea!' Noah said, sitting back up on his bed.

'That's probably it. She doesn't feel anything. She doesn't feel love, fear, right, wrong…' And the old anger had pushed up to the open, right through my wet eyes.

He was waiting there, for me to continue, but I could not talk any longer. I felt my voice trembling in my last words. I could not show the sorrow I had in me, seeing my mother again, after all those years. Nothing had changed in her. *Why am I still looking for something different, a different outcome? The child in me is still looking for approval? For love? Am I still bound to her, letting her hurt me in her senseless ways?*

I briefly looked at Noah, who was looking back at me still. His pale, green eyes were staring at my pain, as he could see it clearly. I had dismissed his body and my attraction to it before, but this time my mind felt too weak to resist. His square naked shoulders were turning in a hug I desperately needed, his bare chest was the right place to bury my tears without the world seeing it. Noah's magnetizing look was turning against his own doubts, the same doubts he shared before. He did feel attracted to me, as he had confessed before and he was again, once more. For a moment, our differences, our contrasting personalities, disappeared, we were connected again, physically this time, and that was a danger I had forgot.

He stood up, frozen for a brief moment as if he was searching for a reason to hold back or another reason to move forwards, and I could count the seconds of him waiting, synced with my heartbeat, growing faster and faster. Then he sat beside me, his hand moving slowly on my arm, his eyes screening my chest, my neck, my mouth. Whatever he felt, it wasn't just friendship. He was walking right over the invisible boundaries we had pulled up, carelessly. He had only me in his mind, and I had pure emptiness in mine. I could feel his skin sliding on mine, friction of pure electricity, there was more than I could perceive. It was electrifying my soul, waking me up to something I could not contain. And then his head moved close to mine, his left hand on my hair, he was hugging me with all the kindness he was capable of. His mouth kissing my forehead, his role was switching rapidly between friendship, passion, family.

'Noah...' I whispered, my voice shifting from excitement to anticipation.

'It's OK. You need this...we need this,' he said, his body moving beside mine, his arms around me.

He lay down by my side, flesh to flesh, like we were one thing only. I could feel his breath on my neck, my chest, giving me the soft chill of intimacy. It felt strong and different. There was passion within and there was safety, protection. What we were joining together wasn't lust, it was beating souls, communicating with one another.

'I've lost you somewhere...in our journey. I'm sorry. I'm here now,' he continued. 'I want you close to me, as I want to be close to you, that's all. The rest doesn't matter.'

'I've lost you too. I wish I knew where this is going, everything...but I feel stronger when you are with me, even more now.'

'Yes, even more now.'

And without us realizing it, his artefact, his heart came out to meet my shell halfway in between our chests. And then we fell asleep. Miles and miles away, Noah and I did it again. We left our bodies to reach somewhere unknown, a place we knew but both didn't have any memory of. We were together, but only one body was moving in the space, as we had fused into one entity. Our minds were one, our voice was the same.

'The threat to our world is growing in size, master.' Someone was speaking to us, a gentle creature, his skin dark, his brown eyes shining along the white marble walls. 'As we try to contain it, they too are growing bigger. It's getting difficult to spread my power…'

'What do you suggest we do, Eleoen?' we asked.

'Maybe you could push them back? To give me, to give us time to even the odds,' he said, unafraid.

'I do understand forgiveness is a power welcome only to a few, especially since some of them have spread so much hate lately. Let me think a little. I'll let you know what we will do about it.'

And the man walked away, his soft golden cape moving, dancing with his quick walk. It was like he was floating above the ground of that immense place. Everything around us was white and gold. Sandy walls ran around like we were surrounded by warm beaches, to the right, to the left, up to the roof. To the front, a very large opening showed the far blue sea, moving under the bright light of the sun.

'He is not wrong, you know?' A woman had just walked up from behind. She had long, brown hair held up by a thin golden tiara. Her face was sharp; she was clearly stating what she felt was obvious.

'Cherish…have you spoken to the people?'

'I did. And of course, they are too busy to pay attention. They don't understand the importance of our message, Love. They are obviously too simple to understand.'

'What their minds don't reach, their hearts will, Cherish. But I do understand why it's difficult for you to accept. Not everything is thinking and searching. Sometimes, the truth will reach us from within, from our feelings…'

'How are they going to remember it if they don't understand it in the first place?' she said, moving to a large brown chaise longue. Long bracelets were coming down from her elbows to her hands, coiling around her fingers in intricate, golden patterns.

'My role is to protect them, to preserve Creation's work, regardless of whether they remember or not. All we can do is to plant the seed of Love, despite the odds.'

'I've heard Eirene is struggling to keep the civilization at ease down the east. Should we send Mnemosy to help her? He might just erase whatever reason they have to fight from their memory…' But Cherish was showing reluctance to her own idea.

'I can't believe my ears. You, the Awoken of Memory, the Awoken of Preservation. You are really thinking of letting them forget?' And we moved back inside, leaving the sunny terrace by itself, basking under the pleasant heat.

'I don't. I don't think it's a good idea, but how are we going to be ready when the time comes, if we can't even hope that the creatures of this world won't kill each other? If we leave them for a moment, it's like starting all over again.'

'It's not them, Cherish. It's the evil that keeps pushing its way in! Since the great battle with Creation, it looks like Nothing has no intention of facing me directly, at least for now. He might try to buy some time, plotting in the shadows, sending his torturers here. I'm not sure how we are going to defeat him. Our power, my power, comes from what I am, nothing more. I can't defeat Death, for once. Creation is gone, gone for good, but I can fight using the memory of the lost ones, using the love they felt for one another. That's the only way I can make the people of the world immortal.'

We walked away from Cherish, who was still sitting by a large, stony window, looking outside, her thoughts flying freely. About to walk deeper into that vast place, we turned back for a moment.

'Tell Philiat and Pragma to go to the city of Atlas. There is a new threat waking up down south. The evil has unleashed a new sorcery. Someone who is allegedly able to turn people into emotionless stones. Athymos she is called. Apparently, she can erase emotions at will. Can you do that for me, please?'

'I will!' she replied, standing up. 'Have you decided what you are going to do with the node? The door is still open, there for the Harpies to see.'

'I'm not sure yet. It's the only way to my brothers' worlds. I'm worried about Soul and Health. I can't feel their power crossing the space to reach me.'

'Which makes it even more risky.'

'Only the Gods can pass through the node, don't worry.'

'They can still see it. If we don't hurry, they will find it! They will find the node. What are we going to do then?'

But the night was gone, and so was our dream. Noah and I woke up to the first light of the new day, still holding on to each other, fully aware of what we had seen. Fully aware that our souls were still bound to one another. His smile was the first thing I saw, bringing me back to a soft reality. I looked into his eyes, searching for answers, looking for an explanation of what I dreamt. I knew he was too. I was sure he was with me all night long, beyond the reality of our world. He moved closer, his lips touched mine briefly, almost as if he wanted to go unnoticed. But he didn't. Whatever potion had brewed in the secret of the night, it had a strong grip on my flesh. So, I reached back, before he could break the seal of our kiss; my hand was behind his head, pulling him closer, closer to my emotions, to a desire of having more. There was no resistance, we turned connection into hunger, friendship into passion; we were about to step over the unspoken deal with no regard, selling our consciousness to the god of lust.

'Sorry, I'm sorry!' I said, suddenly moving away.

'It's OK. I'm OK...' Noah replied, as he tried to tell me he wanted it too. But that was exactly my problem. He wanted it, I wanted it.

'I'm not sure this should happen. I mean, I know we are both craving it, but something is telling me this is not right. It shouldn't be in this way...'

'Is it...because of John?' That name thundered in my head at that exact moment.

'Oh God, no, yes! I wasn't even thinking of him, but I should have.' And my words suddenly detached Noah from me.

'It hasn't been easy, since the day I met him, since I saw you with him. Since that day, in your house, I felt like I was intruding in your lives, as if I was tampering with the life you built together. This is why the distance between us was growing. But at the same time, I knew then, as much as I know now, that whatever this is, we are meant to be together!' That was the first time Noah had let that out.

The sharpness of his will was so clear that it could cut the air in half. He wanted to be with me completely, as I was with John. It wasn't just attraction; he wanted to share his life with me as if I was meant to be his other half. The entire secret about our origins, our fate was feeding that desire from within. He had no one, and he had found the only one that mattered. Again, we were not on the same page. We were two pages of the same book, open right in that invisible line, sitting side by side. We were bound together, but I didn't want him in that way. There was something inside me telling me it was like desiring my own body, my own flesh.

'OK, listen to me, just one second. I don't want to lose you over something that we don't fully understand. I do feel something for you, something very strong!' And his face was lit up again by the fire in his heart. 'But hold on. I don't think what I feel for you is what you think. What I thought too. I blame myself for sending you the wrong signals, I admit that. But also, I do feel you belong to me as I belong to you. More than physical attraction; so much more that touching you just now felt wrong.'

'I don't understand…do you feel what I feel or you don't?'

'I do. But I don't think what you feel—and so what I feel—is what we think it is. Let's wait a bit longer. I can tell you this, I don't want to lose you. You are part of me, and I want to keep it, no matter what. Just, let's wait.'

'You know I'm not good at that… All I feel is this rush to move forwards, into desiring. I want the truth, the whole truth. I want to know what's happening to us. I want to know where we are going. I want you!'

'You think if we are together, the doors into the unknown will get wide open, for us to see?' I asked, finally realizing Noah's deepest desire.

'I do,' he said, after hesitating a little. 'But I don't want you only because of it. Everything is telling me to have it. Especially when I'm alone with you, when I look into your eyes. All I can think constantly is that I want you.'

'OK. I'd say we should discover the truth first. I promise you we will do everything we can to get to it. Regarding having us, together, we can figure this out later. Let's think of it as our second priority. What do you think? Can we do that?'

'I think it's a mistake. But what else can I do to make you change your mind? I will wait.'

'Noah?'

'Yes?'

'That wasn't the first time I saw Cherish in that large terrace. I've seen her before, on my way back from Noah's Bridge, right after meeting you.'

'Does Anita know it?'

'I never told her. It was a brief vision, like five seconds. I had no idea what I was looking at. But she was there, saying exactly the same words: *If we don't hurry, they will find it! They will find the node. What are we going to do then?'*

'If you have seen it twice, it must be important. Let's not waste any more time.'

'I agree. Let's go and meet my mother!'

Chapter Nineteen
Motherhood

∞

Anita was already up when Noah and I left our rooms. Initially, I thought we could give her some time to rest and go to meet Victoria just the two of us. However, she was already up and about, roaming around the main room on the first floor, where breakfast was displayed in a haphazard manner. As expected, it was more of a self-service breakfast, but the food that guests could choose from was disappointing.

She had stopped beside a narrow table where a large, hot moka pot was still steaming, and just beside it, many tiny cups were waiting upside down in a state of boredom. With her fingers on her chin, she stood close to an old man with broad shoulders and a long grey beard who looked at her with confusion, unable to understand her indecision.

'What am I supposed to do?' she asked me, as I walked closer. The old man glanced at me and smiled.

'What do you mean? It's coffee. Just take a cup and pour the coffee in it.' And I moved away, captivated by some chunky croissants.

'Don't they have large cups? I need my usual generous dose, maybe even more, considering everything…' And the man also moved away, probably bored of waiting in line.

'Just get some, and we can get more when we meet Victoria…' Noah said, smiling at me as he grabbed the exact croissant I had my eyes on.

'What is this?' she asked, picking up on our subtle connection. 'What's going on between you two?'

'What do you mean?' I said, ignoring her insinuation.

'You do believe she will show up, don't you?' Noah asked, changing the topic while taking a seat beside me.

'For our sake, I hope so. Let's remember the main thing here: no matter what she says, no matter how nasty my mother can be, we need to stay close to her. We need her *positive influence*' —and I glanced at the old man, trying not to be too explicit—'on our shoulders.'

'Wise words, boy! A mother is always a mother!' the stranger said, smiling at us again as he walked out of the room, catching us off guard.

'We need to be more careful. We don't know who around us can speak English,' Anita whispered, her face making a sour expression as she sipped the strong coffee.

A few minutes later, we left the place and walked out to the end of the road, Victoria's designated coffee shop waiting for us at the right corner. Rain must have fallen in the early morning, as the streets were wet, and some of the stands we had seen the day before were missing. Nevertheless, despite the hour, a lot of people were walking everywhere, some in an obvious rush. For them, the world was the same they experienced the day before, the month before, always. For us, it was a new, risky world. We were moving in broad daylight, pretending we were not hunted, ignoring whether we had been detected in some way. As we arrived, Victoria's face appeared through the large windows of the shop. She was sitting on a tall stool, a heavy cup in her hands.

'She is already here. Let's go!' And I ran inside.

'Hi Victoria,' I said, keeping my distance, as I thought she wanted me to. 'Sorry for the delay; we grabbed a quick breakfast before leaving.'

'So, tell me, why are you here? After all this time?' she asked almost immediately, not paying attention to what I had just said.

'It's quite complicated,' I replied, trying to think of what I could come up with, while Noah and Anita were ordering cappuccinos for the three of us.

'I'm sure it is. Everything has always been complicated for you. Discipline, beliefs, family…'

'I know the truth, Victoria. I know you are not my real mother,' I said, trying to counteract her attempt to hurt me. That wasn't meant to be my opening line but, as usual, her words had a peculiar way to penetrate the armour I kept building over the years.

'I imagine my mother told you…even in her final hours, she managed to stir up some drama…' And she looked away, probably picturing Grandma somewhere outside.

'How much do *you* know about it?' I asked.

'Is this the time when you ask me about your real parents? I knew this time would come. I was expecting it to happen early on. Then you left, and I thought we wouldn't talk about it any more.'

'I didn't leave. You ousted me.'

'My house, my rules. You knew that. What were you expecting me to do after telling me you wanted to leave our faith, your faith? For what? To engage in evil sin?'

'Evil…that's a good place to start from. Let me ask you this, as it feels like, despite everything, you seem untouched by all of this.' And Anita had just returned, maintaining her distance as she placed my cappuccino on the table. 'Does the name Athymos mean anything to you?'

A brief moment of silence fell upon us suddenly. Anita picked up that word right away, understanding what I was asking, worried that I would expose us right then and there. Her feet pointed towards the front door, her hands still mimicking the service she had just provided me with, she was staying in the distance, ready to flee. Victoria, on the other hand, seemed lost when faced with my direct question. Her eyes finally met mine, trying to decipher my intent.

'No, it means nothing to me. What are you asking, exactly?'

'You see,' I continued, almost disappointed that she genuinely knew nothing about it, 'I've spent the last few months, well, technically years, digging into my past. I found a lot of important information, but I think the most important thing I know now is that being with you, back then, might have saved my life.'

'Jehovah saved your life, before you threw everything away...' She was completely oblivious to my words. My hook, my strategy to let her defences down, wasn't working.

'I'm not talking about your faith. I'm talking about your role as my mother.'

'Daniel, why are you here now?' she insisted again.

'I'm here to be close to you again. At least to see if I have a chance to be safe, as I was before...' And those words were like blades in my bones, hurtful lies spoken for a greater good.

'Are you thinking of coming back in?' Her eyes shifted from me to Noah and Anita briefly.

'We all are,' I continued, knowing the two had never agreed to me saying such an impactful lie.

'Why now, why do you need me? You could have come back on your own anytime, anywhere, wherever it is that you live now...' She was reluctant to believe. For a moment, I thought my lie was too obvious to be believed.

'Because everything is interconnected, including you. I know this is sudden. I told you it's complicated. I'm not asking you to do anything. Just stay in touch, let's stay close as I'm starting this journey, as we all are.'

'You know there are steps you need to take. You need to speak to the elders. You can't get back in, just like that. You need to prove to them and to Jehovah that you have changed, that you are finally cleansed of every sin you committed. That you are deeply sorry for your past, for what you were. Then, only then, we can be close again…' And she stepped down from her stool, ready to leave. Her words echoed in my head. I was determined to make her believe my lie, but in my mind, I could only picture Noah and me, falling asleep close to each other. I wasn't cleansed of any sin. I was actually deep in it.

'Yes. I know all of this. But I also know you are allowed to help me step by step. I'm not saying let's be together every day, all day. Just be around. Meet me, I don't know, a few minutes tomorrow to guide me, then the same the day after. That's all.'

'I need to speak to them about it, first. Meet me here tomorrow, same time. I'll tell you what you need to do. I have to go.'

And she walked out without saying anything else. Carrying her bag full of religious magazines and flyers, she left to begin her walk-by preaching. Another Jehovah's Witness, a woman, was waiting for her at the corner, right under the street lights, engaging people passing by in undesired, unpleasant conversations. As the two of them moved out of sight, Anita and Noah asked me about our conversation. I sipped the hot drink from my large cup, and the difficult translation unfolded. They needed to know what I had committed them to, unfortunately without their consent.

'Are you insane?' Anita shouted, spilling some of her cappuccino. I knew she wouldn't be happy about the lie I just told to Victoria.

'It looks like she really has no idea about who she really is,' Noah interjected, changing the subject, his hand slowly reaching Anita's shoulder in the attempt to calm her down.

'Are we a hundred per cent sure she is Athymos, right?' Anita asked.

'Oh, I'm sure of it,' Noah and I replied simultaneously.

'OK, you need to explain to me what's going on with the two of you. Up until yesterday, I was afraid you were going to fall out. Now it looks like you are best friends.' And she put her cup aside, demanding an explanation with her intense gaze.

'Nothing is going on! I said, avoiding Noah's gaze. 'We are just trying to make things better for all of us. That's all. Anyway, I'm sure she is who she is. Victoria is completely and absolutely devoid of any feelings. There were no emotions in her speech. I could almost feel the emptiness emanating from her as she talked to me.'

'So did I, and I understood nothing of what she said...' And Noah raised his hands, almost justifying his response to Anita, who was still looking at him suspiciously.

'So, your plan is to pretend you are going back in...and we're getting in with you? So, we can meet her again?'

'Precisely. I know, Anita, it's crazy. But what else could I have come up with? There is nothing, absolutely nothing that she cares about, except this.' And we left our spot, our feet already carrying us outside.

'I wonder if these things are somehow connected,' Noah said after we left the coffee shop behind, walking around the block with no specific destination. 'We have Victoria on one side and this cult on the other. She has no emotions, no feelings to guide her, so what does she do? She chooses something that can provide that to her, a sort of North Star... Don't you think it's too odd to be a mere coincidence?'

'I wonder what it's like to live with no feelings. I mean, I know of people who cannot taste, who have no sense of smell.. but feelings?' Anita pondered, glancing left and right as we crossed the main road.

Noah had come up with that idea with just a few signals he picked up in the last few hours. In all those months I had spent contemplating the truth, I couldn't see it myself. But he had a point; there was surely going to be more to discover about that. Afraid the invisible mark Victoria had left on us during that brief meeting would fade away, we walked only a few steps from the coffee shop and found a small park right across the road. The air was cool, but the sun was out, so we decided to sit on a stone bench for a while, enjoying what was starting to feel like a strange holiday trip. Many people were passing by, crossing the park to get from one side of the busy city to the other. To our surprise, the old man we had met at the bed and breakfast was there too, sitting a few steps away. His hands held a paper bag, and he was kindly feeding some birds that had the unexpected fortune to be there at the right time.

'Your man is here...' Anita said. 'The one staying at our place?'

'He was looking right at us a few seconds ago,' Noah added.

'Probably he is wondering why three tourists like us are staying in this tiny park when there is so much to see,' I replied.

'Anyway, we really need to check our bank accounts and, most important, I need some new clothes or, at least, to find a place where I can wash mine. Another few hours, and I'll be collected by a rubbish lorry! If I go and look around the block, will you stay here? It's safe if I go. You two are the ones at risk!' And Anita stood up, her determined expression aimed at us, as if she was scolding her own children. Her hands stretched towards us, she asked for our debit cards along with their security PINs and, like it was business as usual, she left.

A few minutes after she was gone, Noah pulled his mother's diary from the small bag he had been carrying for days. Lying down on the hard bench, his head on my legs, he started to read it again, right where he had left off. Our voices silenced by the careful read, the only thing we could hear was the loud noise of a messy city. Buses pulling on their brakes at every stop, cars beeping their horns, people shouting one another across the road in happy greetings, it was a cornucopia of madness. Here and there, some people would walk by, looking at us, how close we were, giving us the weird look of dislike. Although in a mundane city, we were still in Italy, a country open only to its own traditions, from food to beliefs; the new was welcome only under hard censorship, whatever that was.

'I just remembered another reason why I left this place…'

'You lived here?' Noah was still hanging on the mysterious pages.

'I mean the country. If there is something they really share, north and south, is how inwards this nation is. People are giving us the look…they think we are a couple, a lusty couple of sodomites.' And I laughed.

'But we are, in a way... A couple, I mean, ' he said with a quick smile and continued, 'I really can't understand how you could face all this nonsense around your sexuality and emotions and stay strong. Even now, doesn't it hurt having to pretend to your mother?'

'It does, more than I can express in words,' I replied, sighing. 'But, as you said, I knew then, and I know now it's all nonsense. Forget about their beliefs and their ideas about a god who will eventually kill anyone who isn't a Jehovah's Witness. What I never understood is how they can believe that God is love and, at the same time, hate the love we feel as human beings. How can they say we were made in His own image and then say I'm wrong for being who I am.'

'I can only see it in two ways. Either God is kind, like you are, or He doesn't exist at all.' His words had come out naturally, almost without thinking, giving me a sense of peace and warmth.

After a few minutes of silence, Noah resumed. 'Look at this, Daniel. *As my child gets older, less are the chances I'll find them…* She is talking about the Awoken Ones. *I have the feeling I could actually chose what future Noah is going to have.*

If I stay focused, if I keep pushing down this magic, he might have a normal life. But what if I'm wrong? What if I should, instead, find them all? I keep thinking of digging it back up. Am I preventing my child to be who he is supposed to be?' And Noah had stopped reading. 'My mother was obviously in conflict between two possible futures for me. Well, we know she chose to give me the life of a normal human being.'

'Well, it didn't work. Did it?' I said. 'My grandmother did the same. And that didn't work either. It seems, though, they both kept that door open. Your mother with the journals, the artefact buried behind her cottage…Grandma holding on to the box containing my shell. Do you think they knew they could keep it contained only that much?'

'You could be right.' Noah continued: *'If what Dõron said it's true, there are many years of normal life in store for Noah. I want him to grow like a strong, kind man. If the time really comes, it only because it's meant to be. In the meantime, he is mine to love, mine to protect. I'm going to raise him as mine. And this is my promise to the God of Love.'*

And we went quiet again. Siobhan knew there was an expiration date hanging over our heads. She knew she could hold on to the idea of having a normal child only up until his right age. If our families had something in common, it was that the Praetorian was acting behind them with one purpose: hiding us from our real world as long as we needed, before the time came. It wasn't a surprise considering the same Awoken One was behind both women. Dõron was the real hero of the entire story. She had managed to keep two small children, who were thousands of miles apart, safe for years. How much energy did that cost her?

That was motherhood at its finest. Not Victoria, not Siobhan, she was the one who kept our invisible bond alive, our lives under her protection, up until the very end.

One hour later, Anita came back, wearing a new shirt, a new light brown jacket but the same pair of jeans. She had found a laundry shop somewhere near our accommodation and had returned to ask us for the key to our room so she could go back, collect *our smelly clothes*, and get them all done in one trip.

'I know,' she exclaimed, opening her arms in the air. 'The choices were between this and a black jumper with *I love Rome* and pink hearts all over it, and I'm terrified of not knowing whether I'm wearing unwashed clothes!'

'Style over risk! I agree.' And I smiled, thinking how Anita wasn't allowing the overall situation to dictate a poor stylistic and healthy choice.

'Anyway, I have good news and bad news, she continued, handing only one bank card back. 'Noah, yours is working. I have no idea how much is there, but I got you some cash. Daniel, yours I'm afraid will stay forever in this beautiful city…'

'What?' I asked, worried.

'It said the bank was instructed to hold the card. I'd say there is a problem with your account?'

'More like it's in a billions euro in negative. Noah does your mum mention an Awoken of money by any chance?' And I smiled, looking at Siobhan's journal. My mind had quickly run to all the possible scenarios where I had lost everything I owned but I wasn't going to say it out loud.

'Is there anything interesting in there?' Anita asked, looking at Noah's hands.

'Nothing we didn't know already,' Noah said, sitting back up, trying to dismiss the fact that Anita had just found him lying with his head on my lap.

'I found a place where we can wash and dry our clothes in one hour, a few blocks away. I have it on my map here. Hold on, this free wifi is very bad… Here we go, look at this,' she said, pointing the screen of her phone right at my face. 'Shannon's Insta. Please tell me she is not going on talking about her new leggings as she is swinging her legs all over the room!' And I laughed as I could clearly see that was exactly what Shannon was doing. 'Oh, also that silly trend for couples, with Mark…' she added, scrolling on her newsfeed, '…who is more protective, who starts the fights… Oh, I can tell you who, without even looking at this stupid video! I can't believe we are here trying to save the world, without anyone knowing, and she is convincing hundreds of thousands of people to buy those awful leggings!' And she sat beside Noah, her agitation rising.

'Why do you even look at it, let it go,' I said, making her even more nervous.

'I didn't know we were saving the world, just our bloody skins!' And Noah made her laugh, bringing her to a more light-hearted mood.

'Any chance she might be a Harpy?' she added.

'Who?'

'Shannon!'

'Just because you don't like her doesn't turn her into one of them, you know…' I replied, smiling.

'Yeah, but it would make me feel better!'

'Yeah, I know.'

'Daniel?' Her face suddenly turned sad. 'They got married! Mark and Shannon!'

'What? When?' I asked, standing up without much care for the people passing by.

'Looks like in July? The world has really moved on… We've lost, what, fourteen months? Anyway, I'm going. I don't want to think about it!' And she was gone again, our keys in her hand, determined to clean all our clothes, pouring bleach on them, mentally replacing T-shirts with Shannon's leggings.

Once she was gone, I asked Noah what exactly he remembered from the dream we had the night before. We had briefly talked about Cherish, but with the unfolding close encounter after we woke up, the topic had been forgot.

'I think I saw everything you saw. What are you asking exactly?'

'I'm thinking about all those names we heard. I can't recall any of them, but it truly feels like there are many out there, too many for us to find, I'm afraid.'

'And Anita was there! How is it possible? Well, it was Cherish actually. But still, how do you tell them apart, at this stage?'

'Do you think she knows? When she's here and when Cherish takes over?'

'I think she's going through what we went through at the beginning. She's getting there. And I feel it's a strange coincidence that we dreamed about Athymos. Of all the memories we could recall, we chose that one. I think we're pulling the ones we need as we go. I think we should start taking notes, keep a journal, like my mother did.'

'So you think we are…evoking those memories based on how close we are? It would make sense. Cherish was the first one I brought back that day, outside the pub that wasn't there. Noah?' I continued after a brief silence. My hand on his arm, his attention was fully on me.

'Yes?'

'Your man is not just looking at us. He's staring at us… He's been doing it for a good while now. Should we be worried?'

'Do you think he is…one of them? Should we go?'

'It wouldn't make much of a difference. He knows where we're staying.'

Chapter Twenty
What Lies Beneath

∞

Noah and I hurried our way back to our rooms, hoping to reach Anita before she left. Although we couldn't be sure we were followed, we couldn't stand still, being watched by that old man. As we were getting closer, she came out from the front door with a large bag she had taken from somewhere. Our clothes were crammed together at the bottom, and a white sheet was sticking out from the top.

'What else did you put in that bag?' I asked, laughing.

'Our sheets! I don't know if I'm worried about who slept on it before us, or more worried that *they* can smell our scent once we leave.' And she started hurrying down the street, with Noah and me following her, exchanging smiles.

'Does this mean we're moving?' Noah asked, as we entered the laundry shop.

'It might not be a bad idea, Anita,' I said, moving closer as I helped her empty the bag. 'I think that old man might be following us…'

'Are you sure? I mean, he seemed pretty harmless.'

'At this stage, I'm not sure about anyone,' I admitted.

One hour later, after Anita decided the dryer was taking too long — *'considering the risk of even having old men after us'* — we retrieved our still-damp clothes and left the place. Leaving the bed and breakfast's sheets behind without much concern, we moved a few blocks east, close to the Pantheon, where we found a small hotel that had last-minute room rentals available. A little girl was behind the reception desk, and the expression on her face upon seeing me carrying the large bag on my shoulder made both Anita and Noah burst into laughter. Hungry for food, after leaving our belongings behind, we departed immediately. The main square was bustling with people going in every direction. Some tourists were gazing at actors who were pretending to be frozen statues, capturing pictures and chatting loudly.

'We should consider doing the same, you know? If we're still being followed?' Noah suggested, smiling.

'I can't believe my ears. You out of the three of us, you are actually proposing to stay still, pausing our mission…'

'Our mission?' Noah was laughing at Anita's words. 'What do you think we are, secret agents?'

'Look at all these people…they know nothing! They have no idea of the impending danger hanging over their heads,' I said, feeling melancholic. Anita was right, we were on a mission, a mission we did not fully understand. And yet, we were agents sent without secrets of their own, but conscious of the many carried by others, many secrets we could not see through still.

'There! Food!' Anita exclaimed. 'Let's sit and have something to eat over there. We should discuss our next steps.'

We sat down at a small restaurant, a trattoria, where the enticing smell wafting from inside was so strong that it could have turned any Harpy into a muppet. Hungry and captivated by the aroma, we ordered quickly, skipping pleasantries and drinks. The sun shone brightly on the expansive, round church, bathing us in its warmth as we sat between the indoor and outdoor sections, making it seem like we were enjoying the peak of summer. In contrast, some shops on the opposite side of the square were in the process of removing their Halloween decorations to make way for Christmas items. Time seemed to press forwards relentlessly, unprepared for what was to come next, blending seasons and celebrations into a chaotic mixture of randomness.

'This feels so wrong…' I mused.

'That it's probably twenty-five degrees out and they're putting up Christmas decorations?' Anita asked.

'No. Well, aside from that.' And I smiled. 'I mean us being here. I can't stop thinking about John. I should have never left him behind.' And Anita's expression turned sorrowful almost immediately.

'I know all we can think is the worst has happened, but we don't know that for sure. The gateway might be inaccessible after all. I know, I know what you're going to say,' she added before I could speak. 'But the best thing we can do now to ensure their safety is to move forwards.'

'Speaking of which,' Noah interjected. 'Where is the final God hidden? Is she dead? Is she alive? I don't understand. The first time we heard about her, she was said to be gone.'

'I'm not sure if Time wants to find her, or find her artefact. If we can assume we can bring her back once we have it?' And Anita, in the meantime, was studying the drinks menu as if it was an ancient manuscript.

'You mean go back in time again? Like we did for Soul?'

But my question went unanswered. The waiter returned with our food, so we fell silent, attempting to keep our conversation discreet. Over the two hours we spent there, the place went from crowded to empty and busy again, like waves in a vast sink, pouring and draining, with hundreds of people flowing in and out in an endless loop. Eventually, feeling the pressure of numerous hungry patrons eyeing our table, eager for an empty seat, we decided to head back to our rooms.

Below our hotel, on the street, a small shop was serving afternoon drinks and snacks at a reasonable price. Wanting to linger outside a bit longer, we opted to enjoy the cool sunset of the afternoon, perched on a small table and chairs that struggled to accommodate our weight, wobbling precariously on the polished stones of the walkway. While Anita and Noah waited to place their orders, listening to the incomprehensible chatter and laughter of young people next to us, my mind leaped back in time to the troubling events we had witnessed in Varayal. Somehow, we weren't revisiting that topic. None of us wanted to relive the moment we thought everything was going to end. The invisible malevolence that had tried to stop us, its thunderous voice echoing in our ears within that empty space, was something we didn't want to address.

'How are we ever going to confront him?' I said, out of the blue. 'This malevolent, immense threat looming over us, Nothing,' I added as they both looked at me, trying to understand my reference. 'How are we ever going to defeat something so powerful?'

'Remember what we saw last night? I think we never managed to defeat him… He was still manipulating events against us from afar,' Noah added, catching Anita off guard.

'What do you mean, *what we saw?* What did you see, when?'

'Last night, we had a…shared vision, Anita.' I lowered my voice to ensure no one could overhear. 'We went back, who knows when, but we were Love, and he was talking about this evil force existing somewhere, far away.'

'What else did you see?'

'Large white walls, a truly beautiful place and some Awoken Ones.'

'And you! You were there too,' Noah added, surprising her again.

'Well, Cherish was there. She looked somewhat like you, but she wasn't you you, if you know what I mean…' I quickly said.

Anita was puzzled. At first, she asked why we hadn't told her about that right away. Then, she began analysing every small detail of what we had seen, what it meant, who was in it, why we saw it. No matter how many times we recounted the entire story, we couldn't come up with anything more than what we already knew.

'I wonder when that was…' she said, once again.

'When?' Noah asked in response.

'Yes, I mean how many years, centuries ago? It definitely wasn't me. It didn't happen during my lifetime, well, our lifetime!' And she raised her hand to get the waiter's attention. I wasn't sure if she wanted another drink or just wanted to get closer to the boy she found of a *very Italian beauty*.

'One thing I'm starting to believe is that all these…entities, come back in different ways. Some return as they are, magical beings in their true form. Take Iris or Harmonia, for example. She just came back like that. Others return in Human bodies, as if they are being hosted, but why, I still don't understand it,' I mused.

'I think it's because of their strength. Or the strength of Love. Maybe if they're strong enough, they can manifest on their own. Otherwise, they need a host, someone who can carry them until the time is right,' Anita pondered, looking at her hands as she referred to herself as a potential host.

'Like Dõron…' Noah said.

'Like Cherish and me,' Anita concluded.

'So, they're essentially dormant, waiting for the right moment to emerge. What happens to their original bodies then? What happens to the people sharing the same flesh as them?' I questioned, leading them both into a mental labyrinth of further questions.

Throughout the rest of the day, the conversation shifted from one speculation to the next, yet no significant progress was achieved. We revisited the topic of Victoria and our plans for keeping her close. We remained uncertain about the extent of her power and how long we could go without her before the hiding effect wore off. The only thing we were certain of was that we would encounter her again, along with that unsettling sense of emptiness.

That night, back in our room, Noah and I maintained our distance. As agreed, we aimed to separate *our mission* from our emotions for the greater good. In our beds, we eventually drifted into sleep, unaware that once again, we would travel back in time to when we existed as one, truly being. Separated only by an old, silent locker, our distance dissolved; Noah and I once more shared the same body, the body of a powerful God. This time, we could see our face reflected in the serene, silvery lake before us. Our hands touched the mossy grass, and we glimpsed more than just our appearance: our grey eyes, olive skin, and golden, curly hair. Something had occurred or was about to occur, something that troubled us deeply. Above the vast lake, a wonderful city made of silver and gold metal, glass, and beauty peeked through the dense foliage of the large trees. Numerous people were gazing at it in silence. Finally, one of them approached, placing a hand on our shoulder.

'We can't prevent this, Love. There is no power we possess that can be wielded against him.'

'Nothing is willing to annihilate his own army just to destroy this world. What he couldn't achieve directly, he made the universe carry out his malevolent act. No soul, nothing will escape the impact,' another voice chimed in.

However, we could not accept defeat. Whatever immense threat loomed ahead, we could not permit its execution. The world we were living in was Creation's doing, her hands blessing her survival through us, through the love that had seeped into the very roots of that planet. We had existed for centuries, keeping the Awoken Ones content, constructing a world brimming with compassion and forgiveness. Yet all of it would be obliterated in a catastrophic blast.

'I still bear the duty to protect this world,' we asserted. 'I can't simply let it happen. Even in this eleventh hour, I still possess the power to shield this planet from being reduced to dust!'

'Love, the impact will be too immense to evade.'

'I understand, Kathor. I respect your insight into the sheer potency this will unleash upon us. You are, after all, the Awoken of Power. We need to turn that power against it, not shy away from it.'

'Even if we were to fight, it would necessitate all our powers, your entire strength,' another voice spoke.

'What does the Awoken of Hope have to contribute?' we asked, pivoting around, leaving the lake at our back.

'It's the only way, yes, master. We have to give it back to you, if you want to stand a chance...' the one called Asher spoke up. He glanced at the others, reminding them that this was their only option.

'So we shall!' Kathor responded. 'We will return it, without hesitation. There is no happy ending in the final pages of our existence. We may stand a better chance if we reunite.'

Our wandering in a dream of a lost past was abruptly shattered by an unexpected knock on the door. It was just 4 a.m., and someone was calling us from the other side.

'Anita?' Noah whispered, his sleepy eyes pointed at me.

'I'm not sure...'

'Well, guessing won't make it any clearer, will it?' Noah swiftly got up, donned his trousers, and reached the door. He exchanged a quick look with me as I got up, then opened it. Much to our astonishment, there was no one there. The corridor outside lay completely deserted. The faint lights at the walls were shifting from corner to corner, skittering across the tiny space, like a flickering candle fighting against a gentle breeze. But there was no one to account for the abrupt awakening. Noah moved away from our room, heading towards the cold, narrow staircase that led downwards, searching for anyone who might have just left. He eventually returned, his face etched with confusion.

'What in the world?' he said, re-entering our room.

'Let's go to Anita's. If something's after us, it might be after her too.' And I grabbed the key to our room, leaving the door securely locked behind us.

Anita's room was to our left, right next to ours. Her door was shut. From feeling haunted, we now found ourselves haunting back, knocking on Anita's door to rouse her. A few seconds later, a very befuddled, less-than-pleased face appeared.

'What's going on? And why are you shirtless?' Anita asked, eyeing Noah. Her eyes struggled to stay open.

'Something strange happened. Did you hear anything? Like knocking on your door?' I inquired, concerned.

'Yes, just a few seconds ago! Oh, guess? It was you! Mystery solved, Jessica Fletcher!' She turned back into her room, searching for a bottle of water.

'We're serious, Anita. Someone knocked repeatedly on our door! There was no one outside, so we thought maybe they were after you,' Noah explained, perching on her bed.

'They? Who's "they"?' Anita asked, momentarily confounding us. She must still have been half asleep.

'Them!' I gestured to the empty space outside her room, indicating the obvious.

'Maybe it was that creepy man who's also here? The one we ran into again at the park?' she conjectured.

'Anita, we're not in the same place any more. We moved to avoid being found, remember?' Noah looked at me, aghast.

'Oh…' she realized. 'My mind is all over the place. I feel like I've been disconnected from my own thoughts… You're right! You're right. You're right,' she kept repeating that final phrase as she entered her en-suite bathroom, leaving us perplexed by her peculiar behaviour.

'I have to ask again, what's happening?' Noah questioned.

After waiting for an excruciating twenty minutes, with no other strange occurrences from the unknown, Noah and I returned to our room. Anita had repeatedly assured us that there was nothing to worry about except missing a good night's sleep. Back in our beds, we could only gaze at the ceiling, listening to the sporadic footsteps of the occupants in rooms above, shifting beds back and forth. We were either wide awake while they tossed and turned, or perhaps we simply could not go back to sleep. As the early morning hours approached and the sun's rays streamed through the side window, I turned to the other side, meeting Noah's gaze. He teetered on the edge between here and there, attempting to rest to no avail.

'How much longer until we meet Victoria?' he murmured, his voice betraying exhaustion.

'Two hours,' I replied, adjusting a small radio with a clock display. The bedside table looked even lonelier with just that solitary device on it. 'I don't know how I'll face another encounter with her after being up all night.'

'Come here.' And his arm stretched out to reach my hand. 'Don't worry, just lie here beside me for a few minutes. Then we can get up and attempt to erase this tired look from our faces.'

I complied. I had established boundaries just the previous day, and there I was, reeling at the precipice, as if testing a beast that shouldn't be provoked. Once more, our bare chests touched, his warmth transferred from his body to mine, my head nestled beneath his chin, the sweet scent of his skin mingling with mine. His tender lips glided over my forehead, seeking the right place to rest. And there they found mine, as I looked up, poised to reciprocate the kiss we had withheld for so long. Emotions flowed from one heart to another, a trade of dreams and desires crashing together frenziedly. His thoughts melded with mine, his mind merged with mine. Once again, we felt like the first time we met, on that bustling island, away from the dance floor, the shopping carts, among people who were nothing like us. Yet this time, we knew precisely how to navigate the abyss of our madness. We now possessed a map leading us to the treasure we had tirelessly sought.

'How do I become you?'

'How do you become me?' I countered.

'The time to break this curse is drawing near. I know it.'

'We have only one shot. It's so close..'

'Time, Soul, Health, we can be together again.'

'How do we become us?' I questioned again.

'Just be mine.'

Our artefacts stirred to life once more, emerging from our bodies, our essence. They radiated with brilliance, their energy swirling around us, pushing our bodies together, closer. Until we fused into one flesh, one mind. Our souls were left behind as we traversed the stretches of our eternity, reaching the Gods we had liberated at a great cost. We returned to a place we had once called home. A wild, green and reddish landscape stretched out before us. Grey mist clung to the ground and the sky, connecting them as if they were one dimension only. Tall grass swayed silently, except for one spot, where an elderly woman stood, ready to welcome us. Her hands were raised, her face grey. We knew her, we had encountered her before.

'It's time to uncover what lies beneath. Come, brother, the time isn't right just yet, but you're close. Yes, very close...'

'Brother?' we asked.

'It's time to emerge as who I truly am, Health.'

Chapter Twenty-One
The Path We Share

∞

You saw Health?' Anita asked, as Noah and I were bringing her up to speed, sitting at the usual coffee shop, while waiting for Victoria.

'I'm not sure "seeing" is the right word. You know, it was the usual dreaming, feeling...' I replied, sipping the hot coffee.

'What else did she say? Where is she?'

'We don't know. She was there and gone in the space of a few minutes. It felt like we were back home, in Connemara, but...' and Noah looked at me briefly, '...we could be wrong.'

'She was the same woman, Anita. The same one that came to me in the early days. The one that told me *Things are waiting to be… Hurry.* I'm sure it was her.'

'So, hold on. I thought that was Dõron?' Anita was following my same path of doubts and wonders.

'I thought that too. But I think that was Health. Dõron was the one that protected me and Noah for all those years. But I think Health is the one that gave me the cloak. I still remember the night Time came to rescue us from Lëogan. I had told him about the cloak and he seemed shocked in learning that *she* was there somewhere!'

'This means she was also one of the three that I've been seeing so many times. That night we met Time in Castlecross, remember? He was one of them. Now her. I'd say the third one was Soul,' Noah continued.

'So many have been playing a part in all this, it's hard to understand who was who. If we believe the Awoken Ones have been visiting us, but also the Gods,' I started.

'And the Harpies!' Anita added.

'And the Harpies!' Noah repeated, his hands on his cheeks.

'Some have shown in Human form, some in spirit, some in a memory? We were told that Time and Soul could not reach you from afar. It was the memory of them in your soul that brought them back to you. But…with Health it seems to be different. She was, she is closer than they were and, if she did give you the cloak, she is definitely acting, somehow.' Anita was taking mental notes.

'OK. Let's assume that every thirty years this…thing repeats itself,' I said, trying to help her. 'From what we know, some attempts have failed right from the start with Love not even getting close to manifest. This time, the pure presence of Love, although premature, had pushed some of the surviving Awoken Ones to put the plan in motion…'

'Who was left? Iris, Dõron…'

'And you. Cherish was there all along, dormant, but she was there,' Noah added, but, to that remark, Anita made a strange face, still rejecting the idea she was somehow entangled with it.

'Something or someone must have triggered this whole sequence of events, right? Let's say the time had come, I want to believe Health came to me, telling me to find Noah. Dõron must have been moving the plan along as she appeared right at the same time. Now that the Awoken Ones were acting, so were the Harpies. And that's when we got into the middle of everything. Me finding Noah, us finding Time, Time finding Soul.'

'Yes, it makes sense,' Anita said, leaving the table to order some more coffee. 'What are you trying to say?'

'That Health has been there all along, trying to reach us, to help us,' I replied.

'Hiding?' Noah asked, passing his empty cup to Anita.

'Healing, perhaps.' And she left, almost bumping into Victoria who had just walked into the shop.

Her face sharp, a very small, conventional smile was all she could give as she walked in, approaching our table. She hadn't acknowledged Noah's presence, neither Anita's as she virtually swapped places with her. There were no greetings, no satisfaction in knowing the sinner wanted to repent, in knowing I wanted to get back in. Victoria had kept her distance, without sitting in the empty chair Anita had left behind. She had come to deliver a very short, but vital message.

'They say it can be arranged. You have to start the path of redemption, meeting the elders. Considering your…situation'—and the break in those words was painfully intentional—'it won't be easy. It will be scrutinized, and you all have to do it independently. This is not a group therapy. They have never been baptized, so they are starting the normal way. You are not.'

'OK, OK,' I said, trying to think of how we could do that in a smart way. 'It makes sense. They don't speak Italian, so they will need different support, if you know what I mean.'

'I could technically be able to see you during the process,' she continued, ignoring what I just said, 'but I don't personally think it's the right thing to do. I see a very dark cloud hanging over your head, and I don't want that to spill over me.'

'I want to do this, but you have to be there for me this time.'

'Don't push it. I'll see what I can do, but if I do that, if I keep seeing you, I don't want to hear any strange story, any word about my mother or the past. Do you understand me?'

'Daniel? Your man is outside, looking right at us.' Anita came back, cups in hands, unaware of what Victoria had just said. Thankfully, Victoria didn't know what Anita just brought to our attention. As she came in with no pleasantries, so she left us, with no final comments, no goodbyes. She was a pure messenger on a mission, and that mission was accomplished.

'Something is definitely up with that man out there,' Noah said, his eyes pointed outside through the large windows of the coffee shop.

'Under other circumstances, I would say it's just a pure coincidence. After all, we are still in the same area. Maybe he is just roaming around in this neighbourhood, but I don't think so,' Anita continued.

'Maybe I should go and talk to him.'

'Maybe.' And Anita's hand reached to stop me. 'First tell us what she said!

I quickly went through a recap of what the mother of every sorrow had just told me, before she was gone, in the blink of an eye. Anita and Noah were still reluctant to follow through with my plans, but the fact they didn't have one of their own was playing in my favour. I didn't know how long the shadow of Athymos would obscure us from the evil, but there was definitely a Catch-22 there somewhere. If she wasn't part of any faction still, we did not know. We were descending a painful path into my mother's cult, attempting to save ourselves from a premature defeat. *Isn't this what she has done as well, after all?* I thought. How long before Time and Soul would find Health? They were looking for her, but she was presenting herself to us. We found no Awoken Ones, except the only one that didn't belong to Love. Instead, we had disappeared from the world of magic, under her scent of emptiness. My idea was starting to crumble.

Leaving the others to finish their drinks, I moved outside, determined to confront the one who apparently was following us, suspiciously. He looked the same, he was wearing the same clothes he had the first time we met him, back in the first place we stayed. Somehow, I thought that was pretty similar to our situation, moving to Rome with the only clothes we had, looking shabby and tired.

'Hi, we met before, haven't we?' I started.

'I believe we have indeed.' His tone was happy. His face attempting a weak smile, I could barely hear him in the messy, noisy city. 'A few times, actually.'

'Are you from Rome? Or are you just visiting?'

'Just visiting, I hope. So are you, right?'

'Yes. Me and my friends are here to see someone…'

'Your mother…' He still remembered our conversation at breakfast. My suspicion was holding its ground. 'How did that go?'

'I'm sorry,' I said, resisting the inquisitive look. 'Have we met before? Before these last few days, I mean.'

'Meeting…sounds like we parted ways and then reunited again. But we were never, actually.' And at the sound of those words, I looked back inside to the two who were intently trying to read the muted conversation. 'I am where you are. Sometimes as part of a whole, sometimes as just me. You don't recognize me, do you?'

I had no words. I was trying to comprehend his cryptic talk and trying to understand if we were in danger. He didn't look frightening, his voice didn't sound aggressive. All I could do was stay silent, my head turned to the ones I loved, who quickly left their table behind, coming to join me.

'Don't be afraid,' he said, right after Anita and Noah reached us. 'There is no enemy here, not even the woman that just left. Oh, believe me, she is a threat, but of a different kind. You should not be close to her for too long. It feels like she could drag away any spark of will.'

'You know Victoria?' I let out.

'Victoria? Is this her name now? Yes. Any of us would know her. She is unique, if this is the right term to use.'

'Who are you?' Noah asked.

'I'm Eleoen, the Awoken of Kindness and Forgiveness.'

'We know you!' I instantly replied. 'We saw you in our vision, you were with us, back when Love existed.' And I looked at Noah who could recall my same memory.

'We were all together. She was one of us too,' And the old man pointed his eyes at Anita.

'You look different,' Noah said.

'I could not come in my true form. Love needs to come back before I can do that. For now, this gentle Human is sharing the path with me,' he said, whispering, as strangers were coming and going through the busy road.

'We should not be here in the open… We should move somewhere quieter.' And Anita pulled my arm to bring me back to the noisy reality.

'Let's go to the park where we met yesterday,' Noah suggested.

So, we moved away from the traffic, the loud sound of horns and beeps. People were walking even faster than before, probably foreseeing the bad weather coming. We crossed the road and headed to the entrance of the park, finding the place almost deserted. Only a few men were walking at the far side, at the other entrance. Around us, there were only birds craving a merciful gesture. As we arrived at the same spot Noah and I had sat not long before, Eleoen stopped, his face pointing at the sky, his mind packed with unknown thoughts.

'You said you are sharing the path with this man,' Anita started, her personal interest coming right through. 'How does it work? What happens to him if and when you leave?'

'He is one of the Carriers. This world calls them in many names, Hosts, Druids, and Draoithe for your people.' And he looked right at Noah. 'He will go back to his life, whatever that might be.'

'Draoithe…' Anita interrupted, looking at me. 'Wasn't that the strange name that woman used, that night by the island, in Noah's Bridge? She said her kind was able to see in between here and there? And also that other woman used the same name during her explanation around the history of that place. It was all true!'

'Does the man know?' Noah asked. 'What does he know? What if he has a family, things to get back to? While you are in him, is he…alive?'

'I'm the Awoken of Kindness. You think I would take his life just like that? He knows, he is here with me, fully aware of what we are doing. So are you. Have you ever, for a second, thought to do anything different? Has she?' he asked back looking at Anita, leaving her speechless. After all, Anita had never done anything that she had not put her head to.

'This means you will leave his body, eventually?' I asked.

'Eventually, if all goes well.'

I glanced at Anita briefly. Whatever mission we had, and she willingly accepted, had an expiration date. It was good news, after all. If we managed to release Health and Love, Cherish would leave her body for good, freeing her to live her life as she wanted. *Would she be the same afterwards? Is she who she is due to the shared path of that secret dichotomy, or is that simply her essence?* I wondered.

'Why are you here? Did you find us? How?' I asked.

'I'm here because of you. I didn't find you. I arrived just in time for your appearance in this place. I woke up as you appeared in these streets. I had little strength and time, so I sought out the first, right soul that came along.'

'Do you know how many more have returned?' Noah inquired, reaching out to a nearby pigeon that was picking up small stones from the ground, only to be left disappointed.

'I don't know. But unless they returned as soon as you did, I doubt they could locate you. I struggled to follow you as Athymos spread her power over you and this place. Luckily, her obscuring effect doesn't last too long.

'Well, at least we know it's working. I was starting to get worried we were mistakenly taking it for granted.' Anita looked relieved as she sat on a stony bench.

'You can tell? How long does it last?' I had been pondering that question since we left the time bubble back in Ireland.

'It's not just about you. It's everywhere she walks, everything she touches, everyone she comes close to. This sense of…emptiness is spreading everywhere.'

'Do you know why she hasn't joined the other Harpies?' Noah was quick to ask the next, most important question. However, Eleoen moved further away, into the darker side of the park. The weather was getting worse, heavy clouds had started to cast their shadows upon us and the beautiful, large trees adorning the quiet spot. As we followed him, his colours shifted, his grey face was enveloped in another unnatural shadow, unrelated to the real world.

'Here…' he resumed. 'She was here not long ago. As she walked out of the coffee shop, she came here, preaching. She stayed here for a few minutes. Someone sat on this bench right here. She talked to them, her feet positioned here.'

'You can see the past?' Noah inquired.

'No, he can see her traces. I know it sounds mad but I can see them too!' Anita interjected, taking us by surprise.

Like she had done back in Noah's old cottage, she could see beyond reality. 'It's like you can almost reconstruct a complete picture by sensing these tiny spots of nothing.' Her hands were moving around, her eyes adjusting to that newly discovered power.

'Eleoen, do you know why she hasn't joined the rest of the Harpies?' I repeated the question.

'Athymos is not bound to any faction. She is an Awoken One, certainly, but she's unique. Her true nature stems from Nothing, not from Love. And even though evil is her master, the very dark entity himself cannot control her! She feels no sense of duty or loyalty, to anything or anyone. When she existed in spirit, in her full strength, she spread through this world like a disease. She turned hearts to stone, minds to dust. Humans were like empty vessels, emotionless statues.' Eleoen ripped an orangey leaf from its rightful owner, examining it as if he could peer through the pages of history just by looking at it. 'But then, the Great War happened. Like all of us, she had to come to an understanding to survive. We had to find a host to be with, to wait, to slowly fall asleep. So, she found a host for herself in the rush of the final hour. When the time came to find another host, unknowingly and as weakened as she was, Athymos chose Victoria, who unexpectedly managed to shape Athymos's mind and will. Their coexistence was a mutual shaping. The Awoken One influencing the Human and vice versa. Victoria's doubts, Human doubts, turned against the darkness of her other half. Whatever decision she made, she enslaved her own Harpy with it. The tighter she clings, the less Athymos can assert herself. Her host binds her in a prison of nothingness, preventing her from breaking free.'

'Does she know? Victoria? Is she aware of all this?' Anita asked, looking at me, lost in many thoughts. Somehow, my mother's nature had briefly changed. Somehow, she was fighting our same battle.

'How much the host knows, I do not know. She might know but not be fully aware, if you know what I mean.'

'So eventually, the longer Nothing stays away, the weaker Athymos becomes?' I mused aloud. Anita could see my mind spinning, hoping there was still a chance for Victoria to triumph, silencing the Harpy indefinitely.

'What are the odds of Nothing giving up? If there's one thing we know, it's that he's drawing closer!' Anita retorted.

'I know. But if we succeed, if we manage to win this…war…Athymos will be gone forever? Victoria will be free.' Suddenly, one of my lifelong adversaries reversed its role. She was no longer a perpetrator; she was a victim, just like all of us. She was silently battling one of the strongest Harpies within her heart. She absorbed the blame, the hatred, the sorrow from me, from Grandma, from everyone who knew what she had done to me.

'Don't indulge in pity, not this time. Trust me, I sense it.' Eleoen's voice brought me back to the present, as he moved closer. 'There's an invisible bond between an Awoken and its host. We don't choose randomly; we don't take over entirely. Victoria was right for Athymos, and thus she was right for her.'

'Your words echo Revelia's explanation of why Time didn't bring Una back with everyone else. Why some evils just can't be granted a second chance?' I asked, receiving no answer. I could not understand why there was a limit to what can be redeemed, saved. I was the one who could cast the greatest judgement against someone who had been a terrible human being, but there I was, trying to give Victoria another chance. *If I can, why won't destiny?* I thought.

With that, we moved on. My mind remained entwined in my own thoughts while Anita wondered how the duality between Cherish and herself would manifest eventually. If Eleoen's words held truth, she would soon part ways with her Awoken. As we walked to the other side of the park, she asked if, when Cherish lived independently, with her own manifestation of being, she would forget everything once again. In a way, she no longer wanted to. She had struggled to regain her memories, but had grown fond of the incredible knowledge she had acquired.

A few days passed with the same rituals, but not much progress. We encountered Victoria again, this time near her church, to meet the elders and pretended to be well prepared and determined to join the cult. As Noah and Anita didn't speak Italian, and considering my path would diverge significantly from theirs, we were made aware that our mutual support and unity as a group would soon be divided. The fast track remained open for the two of them. For me, there was going to be much *'cleaning and removing'* before I could proceed. While having different paces wasn't a real issue, the prospect of physical separation was unexpected and unacceptable. We had already left our allies behind in Runae and the time bubble; we couldn't afford to lose each other. Whatever compromise was necessary to stay close to Victoria, that wasn't it.

'I still believe this is a bad idea. I mean, it was good to get close to your mother, but we need to draw a line here,' Anita said after her first meeting with the elders. Her face appeared tired and troubled.

'It was a good idea! We met Athymos in the flesh, so to speak. We found Eleoen,' Noah listed, as if trying to convince himself that progress had been made. 'But I agree with Anita. We should end this here.'

'So, is this it? The only reason we're here is to find a Harpy and *one* Awoken?' If Grandma's insights led to the plan we were following now, it couldn't be so simple.

'We're out in the open, not trapped in Iris's dome. Don't forget that. Finding your mother gave us the chance to move forwards,' Anita added after a pause. 'I wonder how many others are out there. Other Awoken Ones, I mean.'

'They should all return eventually, right?' Noah queried. 'We already know some are missing. They might be out there.'

'Could we stumble upon one near a food source? I'm starving!' Anita interjected, her comment momentarily breaking the pressure and bringing a smile to our faces.

'And what's the deal with those people and their books?' Noah continued, with a wry smile. 'I mean, I get the Bible, which is massive by the way. But those other books? Why do you need more books to read the only one that matters?'

'Have you ever...?' Anita began.

'The Bible? Are you crazy? Have you seen how huge it is?' I chuckled, reflecting on how many times I had, often reluctantly, delved into its pages, hoping that the God Victoria believed in would rescue me from my hardships.

A few blocks away, we stopped at a local bar serving Italian delicacies. As if mirroring our sense of urgency, the portions of each meal seemed to shrink with each bite. Eleoen had not come back since two days after abruptly departing without warning. His final words before fading into the misty city were concise: 'I have to go; someone needs me.' And there we were, alone again. Noah's earlier optimism was swiftly erased. Seated at a table near the busy sidewalk, our spot felt perilously close to the street, as if we could be struck by passing cars. A few plants offered a semblance of safety, but the space felt constricted as the waiter served our food.

'I think we should move again,' Anita suggested, taking another bite of a large slice of pizza.

'Yes, but not too far,' I interjected.

'I agree. There's so much food around here that I want to try,' Noah chimed in with a smile.

'I meant not too far from her…'

'I want to revisit something.' Anita put down the remainder of her pizza. I sensed that she was about to steer the conversation from the delectable food to something much more compelling. 'I'm trying to understand how they can locate us.'

'The good ones or the bad ones?' Noah asked, attentively listening.

'We know the Awoken Ones are drawn to your nature, your…let's call it power. What I'm unsure about is whether the Harpies can sense it too. Or is there some other connection between you two and them?'

'If what Harmonia said is accurate, there are Awoken Ones who turned into Harpies. Maybe they've been used as…antennas?' I whispered, as a few people settled at a nearby table, close enough for us to be cautious.

'Could be, but…'

'What else are you referring to?' Noah inquired, shifting his chair closer to the table. If we were being followed, we were being overheard.

'The way Time hesitated to use his power in Varayal. The way he preferred to use Revelia's instead. It failed, and the moment he resorted to his own, we were detected. And if you recall, he specifically warned against using yours for any reason. He knows something; I'm certain of it!'

'From what I've seen, Time may not be who we thought he was, but I don't believe he'd withhold crucial information from us if it endangered us, would he?' I questioned.

'Perhaps he doesn't know yet. Maybe he suspects something?' Anita persisted.

'Yeah,' Noah joined in, 'something is informing them of our whereabouts. Something is linking them to us.'

'Or someone?' Anita proposed.

'Or someone…' Noah and I echoed in agreement.

Chapter Twenty-Two
An Ally in Time of Need

∞

I told you. This is what we are going to do, and that's the end of it.' Victoria's expression was firm but devoid of emotions. On the other hand, mine was struggling to contain the multitude of sentiments I was feeling.

'I don't want to move again! Wasn't moving out of Grandma's house enough? Now we have to do it again?' I complained.

'What do you know about life? What do you understand about the things I have to go through every day? I can't keep going on like this. You're thirteen; you don't understand the significance of this life for me—the things I need to control, the things I can't discuss, the things I have to pray to Jehovah to help me tame!'

'So, just because you're afraid, just because of this man in the other congregation miles away, you're going to uproot us again?'

'He's an elder. He's kind, and he knows how to be disciplined, how to follow God's word.'

'Is that all that matters? God's word? God tells you to go door-to-door preaching instead of finding a better job, a job that can put food on the table, that can feed your son! God also says your son shouldn't go to high school. God tells you to keep me awake all night because I can't find a stupid answer in a stupid book! Where do I fit in all of this? When will I ever come first?' I let out all at once, my rage pouring out.

'God will always come before anything!'

'Even before me…'

'Even before you. God comes first!'

I woke up in the middle of the night, my eyes wide open. I had walked back into old, painful memories that I never managed to forget. That conversation had happened around the same time I had talked to Grandma. She had said the whole situation might not be bad for me. How she could be right was still something I couldn't grasp. In the silence of our room, I turned around. Noah was asleep on his bed, the heavy sheets barely covering his hips, his naked chest rising and falling gently. My head was going back and forwards between the distant memories and recent events. *Was Victoria trying to tell me something? Was she attempting to contain Athymos by imposing a rigid, disciplined way of life on herself and me?*

I thought about it. In those days, the only possible explanation coming to mind was that she needed a man in her life. She needed it emotionally and physically. I was too young to fully understand the mental repercussions for a human being not being able to be close to someone, swept away by passion and desire. But I truly believed she needed to find her half destined to be. Now I knew it wasn't lust moving her actions. She wasn't looking for a passionate love that would burn away her fears. She was fighting her demons from within. The possibility that I was merely trying to justify her actions once again made me sick.

After all those years, I was still just a son who wanted to be loved, who wanted to be the centre of attention. *Is this what we spend our whole lives doing? Growing old, children trapped in aging bodies, striving to meet our parents' expectations in exchange for love?* I questioned myself, attempting to dispel my thoughts. I rolled my eyes, shook my head, and turned around, my gaze fixed on the door. Something strange happened. With a faint click, the door slowly creaked open, just a little enough to let in a gentle breeze. The wall beside it seemed to ripple, as if its surface had transformed into water. Something was shifting from one form to another, bringing an undercurrent of fear. Uncertain if my mind was simply playing tricks on me, I got up, my feet touched the cold floor, sending a shiver of reality up my skin.

'I found you,' a voice whispered. It came from nowhere and yet seemed to echo all around at the same time. My eyes shifted quickly to Noah, who was still fast asleep.

'Who's there? Come out and show yourself!' I shouted, rousing Noah from his slumber.

'It's me, Philiat,' the voice said. Noah looked around, trying to locate the source of that soft sound. 'We saw you, we found you unexpectedly. Being so close to her prevented us from sensing your presence, but then you walked right in, right in front of our very eyes,' Philiat continued. That name sounded familiar—where and when we learned of it?

'Come out and let us see you!' Noah whispered, his voice showing the surging anticipation.

'I can't! I'm too weak. And so is my sister, Pragma. She's still watching over the Harpy; I can't leave her alone for too long. We are…so…fragile.' The voice, a man's voice, was low and quiet. It came and went in waves, as if its owner struggled to breathe.

'How did you find us?' I asked, swiftly dressing. Though I couldn't see him, I felt his eyes on me, on Noah.

'Today, when you entered the place, side by side with your very enemy. My sister and I have been close to her, battling her power since the day you sent us. Before this new world even came into being. Before the impact, before the day this world nearly ended.'

'Now I remember. Love sent you to control her power. Noah, remember the dream we had the other night? Love had instructed Cherish to send Philiat and Pragma to check on Athymos!'

'You've been doing it all this time?' Noah was astonished.

'We never stopped. We can't stop. It's Love's will,' Philiat's voice grew weaker, barely audible.

Caught off guard, the door swung wide open, pushed by Anita's hand. She entered silently, her face strangely pale, her body seeming to shift. Something else walked in beside her, as if she wore a double layer of skin—one of flesh and another of spirit. Her eyes were glowing with a strange light, her expression was dull, as if her body was the one of a doll enslaved by a stronger will.

'One of the Seven…right here, right before my eyes,' Anita said. We had learned to distinguish her voice from Cherish's. Her double was controlling the conversation.

'Seven? There are only seven Awoken Ones?' Noah glanced at me, counting quickly in his head. With the ones we had already encountered, this seemed to complete the list.

'Seven are the closest Awokens to Love. We're all manifestations of you, but seven are the ones who form his core.' Cherish pointed her finger into the unknown, as if touching the bare wall before us. The unexpected guest flickered briefly, becoming visible for a moment. Then six more duplicates materialized, like ghosts appearing in smoke and sparkle, revealing their existence. She continued:

'Philiat is the Awoken of Brotherhood—the love we feel for our friends. Storgén represents the love for our family. Prometheus embodies sacrificing love, Pragma intellectual love, the one for our beliefs. Agapei symbolizes the love we feel for everyone, compassion and empathy itself, and Xena signifies the love for those we respect with generosity, a way to connect with strangers. Lastly, you probably know Eros, whose name has endured through time—the love felt through our bodies, passion and attraction.'

And her magic turned off swiftly, as it came. Of the seven bodies, only the real one remained, his shape highlighted by Cherish, who was holding him in place. We finally knew for sure there were too many Awoken to be counted. It was great news; we had more allies than we could imagine. But they were all struggling to come to life; all of them had lost their battles in one way or another. If what we knew was true, that was the only chance left to make it right. If we failed, we would erase them all for good.

The number of entities depending on us was multiplying fast. My mind turned strangely inwards. John was still populating my thoughts, my worries. *What kind of love did I feel for him? What love am I still feeling? It is love, regardless of what we had and what we still have. Could my doubts be just love shifting from one nature to the next? Is Eros leaving its spot for…what? Philia? Storge? What is he now for me?* I thought.

'So, there are multiple types of Awoken Ones?' Noah asked.

'So there are of Harpies.' Anita replied.

'Let me go, Cherish. I need to go back. Pragma cannot face Athymos by herself for too long.'

'No! Not this time,' she said sharply. 'Last time, this was exactly Love's error. We had come together as one to fight the enemy, but you and the other six were asked to stay with the Humans. To protect them. Love wanted them to have a piece of him to be carried along. And look where we are now. This time we will all be one, the only one that matters! Join your master. We will do the same with Pragma, soon.'

Whatever Cherish intended was not immediately clear, but something felt uncannily similar to what Soul had done in Varayal. He had not merged his power with the multitude of souls he had produced. Instead, he had done the opposite. He had asked them to join in battle as an army rather than one being. If Time had done something similar, it was not clear. I could easily remember what we had seen in the Ancient Mirrors and in Time's vision, but it was different, somehow. We could have chosen one path or the other. We had failed once, as Soul had. It was time to change strategy, and Cherish's will was too strong for us to oppose it. So Philiat gave up, hoping that changing the charted course would be the winning way. His glow grew smaller, directed by Cherish's finger, who could move him as she pleased, like she was conducting a symphony of her own. Without us realizing, my artefact and Noah's heart appeared in the silent darkness of our room, shining brightly. Philiat, turned into a flickering dot, moved right next to my shell, slowly gliding into it, as Cherish's music ended in a quiet adagio.

'And one is home. Next is Pragma. Where the others are, I do not know just yet, but I'll find out soon. You are not alone any more. You found a strong ally here in times of need. But there is more to be done!' And Anita turned back and left the room, leaving us astonished.

We had no idea what just happened. Philiat was now part of our artefacts, and Pragma was going to be next. We had many questions. It was obvious we were going to hunt the other six down, bringing them with us. But the purpose of it was still unclear.

'I'm speechless. I bet she won't remember a thing tomorrow!' Noah said, standing up and moving close to the door.

'I'm afraid so. She just left like nothing happened. It's going to be funny when we tell her what she just did.'

'She knows a lot, Daniel. I mean, Cherish. If only we could summon her to come out and tell us.' Noah was standing by the door, torn between wanting to close it and wanting to go after Anita.

'Neither of them will want that. I'm pretty sure. We have learned a lot anyway. Let's be careful.' And I went back to bed, sitting down restlessly.

'This whole thing has been a never-ending collection of missing pieces. Every time we think we are closer to the truth, the picture gets bigger and bigger,' Noah let out.

'And we find more holes with it,' I added. 'But we know what she meant this time. Remember our last vision? We were surrounded by Awoken Ones, and the plan was to merge together as one to fight Nothing. Apparently, some of them didn't.'

'Because we told them to. Because we wanted the world to continue to love?' Noah sat beside me, his eyes fixed on the dark window. A few heavy machines were lifting fat bins full of rubbish. 'How could that be a mistake? I would have done the same.' After a few minutes of pure silence, he resumed. '*And look where we are,* she said. She is not wrong, you know?'

'Yeah, Anita never is…' I sighed.

If the strange event that happened the night before could change our perspective on many things, our return to the church, meeting Victoria, was still going as planned. The morning after we met Anita in the hall and left at once to grab some food before meeting the elders at eleven. Our walk to the coffee shop was quiet. Noah and I wanted to ask her what she remembered, but that question felt uncomfortable. Anita, on the other hand, was unusually quiet. She said only a few words, and her face looked worn out, tired. Sitting at the usual table, our predictable cappuccinos steaming under our noses, we were waiting for the inevitable to arrive.

'Something happened last night.' Anita started, out of nowhere. We were stunned.

'Did it now?' I carefully measured my words.

'Yes. Remember that sentence I wrote? What is it now? One, two years ago? Never mind… I did it again!'

'You wrote about Cherish again?' I asked. That wasn't the revelation we expected to hear.

'No, no. I wrote a list of places. Look.' And she pulled out a white piece of paper, crumpled as if she had hastily torn it from a notebook.

It was déjà vu all over again. This time, John wasn't there to help decrypt the mysterious words. The list was plain and simple. There were five different locations, but with no specific addresses. Instead, a few details were added, like a map of people and events connected to a specific spot.

Unknown—Home is where your heart belongs.

Unknown—Where strangers come together.

Sicily—By the volcano. Family is everything.

Ireland—Nursing home.

Unknown—Somewhere when it's time??

'Meaning?' Noah asked after inspecting the riddle.

'And once again, I don't know. Just like I didn't know last time.' She sipped her drink with a strange lack of interest.

'There's more…' I continued.

'What else is there?' Anita wasn't mentally prepared to welcome more revelations, especially if they involved her. However, I couldn't withhold that important piece of information from her.

'You didn't just write that last night. Cherish took over and you came to our room to help us, to help Philiat.'

'I did what now?'

In a split second, she was completely awake. I had brought her back to full energy. I wasn't sure where she stood in terms of understanding Cherish and sharing the same body and mind, but she seemed receptive. Thus, the recent events unfolded right there at the breakfast table. Her scrambled eggs were left cold and forgot. Her fork hung suspended above her plate, mirroring her journey into our mystery. Noah and I shared everything we witnessed and what her other half, Cherish, told us while she was in control.

'So, we need to go there anyway? To that horrible place?' she challenged.

'Yes, we do. We have to get to Pragma. But hold on, is that all you have to say about this whole thing?' Noah replied.

'What else is there? I've given up. She's inside me, who knows for how long. She can control me whenever she wants. What's the point of resisting?' She pushed her plate aside, unable to eat. 'The only thing that annoys me is that I can't remember. Cherish has a vast amount of knowledge in her head. Why can't that be shared with me?'

'You're unbelievable! Amidst all this madness, you're thinking about knowledge, about digging,' I said, smiling. That was the Anita we knew.

'Perhaps it's too much to contain? Imagine having to carry centuries and centuries of memories in your head,' Noah added.

'True. Why didn't I think of that?' Her mood shifted again. Anita was walking on the edge of a journey spanning many lifetimes, allowed only fleeting glimpses.

'If you don't remember and you're not physically there, what are we going to do when we get to the church?' Noah's question left us in silence. He had a point.

All we could do was stick to the plan and move forwards. We left the coffee shop soon after and arrived at the Jehovah's Witnesses congregation a few minutes before 11 a.m. At the door, Victoria stood with two more people:

a man and another woman. They had just returned from street preaching and were waiting for the elders. Not long after our chilly exchanges, two more men arrived. As we walked in, ready for instructions on what, where, and when, Victoria moved away, her annoyance evident. Something in her had changed, but I couldn't grasp what it was. For some mysterious reasons she looked stiff.

'You two, this way.' One of the elders pointed to a room for Anita and Noah.

'And you, come with me,' the other one said to me in Italian.

As we feared, we were separated into two rooms. Despite our worries about being apart, we were still among Humans. Mother wasn't a threat, and we would soon leave. After a quick exchange of silent words travelling back and forth between our faces, Noah, Anita and I complied with the request. With Victoria by my side, we took seats in front of the elder. In between me and him, a large, old desk adorned with weighty books was holding the partition between saints and sinners. Six pairs of eyes watched in silence; an inquisition was about to begin.

'As you know, your situation is quite peculiar...' he began, his face serious and authoritarian, contrasting with his attire of a simple light blue shirt and wrinkled trousers. 'Although is my understanding that you deeply regret the lifestyle you've led and are fully committed to following Jehovah's path, your sinful nature will continue to tempt you. You'll have to battle this struggle for the rest of your life until Jehovah's kingdom comes to purify your mind and soul. On that day, you'll be pure again. Until then, you'll face Satan's traps, which he'll constantly place right before you.'

'I understand,' I almost whispered. It was a predictably boring speech, but I had to sound convincing.

'Homosexuality is an incredibly vile sin!' he suddenly thundered. 'The Bible states that men lying with other men will be destroyed at Armageddon!'

'I know.' In my mind, I wasn't feeling any pressure or fear. I knew there wasn't going to be any Armageddon and, if by any chance I was wrong, it was likely to be preceded by Nothing's destruction anyway.

'Giorgio,' Victoria interjected fearlessly, unafraid to overstep. She was a woman, and he was an elder. 'For how long must he show his sincere repentance?' Her face twitched slightly. Whatever was happening to her was getting visible.

'At least six months...' he replied.

'But, during these six months you will have a great opportunity to reunite with your brothers and sisters, don't you think?' the other woman said, smiling at me, oblivious to the situation's gravity. It was as if she hinted at a completely different topic. The brief winking of her left eye took me by surprise.

But my mother did not share the same perspective. She stood up suddenly, her fingers moving frantically. A strong reaction was emerging. Something or someone was unsettling her. Her skin reddened, eyes widened, and her mouth moved rapidly. She moved to the back of the room, walking back and forth as if she was restlessly debating with an invisible fifth guest.

'Victoria, please sit down,' the elder said; his voice, although calm, was showing some dismay.

'Do you think I don't know my son? Do you think I don't know who you are?' she shouted, taking us by surprise. Her voice changed, echoing the same double sound Anita's had the night before. 'I see through your lies, your cries for pity and empathy…those feelings…sorcery of weak minds!'

'Mother?' I could only manage a single word as she transformed, her shadow growing behind her.

Victoria left the elder in disbelief, embodying his worst fears. A demon in the house of God, evil in the heart of his temple. She stood before him, shaking his faith like a crumbling wall. The space around started to tremble, the many books left asleep on the large shelves by the walls started to move and fall down.

'Sister Victoria?' The man's voice was barely audible. Whatever spiritual power he believed in, he had never witnessed it. That wasn't the sort of divine blessing he was convinced to have faith in, all those years.

'I've been enslaved, incarcerated by this hoard of feelings, burning in my head for too long!' Victoria's voice rose to such a loud, deep sound that I believed the others had heard it. 'This curse of crying for attachment, attention, beliefs. I can't take it any longer. Not now that you come along as well! Her thoughts are getting louder now that you are close. Oh, she is so pathetic…' And her mouth enlarged as if she was smiling but no laughs could be heard.

'Victoria! In the name of Jeh...' But the elder could not finish his sentence. As he stood up, his hands on the old desk, ready to reprehend her, she fought back with an invisible power he was not aware of. Suddenly, his eyes froze still, the colour of his skin was dragged out of his body as he turned grey and transformed to stone.

I was in a complete shock. I saw the true power of Athymos right before my eyes. The same magic I was told in my dream, there in front of me. Before Victoria could turn her attention on the two of us left standing, the other woman hurried to my side, her hand on my shoulder, saying:

'We need to get your friends now!' And she pushed me out of the room hastily.

'Guys, we've got a problem!' I yelled, opening the door to the other room. Both of them looked as if they were paralyzed by the sudden magic surrounding them. Tons of books and magazines were sparse on the floor, a sign their boring conversation with the elder had been interrupted before I walked in. They were still holding a Bible on their laps and another book in their hands. The other elder was looking at me, his mouth still agape. 'I think Athymos has surfaced! Victoria is putting on a show right over there. Whatever we need to do, we have to hurry!'

'Oh no, not now...' Anita groaned, as if reluctant to hand the reins to someone else. Cherish was about to switch places with her host, sending Anita into the unknown.

She moved swiftly to my side. Her left hand stretched to Noah, and with the swing of her finger, she extracted the artefact from his chest, leaving him in shock. She turned to me, ready to conjure my shell, but I beat her to it, willingly.

'Pragma, it's time to return to your master. Your brother is waiting for you!' She glanced at the woman behind me, the one who seemed to be just a simple Jehovah's Witness.

Without hesitation, the Awoken responded immediately. A sudden, bright glow enveloped the unresponsive woman, whose body collapsed as soon as Pragma departed to reunite with her brother. With a flick of her fingers, Cherish pushed the shell and heart back to their rightful owners. Her eyes briefly shone like a radiant sun as she said:

'Let's go, quickly! We need to find the others!'

And so, like hunted thieves, we left the room, leaving the elder bewildered by the magic he had just witnessed. Whatever god he had been following, he was now ready to challenge his beliefs for good. As we walked out of the building, a manly scream reached us by the front door. We knew Athymos had finally prevailed against Victoria and released her cold magic on the other elder. We could not hesitate any longer. We had to flee at once.

Chapter Twenty-Three
The Many Ways We Love

∞

With a rush in our feet and confusion in our heads, we followed Anita through the long street and out of that neighbourhood. We still had Victoria's scent on our skin, so we hoped we would get lost, out of sight, if we managed to disappear quickly.

'What the hell happened?' Noah asked, turning the corner from a small street to a tiny one.

'I think Victoria is gone. Athymos has taken over. She killed your man! She literally turned the elder into a rock!'

'What?' Anita let out; the shock on her face was reaching back to me with the same terror I had in my heart. 'Is she in full control of her body now? This way, quick!'

'I'm afraid Love's rising strength is not calling only the good ones. We might be in serious trouble.' And Noah stretched his hand to me as I was falling behind, my body in clear opposition to the rush I had in my mind.

Like mice in a busy labyrinth, we were running through messy alleys and old streets, block after block, losing our own sense of direction. Suddenly, the road opened up to a large square packed with people; tons of tourists were walking up and down the Spanish steps, taking pictures and talking loudly. As my breath was getting shorter and my feet felt heavy, my head started to pound, making me nauseous. Anita eventually stopped, mumbling something about 'the others', but I could not understand a word. I could feel the pressure in my temples; voices and emotions were crashing into my thoughts like powerful waterfalls meeting their dead end. And then I was taken completely. I was moved back to the exact moment I had left, a few nights before when Noah and I had seen Love talking to the other Awoken Ones, telling them the end was near.

'What is the Awoken of Hope having to say about this?' Love was asking again.

'It is the only way, yes, master. We have to return it to you if you want to have a chance.' And the one called Asher looked at the others, reminding them that was the only option they had.

'So, we shall!' Kathor replied. 'We will give it back, no hesitation. There is no good ending in the final pages of our existence. We might fight better as one.'

'We will, but on one condition!' Love said. 'Whatever happens to me, I won't let this world end. People will survive, Humans will rebuild. But I can't let them live without love. They must have it. It belongs to them! The Seven will stay, not part of the whole, this time.'

The group was taken by surprise. Many raised their voices, objecting to his decision. If they were going to make it, if Nothing was going to be stopped, it would require every inch of strength they had in their hands, especially the strongest ones.

'Love, are you sure this is the right thing to do?' Cherish said, her voice low, her worries passing through.

'I am. I would ask you to stay too, to give them the power to remember, but you are the strongest beside the Seven. I'll need you by my side.'

'Master, how long before the impact?' the one called Mnemosy asked, looking at the blue sky. A shining dot was blinking in the pure blue above, leaving an almost invisible trail behind.

'Eight days, and it will be colossal...' Kathor replied before I could speak. 'It will impact in the northwest, by the great glaciers, north of the green valley. It will spread fast, melting the ice in a few seconds. The world could be washed away, if not completely destroyed.' And her hands were pointing to the far land, over to the stunning golden city that stood quietly on the horizon.

'We will contain it. We might not be able to stop it entirely, but we can contain it!' I said.

'What about the other Gods? Any chance any of them are still out there?' Cherish asked, moving close to the edge of the crystal lake.

'If they are, they are still facing him. I can't hear my sister's voice any more and neither can I hear my brother Soul. We are on our own, I'm afraid.'

'Daniel?' a voice shouted. 'Daniel! Are you OK?' Anita was back, and I could hear her voice thundering. I was back in an instant. The world had moved millennia ahead, in the present. Noah was holding my shoulders as I was bending forwards, my hands still on my head. Anita pulled my chin up, looking into my eyes, searching for answers.

'Another one?' she asked.

'Yes, the same one I had with Noah, with the Awoken Ones. It's true,' I continued, pulling myself together. 'We didn't get the Seven with us in our fight against Nothing. We wanted to stop him, but we could not take them from this world, from the people.'

'Right, listen to me, both of you...' And Anita pulled us into a narrow alley, away from indiscreet ears. 'These Seven, their names sound very much like the Greek definition of Love. All of them, their nature, their pure definition.'

'You are saying there is a connection?' Noah asked.

'I'm saying this is where the idea comes from! Like the night of Halloween. These things happened ages ago, and with time, they have turned into myths, legends, culture, religion, even! I think it's all connected. These pantheons of Gods, their names, the Awoken Ones, the never-ending fight between good and evil. These are all things that come from the same story.' And her face looked enlightened, proud of reaching a difficult, remote truth.

'And I think I know why nobody knows it; nobody remembers,' I said, looking at the edge of the tiny road, watching people passing by, unaware of the madness we witnessed. 'Nothing didn't strike this world directly. He did face Love; we know what happened then, but he didn't turn to Earth directly as he had done with Varayal. He sent something, a meteor or an asteroid. Something like that. I saw Love organizing the counterattack with the Awoken Ones, trying to stop it. I'd say they failed. They might have managed to reduce the impact, but something did crash on Earth, somewhere in the west, near something he called the ice cap. If what I saw is true, the collapse of the ice flooded the entire planet.'

'The Deluge?' Anita let out, as she was collecting another legend into her book of facts.

'Why did we not use the Seven then?' Noah asked. 'And why did I not see what you just saw?' He was puzzled.

'Because we knew the world would face a hard reboot. If people could survive, their feelings had to be preserved at any cost. We left the Seven to protect that, as the world was going to heal again.'

'OK, we need to move. I don't think we need to stay in this place any more. Definitely, we are not going to meet your mother again! We have to move ahead.' Anita was looking around, as if she could see threats in every corner. Something was approaching from afar.

'To Time and Soul?' Noah asked, happy to progress in our quest.

'No!' she said. 'To the other five, wherever they are. Let's go, we won't be going back to our rooms. We are not leaving much behind, anyway. Let's find a quiet place to think about where to go next!'

But before Anita could turn around, a sudden flash, followed by a sibilant sound, struck her from behind. Her body glowed briefly, her eyes still pointed at mine turned into two golden stones. Her cheeks, her face, her neck lost its colour for a moment to then turn quickly back as they were. On her mouth, a small expression of pain turned into a quiet moan.

Victoria was only a few feet away and was walking slowly towards us. She was accompanied by a shadow, double her size; long blurry arms were extending beyond Human reach. Her mouth was open; a voice spoke without Victoria's lips moving:

'Sorrow, happiness, attraction, repulsion, love, hate. What else can these people create in the vain attempt to be alive?' And her right arm swung in the air, Victoria's following right after, like a delayed carbon copy.

Another flash entangled to a sound travelled from her to us, crashing against an invisible wall a mere step away from me. Anita's hands still on my shoulders, she was frozen still, her long-silent companion shifting behind her, shielding us from Athymos' attacks.

Noah was looking at the Harpy and Anita, back and forth, unable to move, to run. Whatever magic the enemy possessed, she could not only petrify skins and bones but also wills and minds.

'Just let go...' Victoria resumed; she was standing right in front of us. 'Let it all go, empty your mind from all this

heavy burden, don't you think it's time? Let me show...'
But the Harpy suddenly stopped talking.

Victoria wasn't moving and the evil wasn't pushing her magic on us. My mind went to Time. It had to be him. *He has frozen the space around to save us once more*, I thought. A few moments later, towards the end of the road, something strange manifested openly. A weak, white shadow was moving from one place to another, bouncing from wall to wall. Another one slowly appeared beside us, small, short; its shape was the one of a little boy. His dark olive skin, his green eyes, and his small hands formed into our reality. His finger pointed at Victoria; he said:

'Here, that's much better.' And Anita crashed onto my arms; Cherish was gone silent again. 'She is very, very powerful! I can't beat her, but I can confuse her a little. Get up, we need to move quickly. I'll make sure she won't remember where she saw you last!'

With Anita's arms on mine and Noah's shoulders we resumed our run and disappeared in an alley to the right. Our eyes led by the bouncing light, we were following it with no question, trusting it. Whatever new ally we'd found, it had rescued us right when we needed it. Suddenly as we reached a large apartment block, the white glow ghosted inside. The front door moved a little, making a cracking sound, inviting us in.

'I suppose we go in?' Noah asked.

'Yes. It's not them. I don't see their traces anywhere,' Anita said; her body was getting back to full strength. 'I know now how it works. It was the same in your house by the lake and at the park with Eleoen. Actually, it might be him.'

With our trust in Anita's ability to master her new skill, we followed her inside. In the dark space around us, we hadn't entered the building but a space in between realities. As predicted, the old man we'd learned to be Eleoen was waiting for us. He looked different; his body had changed overnight. He had left the Human host behind, finally able to come back in his true form. If we were responsible for this change, our power was growing fast. The Awoken One wasn't alone this time. He was accompanied by two more, a young boy and a teenage girl. She looked like a doll. Her hair was shining gold, and her blue eyes pierced the space like diamonds. The younger kid moved his messy dark hair to the side, revealing an intense olive skin. With his cheeks up and his pointy nose, he looked like the happiest child in the whole world.

'This is Mnemosy,' Eleoen started, his hand on the boy's head. 'And she is Ashtar. Forgive his appearance; his body is strongly connected to his being. As his power is not fully under control, he keeps forgetting his age, resetting it to the day he came to be.' The three of us looked at him, surprised. 'She is the Awoken of Beauty. I was looking for her sister, Ashtra, when I felt your presence again. I'm afraid she is still lost in between this world and the next as her power cannot grow in this madness.'

'I have a third sister, Ashrat, the Awoken of Emotional Intelligence,' the girl said. 'I know she is out there somewhere, but I don't know where.'

We were, once again, taken by surprise. There were so many Awokens we had no idea even existed. There was a connection between us and them and between them too that we could not fully understand or remember. My mind turned inwards, thinking about how we could have reached them all while we were fighting against time, against Harpies, and with a goal to accomplish, a quest too big on its own for us to be able to help them as well. As he could read my mind, Eleoen moved beside me and said, 'Again, don't worry too much. You have a path to follow. We won't be taking that away from you, all of you. There is only so much you can do as you are trying to protect this world and avoid evil at every step.'

'What about the others? There are so many of you; how can we find them all? How can we protect them?' I let out.

'They are here because of you. They will find you, in one way or another. As I found you…'

'What about her sisters?' Noah asked.

'Ashtra won't be manifesting,' the girl said. 'Not until this world has found its balance. As the Awoken of Goodness, she faded away when the evil took its seat in these lands.'

'We are looking for the Seven,' Anita said. 'We have found Philiat and Pragma. They were watching Athymos closely. But where the other five are, we don't know yet…'

'You are the Awoken of Memory, or Remembrance and Protection. You should know how to find them all.' Eleoen was puzzled. *He believes Anita has the ability to scan the entire planet and get to them?* I thought.

'What about those places you wrote? What if the answer is there?' Noah asked, feeding my thinking further. If the Seven were all the strongest form of Love, we might have a way to find them, hidden in Cherish's words. Anita quickly took the piece of paper out of her side pocket and flattened it right before our eyes. 'Sicily and Ireland…this is quite clear,' she said.

'Yeah, but where?' Noah asked.

'By the volcano, family is everything. One is by my grandma?' I said, thinking out loud.

'And one is where I work? The nursing home?' Noah continued. 'That's a strange place to be.'

'Not if it's Agapei, the love we feel for everyone. The love we show as compassion.' Anita was getting somewhere. 'Which means Storgén is with your grandma. The love we feel for family. But the rest… It's really hard to understand what it means.'

'If you are right, why don't you just try one?' Eleoen said, smiling.

'We go to Sicily! It's the safest place we can start from. If Storgén is there, we will know we are on the right path.' I was worried but excited to go back home, right when I needed to feel I was actually getting into something, belonging, loved. After being under Victoria's dark shadow, the only antidote I could think of was Rita-Louise. The only one who knew me, the real me.

'What about you three? Will you be able to come with us?' Noah asked, his hand already reaching over.

'We are where you are, when you are, and whatever you do, we will be doing it too.' And Eleoen faded away, followed by Mnemosy and Ashtar. They had vanished right before our eyes, flickering into our imagination, they were gone, somewhere by our side.

As our next step was set, Noah and I knew the charm to spell. Our artefacts came out in the dark space, blinked three times, each time brighter, eventually enveloping the three of us in a vacuum of light. The scene was repeating. As the Awoken Ones had done a few seconds earlier, so we disappeared, leaving the old, messy city behind, away from the evil we had craved, the wicked Harpy we had come too close to. It was time to move further, to continue our journey in rescuing the missing pieces, the Seven, John, Daisy, and everyone we loved. We had entered there alone and we were leaving with more allies than we could hope for.

As we travelled through space, it felt like we had moved through time too. If I didn't know better, I would say we moved back to summertime. The heat of the lonely island was still holding strong well into mid-November, making us feel out of place. Guided by my strong will, we appeared right at the front gates of Grandma's home. Everything was exactly as I left it last time I visited her, looking for answers, gaining the very source of our power, my shell. The front garden was unusually overgrown, as if Carla, for some reason, had stopped tending to it. The front door looked shabby too, more than expected in such an old house. A few envelopes and letters were scattered on the ground, soaking wet, waiting for a collection that didn't come. All around, the world continued its duty with little regard. We were stepping between past, future, and present in a very strange mix.

'What's all this?' I said, worried, as I picked up the mail from the dirty ground. 'It looks like Carla hasn't been here.'

'Is there another entrance, perhaps?' Anita asked, though she knew there wasn't. She was pushing away the terrible idea as I was, fiercely.

'Please tell me we travelled through time as well, not just through space,' I said. 'This doesn't look good. Why does it seem like nobody has been here for a long time?'

'Is there no way in?' Noah asked.

There was no other door to knock or bell to ring. That one was tightly shut, and nobody had come to answer. The only thing left to do was to visit Sara next door to see if Grandma was staying with her now. But I soon learned that house was empty too. The curtains of the front window were wide open; inside, only a few pieces of furniture were left, covered under dusty sheets. My heart was beating fast, sinking by the second. How far ahead in time had we travelled? In and out of Iris's magic, we had lost weeks, years, time we could never get back. How many horrible things might have happened while we were playing Gods, trying to survive? How many others hadn't made it to that day?

Anita reached my shoulder with her hand, pulling me away from the empty home. Noah was looking at me, sad. An anticipation of sorrow was using him to hit me, punch me in my stomach. As my pain reached my eyes, tears about to surface, a familiar, ugly face appeared; someone was walking up the front road. Carla was carrying the heavy burden of food. *She is taking care of someone else now?* I thought, and I almost hated the idea.

'Oh, Daniel? What are you doing here? Where have you been?' she said in a strong dialect.

'Carla, what's going on? Where is Grandma?'

But she couldn't answer. She was in shock and sad. Her puffy brown eyes were darting around, her face looking even uglier than usual. She suddenly dropped the bags on the ground and hugged me.

'We have been looking for you for so long! Sara tried to reach out so many times...eventually, she gave up. And with the months, after...' She stopped for a moment. She couldn't say it, and I was getting sick just waiting for those words. 'With time she gave up everything. Sara passed away a few weeks ago... You know, they were inseparable. She couldn't bear the idea...'

'Carla!' I said firmly. 'Where is Grandma?'

'La Signora Rita-Louise passed away a year and two weeks ago...' Her face turned away, hiding the tears I couldn't shed.

That wasn't possible. I had been there only a few months before. So it felt like. I did not feel anything; I did not sense her passing. With all that magic surrounding me and her, how was that possible? How could she silently leave me? Although Anita and Noah could not understand a word, they could see bad news had landed on my heart. I was angry and mortified. I had left her alone again. I had taken the box with the shell and left her on her own, selfishly. Noah's hand reached mine in between pain and shame, holding it tight, sending me into a frenzy.

'I still have the keys. I didn't know what to do after she was gone, you know? Your mother never came back afterwards. Do you want to get in? Let me run home and get them for you!' And she was gone before I could say a word.

Anita and Noah said nothing. They were holding on to a silence that meant the same things that were running through my head wildly. His hand still in mine, Noah was looking at the old building, guessing what must have been for me, what it must have felt like, in all those years. A few minutes later, Carla came back, embarrassed even to walk between us to open the front door. She felt she still had the responsibility of keeping the house in order, but after a while, she had given up, and now she was facing my tribunal, my silent, unfair judgement. The walk inside was the same I had taken for years. Same walls, same freezing tiles. But everything was dull, cold to any touch. Grandma was gone, and so was the very spirit of her kingdom. Carla had left the key on the kitchen counter and moved to a quiet corner of the room, trying to be invisible in the shadow of the walls. Anita and Noah walked around, looking for answers we were not going to get, ever again. The last Praetorian was gone. We were next in line.

'How many others will go while we are playing this sick game?' I let out, moving Grandma's stuff from a lonely coffee table. Everything was in order, as Carla had kept her work to her best, up until the very end, but dust had multiplied with the weeks and months. 'I left her behind, and she is gone. I left John behind, and most likely, he is gone too...'

'Don't say that!' Anita replied, worried.

'I couldn't even say goodbye…the one who saved me…many times. And she went, without me by her side…' And I started to cry.

Sorrow and shame were fusing with desperation and anger. My heart was twisting as if it was convulsing, faster, louder. The less the other three talked, the more I could hear my voice blaming me, pushing me to hard self-judgement. In my head, she was going to be rescued too, as we were going to release Love; I was going to trade my sacrifice for her sanity, having it back. But it had gone backwards. She was sacrificed for a God I wasn't even sure we could bring back. My leap of faith was getting wider, unsustainable. I was facing the defeat of my life, unable to move anywhere, in a house I always felt was mine. My protector was gone, and so was her magic. I was alone, I was Noah when his mother passed away, I was Anita when her parents left, I was anyone who has nobody they need to survive, to feel alive.

'Forget about this God. *She* was Love to me. Not the Seven. She was all kinds of love. She loved me in every way possible… And I wanted to repay her, free her from her burden, tell her I knew. Tell her she kept me safe like she promised, the day she got me. The last words we said were the ones of strangers. She could not remember me any more, she never will…'

I was pure desperation. My head could not stop the free fall of my heart. My legs went weak; I held on to the side of the door, between the sitting room and her bedroom, trying to reach that same bed we had talked by the last time I had seen her. How much more would I lose?

Chapter Twenty-Four
The Seven

∞

In my mind, we spent weeks sitting in that quiet house, waiting for a reason to move ahead, to continue pursuing our main goal. That was not what I expected. Somehow, in my distorted dreams, I could see Grandma sitting in the same chair where she was sitting the last time I had been there. We would walk in, exchange greetings, play that little game of introducing ourselves to each other for the hundredth time, and then we would find Storgén, just like that. But we had only been there for about an hour, our voices muted by my sadness. Carrying out the same old duty, Carla had moved at the kitchen sink, shifting a few items around. Her movements were clumsier than usual, as if she were influenced by something entirely foreign to her. Despite her sorrow and sadness, within a few minutes, she had already prepared a moka pot for some hot coffee. As I walked into Grandma's bedroom, my eyes were drawn again to the incredible number of pictures she kept by her bedside locker and on the walls. There were so many. Some displayed their old age, the black and white tones turning grey and yellow. Grandma, however, looked young and beautiful still, more similar to how she appeared in my vision by the harbour than how she looked in her latest days.

In some pictures, she was by herself, in a stationary pose, her gaze turned away from the camera. In others, she was in the company of her long-time best friend, Sara, both of them smiling and happy. Next, she was holding the first orange of the season at the back of the house, in the large garden she loved so much. Rita-Louise's presence still lingered in that silent home, her memories everywhere I looked. *Where does everything go?* I wondered. *Every connection we make, every laugh we share, every tear we shed…where does it all go?*

And there it was, the same old picture I insisted on discussing with her last time I visited. It was still staring at me, trying to capture my attention. Victoria, Grandma, and everybody else were there, including the three shadows in the background. Suddenly, a thought emerged in my mind. It was time to check with Noah and Anita if I was just imagining that strange multiplication of people or if they could see them too.

'Noah, Anita, take a look at this for a second…' I said, walking back to the kitchen with the mysterious picture in hand. 'I saw this photo last time I was here, and I think there's something odd about it.'

'Well, it's an old photo,' Anita replied after studying it for several seconds. Her eyes darted around, as if she was trying to keep Carla in the dark.

'And it's faded, especially on this side…if you know what I mean,' Noah chimed in, mimicking her same behaviour. They were subtly indicating that they could see them too but didn't want to say anything while Carla was nearby.

'La Signora Rita loved her pictures!' Carla interjected. 'Her family meant everything to her, as it should. Something your mother never understood!' Her actions were scattered, and she seemed unsettled.

'Yeah, we had this conversation before.' I could recall how she couldn't accept the fact that Victoria had chosen strangers over her own family. Talking about her now felt different. After realizing she had been fighting against Athymos for that long, and losing her battle right before my eyes made it difficult to talk about her again. I could see her face, her mouth frozen but the Harpy's voice coming right through. Her face was Una's face. *Am I pitying her now?*

'You'd think she'd be here now, with you… Or that she would have stayed. You know she came back just to organize the funeral? Once that was done, she was gone. She didn't even show up at the service or at the graveyard!'

'She would have never set foot in a Catholic church, you know?' And then I realized my mother had made no mention about Grandma's passing. *She knew and she didn't tell me.* I was angry again.

'By the way, those others didn't come either. But maybe they're gone too? They look older than la Signora.' Carla moved back to the cooker, removing the whistling moka pot from the flames. She was alluding to the same three figures I believed nobody else could see. I was in shock.

'Carla, do you mean you can see these people here?' I asked, holding the picture closer to her face. She looked at me with a strange expression, as if wondering if I'd gone mad.

'Of course, I see them. I'm not blind!' Her voice trembled slightly for a brief moment. 'These are family, well, family to you…your brothers.'

What did she just say? I thought. *I must have gone insane. She didn't just see them; she knows who they are? Who told her? What's going on?* My confusion was evident, unabashed. But Carla went back to the task of serving coffee. A moment later, four small hot cups were steaming right under our noses. Anita smiled and moved her cup away. She couldn't drink such a short, strong coffee, no matter what. Also, she wanted to bypass the formalities and engage directly with Carla.

'Carla!' she exclaimed, her voice firm. It wasn't Anita's voice. 'I see you…but why you're playing this game is beyond me. Why didn't you reveal yourself earlier?' Noah and I were taken aback.'

'I see your eyes still see through…' Carla's voice had changed as well. The Italian tongue was gone and with it, the heavy accent. Whatever was happening, it was a dialogue between Cherish and someone else.

'Let's set Carla aside for a moment. We need you!'

'Anita? What the hell is going on?' I asked, but my question fell flat.

'I suppose I can come clean now.' Someone spoke through Carla, her body moving like a pawn under someone else's will. A grey shadow manipulated her body, as if a twin was shifting behind her. 'I've been here for quite some time. Over the past year, I was just a pure soul, haunting the corners of this old home. I'm bound to this place, a final remnant of a family. I couldn't be moved away from here. Please forgive me.' And Carla's double grew brighter, more visible. 'I had to seize my chance now, and Carla was the only way in. I've been waiting quietly for the right moment, even before, when Daniel came back to retrieve his shell. Rita-Louise couldn't assist him any longer, so I stepped in. I provided him what he needed, shared what he needed to know. Since the other half of the artefact was still missing, I couldn't fully come to life. Instead, I chose to remain in the shadows of these old walls a bit longer, to keep Rita-Louise safe.'

'What are you saying? It wasn't Grandma who spoke to me that day?' That couldn't be possible. She revealed things that only she could know.

'She was and she wasn't. I took over her mind and soul long enough for her to tell you what she wanted you to know. If I had come out then, your other half wouldn't have been there too, with his artefact. It was too early. I knew you would come to rescue me, eventually.'

'So, you are Storgén,' Noah asserted, and Carla's double nodded a silent yes, finally leaving his hiding spot to come to life.

His form changed; it wasn't Carla any more, as we knew her. His host had gone silent, frozen in time, allowing our secret conversation to flow. A long-awaited truth was going to unfold, without any unwanted witness to see, to know. The Awoken One had materialized just a little to let us see him, his pointed face sharp, his cheeks popping up like grey peaches; a shy smile was still asking for apologies. He was taller than Carla; his body moved from being a shadow to instead projecting his shade on her, his hands large, and it felt like Storgén could embrace us all.

'I thought our end was upon us. I kept hoping, holding on to my duty, but you didn't come back, and my strength is gone. Well…it was. I can feel you again; I can feel my energy rising up again.'

'Storgén,' Anita said, her voice still Cherish's. 'Time has come. We found much more than we could hope for. We are here for you. You need to be with Love again.'

'We have found Pragma and Philiat, and now we found you. It's time, Storgén. We need you with us,' I added.

'We still have to find the others, and there is really not much time; we need to hurry!' Noah was emphasizing the urgency, rightly so.

'Very well, then. Mind Carla. She might be a little confused.'

And Storgén shone instantly; in a bright flickering of pure light, he disappeared from sight, his power reduced to a single atom, moving across the room to reach us. As the magic dissolved, Anita suddenly came back, her clear voice shouting to hold Carla as she was about to fall down on the floor. The latter had no idea what had happened to her in the last hour. Between greeting us in the house and the full manifestation of Storgén, the Awoken One had taken over, removing the host from leading her own body and mind.

'It's OK, Carla. Don't worry; you just got very emotional because…you know, all this…' The lie came out of my mouth without even thinking. 'I made coffee for us. You want some? That might give you a kick!' Whether my lie had worked or not was not clear. Carla looked at me, then Noah and Anita, then at the still-hot moka on the cooker, her face puzzled.

'Yes, it must be the emotion…taking over.' Carla's raspy voice and thick accent suddenly returned. She was back herself; her hands were already holding the hot cup of coffee. We had successfully removed the unknown guest and his memories from her mind. As the rightful nephew and owner of that large house was back, Carla passed the duty on, finally moving ahead. A few minutes later, she left, a disturbed and sad expression still showing on her face.

We were left alone, in the silence of a cold keep; we had finally stopped running. Somehow, we all felt we could stay in there a little longer, safe, unseen. Although no magic spell was holding between us and the evil, the three of us agreed we could use some rest, finally free from a long hunt. Three of the Seven were already with us. Where the others were was not as urgent as pausing a little and, perhaps, getting some food.

'If we run again,' Noah started, looking at the garden at the back of the house, 'we bring our stuff with us. No more leaving things behind. We are without clothes again!' Anita and I smiled at his usual emphasis.

'I'll check if the water is running, the boiler, the gas. We might hold on to this place to collect our thoughts and get some time to rest?' I asked.

'Yes! A shower!' Anita's eyes lit up at the idea of getting clean again, our pain and tribulations washed away down the drain.

'Let me check some stuff. Then we go buy some food, some clothes. Anita'—I pointed to the left side of the house—'there is another large bedroom just that way.'

'On it. Sheets?'

'We might need to buy those too… Leave it, Noah,' I immediately said as he was walking into Grandma's bedroom, ready to pick up his part of the duty. 'I want to do it…I need to feel it.'

And he came close to me, his arms on my shoulders, his neck touching mine. He knew what I was feeling and, without any words, he was telling me exactly what I wanted to hear. This time, Anita was smiling at us; her look had no judgement. Somehow, that was something she could accept. Or perhaps, Cherish had taken over again, happily seeing the two parts of Love, somehow, coming together.

The walk around the small village quite soon turned into the walk of shame. Everywhere we went, I could hear people whispering behind our backs. At the grocery shop, Tina, the old woman at the till, said to the next customer in line who I was, adding how disgraceful it was for me to show up only then. On our way from the supermarket to a phone shop, we met a few people who knew me. After some formalities and greetings, they exchanged some nasty comments even before we could walk far enough to not hear them.

'Of course, I'm here now to inherit the house; makes sense, right? I'm the grandson not her son!' I said, angrily pulling some phone chargers from their hangers.

'Let it be, let them talk…' And Anita pulled some items from my angry hands. 'We don't need six chargers now, do we? By the way, we need to get at least one Italian SIM card.'

'Make two,' I replied. 'I want to call Eléna, my sister. I'd like to see her again, you know… Before we leave again…' And Anita knew I was about to add, 'In case I won't see her again,' so she moved closer and put a finger on my mouth, nodding her head.

'Yes, Anita is right. If you only knew how many times I heard this kind of comments from the people back home,' Noah was shouting from across the aisle, feeling my pain. 'The joy of living in a two-by-two village!'

'Oh, I keep forgetting that! Yes, Noah's Bridge would be pretty much the same size.'

'Yeah, but you got better weather.' And he showed up with a small tablet in his hands. 'What? It's very cheap,' he added after Anita gave him a strange look.

'What is that for?'

'We are still civilized people, are we not?' He smiled. 'We can watch something tonight,' he whispered close to my ear.

'There is a TV in the house…in the sitting room!' Anita replied, moving away to the till. She was clearly reminding him that there wasn't going to be a romantic movie night for just the two of us in the foreseeable future.

'The TV is in Italian!' he shouted. 'You know what? I think she is really enjoying all this…bossing us around, telling us things, leaving mysterious messages behind…oh, and I *want ice cream after dinner!'*

Noah was unusually happy. Despite the difficult situation we were in, his mood was lifting us up, making us feel normal again. So, Anita and I went along, letting him have his tablet and ice cream. Finally acting like decent beings, we had our showers, made dinner, and ate without needing to look over our shoulders. The constant rush we felt was finally releasing its grip, allowing us to enjoy our conversations, this time not revolving entirely around our quest.

I shared some funny stories about the time I used to live in that house, like when I broke my arm falling from the giant cherry tree at the edge of the garden or when one night, Grandma had woken up to the shaking of the house, the volcano causing the foundations to move. Her sleepy look on her face, she had walked around slowly, with no fear at all, looking for her fancy top.

'Last thing you want is to go outside, with everyone in the streets, wearing an old, worn pyjama top!'

'Of course, with all that panic, she would think that!' And Anita laughed heartily.

'What's going to happen to this house? Victoria is not coming back, is she?' Noah asked, his eyes scanning everything around the room.

'With all the places, I hope this is not the first one Athymos will look for us in,' Anita replied.

'No,' Noah added. 'I mean as a legacy…I don't think she will claim this place, will she?'

'No, I don't think so either,' I said. 'She doesn't feel this place is hers. She never did… And like Grandma said, '*the house doesn't want her*'. I don't think she will ever come back, to be honest.'

'Oh God, I just pictured those books again! The ones at the church. I don't know what was worse. Your mother or those books.' And Noah laughed.

'His mother! Books are always good.' And Anita moved away, smiling, putting the empty dishes in the grey sink. Noah's face showed a funny disagreement.

'Everything is going to change, isn't it?' I let out, standing up, helping Anita clear up the table. 'We will never be going back to the life we had…'

'I think it has already changed,' Anita replied.

'We have already skipped months and months of everyone's lives. I wonder what has happened in the nursing home…'

'And to Harry…Mark and Shannon!' I added.

'Oh please, she must still be there throwing her legs up in the air on her social media.' And at that, I laughed.

'Speaking of the nursing home,' I continued. 'Now that we know we were right, is that where we should be heading next? If Anita is correct, Agapei will be there.'

'Do we have to leave this place? It feels so…normal, peaceful,' Noah said unexpectedly. This time he was the one slowing down, wanting to stay still for a little longer, in that place. Rita-Louise's magic was still at work.

'We can always come back here. We have the key.' And I moved to the sitting room, checking if the infamous TV set was still working. My hands full of old dust, I spent a good fifteen minutes sitting on the cold floor, trying to get the old device working again. The power was on, but all we could see on the screen were statics. As the other two were done with domestic duties, Noah came close to me, sitting in a bumpy armchair, his knees close to my shoulder, his left hand on my head. Busy topping up our phones, Anita missed the clear signal of intimacy between me and him. As simple as that gesture was, it was clear we had moved to another level of complicity; we were getting closer.

'I know you want to,' she said, handing my phone back to me. 'but I think it's best if you don't tell your sister you are here. I'd text her, tell her you are alright. After all, we have been gone for so long, she could be worried…but I wouldn't risk bringing her in all this.'

'You are right…' I let out, sad.

'I shall look forward to the day she isn't!' Noah added, smiling.

After spending a few hours watching grey pixels blink on the broken TV and taking the chance to talk about all the things we had left behind in our lives before the madness, we felt tiredness finally catching up. The air had grown colder, and a soft breeze was slipping in through the large patio doors left open. Anita quietly moved outside, looking at the sky growing darker, her eyes focused on the large garden being swallowed by the night. The similarity with what our future might look like was too strong to be ignored. Her mind and face showed a worry her other half had been carrying for centuries. I walked out, ready to leave for the night, when I caught a glimpse, a whisper in Cherish's thoughts.

'I knew this was a mistake…but I also have to admit you knew best. We had to leave the Seven behind. If we had a chance of saving Creation's making, we had to preserve the true nature of you, in their hearts. What else could they have been, without love? Animals in Nothing's hands. They would have destroyed each other, slowly, painfully. We might have sacrificed everything only to have them succumb to something worse. A painful agony, turning into feelingless beings. Millions of Athymos's copies…'

'You are getting stronger,' I said, looking at Anita.

'You are, and so am I. You are stepping right at the beginning of the end, where everything changes. We are at the turning point. Soon you will have to leave this human existence behind… The time is approaching fast.' And she looked at me, right into my eyes, almost urging me to hurry up.

'So, what is going to happen to me? To Daniel?' But Cherish was not answering, her eyes capturing the space behind me. 'I have been giving it a lot of thought… What's going to happen to me? If we manage to bring him back.

Love is the only one that exists in a Human body. Time, Soul, they were who they were, enslaved in their own prisons, but they were still…them. Love, on the other hand…'

'This is something that goes beyond my knowledge. The moment we stopped existing, after the blow, something else happened. Someone else's power had made this possible.'

'You mean Love manifesting in Human bodies?' I asked.

'Yes. This is not Love's making, and definitely is not Creation's. You should have survived as a God, weak and hurt but as one. Or, if Nothing was capable of destroying you, you should have disappeared entirely, and me with you.'

'What's going to happen? What's going to happen to Anita?'

'There is so much that might happen… I don't think it's wise to put our minds into unknown possibilities.'

'I don't have much left, but John and Anita are too important to me. I need to know what is going to happen.'

'It looks like your true nature was broken in two by the evil. You will have to reunite your souls, eventually. And one of you will have to give in, I'm afraid.'

'One of us?' Noah had just joined the conversation, shocked.

'You are the carrier of something inhuman. You can't exist with and you can't exist without. You have seen the same duality in all the Awokens we have met. You can still see it in me.' And Anita turned her face to her own hands.

'This body is carrying the weight of my nature. Eventually, she won't be able to contain my growing power. I'll leave her behind, forever. This or death. We know we have no other path.'

'What about the ones that existed in their true nature?' Noah asked, moving beside me.

'Iris, Asher, they are barely living…but they are living without the support of any Human.'

'So, Love will leave us behind, eventually?' Noah went on.

'We are the result of a curse, Noah,' I said before Cherish could speak. I knew what she would say. 'Love didn't possess us. Love was born in us.'

'So there is no way out? We can't exist without?' Noah was finally showing reluctance. Since the day we had met him, he was hungry for what was going to come next. He wanted to move forwards, discover, become something else. Now, in the space of a few hours he had done the opposite, twice. His eyes were locked to mine, he had grown fond of me, Anita, the life we could have had together. 'There is no other way, is there?'

'Correct.' And Cherish's spirit had gone dormant again, leaving the three of us in the depths of our confusion and worry.

Chapter Twenty-Five
The Curse of a Shining Star

∞

Noah and I were lying on the same bed where I had sat long before, engaging in conversation with a fragile mind while seeking answers. His new clean tablet flickered brightly with the images of a video he had put on. Our eyes were fixed on it, but our minds were travelling miles away. As we got closer to our goal, the idea of an imminent end grew stronger. Regardless of whether we emerged victorious or not, there was no happy ending for us. We had persistently pursued our quest for answers, only to find that the answers we discovered were not the ones we were seeking.

Anita had gone to bed just a few minutes earlier, after sitting beside the two of us for a while. Unable to escape her heavy thoughts, she had chosen to silence her restless mind with the power of deep sleep. In contrast, Noah and

I were unable to quell the darkness that troubled our souls. Midway through what was supposed to be a funny film, Noah hit the pause button and set the tablet aside, forcing me to return to the quiet solitude of that home.

'I think we can induce our visions if we try,' Noah said.

'What do you mean?'

'If Anita is learning to do it or if Cherish is now capable of doing it, then we can do it too, don't you think?'

'So, you want us to try and summon Love's memories?'

'We need to know, Daniel. We must prepare ourselves for when the time comes. With our current knowledge, we can only sit here and worry or delve deeper and choose what to be concerned about. I don't like the idea of any of us going away, especially if it's only one of us. If we stay, we stay together. If we die, we die together!'

'Together…' I let out, glancing at the many pictures hanging at the wall. Grandma was looking at us. Iris's voice repeated in my head: *'Daniel's love for you, John, was of a different kind. We didn't push for it, we never planned it. If there is something we couldn't do, it was to make Love be any different than what He is.'* If I die or I live, should I not do that with John? *My John*, I thought.

'Together,' Noah repeated. 'After all the things we have been through, I see no other way. Forget about Love and Time and Soul for one moment. Even if we manage to get him back, how can we let it all slip away?'

'You are really changing indeed.' And I smiled.

'What you mean?'

'For a good bit, I was worried you were in this alone, on your own. I was worried you didn't care about me or Anita or what was going to happen to us.' And Noah's face turned away, regret and shame were sitting on our same bed, beside him, beside me. 'But I don't feel this way any more. I see you know. I see you care about us, about me.'

'We were drawn together by something else, by a spell. Now I'm drawn to you because of you, nothing else. I wanted to have more, now I'm not so sure.'

'If we do survive this, if we all do… You know how I feel about John.' I was dangerously putting Noah on his old path by pushing him away. He wanted me and my safety, I was thinking about John's.

'I do. But I also know how you feel about me.' And Noah's hand moved to my face, gently, soft.

'Last time we nearly triggered a vision almost intentionally was in Rome.' And the vision of Noah and me, half naked on a small bed, was making me uneasy.

Noah moved his new tech toy aside and turned towards me, his legs crossed, sinking into the soft duvet. I mirrored his posture, facing him just a few inches away. Our knees touched, and our hands rested in between, holding on to each other's hope and fear. The space around us was as dark as the night outside, and a small, aged bedside lamp cast our shadows across the room and its furnishings. Whatever form of dark magic we were about to conjure, it would reveal the unknown right before our eyes.

'How do we know where and when to go?' I asked.

'Let's focus on the last thing we saw. It might work.'

'Alright, I hope we don't accidentally teleport ourselves somewhere without Anita. Without her, our chances aren't great.'

With our eyes closed and our hands holding firmly together, united by the desire for knowledge, our artefacts emerged, shining, brightly enveloping our faces in a pale, white glow. The pulsating force was stronger than ever before, fuelled by our will, accompanied by an unnatural warmth. In mere seconds, the air around us grew hot, and our skin turned red from the intense fire surrounding us. And then, up became down, and the top became bottom; gravity ceased to exist as our bodies soared through the hot air, racing through the deep blue sky. Once more, we were united with the multitude of awakened souls we had brought along, united in our battle against the enemy.

A familiar, gleaming star welcomed us, its intentions dark and malevolent. Moving faster towards our trajectory, it was aiming at the world we had vowed to defend. The higher we ascended into the atmosphere, the vaster it seemed. A colossal, aggressive stone had been dispatched to overcome Creation's design, aimed at our destruction.

'Something is pushing its will on it! The speed is too high, the heat is too strong for this kind of meteor!' Kathor shouted, as her body was shifting in and out of our magic.

'There is darkness all around it,' Cherish added. 'I can almost see its hands pressing! Over there, where the space is piercing through, the evil is there!'

'Nothing is not just sending a mere emissary of death. He is accompanying it with its own power!'

'We won't be able to face it alone. Call the Seven!' another Awoken shouted.

'No! We will face it now, the many of us!' we replied.

'Over there, where space is torn asunder, evil's presence looms!'

'There is a terrible evil walking right on its surface. We can't face this alone! Summon the Seven!' another awakened voice cried out.

'No! We'll confront it now, with our combined strength!' we countered.

As we reached the scorching surface of the speeding projectile, we encountered our most formidable foe. Bodiless yet mighty, its will was the essence of everything that existed—dark, vast, and intensely diabolical. Its rage against us was palpable in every aspect we perceived. Amidst the trembling soil of the celestial body, another presence was approaching us—steady and untouched. Its golden feet hung in space, its large hands extended a deadly invitation, its face distorted by an unsettling grin. There was no body, only a dark, dusty mist accompanying it, taking the place of limbs and will. The hurtling rock had a rider, a master who awaited our arrival. As it advanced, its form grew more ethereal, vanishing from sight, returning to nothingness. A voice thundered:

'And so, another one comes to his end. The first abomination, the first...God created by something no longer wandering this void.' Its voice resonated, a blend of metal and fire. 'Your creator is gone. Why don't you follow her footsteps?'

'We care not for your words!' we responded. 'Skip the pleasantries and return to the void from where you came! This world is beyond your grasp, and that of your master!'

'Ha ha ha ha. We are already here…we are already there. This is the sole existence permitted…' Its laughter echoed, a dark disdain for all we stood for.

'Awoken Ones!'

The clash was cataclysmic, beyond prediction. We collided with a wall of pure emptiness, our powers rebounding to their respective sources. The adversary moved with elusive speed, untouchable, unstoppable. Every strike we launched proved fruitless, crashing into the rocky soil and shattering upon impact. Its assaults left us untouched, its strength insufficient to breach our defences. Caught in a standstill against time, we found ourselves unable to best each other, vulnerable to our own defeat. Time was of the essence, no room for hide-and-seek. In a matter of minutes, we would reach Earth, returning to where we had begun, mounted on the steed of death and devastation.

'It's leaving a trail behind.' Cherish's voice whispered within us. 'But it's just one. We are many.'

'Alright! Let's do it!' we responded.

Multiplying of beings left our essence, scattering all around our enemy, taking it by surprise, leaving it unprepared. The dance of war turned on our side. We trapped it in a circle of pure power, limiting its moves, we were ready to strike the final blow. And so we reached it, like tens of bullets tearing its essence apart, pushing it through the cracks of the asteroid. Our power drilling down to the core, using the evil as tip of a piercing machine, was ending it completely.

But unknown to our ingenious minds, the sinister evil held another card up its sleeve. We had fractured its weapon into two fragments, but its trajectory remained unchanged. The solitary menace split into two colossal projectiles, both aimed at our most cherished realm.

'You never learn,' a deep, thundering voice said. Nothing was smacking our effort with the bare power of his will.

'There are two of them now!' Asher exclaimed, fear-stricken.

'This is beyond repair! We can't stop them both!' another Awoken added.

'Where there is Love, there is power!' we declared. 'I would do anything for them. Anything to shield them from this merciless malevolence.'

Our light blazed brighter, our power expanded, our essence stretched from fragment to fragment. Invisible hands seized both segments of the lethal rock. Prepared to execute the ultimate sacrifice, we were ready to rend ourselves apart, immolating our souls for the sake of protection.

'And this…is…it!'

Nothing had awaited that precise moment, the anticipated leap of faith he knew we would take. His power surged against us, penetrating our core, generating a cataclysmic burst of energy. He knew our moves, our will, as if he could claim it for his own. A blade of dark emptiness found us stretched apart, lacerating our soul and our mind.

In the surging explosion of our matter, an unexpected force surged behind us. What felt like a new magic emerged from space to confront the evil we could not conquer any longer. As the energy blast dissipated into the void, fragments of our magic rebounded through the dark expanse, permeating Nothing's essence, distorting it, corrupting it. Like a dying God, we offered the ultimate sacrifice. We vanished into our collapsing will, plummeting towards our demise, the image of the Humans we cherished dissolving in our lifeless gaze. In our final, fading breath, a being of pure magic grasped our hand, her whisper weaving a tender farewell.

'By the grace of the beloved mother of us all, it comes to you the balm to dying wounds. May you find the path to your heart and heal. My brother...'

The crush of our divided magic was like two bullets shaking the very centre of the Earth twice, pounding it, destroying it. Like the dead meteors turning into dust, so were we, our souls gone, our beings ripped apart and left behind, sinking into the depths of ice and the Earth's crust. Our last glimpse of life had been the realization of defeat, dashing into our end, the image of the Humans we carried in our heart, dissolving in our lifeless eyes.

With our collapse, two large cavities formed, the blast eradicating the life of our dear world, putting an end to nations and kingdoms, Humans and civilizations. The raise of the raging water came right after, pushed by the blow, flowing out of its banks, oceans claiming the long-waited lands back in their folds. In our last, dying breath, someone of pure magic held our hand, her whisper enchanting a soft, sweet magical prayer.

Noah and I returned to reality, our artefacts fading into our chests. Silence enveloped us, a tribunal of myriad questions suspended in the air. We learned what had transpired, but we were unable to speak of it. Our eyes locked, our faces connected, our knees still touching. We felt the cold air rise, filling the void left by the intense heat we had endured. And thus, it concluded. This was the true event we had witnessed through a different lens, in the initial days.

There were no stairs, no festivities, no Gods. Noah and I were traversing the path of a ritual destined to shatter the curse, reuniting our souls. The same curse we now understood had manifested. Love, unkillable, was torn apart in a bid to preserve Creation's work. The deity had fallen into Nothing's trap. The radiant star had not been dispatched solely to annihilate the world — it had a broader purpose. It was meant to draw us into the open, to trap us in an eternal conflict. Nothing anticipated every step of our journey, seizing the opportune moment to intervene. This was his sole method of evading Creation's constraints. Love could not be eradicated, but it could be silenced, fragmented for eternity.

'I can't imagine the level of destruction the world had to endure…' I said, breaking the silence.

'It surely must have killed most of the people on Earth.'

'How long was Love trapped? How long before he was born again?' Now that I knew how it all began, my mind raced through the pages of history, eager to reach the final days where Noah and I became the main characters of that eternal curse.

'Creation's spell has worked on Love and in every incarnation of it. Including the Awoken Ones. I mean, they have returned,' Noah added. 'They've returned many times…'

'What was said about Nothing? Do you remember? That he wasn't able to face us directly? Did you see what happened when Love was destroyed?' I asked, my eyes shining with a sudden realization.

'He looked wounded, as if Love's essence could actually harm him?'

'I think so…and I believe this is the best news we've received so far.' But Noah looked at me, puzzled. 'Think about it. If he can be hurt, he can be stopped!'

The morning light illuminated the room, revealing our bodies lying randomly on an unused bed. Anita entered, ready to wake us up, noticing that we hadn't crawled under the sheets and had fallen asleep in an odd position. Whatever situation we were caught in, I was relieved it wasn't compromising. As she drew nearer, I sensed her presence and woke up.

'Anita…is everything alright? What time is it?'

'It's still early. Did you fall asleep like that? Did you at least get some sleep? You look wrecked!' And her hand brushed my tousled hair from my forehead. 'Come on, make me some of that dreadful coffee, will you?'

We left Noah behind to allow him a little more rest. I wanted the chance to catch her up on everything we had learned. While I thought I was bringing the most significant revelation of all to the table, she didn't seem surprised.

'Don't you have anything to say?' I asked, sitting at the kitchen table. Six egg yolks stared at me, awaiting a beating.

'I'm thinking. You know, lately I feel more and more familiar with everything that's happening to us. I mean, if you consider how shocked I was at the beginning...' And she tried to sip her tiny coffee, her face twisting into various expressions. 'Oh, I'm not getting used to it. No, I don't mean the coffee...' And she chuckled. 'It's more like it feels familiar. Like I knew, but I had forgot.'

'Do you think you're getting closer to Cherish's mind?'

'I think so. And that's a good thing, because she holds a lot of knowledge somewhere in there.'

'I thought you didn't like the idea of being part of this...marriage.'

'I didn't. But I'm changing my mind. Though I'm not changing my mind about this awful coffee! I'll try and make a cappuccino...' And she carelessly tossed the small coffee cup into the sink.

'Now we do know how it all came to be,' I continued. 'And you were right in saying something must have happened to the Humans of this world. Their history was indeed erased. When? I don't know, but it was definitely a complete destruction.'

'And Love left the Seven behind. Somehow, you knew they would survive. Perhaps you hoped for that to happen.

And throughout all this time, the Harpies have dominated this world, challenged only by the few remaining Awoken Ones,' Anita replied, sitting down and gazing through the patio doors.

'Yes, and the most terrifying, the one riding that meteor, we have seen him before, at the house by the lake. It was Death, Anita. I'm pretty sure he is the Una of our world.'

'Do I smell coffee?' Noah appeared a few seconds later, probably awakened by the sound of Anita's discontent rolling at the bottom of the sink.

In the quick hour we spent preparing and eating breakfast, we came up with a plan for where we were heading next. We were right about Storgén, so we could count on finding Agapei in the nursing home, just as Cherish had indicated. Believing we would be back soon, we left everything we had in Grandma's house. As we pulled our artefacts into motion, ready to teleport the three of us back to Ireland, I could still hear Noah's voice complaining about bringing all our stuff with us.

With the magic unfolding, my mind made the same shameful connection it had done before, stuck between Noah and John, reminding me of how I was trapped between them and my feelings for them both. John's face took centre stage in my thoughts as I tried to bring us back to Ireland with the sheer power of my mind. Then something happened. While we were travelling through space, a sudden pressure pulled my hands away from Noah's, shaking my body frenetically. In that brief moment of hesitation, as my mind confused feelings with will, my power clashed with Noah's mind, parting away from him. Anita and I landed abruptly by two large magnolia trees.

'What happened? Ouch! I think I broke something...' Anita shouted, holding her arm, her left shoulder in pain.

'Where is Noah?' I asked, terrified.

'Daniel, we are at your place, look!'

I had never been so worried about being back home. Something had gone wrong. My mind had chosen the wrong destination, almost on autopilot. We had lost Noah, who was, in the best scenario, alone in the proximity of the nursing home, without us by his side. The last time we were at my place, we were surrounded by Harpies, close to being captured, to be killed.

'No... No!' I exclaimed, desperate.

'Quiet,' Anita whispered, her hand on my mouth. 'Last time we were here, tons of Harpies were about to flay us alive.'

'This is my fault,' I said, muffled under Anita's hand. 'My mind went to John for a brief second... John, Ireland...'

'We will talk about your driving skills later,' she said. 'We can't stay here in plain sight. Is there any chance we can get inside?'

'We never entered the house, remember? The keys were in my car! We had to flee. But there is a spare key in John's shop. If that's not locked.'

'Let's go!'

Anita and I ran across the land and onto the tarmac between the house and the large shop. Although it was early in the morning, the usual heavy Irish clouds were turning the day dark, allowing us to take advantage of being unobserved. If the evil was still watching over that place, we did not know. All we could do was hope for some luck. If we weren't pushed by the circumstances and wore ordinary t-shirts with random designs, we could easily pass for two ninjas, moving stealthily, like cats on feathers. As we approached the side entrance, the door swung open, letting us in. The place was empty. There was nothing left inside. John's work was gone, the floor was clean, and the multitude of tools he used for his artwork had disappeared.

'Everything is gone!' I said, my hands on my head.

'There is no way they could be interested in taking John's stuff…' Anita was moving across the room in disbelief.

'It wasn't them. How long have we been gone? Someone took the house, Anita. Probably the bank…' I was desperate. Everything I owned and loved was disappearing, one thing after the next. I was being stripped of everything that felt like mine, that made me who I was. If releasing Love could cost me my life, the trade was impossible to accept. *Losing my house, my things? Was there a need to be so surgically precise in inflicting this pain on me?* I thought.

'It's like being erased from history. We could be easily dead to them, to the world,' Anita said.

'Let me see. We used to keep the key of the house at the top of the doorframe. Here it is!' I said, passing it to Anita. 'But, is there any point in walking in now?'

'Well, it might be better than staying in this empty room. Let's hope there is no one inside.'

And we were in luck again. The lock hadn't been changed and nobody was in the house. Like John's garage, our home had been ransacked from top to bottom. There was nothing left. Our things were gone, not a piece of furniture left except the kitchen. Ironically, John's favourite chair had been spared by the rightful thieves and it was holding a quiet spot in the corner of the sitting room. My mind couldn't help but think of the night John had used it to prevent the magic from taking us away. *If only it withstood such power*, I thought.

'Oh my God…it's like being mugged!' Anita said, moving across the large kitchen with her hand still on her arm; pain was becoming visible on her face.

'They took everything! It's all gone!'

'OK, OK. Let's not panic. This is not why we are here,' she continued. 'I mean, we were not even supposed to be here. So, how do we get back to Noah?'

'We got here because of me, he must have landed at the nursing home. That's where his mind was at. But how do we get to Connemara?'

'The old way. There is nothing else. We need to get to town. Let me see if my phone is working here. No service. The Italian SIM card is not working.'

'What about my neighbours?' I asked, peeking through the hall window. 'It is going to be a shock for them to see me again, but what else is there?'

'Daniel?' a trembling voice said. Someone had heard us from upstairs.

'Harry?' Anita and I said out loud. We could not believe our eyes. Before we could add anything else, he stormed down the stairs; his arms, preceding his intention to hug us, went wide open. He sounded desperate and relieved at the same time. After so many years of friendship, that was the first time I saw Harry's love for me for what really was: silent but incredibly vast.

'I thought you were dead! You disappeared and you disappeared, John was gone too!' he cried.

'I'm sorry Harry. We didn't leave of our own will. I'm going to explain everything.' I could not bring him up to speed there and then. He deserved a full explanation but we were in a rush and exposed in the open.

'We thought the house had been taken over by the bank?' Anita asked, moving towards the front door.

'It is. I've tried to keep them away from it. I sold everything I could sell to pay it out, but little by little there wasn't much left.' Harry's face showed sorrow mixed with guilt. 'They are collecting the keys tomorrow. I came here to…see this place one last time.'

'Admirable,' Anita let out, her voice mixing with Cherish's. 'Let's get out of here!' And she pulled the front door, only to find it locked. Despite trying and trying again, the lock would not release its grip, trapping us inside. There was still magic holding that place in a freezing frame. Whether it was with us or against us, we were about to find out.

'Daniel…' a voice whispered. It was coming from behind us and above our heads. It was coming from the walls around. Harry was petrified.

'Who's there?' I shouted, my hands clenching suddenly.

'You need to leave…they are watching…' the soft, feminine voice continued.

'I don't sense them. Where are they hiding?' Anita asked, her voice completely changed. Cherish had taken over in a time of need as she was scanning the place around, her eyes piercing the walls.

'Daniel, what's going on?' Harry was holding my arm firmly, his eyes on the ceiling.

'Who is there?' I repeated. I didn't have Cherish's magical sight, but we were all blind to the impending threat.

'Someone else, something else is here,' Anita said. 'It's part of us, part of you… There is more than one, but I can't understand which is which. But there is an Awoken One in this house!' And she gently touched a wall, looking for something I couldn't see.

'There is what? Daniel, Anita, what's going on?'

'It's a long story, Harry. You need to trust me and stay beside us at all times!'

'Its core is weak, but its soul is imprinted everywhere,' Anita continued.

'If you are one of the Seven, if you are here, come out! We don't have time. You need to come with us!' I shouted into the empty space of the house.

'He is gone, gone with Daniel's love…you need to leave now…' The gentle voice took us by surprise again.

'Your will is strong, but your body is damaged…' And a soft glow moved across the room, sparkling.

Tiny dots of light had descended upon Anita's body, right where she had hurt herself with the fall. In the bright, warm embrace of that new magic, we found our energies renewed. Anita came back in a snap, stunned by her own healed body. Before we could even question who had gifted us with that blessing, Love's white cloak materialized in the middle of the room, between us and the front door. Our immediate future was calling us from afar, prompting us to move further before it was too late. I could feel Harry's hand gripping stronger to my arm, the magic was presenting itself to him in plain sight.

'My cloak, Anita,' I said, touching it, vividly remembering both times that very same gift had rescued us from evil. 'Something is going to happen…' And my hand moved on Harry's. We needed to be ready.

Suddenly it felt like thousands of snakes started to crawl on the floor, shaking the foundations of our will, wobbling our skin and our souls. Tens of Harpies walked in, penetrating the walls as easily as a cold breeze through an open window, swishing from every corner. Dark were their clothes; a grey glow covered them all, dancing in a terrifying manner. One of them came closer and stood right in front of our petrified eyes. Anita and I were holding our ground, back to back, hand in hand, right in front of our friend. Between us and the evil, only the shining cloak.

'This sorcery won't be of any help,' it said.

'She is Lytas, the Harpy of Anger and Madness,' Cherish whispered. 'She is known to be the one that drives people insane through rage and suffering.'

'And you will…' the Harpy replied, smiling through her deformed face. Her eyes were two dark cavities pushed to the sides, no ears, no nose; she was pure agony to look at.

The first blow struck like a flash, from its executioner right towards us, bouncing back on the cloak standing as protection. Harry jumped back, terrified. I was holding him as firmly as my determination to spare him from any harm. A few more came in sequence, leaving the Harpy surprised, driving her mad. With every attack, I felt closer to our end, in an immeasurable pain that failed to fully manifest. Then another Harpy made its move from the other side of the room. Its hands brought together in prayer, its skinny fingers were almost without flesh, bare bones piercing through the rotted tissues. The dark sleeves of its cloak slipped down to the elbows, and a vortex of pure energy left the centre of its body to hit us hard.

While the powerful blow was not able to breach the cloak's defence, it could still destroy everything else around. In the loud clash, we were pushed to the ground, the walls ripped apart, the roof, windows, and the entire front of the house turned to dust. A few moments later, the three of us found ourselves outside, the garden in front of our eyes. If the cloak barely resisted that evil, we knew there was no chance for us to stand against what was coming next. A large, horrifying creature was joining the army, sliding through the grass as it levitated over its deadly power. Everything it touched turned dead, crushing the life out of every single leaf, every living stem. Its feet, knees, and hips unnaturally shone with a golden glare, its hands were so large that they could have grabbed us all in an instant. Death had come to reap us, to accomplish Nothing's plan without hesitation.

'Finally…' he said, his voice dragging like the deep sound of a flute, warping the space around. 'They say it's your nature to escape me, to survive Death… Let me show what the truth is…'

Chapter Twenty-Six
Death's Enemy

∞

His first move was meant to be the only one he was mercifully going to make. He had come to destroy at once; he was not going to play with his prey, tormenting us, slowly vanishing us. He struck with the power of a black hole, sending us the ripping magic of annihilation, pulling our souls out of our frightened hearts. I could feel the inside of my body pushing against my skin, my core trying to escape through the fractures of my own flesh. One by one, all the Awokens I was holding within myself were dragged out in the open like fireworks were exploding on the spot, spilling out from my true nature.

What we had accomplished in months, years—Death was erasing in a few seconds. Our ally and protector was burned in an instant, leaving a trail of white and golden fabric all over the air, all over the space surrounding us, turning it into a dying nothing. The large magnolia trees John and I loved so much were torn apart, their leaves annihilated, the grey power of sickness rising up from their roots. If I was going to succumb as well to that deadly power, Anita instead was showing an unexpected resistance. Cherish shielded her from within; her body untouched, she suddenly stood up right in front of Harry who was lying down unconscious. Her hands closed in a sign of war, her unexpected resistance left Death surprised.

'Have you not learned?' she shouted, as her dark hair was whipping the air, her eyes turned to pure gold. 'There is only one power able to resist you, to face your destruction and preserve the innocents, to preserve everything we care...'

'Be gone, witch!' And Death struck again, what was left of the house blown away into thousands of pieces of debris, pushing me further back. I could see, hear, and feel everything happening around us but my eyes were locked on Harry. He wasn't moving and I was prevented from getting any closer and making sure he was alright.

'You can erase, destroy...' she continued, unchallenged, 'but Love and the memory of the ones we cherish will always survive! You cannot overcome Love.'

'You are pathetic, your Love is just a little, insignificant Human and, like the rest of his kind, will die by my hand!' Once more, Death unleashed his full strength on us, aiming at me from far off, dusting every inch of ground standing between the two of us, unable to touch me, to take my life with it.

'I'm Cherish, an Awoken of Love, the protector of Memory, the protector of my God!' Cherish was moving closer and closer, her arms stretched in the air; she was finally showing her true nature to me and to the Harpies who were now doubting their confidence. Philiat, Pragma, and Storgén had moved close to Cherish, standing side by side. With them, Eleoen and Mnemosy joining the fight, they were forming a pointed shield, aiming at the large enemy.

'It's time,' the voice I had heard before, in the house, whispered once more. 'He has found Agapei. Get him back.' And the white cloak reappeared out of nowhere, its fabric recomposing right in front of my eyes, pulling back its shape and power.

In a blinding glow, someone walked through space and reality, the white gift now landing on his shoulders. Noah had teleported himself on his own, without the power of our artefacts, his face smiling at me. As his feet touched the ground, another Awoken left him to join the fight. The fourth of the Seven had reached the others in the attempt to push back Death. Agapei joined the fight against an enemy we could not overcome, increasing our resisting power, reinforcing our line of defence.

If what the voice said was true, we were meant to escape again, once more running away from an evil we could not match. But Cherish's plans were moving in a different direction; she was determined to end the hunt once and for all.

'How? Daniel, what happened? How did you…' Noah said, looking at his hands and the white cloak flapping with the power of the two clashing magics. 'Oh God.' His eyes enlarged, fixed on the war unfolding, on Harry's body lying on the ground.

'Noah, we need to run! We need to get to Harry and leave at once!' I let out, grabbing his hands.

'Anita! We need to go!' Noah said, trying to walk towards Harry, against a violent, opposing energy.

'No! It's time to end this, now!' Her voice was getting louder, vibrating through the waves of power roaring in the space around. 'Go, get the other two. I'll find you!'

But before I could oppose the idea of leaving Anita behind, flashes of violent rage started to penetrate the wall pulled up by the Awoken Ones, piercing it through, cutting the air behind, cutting our skin like thousands of shattered glasses. Cherish pushed us to go once more, determined to give us a chance to escape our malevolent fate. As if evoked by their own desire, the two artefacts had come out in the open, against our will, leaving the Harpies stunned.

In the warping motion of the white cloak, Harry, Noah, and I disappeared instantly, leaving the factions at war to their own destiny. The last, brief moment we witnessed was the Awoken Ones taking advantage of our departure, as the Harpies had remained still for a few seconds, striking a blow so strong that Noah and I felt it, as we had appeared in a new, unknown place.

'There is nowhere they can run.' Death's voice was deep, his horrifying face looked like he was crying a slow, dying breath. 'For all of you…there is only me!' The ground was pulled from its roots, up in the air, the other Harpies pushed aside by the blow. Cherish and the other Awoken held the spot, resisting the attack.

'Like I said, life is not your real enemy. We are not afraid to die.' And Cherish pulled her arms ahead, her hands stretched open in the burning air. 'Death's enemy is Love and the memory we hold on to about everything and everyone we loved, and we have loved for centuries, we have loved since the beginning of time!'

Whatever spell was cast in that moment, it had a power unknown to the Awoken Ones, even to the four closest to Love. Something else was secretly playing in the fight, swinging the balance, tipping onto Cherish's side. As every strike ripped their flesh and their souls apart, the fighters healed right after, like time was moved back, rewinding the pain and destruction Death was sending against them.

'No, No, No!' I shouted before I could think to look where we landed. My heart was beating so fast I almost fainted. My eyes fixed on Harry, my hands over his body in a split second. On his face, cuts and scars recalled the last few minutes right into my mind.

Harry's heart had stopped sometime during the attack. His body still warm, his soul left behind, at the house. I started to cry as my mind hurried to find a way to undo that horror. I could feel my stomach turning upside down, my legs shaking, my arms weak. Noah's hands on my shoulder, he could feel my desperation as if it was his. He was crying with me, for me, for Harry.

'This can't be,' he sobbed. 'We'll get him back; we have to go back and fix this...'

'We left Anita behind… It's all gone wrong. I don't want to do this any more…' Desperation was consuming me. Noah was looking around, looking for that virtual door we crossed, hoping to see it still open and Anita following us through. 'How did we do it? I thought we controlled our artefacts with our will… I would never leave her behind!'

'Something is happening to us, to our power,' Noah continued. 'How is it that we parted ways right after leaving your grandma's place?'

'You mean someone else is controlling us?' *If it's true, maybe that same someone could bring him back?* I thought.

'I think Love is getting stronger. There is another will here, in between us…' Noah moved around, in the vastness of nothing. 'I've seen this place before.'

Soft, grey hills ran from place to place. Against the silence of the long grass enveloping the entire space, waves were crashing onto the shoreline, over and over. We had seen that place not long before. In our vision, the third God had talked to us, right there. Among the reddish wildness of Connemara, she had come out of the heavy fog to welcome us. It was like we had seen the future and now were waiting for her to present herself to us, once more. But we spent several minutes waiting, looking around, lost in the quiet vastness, our minds screaming for help, the help we needed to save Harry and Anita. Suddenly, the sound of a burst bubble took us by surprise.

'Oh!' a voice thundered, tiny hands on a rounded face, worried about an impending danger.

'Trusk?' I exclaimed, torn between sorrow and happiness.

'How? How did you find us? Where are the others?' Noah asked, running towards him, hugging him at once.

'Fhe dome is gone!' Trusk said, his hands trying to depict the horror he had witnessed. 'Iris is dead! Fhe big scary people desfroyed everyfhing!'

'No!' I exclaimed. 'Where are Time, Soul, Revelia?' As if my question had been heard through time and space, another bloop came out of nowhere. Revelia magically appeared behind us, her face sweating, the strange colour on her face showing the same fear Trusk was carrying.

'Where is Anifa?' Trusk asked.

'Daniel, Noah! I thought I was going to meet my end right in this strange land!' And Revelia ran towards us, her heart thundering through her chest. 'Who is this Human? What happened to him?' And her hands went over Harry's body. She was inspecting him as if she knew already the answer, as if she knew how important he was to me. She was looking for a sign he could still be saved, somehow.

'There is so much pain, It's unbearable.' Harmonia had joined us without us noticing.

One by one, all the ones I knew and cared about were coming back to us. All except Harry and John. Whoever was trading a life for another had a very sick sense of humour. Time and Soul finally walked through the passage their magic held open, their hands glowing, their faces sharp.

'The Awoken One is dead,' Time repeated. 'We were attacked by many, many Harpies!'

'How?' I asked. 'I thought the spell could not be broken.'

'Another Awoken manifested, right outside the dome, attracted by the remains of your presence. She appeared lost and confused, she could not fight them all, so Iris went to rescue her, a decision she paid with her life.' Soul was showing sorrow and pain in every word. 'This body has parted ways from his own soul...' he continued, moving closer to Harry and me. 'Don't surrender to desperation. I can find him, anywhere he may be now.'

'Can you bring him back?' But my question went unanswered. Soul looked at me, I could read through the reflections of his crystal face: he wasn't bringing any relief to my grief.

'As the one who cast the spell was gone, we got exposed. Soul and I managed to snatch the one called Ashrat from their evil hands before running away,' Time continued. Once again, he felt distant, cold.

'Ashrat?' Noah asked 'We have met her sister! She is here with us!'

'You moved back in time, didn't you? You should have appeared on the next thirty-first of October.' I had learned that lesson at my own expense.

'We did. But we did not get back to this present immediately. There is a great evil in the future, a very powerful one.' Revelia was moving slowly, looking around the quiet space. 'I didn't see it through my magic; I saw it with my true eyes, I felt it in my bones, under my skin. That's the present of tomorrow.'

'Revelia!' Time snapped. Whatever she was going to tell us, we were not going to like it. If I knew Time well enough, I was sure he was preventing her from sharing the truth about our fate. We were hanging on a very thin hope, sliding on a sharp blade. A little push and we would fall dead.

'You saw the future? Our future…' I asked, seeking an answer.

'Daniel?' Noah's wasn't following.

'We were not under the spell this time. If they moved ahead, they must have seen the future with us in it, our future… Isn't it right, Time? Soul?'

But the Gods were not conceding. Whatever truth they were withholding from us, it was scary, petrifying. Turning to Harmonia, Revelia, and the new Awoken One, my eyes were demanding an answer that would not come. At last, Trusk was my only hope. He would not lie to me.

'Trusk? What did you see?' But his mouth was painfully staying shut. Moving closer, down to my knees, I put my hands on his shoulders, his wings flapped briefly. 'Trusk, tell me, please…'

The little Chomp could not find the strength to talk. His hands folding into fists, his wings lowered, tears started to fall on his rounded cheeks. He was fighting against his will, against his fear. Whatever he had seen, it was hurting him from within. Noah was looking at us, children of the same terrifying destiny, kept in the dark against our will.

'Time, Soul…' Noah continued. 'We have found several Awoken Ones, not just Ashrat. We have also found four of the Seven.'

'But we have lost them as quickly as we found them. We have also lost Anita. Her Awoken is facing a horrible fight with many Harpies, some very powerful. They all are fighting for their lives!' I continued, dismissing an uncertain threat with a more tangible one.

'They won't resist, Time!' Soul's face had flickered a little, like emotions flowing freely through the cracks of his diamond shape. 'If those are like the ones we have met, they will need all the help we can give them.'

'No!' Time thundered. 'We have a chance finally, in a very long time. They are here, with you and me. We are so close.'

'I won't leave my friend behind!' Although as small as an annoying weed, I was facing the large God face on. My will was growing fast, pushed by fear, sorrow, and loss.

'You can't win this battle alone. Remember the reason why we are all here!' Time wasn't letting go. If the master of past, present, and future was suffering from the long waiting more than anyone else, I did not care.

'We need them. We need all Awoken Ones, don't you understand?' Noah replied, holding our position firmly. 'We are made of all of them, they are a piece of us, we need the Seven, we need Cherish, we need everyone we love!'

'I left John behind, I left Anita behind. I lost my best friend just a few moments ago. I lost so much you can't even begin to understand. I'm done doing this. I'm done doing this under your rule!' As if the words could build in an unexpected charge, the ground below my feet trembled, a surging power ran across the field, electrifying waves were pulling the grass right up.

Something was moving through my body with the bare power of my desperation. It was just me no more. Noah was right, someone else was taking over, abruptly, violently. Trusk moved a few steps away, his eyes enlarged by the shock; arms down, he was looking for the only last friend he knew well, Revelia. In return, her eyes turned red once more; the aim was me, the fixed point in the book of the future events.

'Come to me...' she whispered, just a few seconds before the exact same words came out of my mouth. 'For the ones that were left behind, for the ones that have given up, and the ones that cling to a broken hope...come to me.'

'Daniel?' Noah's hands moved slowly towards me, full of magnetic fear, attracted by it.

The moment our bodies were bound together, with the bare touch of his hand on my cheek, the space around brightened enormously, swallowing the skies above and the far sea. The red of the land turned to fire, the soil trembling from the power of lightning. We became the very centre of a magic explosion ready to go off.

'We are the ones called to protect. We are Death's enemy!'

The engulfing light rapidly moved from part to part in the entire space, capturing Harmonia and Ashrat in a blinding shot. And then everything went dark and dull. We were gone in a thundering warp, unseen, unchallenged, leaving the Gods, Trusk, and Revelia alone in the vastness of the lands. The entire house John and I built for ourselves was long gone. There was nothing left but ruins. The dust was mixing with a myriad of branches and leaves, the magnolia trees were turned into nothing, petals floating in the air filled with the sour taste of death.

In between the rubble, one body was lying down, dark, long hair entangled with thorned roots and leaves. As if the spell of grievance had already sung its last chord, the white petals laid all around, the final prayer had already been said.

'NO!' Noah shouted, his voice getting lost into nothing.

I could not speak. My lips sewn together by thousands of thorns, I could not make a single sound. If I knew pain and loss, I did not know then the real magnitude of sorrow. Anita was gone, the only one that had been beside me all along, even before we really knew we were bound together, had traded her life for mine.

The many memories started to flow in my head. Anita and I were sitting by the trees, laughing, talking, victims of the bad habit of smoking. We were connected, pieces of a puzzle we could not see entirely, but together we could still see fit. The nights we had spent, talking about my dreams, were popping up like flowers in springtime. She was handing her soft hand to help me understand. She was there like she always had been.

'So you came.' A slow, rattling voice was welcoming us back. 'You know what it means to be Death?' And a large being moved beside me, his face deforming, disappearing, and reappearing in a nauseous loop. 'Tell me, do you know what it means to be me?'

Without thinking twice, Noah ran past Death towards Anita whose hands were bound together, trapped in a deadly spell. His attempt to free her was a repeated failure. He could not touch her, he could not move her from her spot. Her head covered with grey dust, her body as cold as the deep ocean, Noah could not reach her.

'Your friend,' the evil continued, 'could not stop talking, declaring her will against ours…' And multiple Harpies started to appear all around us. 'You, on the other hand, you are not saying a word…'

The evil whisper was cutting through my flesh from one part to another, reaching my broken heart. He was right, I could not say a word. I was sinking fast, in a free fall of misery and pain. He was right, there was no speech that could match my feelings, a silent devastation folding its grip around me. If that was the price of our quest, I wasn't going to fight any longer. I was done with losing, I was done with crying. I was done.

'Now, let her go!' he continued. 'Release your spell and let me finish the work I've come to accomplish.

And his hand rose from the dark fog, holding a long, silvery stick. On top, the shiny, curved blade of death was reflecting my face, wobbling into its metal. In it, I could see myself crying, I could see myself holding Anita in my arms. *Is it showing me the future? Is he letting me grieve her before ending me too?* I thought. But beside my mirrored form, someone else was standing. I could see her old face, a weak smile welcoming me.

'I said…let her go!' Death repeated, his blade pushing against my neck, pouring blood from my skin to its metal.

'He can't!' another, familiar voice said. 'He is not the one holding her in between life and death. I am!'

Chapter Twenty-Seven
The Healer

∞

The long waiting came to an end. We'd known her since our time begun, but we could not see her. She had been there by our side as long as eternity goes, without us realizing it. Hints, helps, daydreams, and nightmares, she had come in the same form, over and over again. This time, she was abandoning the land of mystery, the kingdom of hope, to sit on the rightful throne of the God of Health. She had come to keep us alive in a time of need, when the other Gods had failed us. She was holding the keep like a wise queen.

'What is this new magic?' Death shouted, pushing his blade further into my skin.

'This is no magic, and it's not new. I'm as ancient as time itself, I'm Creation's child born out of Love for its making.'

Out of a warm embrace, Health glowed in a comforting light. Surrounding the space, her power was moving across, touching every particle, every single atom with its blessing. The cut in my neck healed instantly, filling my lungs with strength, my heart with fire. My sorrow shrank in a blink. I was back myself, with the same determination I felt the moment we left the other Gods behind.

'Hands off my loved ones!' I shouted, Death stepping back, terrified. 'I can't destroy you, but I can send you into the dark, empty abyss you belong to!'

A surging power, a flowing force of emotions pushed the shell out of my heart, pulsing strongly, calling Noah's artefact into a joint gravitational pull. The Harpies scattered away, horrified by the clear omen. The fight was going to end soon, with no hesitation on Love's side. And so it happened. Like strings of a melancholic instrument, waves of light pushed the heavy dust away. Strong waves of joy, laughter, and tears were bonding in a chain reaction, multiplying in size and strength.

'You can't kill me…and you can't escape me,' Death let out, as the very fibre of the evil was shredded apart, reducing into nothing, leaving behind a mere whisper of a cry. In a few moments, all the Harpies disappeared; their master was long gone, pushed into the darkness of his home.

The space was finally free from its deadly grip. In the aftermath of a quick war, Noah and I were the only two left standing, witnessing the appearance of our new ally.

'The news of this new defeat will spread fast…' Health said, her body blurring into multiple dimensions, unable to come to a physical form. 'We need to hurry our steps. I'm almost ready, but another difficult stretch is needed.'

'I know you, don't I?' I asked. 'We both do. We have seen you before. Why are you not like Time and Soul?'

'Because my power keeps me alive without my key. Although my sceptre is lost, I can still heal in this form, not more, nor less…'

'Can you come back to us, as your true self?' Noah added, as we were moving close to him, still holding on to Anita's spot.

'First, let's release your friend. There is an Awoken who protected her from within, as I shielded her mortal body. Yes, let's hurry!'

Even in between existence and spirit, Health's magic had been at work without us knowing it. Now, as we could finally see with our own eyes, the God moved her essence into every corner, like a soft, warm breeze, pulling Anita's body into the air, turning dust into sparkles of life — hundreds of fireflies blinking frenetically in the night that had landed on us. Her eyes open, Anita came back to us, as she had never been touched by the evil. Cherish was still with her, bound to her soul for the journey ahead. The same journey we didn't hope we could still make.

'Anita!' I exclaimed, hugging her tight. 'Are you OK?'

'We thought we lost you!' Noah's arms around us, tears in his eyes.

'I'm OK! I think,' she replied, smiling. 'I have something important to tell you! Death's sceptre, it's important!' she added, leaving us surprised. Whatever she had gone through while we were apart, she'd managed to increase her knowledge, always after knowing more.

'Daniel,' Health interrupted. 'Open your arms.' Several shining lights reached me, disappearing as they passed through my chest. 'The Ones are back with you. You still miss some, but I believe she knows where to find them.'

'Do you?' Noah and I asked, looking at Anita.

'It's not all,' Health continued. 'You probably know by now, I need to be part of the rite for you to be successful. Unfortunately, my sceptre is long gone, lost, forgot. You have tried before now, many times, ignoring how important this missing artefact is. I need it, we need it!'

'So, it's true. We have never found you before? Is this why we have failed every time?' I asked, my arms still around Anita. I could not let go.

'A few times you have…briefly, but never with my key; never knowing what you were really after. You see, the spell cast against me by the evil was supposed to destroy me. With his limited knowledge, Nothing didn't know I could come back as I healed, slowly but surely. I've tried many times, and every time, when the time was right, I pulled your memories out of oblivion, starting your quest.'

'How long does it take?' Anita asked, already a few steps ahead, knowing the answer.

'In Human years, thirty years. This is when I get to my full strength—as strong as I can be to hold my key again.'

'So it's you!' Noah exclaimed. 'It's you the reason why this repeats every thirty years. It's you why only now and not before?'

'Yes. And besides many different unknowns that have happened, this time, you have also managed, somehow, to give me more time, more than expected. You have literally disappeared for almost two more years.'

'The dome!' Anita exclaimed. 'We moved ahead, disappearing from time and space for so long!'

'It looks like it was not all bad, after all…' I said.

'How are we connected, to you I mean?' Noah continued. 'Every time we failed, how did that reset the time for you? Could you not keep your strength for yourself?'

'My dear.' And Health moved back a little, where once the magnolia trees stood. 'The curse you have, trapped into your soul, into your hearts, needs to be constantly fought. Failing to fulfil your destiny in becoming one again, involves losing your essence, every time a little bit of you goes without coming back. I, for my own duty, I've been using my whole power to keep it together at the expense of my own energy. It requires almost everything I am. Then, at the turn of the tide, when you awake to your fate, I start healing again. You become stronger and in less need of me.'

'So this is the rite? This is how the rite would work?' I asked, finally releasing Anita from my hands, letting her stand on her own feet.

'In a way, yes it is. Once all Gods are back and in full strength, Love will be able to break the dark spell. I can heal your renewed essence, Soul can merge the two entities into one and Time can hold on to the split of the smallest of seconds for you to exist, to form again within the space. Now' —and Health turned around, opening her arms wide, her light flickering fast—'the others are waiting for you, worried.'

Like a fulfilling prophecy, the God made us reappear in the same place where Noah and I had stood the first time we had met her, in our vivid dream. The harsh, red landscape was the one we knew well. Connemara was silent and welcoming, its magic quietly listening to voices in the far east. Time, Soul, and the others were debating on what to do. Some wanted to go and find us, while the Gods were resisting. Somehow, they knew we would come back, with the strongest ally we could find in times of need. So we moved closer, Health's presence being almost undetectable. Revelia and Trusk ran towards us, their hands travelling through space fast, eager to hold us once again.

'You made it,' Time said, smiling.

'Health?' Soul's face suddenly brightened, joy filling his energy, magnifying it. As an instant connection fed through the Gods, back and forth, Health shifted into a more tangible nature, taking the others by surprise.

'After so long, we are all together again,' Health said, smiling.

'This is the closest we have ever been in a very, very long time,' Soul added.

Although joy and happiness filled the air around us, my heart was still troubled. Harry's body was still lying on the cold grass: a few flowers had been placed around his figure, and I knew that was the work of Revelia and Trusk who, amongst allies, were the ones who understood how important he was to me. It didn't matter how close we were to victory. As Anita ran towards Harry, went to her knees on the grass, I could not stop thinking about how close she had come to death too. *Why wasn't Harry sharing his life with an Awoken One? It might have protected him, saved him*, I thought. My eyes fixed on the Leonty; she was looking back at me, a red flash moving quickly in her irises. A smile briefly popped up before I spoke.

'It's time to go back,' I said, grabbing everybody's attention. 'I won't wait any longer. We have to go back to Runae.'

'Daniel, I've tried.' I was expecting Time to challenge my call again. 'I've folded the past on itself over and over again. It does not work. A dark cloud is holding its grip on the flow of time, preventing me from reaching the node at any moment in the history of Runae.'

'I don't care. Whatever is keeping the passage closed has to give. We must go. I want to bring back Trusk and Revelia to their homes. I want to make sure their people are safe and well!'

I looked at Trusk again. His eyes were craving help, his trust fully on me. He truly believed in me and that I loved his kind, as I had proved many times before. He moved his tiny, hairy wings up, his hand holding strong to mine, sending electrifying waves through my body. Whatever magic the Chomps held, this was of a new kind. At the touch of our skin a new power manifested; strangers had become brothers. Once a foreigner in his land, now he was a foreigner in mine; we had become family. We had turned into what belonging really means: trust, love, protection above any difference of kind and race. We were all beings made of the same matter. Inside, our hearts beat the same warm, embracing music. And so, another living creature came to exist again, manifesting its presence under the many surprised eyes scattered across the field.

'Here she is,' Anita said, Cherish's voice speaking through her. 'Xena, the daughter of Love, the Awoken One Protector of Connection, the one that moves the souls of the most different living beings.'

'I've been here for a while, I think,' Xena said, her voice soft, gentle, 'but I could not come to light yet. My master has reached the breaking point of realization. So I come to be now, once again, in the midst of so many different kinds. Gods, Chomps, Leonty, Humans.'

'You are one of the Seven! You were with us all this time?' Noah asked, smiling.

'No. I was with them,' Xena replied, her hands on Revelia and Trusk's figures.

'And the other two are waiting,' Cherish added. 'We must go now. We need to find a way to go back to Runae, as Daniel said.'

The fifth of the Seven had joined the pack right from within our hearts. If we only suspected it then, it was clear now that the Seven would come to us like any other Awoken One. They could have been holding on to a spot, like Agapei and Storgén. Some others would float into nothingness, close to our essence, ready to manifest when the time was right. Our numbers were growing fast, so was the rush to complete our mission. Noah's will was becoming everyone's; we had to move forwards. As Health said, we had been detected by eyes darker than the ones we had already faced.

Anita and I knew at least another missing being was held prisoner in Runae. I knew who was watching over whom. I had him beside me for a long time. I had him in my own house; a presence Cherish had detected as we walked into the empty home before the battle. Health wasn't the only one who was standing watch. One of the Seven had been there all along, and he was now gone, gone with the love of my life, in a stranger's land, waiting to be rescued.

'What do we do now?' Noah asked. 'How do we open the gates to Runae?'

'We need the evil to turn his eyes somewhere else,' Soul replied. 'That should allow us to make it through.'

'Before we do...' Health interrupted, her shape changing, becoming more and more visible. Her face coming to us as we knew her, old but firm. Her eyes forming, we could see her power slowly growing in the presence of the other Gods. 'Let's fill the empty spots with what you know your past was made of.'

The old lady moved closer to us, in front of an eager audience whose desire had finally been listened to. She spoke slowly, her voice coming from behind her, and from between us. It was like nature was speaking directly to us, from the ground and from the silent lakes behind her. Noah and I could feel our own presence, but we couldn't see each other any more. We were someone else, taller, softer, almost ethereal.

'The day of the great war, much more than good against evil occurred. Far beyond the notions of life and death, being and non-being, the struggle played out among the

Gods. Realizing that the dark power could not be overcome, understanding that the evil's magic could not be extinguished, Creation had cast a spell upon her children, upon her Gods. As the very essence of who she was, what she was, in exchange for her own life, she bestowed upon you and me, Time and Soul, the gift of immortality. Her power was granted to us—the greatest gift of all. We were now impervious to destruction and beyond the reach of Nothing's will. However, as our adversary drew nearer, after enduring endless battles against us, he finally understood that he could not absorb us into his malevolent existence. He needed to find another path.'

'So you're saying that Creation wasn't killed... She sacrificed herself by bestowing all her power upon you?' Noah asked, bewildered.

'Exactly,' Health replied with a smile before continuing. 'I was there to see it. I was the first one to confront the pure wrath of evil. He exerted his strength against the world I had sworn to protect, Talush, tearing it asunder from end to end. When I felt his blade's sharpness upon me, our mother came to save me. She told me to leave the fight to her and to reach my brothers, seeking rescue and the chance to rescue, to forewarn them of the impending peril. I reached Soul when it was already too late—for him, for me. Strangely, at the edge of Varayal, for a fleeting moment, I sensed Love's presence. It was faint, like a whisper, as if the future had reached into my past to guide me. That's when I realized whom I should approach next. And so, I arrived here, as the tide turned.'

'It wasn't just a whisper,' Revelia interjected. 'It was the future, our present, intruding upon the past, wasn't it,

Time? I felt someone entering that reality just as you reached for the tiara and I felt it again as we were facing Nothing by the Varayal's node. You must have felt it too.' But Time paid no heed to her comment.

'Where were Time and Love amidst all this? Why couldn't they come to rescue you? To save Soul?' I inquired, even though I already knew the answer.

'Both Time and Love were engaged in a prolonged battle against Nothing's forces. On Earth, what you call Harpies—minions of evil—were too numerous to defeat, even with the support of the many Awoken Ones that Love had summoned. They faced a choice: find me, find each other, or safeguard Creation's realms.'

'After Soul's defeat,' Time continued, 'he came to me through hatred and defiance. He enslaved Runae through the hands of the Crimson Queen. I was imprisoned under her will. During my silent captivity, I fomented resistance through my world's people. One by one, they succumbed, except for the Chomps and a few Leonty.'

'And he also turned his attention to Earth.' Cherish spoke. 'Mobilizing his army through dark power and annihilation. This time, we unexpectedly presented a more potent resistance. In response, he deployed his most formidable weapon against us, against humanity. He wanted a direct confrontation, luring us into a trap. Love was torn in half, annihilated.'

'But not entirely,' Health interjected. 'This is where I intervened. This is when I first employed my power to save you. Nothing's curse was meant to rend you eternally. I converted the curse into a cycle of rebirth. Try to understand…I couldn't defeat him or overcome his power, but I could offer you an escape. As mine and Love's powers merged, the curse ricocheted partially, striking hard and damaging our enemy. A shard of our essence infiltrated his core, a piece of Creation within the depths of her foe's nature.'

'And then, the cycle began…' Noah added. 'From that moment onwards, we've existed in an eternal loop of birth and death.'

'In the silence, somewhere in my mind, I can see it…' Anita was back among us. 'Cherish was there, but…when did this happen?'

'In Human years? Nearly thirteen thousand years ago. That's when Nothing dispatched its destructive machinery against you and your realm.' Health moved towards the placid lake on our left. 'Much of your world fell into an extended, freezing winter. It persisted for many Human lifetimes. The inhabitants diminished to mere thousands, clinging to a slender thread of hope for rebirth.' Her hand reached towards the water, yet unable to make contact with its surface.

'Health,' I interjected, 'how can we succeed without your artefact?'

'As with all things I touch, I could heal it, reshape it.' Noah and I exchanged a fleeting smile, acknowledging her words. There was still hope.

'Where was the artefact destroyed? Was it in Talush?' Soul chimed in.

'No, it was here, on Earth. The impact with Nothing's meteor and his power scattered it across these lands.'

'Here, precisely here?' Anita questioned, gesturing at the very ground beneath our feet.

'Not too far. You know the precise location. You've seen it before, the first time you were brought into Daniel and Noah's magic.'

'Noah's Bridge...the island.' I said, looking at Anita. 'The first time you came with me, remember? We were dancing, and you followed me to the other side...'

Once more, events unfolded, seemingly with a specific purpose. We had come to terms with the idea that we were following steps charted by destiny long ago. But the way every detail seamlessly fit into place still astonished us. Our presence was ordained in every place we had been. The trip to Noah's Bridge, the island, Noah's touch while Anita and I were dancing. Cherish had been present throughout; she had to be involved in our every move. We had been stepping carefully around the core of our enigma without us knowing.. Unknown to us, we had been near Health's artefact, tantalizingly close to what we most needed.

'Soul,' Anita asserted. 'You mentioned diverting the evil's attention elsewhere. How about we look for Health's artefact remains and unleash her magic in a visible manner? I can't imagine anything more visible than that...'

'If it works, could we reach Runae and set everyone free?' Noah inquired further.

'We'll go but as Humans!' I let out. 'I don't want anyone harmed, including the inhabitants. The Awoken Ones can remain concealed within our hearts, but Soul, Time, you must remain invisible. Trusk, can you employ your magic to hide yourself and Revelia?'

'I can'f any more! Since fhe Flare vanished!' Trusk looked at both Time and me simultaneously.

'That can be remedied.' Time extended his arms, his green clepsydra pulsating vividly. A tiny red spark emerged, expanding through space. The Chomps' Flare resurfaced right before our eyes.

Health briefly glanced at me, a smile passing between us. I understood that she shared my sentiment. While this was our life's mission, no other being should suffer or bear the cost. We would proceed with caution, our magic concealed.

The plan formed instantly. We were bound for Noah's village again. Once Health's artefact was secure in her hands, our magic would attract the devil's attention. At significant risk, as we neared the culmination of the ancient rite, we would deliberately expose ourselves. This was the sole way to exchange the safety of our mission for the well-being of our dearest loved ones.

'Before we go, Time, Soul, Health,' I said as I held Noah's hand. 'My friend deserves your magic, one last time.'

And the three Gods moved at once. They knew what I was asking. No questions came forward. The three moved in a circle around Harry's body. Their hands in a gesture of prayer, a bright magic unfolded before our eyes. Harry's body lifted from the grass, a glowing power surrounding him was bringing him right up.

'May his soul find him in its long journey.'

'May his days be counted no more.'

'May his body be preserved for eternity.'

A large stone formed right from the ground up. Its shape was tall, its surface was shining like a large crystal. Harry's body was transformed, nestled in an immortal symbol of remembrance. A few words made of gold appeared soon thereafter:

To the ones we love. In our hearts is where every laugh, every memory, every tear finds its place to rest forever.

Chapter Twenty-Eight
The Sceptre

∞

The despair left behind by the evil force was the only presence in an otherwise quiet and old forest. Amidst the woods and the gentle lapping of water from the distant lake, the ruins of Noah's old home mingled with the aftermath of Iris's defeat. The dome was long gone, but remnants of its power still floated in the cold air, like the sparkles of dead magic too weak to settle. In the shadow of the trees, a few Harpies moved slowly, their smoky essence shifting back and forth from reality. They wondered when their master would return.

Unknown to them, Death had faced Love's and Health's power in a distant land. Despite the long wait, they were unaware that he had already returned, accompanied by others who had been cast away during the battle. His golden sandals rattled against the dying grass, announcing his arrival to the few present. After inspecting the empty spot left by the destruction, he spoke.

'This was a great work. There is no deceiving they can master any more.' His voice emitted a horrifying whistle, though his slaves were not victims of any terror.

'One of them is dead, my master. But the rest managed to escape. They have powerful allies protecting them.'

'Their fate was long foreseen,' he continued, closely inspecting the once upside-down tree, now dead. 'I will find them again, soon.'

The wild branches of the ancient trees started to crumble upon the touch of the large Harpy. Rotting rapidly, the surrounding nature transformed into pure demise, bearing witness to the nauseating, dark green glow pulsating from the scythe he held in his contorted hands. Something lurked in the Harpy's mind. A memory from long ago resurfaced, a memory from the time he was granted the power he now possessed.

'This world and everything within it is an abomination.' A deep, slow moan reverberated in the aftermath of destruction and Love's defeat. 'I have come to reclaim it all, to bring it back to where it belongs. Yet, something resists me now, a disease spreads inside me, against my will. I cannot fully annihilate it, cannot undo the creation of these...these beings who call themselves Gods.'

'You have achieved your desire, you the Supreme Emptiness.'

From a small hill at the centre of a tiny island, beside a dead tree, Death gazed upon the world with his evil eyes. He had landed back on Earth after riding the carriage of destruction before it was gone to dust. Falling down to the unprotected planet, he had survived the crash, protected by his dark magic. In the far distance, giant blocks of ice were detaching from their roots, crashing into the sea, melting under the fiery impact of one of Love's two halves. Red and white clashed and merged into a deadly avalanche. To the south, a raging red light glowed over the horizon. A second impact had occurred, between land and ocean, turning water into hot steam, raising the deep blue into the purple sky.

'I have not,' the voice continued. 'The end of my enemy has been temporarily averted. I will now delve into the depths of my own existence, to eradicate the spell cast upon me.'

'My Supreme Emptiness,' Death said, perplexed. 'You have already destroyed the creator of the Gods. You merged her power with yours when I came into being. What else can they possibly do against your terrifying will?'

'I did so. She shall remain dead for eternity. However, her children wield a stubborn magic that cannot be extinguished. Or so it seems. Nonetheless, you will retain control over this world. Annihilate everything that exists, reduce every living being to nothingness, and deliver them to me. In one way or another, they will all perish by my hand.'

'You have bestowed upon me great power, my Great Emptiness. But this world is vast, very vast,' Death looked up into the sky, hoping to catch a glimpse of his benefactor.

'At your feet lies the remains of one of the two who dared to violate my true essence. She is dead. These Gods will attempt to return, seeking to impose their will on what is right and true. Through their magic, they will seek amulets containing their powers. You must prevent their return. Open your arms, now!'

Without hesitation, the Harpy obeyed. His eyes transformed into large, rotating cavities as he received a second gift. His hands contorted, his feet and legs expanded, and he transformed into a giant, dark being. From the ground, hundreds of golden pieces, the remains of what once was Health's artefact merged, reshaping the surrounding nature into an obscure vortex. A long branch broke from the dead tree by his side, joining the unfolding dark magic. After a few moments, a long sceptre materialized before its rightful owner. A shining, metallic blade curved at its top. Death's supreme weapon was finally complete, ready to execute the merciless act.

'With this power, you shall be my hand, a pure embodiment of my will. With this, you will imprison the Gods in the emptiness to which they belong. Go now, and do not fail me. I will return to you.'

Nothing had truly changed in Noah's Bridge. Despite our defiance of the laws of time and our experience of losing weeks and months in that world, the village remained unaltered, trapped within its own magical dome. Everything appeared as we remembered: the trees, the hills, the grey clouds ushering in impending rain. As we reached the familiar hill where Noah and I had first met, our group suddenly diminished. The Gods became invisible to the naked eye, Trusk extended his magic over Revelia, and only we Humans were left with the freedom to navigate the surroundings.

'It's déjà vu all over again!' Noah exclaimed as we descended the hill towards the bridge.

'What is déjà vu?' The Leonty's voice drifted between our minds. She was somewhere nearby, invisible.

'It's when you see things again, as if you're experiencing events twice,' Anita replied, disregarding how that might sound to Revelia, who possessed the same ability at her command.

'But it's nothing like your power,' I added. 'We use the term for things that happen in a similar way to how they happened in the past.' I wasn't entirely sure I had clarified the distinction.

'It is strange,' Revelia continued. 'I do feel like I've seen this place before. But that's not possible. I've never been here. Yet, it feels like this is going to happen again?' Whatever future the Leonty saw ahead of us, it was a manifestation of her true power.

Ignorant of the risks and trusting that we had all the Gods with us—hidden but present—we hurried across the bridge. On the other side, the village greeted us in silence. A few people moved about, engaged in their daily lives. Elaine's Inn stood to the left, seemingly waiting for us to enter once more. Two Christmas trees, drenched by the early rain, flanked the front door. Shops on both sides of the street were adorned with decorations and illuminated with lights. The cold, tranquil afternoon gave way to more cheerful music, and distant singing could be heard as people exited their favourite pub.

'Pub crawling,' Noah mused, sighing. 'I really miss that feeling…you know, being carefree?'

'We can't be this close to Christmas, right?' Anita asked, her left hand briefly brushing against a wreath hanging on someone's door.

'If looks beaufiful! All fhe colours…whaf is if?' Trusk's voice reached us from behind. 'Revelia, look! Fhe strange creafure is looking af us! Can fhey see us?'

'No, Trusk,' I said, smiling. 'Those are toys…machines that appear to be alive but aren't.'

'This is very strange,' Revelia commented.

'I know. Our world can seem strange to outsiders,' I replied, as we crossed the main street, making sure our two invisible friends stayed close.

'No, Daniel, I mean all of this. It really feels like we've done this before.' And I felt a slight push from behind as Trusk bumped into my legs, startled by passing cars.

Across the wide street, older buildings huddled together, as if afraid of the growing cold, seeking warmth in each other's presence. Among old cottages and small shops, a large church stood alone. In front, a round courtyard filled with benches and Christmas stalls partly obscured the ancient doors left open for the evening mass. At the centre, atop a few steps, the local priest shook hands, welcoming people inside. For a brief moment, I thought that would be a great place to temporarily hide Revelia and

Trusk, as their invisible passing was, through pushing and poking, taking the crowd by surprise.

'What was that?' one person remarked.

'Jeez, I think I won't make it to all twelve pubs tonight!' another slurred.

'Welcome, Mrs Murphy!' The priest's voice carried to an old lady who had just reached out. 'I was expecting to see you tomorrow for the Christmas Eve mass. Never mind, it's nice to see you here!'

'Daniel, it's two days until Christmas!' Anita exclaimed, her eyes wide in shock.

'Time?' I let out. If we had moved ahead, it was definitely work of his magic.

'I had to,' he whispered across the air. 'The surroundings were filled with enemies. This is the first opportunity I could find it empty.'

'This smell...' Noah added, slowing down as we walked past a chip van parked on the corner of the square. 'I'm so hungry...'

'We definitely need to get some food. Let's get this done and then we can eat, I hope,' I responded.

As we turned the corner, the lake came into view in the distance. Towards the end of the street, the peculiarly shaped building Anita and I had visited before stood closed. The 'something something summer solstice event' was a distant memory, yet a vivid image of a young girl in odd attire flashed in my mind. We picked up the pace, driven by our newfound hunger. At the lakeside, a partially still dock extended, with half of it submerged in the icy water. Flanking the precarious structure, a lone boat moved slowly.

'We're in luck!' Noah exclaimed.

'I wouldn't call that luck.' Anita's finger indicated the obvious state of the small wreck.

'It's floating…should be fine?' he retorted.

'It doesn't matter!' I said. 'Time will teleport us to the other side.'

'Someone is approaching!' Revelia whispered, capturing our attention.

From the far left, exactly where the painters once stood, an old woman walked slowly. Her clothes were simple, her face grey. She was gazing at her feet, cautious about where to place her trust on the soft ground.

'It's just a local, let's go!' Noah exclaimed.

'This is not what is supposed to happen…' Revelia's voice wavered again, her red eyes glowing in the night. 'We did all of this, and it's not going to work!'

Before the Gods could manifest, the woman disappeared from the distant landscape and reappeared right beside us, causing us to jolt back, petrified. She stood still, her face lowered, silent. A sudden smile crept onto her cheeks, and her eyes lifted slightly, darting left and right. She counted us, mentally listing our presence. Her lips moved imperceptibly, mumbling words too faint for us to hear. As I tilted my head slightly to get a better look at her, Time and Soul manifested behind us.

'Daniel, Noah!' one of them called out.

'This is not what you think!' Soul continued urgently. 'This being has no core. She is evil!'

The old woman's aged features brought with them a sense of horror. She stared at us, her smile malevolent, her eyes as dark as the approaching night. Raising her left hand into the air, she began to conjure her magic. Trusk's protective barrier dissolved immediately, leaving him and Revelia exposed. Anchored to the spot, Noah and I reached them, positioning ourselves to shield them from the evil, prepared to fight. It was us against one of them; the battle was one-sided, its conclusion already foretold.

'Do you truly understand what Love is?' she sneered, words sliding through her teeth. 'It's an illusion. A convoluted way of clinging to something you're desperate to belong to...'

'Who are you?' Noah shouted, his eyes shifting from the old woman to Anita, secretly hoping Cherish would emerge and aid us.

'I am Despair,' she replied, her head turning back, waiting for someone else... 'And what hope remains when I am here to counter it?'

Her mouth opened wide, releasing the tension she had been carefully holding back. A disturbing cry echoed around us, stabbing into our ears and hearts. Waves of sorrow enveloped us, entangled in a melancholic and painful embrace. Soul's form began to flicker, his true nature resonating with that malevolent power, absorbing its malignant effects. On the other hand, Time held his ground, untouched by this sorcery.

'What kind of spell is this?' he questioned.

'She's Desolos, a Harpy,' Anita answered, her hands covering her ears, dropping to her knees in pain. Someone else materialized in her place, ethereal and combative. 'She's binding us in a state of vulnerability. But she's doing something else as well. She's alerting the others to our location!' Cherish's prediction materialized quickly. From the distant corners, grim shadows multiplied, soaring through the air, intent on reaching us.

'Soul, we need to move!' Time shouted. But the God of Souls couldn't budge. His crystalline essence and its myriad facets flickered frenetically.

'Get in the boat!' Health appeared briefly behind us. 'You and the others need to get further away!'

'My brother is here, and so are the others!' Harmonia whispered, suddenly manifesting and radiating amidst us.

Noah's hands were already reaching for the boat, pulling Anita up from the ground as Revelia leaped in nimbly, like a cat pouncing on its prey. Trusk was already floating on the water, a few inches above the surface. Balanced precariously, I joined the others, just a second before Time's power swung into action, propelling us away from the shore with a forceful sweep, cleaving the water in two. The Gods' figures grew smaller as fast as the number of Harpies increased.

On top of the shifting grey cloud, one figure loomed larger than the rest. We recognized him and the power he had previously unleashed upon us. Though Love's and Health's magic had banished him, it hadn't been for long. He was returning in full strength, fuelled by revenge, his evil intentions evident in his monstrous form. Midway through our escape, the boat slowed, its energy draining, nearly glued to the still water. In the silence of the dark night, the screams of the devil's army reached our ears, amid the green flashes that lit up the pitch-black background. Time's energy pulsed violently, countering the attacker, shielding Soul who struggled against the void that sought to thwart us.

'We should go back and help them!' I shouted, my gaze fixed on the distant horizon.

'Whether we move forwards or go back, we need to figure out how to push this thing!' Anita's hands clung tightly to the boat's sides, her feet already submerged in the rising, cold water.

'Trusk,' Revelia interjected, 'can you pull us?'

'You are foo many! And I don'f know where fo go...I can'f see anyfhing!'

'This is a mistake!' I declared. 'We must go back and help them!'

'What about the sceptre? Don't we need to find it before they reach us?' Anita asked, lifting her legs above the frigid, rising water.

'We'll split!' Noah's unexpected suggestion caught us off guard. 'Daniel and I will go back. The three of you should proceed and find it. Anita, remember that Cherish can locate the artefacts. You saw where mine was buried. Trusk can fly with just the two of you.'

After a few moments of hesitation, amidst the compelling screams of the enemy in the distance, we acted swiftly. Noah and I evoked our artefacts, employing a spell we knew well. In an instant, we vanished from sight, reappearing beside the Gods. Revelia and Anita floated in the air as the boat began to sink, and their destination lay just across the other side.

'Daniel? No!' Time shouted, pushing away multiple Harpies converging on him.

'It's going to be OK!' I reassured him.

The evil was opposing our will at its best. Desolos, Strife, and the other Harpies pushed against our power, moved by Death's command. We were surrounded with no way to match their magic. With every move they made, Time's clepsydra blinked slightly, anticipating their actions, rewinding the exact moment, leaving them trapped in a powerless loop.

Noah and I moved beside Soul, helping him stand against the nauseating emotions Desolos was sending our way. The more her cry infiltrated his crystal skin, the more his power spiralled out of control. The ground started to move, sand wobbling in the dark, taking shapes of bodies with souls made of pure magic. They rose from the dead matter, turned into allies. Strong in will, inconsistent in flesh, they fought the Harpies only to succumb to their attacks, turning into the same dust they were made of. For every one that fell, another one would rise up. My shell and Noah's heart moved closer, shining brightly, forming a shield the Harpies could not overcome. Two of them challenged the united front, getting instantly pulverized by its touch, but Death was ready to bring them back from the land of nothing, reforming their shape and their diabolic faith. Both sides at war, it was a never-ending loop of death and life, regeneration after regeneration, no faction could step closer to victory.

'Give up now!' Death shouted, his blade materializing in his deformed hands. He moved fast, swing after swing, pushing us back, his magic mysteriously grown. Someone was giving him strength, aiding him through the impossible. The Harpy successfully opposed two Gods and us, moving unchallenged. Eventually, he reached us, crashing his deadly sceptre between our artefacts, pulling them apart.

On the other side, far away from the battle, Revelia, Trusk, and Anita were running across the small island, inspecting it from part to part. There was nothing else but trees and rocks. No signs of lost, ancient artefacts, nor evidence of a scattered collection of past magic. Cherish's eyes were blind to the only thing that mattered.

'What are we looking for exactly?' Revelia asked, following Anita.

'It's hard to explain. The Gods' magic leaves traces. Like a shining beacon in the dark. But there is nothing here, I can't see anything,' she said, moving randomly, retracing her steps, blinded by the obscurity of the night.

'Maybe if's nof here any more?' Trusk followed closely.

'What did you say?' Anita suddenly stopped.

'You know?' the Chomp continued. 'Like for fhe Crimson Queen. She had fhe key. She fook fhe key.'

'This... Oh my...' Anita's voice changed. 'This is what I saw facing Death. His weapon, his blade is mounted on a sceptre...'

'The Harpy's weapon?' Revelia asked, puzzled.

'It contains the fragments of Health's artefact. I've seen it glowing with that same power belonging to the Gods! It must have been forged that way to prevent Health from coming back! Nothing gave the clepsydra to your sister for the same reason.' As Cherish's words emerged, so did her intention and our future in Revelia's mind, whose eyes immediately ignited.

The hints, the worries—the Leonty was right. Something had recently happened and was going to happen again. We were merely revisiting the past all over again, step by step, without being able to change it. This time, Anita had managed to grasp the risky reality but, once again, it was too late.

'We have done this!' Revelia exclaimed, grabbing Anita's hand. 'Several times. We have been here before; everything that has happened, has happened before!'

'What do you mean?' Cherish's eyes were locked on to Revelia's magic.

'We have done this before. Something over there, by the Gods, will happen. Time will turn back the present to try once more. But every time it's the same!'

'This is because history cannot be changed,' Cherish replied, looking towards the lake where the battle had reached a tipping point. 'Unless one of us stays out of the loop, we will never learn what will be. We have to go back and let Time know!'

But Cherish's plan was a mere fight against the unstoppable flow of Time. The Gods, Noah, and I were pushed to the limits of survival, Death's blade cutting through our very essence. Health's magic moved across the land, healing us but with great difficulty. And so, the piercing of our hearts found its long foreseen future.

I knew that moment, I had seen it before by my house, in the early days when the nightmares had begun. I stood there, waiting to be reunited with the half I had been parted from. Alongside us stood the three Gods, ready to celebrate us in the pure essence of our powers. But the evil managed to overcome our shield; his attack found us weak. Death's blade swung in the air, a shining light in the dark of the night; he was aiming at Noah's heart.

In a terrifying strike, the merciless blade penetrated our shield; Noah's body, too fragile to overcome the deadly magic, collapsed in my arms; his artefact had lost its own heartbeat, turning grey like a gelid stone. I was petrified, violently pushed into a devastating reality. He had taken Noah's life and my own heart, hope, and will in one move. That was the end of our journey. That was the end of our dreams, our purpose together. That was the end of another innocent life. In the blink of my shocked eyes, the Gods shouted.

'No!' Time's voice thundered, reaching the vast end of the lake, flying over Trusk, who was carrying Revelia and Anita to the other side as fast as he could, against the repeating odds.

The green artefact exploded in a massive light, turning shadows into bright day, Harpies into transparent veils. The space froze around us; our movements were held still. The last sparkle of life about to leave Noah's eyes, as he faced me, was halted. His soul trapped between now and then was holding its spot in between my arms. In the split moment of turning back the pages of that bloody history, someone's whisper reached Time's ear.

He paused for the smallest of existing seconds; his hands raised still, the wheel pendant on his neck glowing in sync with his artefact. Red eyes behind his head were telling a vital secret. Instructions of avoiding an imminent mistake were laid out at once. The God's spell was going to trap us again, indefinitely.

Chapter Twenty-Nine
The Loop

∞

Nothing had truly changed in Noah's Bridge. Despite our defiance of the laws of time and our experience of losing weeks and months in that world, the village remained unaltered, trapped within its own magical dome. Everything appeared as we remembered: the trees, the hills, the grey clouds ushering in impending rain. As we reached the familiar hill where Noah and I had first met, our group suddenly diminished. The Gods became invisible to the naked eye, Trusk extended his magic over Revelia, and only we Humans were left with the freedom to navigate the surroundings.

'It's déjà vu all over again,' Noah exclaimed as we descended the hill towards the bridge.

'Revelia!' I called out, looking at the figure of the Leonty halfway down the slope. 'Trusk, why is Revelia over there and not under your magic?'

'Daniel, I'm still here...' The Leonty's voice was close, her shape hidden from sight. She was still beside us, protected by the Chomp's power. As Noah and Anita turned their heads to the same spot I pointed at, Revelia's double disappeared. Our faces met each other in disbelief.

'There is something strange in the making here...' Revelia said, coming out of the Chomp's spell, her ruby eyes scanning the landscape ahead. 'There is a known but short future lying out in front of our eyes. It's like a brief, repeating moment...'

'Can you see it?' Anita asked, her face pointing to the invisible ahead.

'We have been here before. Many times. It starts here, but it ends here too...how is this possible?'

'Time? Can you help us?' I asked, sure he had heard the Leonty's question.

'She is not wrong.' The God manifested in front of us, his golden cloak reflecting the flickering light of the sun piercing through the heavy clouds. 'This is my own power, I can sense it, but I don't know why it's happening.'

'Why and when...' Anita added.

'If you did this, when did you? Have we been here before, with you, Soul, all of us living this very moment?' Noah's question was the very same one rolling in our own heads.

'I'll figure it out. We need to hurry!'

And Time shifted into the invisible realm as he resumed his fast walk down towards the bridge. After a moment of hesitation, we all moved at once, our heads still hanging on to the wonder of that new magic. At the other side of the river, the village greeted us. People were walking up and down, talking to one another, keeping up with their busy lives. A few blocks away, Elaine's Inn welcomed us back. Through its messy windows, amidst randomly placed Christmas decorations, I could see Aoife talking on the phone. The entire street was loudly announcing the upcoming festivity, joining the cheerful faces of people greeting us, sending us the clear signal that we had come close to the end of the year.

'Pub crawling,' Noah mused, sighing. 'I really miss that feeling…you know, being carefree?'

'We can't be this close to Christmas, right?' Anita asked, her left hand briefly brushing against a wreath hanging on someone's door.

'If looks beaufiful! All fhe colours…whaf is if?' Trusk's voice reached us from behind. 'Revelia, look! Fhe strange creafure is sfaring af us! Can if see us?'

'No, Trusk…'

'*Those are toys…machines that look like they are alive, but they are not,*' Revelia whispered, interrupting my words, repeating exactly what I was about to say. I was puzzled. 'This is very strange… We did this already. There is a big building over there, with a large courtyard. *"I'm so hungry,"* Noah says. *"We need to get some food, alright…"* you say…'

'Revelia?' I asked. 'What's happening? Why are you looking at our future? Is there something coming?'

'It's not the future, it's the past!'

'How can it be the past if it's going to happen later?' Noah looked at me and Anita, perplexed.

Crossing the large street and turning the corner, we found ourselves in the old town, Noah's Bridge's very ancient heart. Amidst tons of old cottages squeezed together, a large open square held up a much older church. The number of people walking around suddenly multiplied, their voices growing louder, challenged by the Christmas carols coming out of large speakers placed at the four corners.

'Welcome, Mrs Murphy!' The priest's voice carried to an old lady who had just reached out. 'I was expecting to see you tomorrow for the Christmas Eve mass. Never mind, it's nice to see you here!'

'Daniel, it's two days until Christmas!' Anita exclaimed, her eyes wide in shock.

'Time?' I let out. If we had moved ahead, it was definitely work of his magic.

'I had to,' he whispered across the air. 'The surroundings were filled with enemies. This is the first opportunity I could find it empty.'

'This smell…' Noah added, slowing down as we walked past a chip van parked on the corner of the square. 'I'm so hungry…'

'We need to get some food…' But I suddenly stopped. Revelia's words were repeating in my own head. She had seen it happening, word by word. If she was right, that was our future but also our past. We had done it before but it was still feeling like we were doing it for the first time.

In the midst of the busy crowd, my eyes started to dart left and right, searching for a hint. Something important was missing; we had overlooked something that could make a difference, whatever that was. Between two shopping carts, at the far end of the courtyard, two well-known faces briefly popped up from nowhere. Their heads appeared for a tiny second, bodiless, like they were floating in thin air. Flat nose and chunky cheeks for one, green skin and red eyes for the other—Trusk and Revelia. For whatever reason, they had left the group and moved away. *Curiosity found them weak,* I thought. *They wanted to explore our world a little longer. Oh, guys, this is not the time!*

'Hold on here,' I said, looking at Anita and Noah. 'Our Runae folks were left behind.'

'Where is he going?' Trusk whispered, his voice coming from somewhere, creating a warm, almost undetectable fog that broke through the cold air.

'Trusk?' Anita said, looking somewhere close to her feet. 'Daniel!' she shouted. 'They are here!'

But I hurried my steps too fast to hear her words. At the far end, the yard was enclosed by a large number of trees running around a circular area. Here and there, a few lonely benches stood frozen in the chilly afternoon. Holding their positions, Anita and Noah were watching me roam around randomly. Then I suddenly vanished from sight.

'What's going on?' I asked the two who welcomed me inside the Chomp's magic. 'Why did you move away?'

'This is not us...' Revelia replied, a sense of urgency surfacing in her voice. Somehow, her skin had grown greyer. Two shadows weighed under her eyes. 'The versions of us from your time are still with Noah and Anita. It's hard to explain at once, but we came back in time to warn you!'

'You are from the future? Did Time send you?' I asked, looking away to where the others stood, their faces visibly worried.

'No. We come from the past. I asked Time to send us further back, to right before we arrived here. There is something important you need to know, and you must avoid repeating the same mistake we have made, several times.'

'What is it?'

'You are heading to the small island, looking for pieces of a key. They are not there. They were taken by the evil and turned into Death's sceptre. This was Nothing's way of making Health's return impossible!'

'What? How do you know that?' I replied. Trusk was keeping quiet.

'The one who's sharing Anita's mind told us as we were looking for those pieces. But this is not the most important thing.' The Leonty rushed her words. 'The evil of this world has caught up with us. They will find you soon, very soon. In the despair of the moment, Time saved us all by turning back the wheel of history to the same moment we arrived here, only to end up doing it again. We have been walking our same steps over and over!'

'OK, OK…' I repeated, trying to make sense of Revelia's explanation. 'How do we fix this?'

'Every time, I managed to understand a bit more about what was happening to us. The version of me before your current present managed to warn Time, asking him to keep me out of the loop so I could come and tell you how to break this cycle.'

'So, you are out of sync with history now? There are two of you…and two of you too.' I looked at Trusk again, who raised his hands as if he had no say in the madness unfolding.

'Don't worry about it. This will fix itself if things go right! Now, before we set this in motion, there is something Trusk and I have been wanting to tell you for a while…'

A few minutes later, the Chomp's magic left me behind, and I came back into the land of reality, surprising Anita and Noah again. Once I joined the group, their questions landed on me mercilessly. On my side, the expression on my face conveyed much more than they could possibly imagine.

'Something has happened,' I began, pushing Anita and Noah away from the crowd. 'Well, not exactly. Something will happen, soon.'

'What is it? Where did you go?' Anita lowered her voice, suspicion taking human form. In her eyes, any stranger walking close to us turned into an enemy.

'Revelia and Trusk have come back in time. There are four of them right now, in this reality. Them'—I pointed my finger to our side—'and two more. They said we need to change our future, or we will be stuck in a loop we have already been trapped in. Let me explain,' I continued, stopping Noah from speaking. 'Health's key is not on the island any more. Nothing has forged the shattered pieces into Death's weapon. He has it, and Cherish knows it. She will realize it when it's too late. The Harpies will find us in a matter of minutes and will push Time to send us back in the past to avoid something terrible.'

'Oh my God!' Anita exclaimed. 'I've been trying to recall that memory for quite some time. It's true! I saw it during our fight against Death. Right before his blade found me, I had a flash of Health's power running through his weapon. Somehow, I had forgot it again.'

'What will happen?' Noah pressed his question firmly.

'It doesn't matter. We won't see it happening,' I replied, moving the two to the corner of the large church.

'There is something else, isn't there?'

Once again, Anita could see through the folds of my challenged mind. There was more indeed, something else Revelia had taken the chance to tell, in the secret of the Chomp's Flare, unseen by Time and Soul. Trusk could not hold on to the secret any longer. The promise he had made to Time, after Iris's dome had collapsed and they had travelled to their new present, was not holding any more. They knew what was going to happen but were prevented from sharing it with us.

Somehow, the secret had moved from one bearer to the next. I wasn't going to tell Anita and Noah what our fate was going to be. If they knew, our next steps might change in a dangerous way. In my mind, I was getting ready to admit my future was long written. I had learned to accept there was going to be only one end, but I could not say the same about Noah and Anita. All they needed to know was how to escape Time's loop. Whatever else was going to be laid out after that, there was no way of letting it out.

'So, I saw it right.' Revelia shifted the conversation back to where I wanted it to be. 'We are repeating our own small window of events.'

'You and Trusk are hiding somewhere, waiting for us to change the future. We have to get Death's scythe.'

In the dimming light of the night, we left the town centre behind. Most of the crowd had disappeared; some people were attending mass, some were celebrating with their loved ones in different restaurants and pubs. We were walking our own past and future as it was written, running towards the lake, ready to change what was needed for us to accomplish our goal. If we wanted to lay our hands on Death's weapon, we had to confront the Harpies still.

In my head, I revisited Revelia's words about the future, my own future. John popped up once more. I knew I had to see him again, find him, perhaps rescue him, but *what are our days ahead together going to be?* After my unacceptable explanation of why months and years had passed before I could get him out of Runae, what would I say next? *John, I have some other bad news…* I was attempting to come up with something to say in my own head, forgetting the upcoming peril, the imminent change of plans. *Maybe*, I thought, *we could change that future as well?*

'If we are trying to change the events,' Noah said, his voice tired from the long run. 'Why are we still heading to the lake?'

'We are about to face many Harpies and Death on top of it. I don't want any strangers to be caught up with it. Let's make sure it happens there, away from people's eyes,' I replied.

'If the Awoken One is correct, my key is in their hands.' Health appeared in front of us, her eyes inspecting the shoreline as she looked towards the far east.

'Time,' I said, as the God manifested beside her, 'whatever happens, do not send us back. This is our way forwards, even if we finally meet our end. Cherish,' I continued, looking at Anita, 'you need to come out now. I know you have enough strength to do so. Soul, we are about to meet someone who has a very peculiar effect on you. Can you use your power to tame someone's will?'

'I can, but I do not know the evil of your world and the extent of their powers...'

And as predicted and unknowingly witnessed several times in a row, the old woman appeared like a tiny, grey dot in the darkness of the night. She shifted a few times, coming closer. The first of the Harpies was about to unleash her dark magic.

'That's Desolos, the Harpy of Despair. Do not let her talk,' I said to Soul. 'Don't give her the time to open her mouth. As soon as you can, cover her magic with yours.'

The old evil moved close enough for us to see her face, pointing at her feet. Her eyes were moving right and left, a smile creeping up under her grey cheeks. Her wrinkled hands held together, moving frenetically as if she was savouring the upcoming meal. Her head finally lifted, and she was in shock. Her attempt to talk was somehow prevented. She looked confused, stalled by two wills fighting one another. Soul's magic moved across the short distance between us and her. His diamond shape turned bright, a tiny star in the darkest night; his face glowed with a strong will as he subjugated her wicked consciousness.

'And now, be gone!' Time's hand moved up, swinging in the air, bursting the Harpy from within, turning her into ethereal smoke.

'They are here!' Noah shouted, his hand seeking mine.

As expected, they came in great numbers, their anger speeding up their motion. Like fog spreading fast, they covered the black sky, scattering like a disease. Behind them, Death was conquering the world. His walk was heavy, the ground shaking and dying under the weight of his golden feet, his chest shining with a large cross. His hands were free, and no scythe could be seen. He had come to reap us with the sole power of the greatest evil. The one called Strife left the smoky pack, a disturbing look on his face; he was introducing us to the battle.

'You have come to meet your end, I'm afraid...' he started. 'You cannot overcome our power, just as you could not overcome your own troubles, your disagreements with one another. This here'—and the Harpy pointed his hands to his many companions—'it's an army. You are nothing; each one of you is alone.'

'Hold your tongue, brother!' Harmonia left my body and joined the fight. 'There is no space here for division and sorrow!'

'No.' Another Harpy rose from the group and moved closer. 'It's time to show you what pain is made of!' And

Algos moved his long, skinny hands to his head, pulling down the hood that was hiding the horrifying deformity of his face.

Blades of diabolic infliction formed around his body, travelling fast towards us. As my hand found Noah's, our artefacts came out in the open, shining brightly, forming a shield of protection around us. A few more Harpies turned their eyes on us, unleashing their dark power in an attempt to break us apart. With Soul focused on holding a revived Desolos's mouth shut, Time was the only God left who could stand by our side, fighting the increasing number of Harpies. His power in the making, he rewound the seconds before every attack, bringing the enemy back to their own steps, trapping them in a bubble of space where time would not flow.

To the left and right, we were pushed back, our bodies finding each other's shoulders. At the edge of our resistance, Death came to tip us to the other side, to send us to the oblivion he had envisioned for a long time. His presence was large; he took the space between the Harpies, his blade had suddenly appeared in his large hands, and he was swinging it in the cold air. A few times he attacked from the ground, a few from the sky, but his aim was the right centre of our hearts, right where our artefacts stood, coming together slowly. In the strongest of the swings, he planted the scythe firmly into our shield, electrifying the ground and our souls. His long, dark sceptre glowed a little, cracks suddenly appearing on the blade in front of his angered face, leaving him in shock. Whatever gift he had received was disappointing him, failing him. Something was resonating with our own power, finding it amusing, almost attracted to it.

'I've grown tired of your resistance!' he shouted, irate. 'Why won't you just die?' and the pressure between Noah's heart and my shell multiplied, pushing us to our knees.

Close to breaking apart, I looked at Noah, whose head synced with mine, his green eyes storming against mine. We were about to repeat history, but this time I had told the God not to intervene. *Did I bring us to our own end?* I thought. Once more, an ally we had learned to rely on, despite his size and appearance, came to our rescue. Trusk's Flare moved over our heads, making us disappear at once, leaving Death unbalanced and causing him to crash to the ground.

'Trusk?' I let out, my voice echoing into the empty space we had been moved into.

'I told him,' Revelia said, her hands on my shoulders. 'We are close. Once the blade reaches him, it will all be over...' And Noah looked at me, worried.

'It's exactly how it needs to happen,' I replied, a brief smile popping up on my face. 'We need Death's sceptre close enough to take it. It started to break apart. We need him to unleash his wrath on us once more.'

'Are you saying we need me to die?' Noah was in shock.

'No!' Anita exclaimed, her voice doubling, mixing with Cherish's. 'Time needs to freeze that exact moment. Once done, I and the others will take it from him. Revelia, there is something else you need to do...'

And suddenly, we were back in the open. Noah and I moved in front of the large Harpy, ready to face him while Revelia appeared beside Time, her red eyes sharing the secret of our plan. Surrounded by many enemies, we were as if shrunken into a tiny spot, a few steps away from the shoreline. As they moved against us, enveloping our souls in heavy grey clouds of evil, Noah and I came together once more. His hands bound to mine, his face locked into my eyes, a blinding light of pure energy exploded into the space, scattering away the many Harpies, leaving only their master standing.

His diabolic will repeated the same desperate move; he planted the blade at the very centre of our shield, a few inches from Noah's back. With full trust in me, Noah didn't stagger. His eyes fixed on mine, he was silently telling me he was there with me, for me, for us. If Noah had a path laid out towards something, that was it. He was ready to stand between the evil and his loved ones. I was determined to break the same curse our destiny had shown to us many times before.

So Cherish's hand moved on the instrument of evil, followed by Harmonia, Agapei, Xena, and all the Awoken Ones we had found along our journey. Under the petrified gaze of our enemy, his sceptre started to break into many parts, losing its strength. Time was brought to a standstill, a frozen moment. Revelia and Trusk were sent back to our near past to fulfil their destiny, and there we were, about to take back what belonged to us.

Chapter Thirty
The Gods That Once Stood

∞

Suddenly, we were pushed away by a powerful explosion. Death's weapon had shattered into pieces, releasing a blast of energy that brought us to the ground. In the empty space left by that new magic, one of us was still standing, finally materialized into our reality. Health was holding the spot, her hands brought together, magnetizing the space. What was once trapped by the enemy's will was reforming under our stunned eyes. The sceptre had reshaped from bottom to top, a golden snake folding around a silvery stick. Its eyes briefly shone with a warm, soft light. Health grabbed it with the authority of a true God, returning in full form. Her cloak appeared on her shoulders, and her power was about to be unleashed against our enemies.

'How was it?' she said, planting the sceptre into the ground, between her feet. 'I've grown tired of your resistance!'

Through the years and centuries, they had reverted to their true forms. Health, Time, and Soul had come together, standing side by side, calling me and Noah to join them. As we stood, the entire place transformed from night into the brightest day, releasing a surge of pure energy across the land. The Harpies were pulverized, reduced to ash under the gaze of the only one left: Death, who was slowly walking backwards, afraid of what was coming next.

'The Gods who once stood united are here in front of you. Where is your master? Where is the one we have opposed since the beginning of the eras?' Health said.

'Call him!' Time added. 'Tell him we are here to fight him once and for all!'

'I see it again! I see Runae again!'

Revelia appeared out of nowhere, and with her, the Trusk of a recent past stood a few inches away. Those who had travelled back in time were the ones destined to stay. The only ones who had seen two versions of the same history were calling us to our next step.

'He knows!' I exclaimed. 'His eyes have left Runae. We have to go now!'

'It's open. The flow of time is open again,' Time added. 'Hold together, we are going home.'

As the universe shrank to a single dot, we disappeared in an instant, traversing galaxies with the sole power of Time's magic. Left behind, the seemingly unbeatable enemy stood powerless, deprived of the gift given by his master. In the dark of the night, Death knew we had moved a step ahead. Whatever Nothing's response to his defeat would be, he felt comforted by the idea that his biggest secret had remained hidden in the unknown.

Once again, we reached the exact world in which we had started our difficult journey. In the snap of a finger, we found ourselves at the node, a smaller replica of the same island we were back on in Noah's Bridge. The sea surrounding us was calm, and Erion was shyly raising its head above the hill on the other side. All around the horizon, a brownish halo embraced the lands, sending us a clear sign of a terrifying omen.

'Where is Aura?' Noah asked.

'We are not moving,' Revelia replied. 'The pages of time are not folding, either backwards or forwards.'

'Why?' Trusk asked, his hand still holding mine.

'Because something terrible has happened here.' Time showed sorrow in his eyes. 'I'm screening through the events, looking for the right moment to land.'

'What happened?' I asked. 'Where is John, Treekan?'

The answer came instantly. Not in words or conjectures, but through space and reality. Time moved us again, to the heart of Trusk's village. Nothing resembled the place we remembered; everything was turned to dust, yellow and brown ashes floating in the air. A few homes still stood between life and death, their doors unhinged, their low windows cracked. The river that cut through the hills and the side of the village was gone, dried to its end. The Chomps' heartbeat had ceased sometime in the distant past. Unable to accept the harsh reality before us, no one spoke. Our faces showed disbelief as we scattered like hunters, searching for signs of life, hidden gems preserved from the evil's wrath.

'Joooohn!' I shouted, the dusty air filling my lungs, each breath like a stab to my chest.

There was no sound, no signs of survival returning to give us hope. We were late, we had been late for a very long time. The passage to Runae was lost since we had freed Soul. Nothing had seen us defy his wicked will; his gaze had been on the Gods, and he knew Time had been released from his spell. It was only obvious for him to turn his attention to the world we had come to love. John's fate, along with everyone else's, had been sealed back then.

We had gone hunting for Awoken Ones, the Seven, Health's key, clinging to a hope we should have never entertained. Fools running in a circle, we had to pay the price of a costly war, sooner or later. At the top of the hill where Treekan's home once stood, Revelia was consoling a dear friend, down on her knees, her arms around Trusk, who sobbed loudly. I ran towards them, nearly crashing onto the little Chomp, who looked at me in despair.

'I should have known better.' Revelia's words were sharp, like the pain she was inflicting on herself. 'I could not see anyone's future. I should have known!'

'Is there anything he can do?' Anita joined us, her hands on Trusk's shoulders, her eyes fixed on Time.

'He brought them all back before, didn't he?' I asked.

'Yes,' Revelia said, lifting Trusk's face towards us. 'I'm sure he will bring everyone back once more…' But the Leonty's expression held very little hope.

Some of her power shone through it, her eyes flickering a pale red. Whatever she was attempting, it seemed feeble. Her nod of defeat sent us a clear message. The future depended on too many factors, too many wills entwined in the game of life and death. We were still teetering on the edge of the greatest danger, and predicting what lay ahead was almost impossible.

'This is not how they will end, Chomp!' Time said, moving closer. 'They all will be back, once our quest is over.'

'Why not now?' I asked, ignoring the glimmer of hope the God had just granted us. 'Why can't you do it now?'

'Look around you! The entire planet has been reduced to nothing. Rewinding the past for every single existing atom would require most of my power and a considerable amount of time we don't have.'

'What about you, Health? Could you not help? Soul?' Noah added.

'You all must understand, we have never come this close. We cannot risk.' Health's response was disheartening. If I had learned to expect emotional distance from Time, seeing her align with him was painful.

'As I said, they will be back once we have accomplished our mission.'

'We are our mission!' I interrupted, pained. 'Noah and I, Love. We are our mission. And I won't sacrifice everyone we care about so that the very God who embodies this love we feel can come back!'

My words hung in the air, heavy and charged. An unbearable weight had grown within me, something so potent that it had even slowed Noah's hunger for what lay next. He now stood beside me, his hand reaching for mine in agreement. Beside us, Anita looked at the Gods with her typical judgemental expression. We held the space between the Gods and the last two surviving residents of Runae. After a few moments of silence, Health looked at her brothers, seeking some mysterious approval. Once the two conceded, she spoke again.

'Daniel, Noah...' Her voice was soft, carrying an intimate tone of confession. 'It's time to look at the very reason why we are all here. Love is not our true mission. Love is a vital, critical step towards something greater. Love is the first God, the very first one born out of the feelings Creation had for everything that existed. We all came from you and her.'

'Don't!' I interrupted, nearly in tears. 'Don't tell me there's more... There's always more... We'll never reach the end of it; we're already paying the price. We've been paying it for a very long time. And for what? For something, a goal that keeps moving ahead and ahead!'

'There is more, but there always has been. You weren't...we weren't ready to even dream of such a possibility,' Soul replied. His essence merged with mine, his face emanating empathy and sorrow.

'Daniel,' Health continued. 'We need Love to bring back our mother. The creator of everything that is. Love's true power lies exactly in this.'

'So, you've been orchestrating all of this for centuries.' Anita spoke, her hands clenched in anger. 'You woke us up, put us through hell, made us lose people we love, only to use Love as a key to bring her back? Is this what Love is? Sacrifice?'

And that final sentence struck me like lightning. *What could be the supreme act of love if not sacrifice? What other power, which other God could make that exchange?* My mind whirled. Before I could say anything else, a radiant light manifested between Noah and me. It formed from thin air, moving slowly and hovering in space, searching for a form to take. The sixth of the Seven returned, ready to reveal its true nature at last. Just as Cherish's words had foretold, it was appearing at the precise moment it was needed.

Prometheus was walking in a renewed form, radiating a warm sense of peace and an embracing acceptance. He had finally come to show us we were ready.

'The waiting has been long, but my existence is accompanied by great pain...' he said, his body almost Human, turning to gaze at those around him.

'Prometheus,' Cherish called from behind Anita. 'The most Human of us all.'

He raised his left arm, placing his hand on my shoulder. There was much he wanted to convey, but words were insufficient. In that gentle touch, he shared the consciousness of the past, drawing my mind into events long gone, when he existed to support Love's will in safeguarding the people of Earth. Permeated with the intimacy of his mind, I saw through his eyes, felt through his heart.

Several Humans were moving about, their faces pale, having witnessed the end of humanity as they knew it. Nothing else was left but devastation and destruction. At the outskirts of what had once been a magnificent city, towers lay in ruins, homes washed away. Everywhere, cold winds carried the mournful whispers of death. Amid countless bodies, a distinct figure stood in shock. Golden hair wafting in the air, eyes resembling faraway stars. Dark-skinned, almost greenish, he gazed at his hands freezing under the weight of heavy snow.

'Is this what we will have to endure, from now on?' A similar being to Prometheus appeared a few steps away.

'We were asked to do so, Agapei. And we will, no matter the cost.'

'We could have saved them all if we had joined him in battle...'

'No, we would have faced the same fate.' Prometheus was traversing the land, unseen by the troubled survivors. 'Instead, we were left to give them hope...to help them resist, waiting for the day he will come back.'

'What can we possibly do? These lands are cursed. A long, very long freezing winter is in front of them. The Humans won't make it. They will all die. What can we possibly do?' Agapei's eyes gestured towards the mounting misery.

'I'll do the only thing I can do. I'll give them my power. I'll give them everything I am to let them hold on long enough.'

'This would be certain death!' The Awoken One pulled his brother by the arm. 'Why are you raising the heat of your core?'

'Because this world is dying, brought to its end by dark and ice. They need this gift; they need my fire to survive!' As his brilliant red burning magic intensified, I was brought back to Runae.

The sixth of the Seven had disappeared, joining the others within my soul. Breaking the silence that had gripped our minds, I returned with a newfound understanding. I had finally reached a decision.

'Bring him back to me,' I told Time. 'Rewind his past, and his alone. We will ensure justice reaches every corner of this land when this is all over.'

'I need to determine when it's safe to remove him from his natural history…'

'Do the Ancient Mirrors still possess their magic?' I inquired.

'Hold this spot,' Time instructed the silent crowd. 'We'll be back shortly.'

With no alternative but to heed his words, Anita, Noah, and everyone else were left behind in an instant. Time and I found ourselves at the place where the Chomps' Flare once stood, surrounded by rubble and ruin. With a sweep of his arm, the surroundings shifted again, the large structure that contained the history of that world reappeared, its massive doors ajar.

'This is just before Nothing turned everything to dust.' Time moved swiftly. In a few steps, we reached the far end of the vast room, the Mirrors suspended in a frozen moment. 'It will take only a few seconds for me to locate your loved one. Once done, we will need to extract him from his timeline and bring him with us. But understand, it's not as straightforward as it may seem.'

A familiar magic surged through the expansive chamber, reshaping it, morphing space into landscapes, memories, and people. Sequence after sequence, I watched Time scan the past rapidly, occasionally slowing to pinpoint the precise moment he sought.

'So, you call this…what's the term?' Treekan asked, his hands brushing the fresh paint on the eastern wall of the building. The glittering paint showed the figure of two men holding hands. Beside them, a few smaller ones resembled the shape of the Chomps.

'Art. We call it art,' John answered, smiling. Seeing his face once more and hearing his gentle voice sent me into a whirlwind of emotion. He was exactly as I remembered him, his sandy hair tousled by the waves, his eyes an irresistible magnet. His voice resonated like the call of my vast universe. 'It's a means of expressing how we feel, how we perceive things.'

'Art…' Treekan echoed, his face glowing.

'You think about the things you love the most and try to convey them without words,' John explained, running his hand across his forehead to wipe away the sweat. A wide blue streak marked his nose and right cheek, eliciting hearty laughter from the Chomp.

We moved again, increasingly swift. Weeks passed in a blur, my mind racing to keep pace with the tumultuous events unfolding before us. Laughter filled the air. John was in tears, laughing at one of Reela's reactions to something Daisy had done. But the scene changed once more. Day became night, morning shifted into evening. John sat by the river where the edge of the Chomps' dome once stood. His hands pressed against his cheeks, he was crying. A few steps away, a small cross was planted in the ground. On it, he had inscribed the name of the sole connection remaining to his true identity.

Daisy was gone, and with her went his hope that I would ever return and bring him home. Beside him, an otherworldly presence was offering a silent companionship.

'Stop!' I shouted. 'Time, stop here!'

'This isn't the right moment, Daniel. If we take him now, we don't know what we might inadvertently prevent from occurring.'

'It doesn't matter. In one way or another, we will erase this future anyway. Now, let me reach him!'

The ethereal memory expanded enough to fill most of the space, its boundary touching the ground. I could step through that invisible doorway between the present and the past. As I moved forwards, the passage collapsed, leaving me in John's reality.

'John?' I whispered, slowly approaching him. He turned around immediately.

'Is this real? Are you truly here?' His broken voice struggled to traverse the short distance between us.

Skipping my own steps through his history, I hugged him immediately. My arms drew his body close to mine as if I couldn't believe I had finally laid eyes on him again. He looked both the same and different, sandy beard lending him a dishevelled appearance, merging with his long hair, his eyes suddenly bearing traces of age. Shock melted into tears, sorrow into anger, anger into desperation. We both journeyed rapidly through all the emotions harboured in our hearts, drawing each other closer, fusing our souls as we had never done before.

'This is real. Oh my God, Daniel...' John's tears were uncontainable. His hands moved frenetically as if he had to make sure I was truly there and not a mere, disheartening vision.

'It's real. I'm real. I'm here to take you with me.'

'Where have you been? I waited for you for so long. Something dreadful is happening in this place.' He stood up, abruptly tethered to the reality of recent events. 'I missed you so much. The Chomps, this place was extraordinary, it has been for a while, but something evil has come... And Daisy...our Daisy is gone!'

'It doesn't matter, John. I'm taking you away. Everything will be OK!'

'It will all be ok... Pathetic!' a sudden, dark voice thundered from above our heads.

Something else, someone else intruded into John's past, actively meddling with it as if it possessed Time's power in its grasp. The landscape shifted instantaneously; the once-green valley transformed into a dark desert that devoured the river, the trees, and all else.

'You don't understand, do you?' The roaring voice was shaking my heart from within. 'There is no time in me. There is only now! I will erase you from existence, just as I have done before, and this time, for good!'

A vortex of time and space began to whirl violently, tearing at the fabric of reality, pulling John away from me as I was flung upside down, spinning in all directions. Time's voice resonated in my mind, shouting for attention, yet my focus remained solely on John, who materialized and dematerialized amidst memories of times past. I was revisiting his history tenfold faster than I had with the God, making me sick.

Suddenly, everything ceased. I landed abruptly on burning ground, amidst Chomps screaming and fleeing for their lives. At the far end of the crumbling village, John struggled to support a heavy mound of debris and shattered walls on his shoulders. Beneath his legs, Reela cowered in fear. A monstrous, massive dark hand descended from the sky like a black cloud, obliterating the world beneath it. Nothing had scripted the conclusion of Runae with his unmistakable signature. I had no doubt in my mind—that was precisely how it ended. No future could arise after confronting such overwhelming evil. Racing towards them, I caught John off guard. His heart and thoughts consumed by impending death, he managed to utter my name only briefly before Reela, who couldn't move, followed suit.

'I'm here to take you away!' I reiterated, assisting him in lifting the heavy debris.

'Daniel, it's over, it's all over!' he shouted, his face stained with blood and dust. 'Where did you go? I had you with me for a few moments a long time ago, then you left me again, you disappeared into thin air! Help us, please. You can't leave me again; you can't leave them!'

'It's going to be OK, John. I promise. We will change all of this soon. Give me your hand!' But John didn't release his grip.

As I traversed his past, being pulled away by Nothing's malevolent force, I had genuinely existed in his world for a brief instant. I had arrived, raised his hopes, only to abruptly abandon him once more. He had managed to forget me once more, living his life among the Chomps. He had been there for them and with them until the very end. After his difficult journey in finally embracing the path fate had laid out for him, I had come to meddle with his choice of being a part of that world. And now, I had returned, squandering all the pain and effort he had invested in forgetting me in an instant. In his eyes, I saw a mix of joy at seeing me again intertwined with desperation. He had relinquished the idea of us reuniting, yet even with me present, he refused to change his decision.

'Reela, I promise we will fix this! John, please, you need to let go and come with me!'

'I can't, Daniel… I've waited for you to return for so long. I waited and died, waited and died over and over again, yearning for this moment. He won't let me…'

'Who won't let you?' I moved closer to him, attempting to free Reela from the debris. Yet, my strength seemed to vanish, leaving me powerless. Though I could traverse their past, be seen and heard, I was prevented from altering their fate.

'He won't let me go.' John spoke, tears mingling with blood and grime on his cheeks. 'His hands are upon us. He won't allow you to take us away.'

'I'll find a way. Time?' I cried out, screening the surroundings. Desperation seized my heart as I stood alone on the brink of my greatest failure. Around us fire and death were mixing fearlessly.

'Daniel, my love… It's going to be OK. Yes, it's going to be OK.' John's voice shifted, his eyes transforming into pure gold. 'I love you. I loved the life I shared with you. I cherished your laughter, your tears, the way you turned my world upside down. I loved you before I even knew your true nature, and I loved you afterwards. I always will, forever.'

A radiant light emerged from his body, enveloping John's form before moving towards me. Large enough to take shape, the final Awoken One materialized, his countenance serene, a smile greeting me. His hand lifted, and his palm's brief, warm touch resonated within my heart, igniting a fiery blaze. He was channelling the pure power of memories, the multitude of moments preserved in the collection of life.

John smiled at me, seated on the cold airport ground where we first met each other. I could behold his drawings once more, his sandy hair falling over his gentle eyes. We were there, we were home, and everywhere that truly mattered. In the intimacy of our shared bed, in our playful runs around the kitchen island, we were everything to each other. We were there during the pivotal moments, when it truly counted, when I needed it the most.

He was conquering the world and my world with the magnetizing power of his smile. I adored his soul, I craved his body so many times that I could not recall them all. Once again I was letting him walk a few steps ahead, on the road, on our walks, so I could see him opening the way. The large shadows of the magnolia trees were back on our heads as we sat down in our favourite spot, in a hot summer afternoon. He was recreating a sleepy Daisy on a white canvas. Paint on his nose, on his hands, on my hands, on our bodies. We were the only thing we both desired. He was my only desire. He was present even after Noah, after the nightmares. In a foreign land, he waited for me, clutching the promise I had made, the pledge to our unbreakable love.

As John's spirit bestowed upon me our final ethereal kiss, an excruciating pressure built within my head, beneath my skin. My teeth ached, and my eyes felt as if they would burst from their sockets. Just as I felt I was about to merge with the melting matter surrounding me, Time summoned me back. The portal between events reappeared, yanking me away from the one I loved most. Like a thief, I had kindled his hope, only to rob him of the only thing he had left to offer: Eros. With the last of the Awoken Ones, Time executed his frigid, emotionless, surgical procedure, dragging me back. Touched once more by his gentle hand, we teleported back among friends, who saw me collapse to my knees in desperate sobbing.

'No, no!' Anita cried out, rushing towards me. 'What did you do? What did you do?' She demanded answers from the one she knew had wrought the unloving magic. Fury welled in her eyes, transforming her into a mirror image of Cherish, embodying the fragment of Love that composed her. 'You were meant to bring John back. Where is he? What have you done?'

'What happened?' Noah joined her in a comforting embrace. His hands on my shoulders pounded my soul, memory after memory. 'What happened?' But no explanation was forthcoming. Time receded, his face impassive, a trace of remorse faintly visible. On the other hand, Soul had departed from the group, the weight of my grief and despair burdening him with the agony of numerous lifetimes.

'The many things that were created were born out of love,' I wept with a broken heart, my voice quivering, vibrating like hundreds of echoes suddenly ricocheting through the air. 'All the things she created, the matter we are made of, stem from love. And where are they now? How do we recover from such pain and desolation? What remains to be salvaged if, to achieve it, we sacrifice the very thing that should remain inviolate?'

As my words rose and tears flowed, Cherish finally revived, manifesting as a luminous apparition hovering above Anita's shoulders. Her ethereal hands extended skywards, summoning the multitude of beings we had gathered on our arduous journey. One by one, the Awoken Ones we had liberated appeared, circling me, weaving a mournful melody. The choir of Love rallied around him, guarding me, sharing the heavy burden, bearing it themselves to afford me the opportunity to confront the agony of losing John.

Just as our journey had commenced, it now approached its close. With Noah's hands upon me, Anita at our side, the power of Love awoke at the moment of my greatest suffering. With the Seven at our flank and the multitude of others, the ritual set its foundation for its final enactment.

Chapter Thirty-One
The Rite

∞

'Sister?' someone behind me said. 'Is it really you?'

'Ashtar! You're back!' the other Awoken One exclaimed, breaking away from the group, tears in her eyes as she embraced her sister, who had emerged from my form just moments before.

Whatever trials they had undergone, whatever parting they had endured, their affection remained evident to all of us. Three nearly identical figures were weeping and hugging tightly, nearly melding into a single soul. Ashtar bore a striking resemblance to her sisters. With her blonde hair, she was as beautiful as her doubles, her eyes resembling freshly steeped tea, pale and sweet, glistening like honey in the sunlight. Watching them, Eleoen offered a brief smile before approaching me.

'Everything you feel, we feel.' He spoke. 'All that makes you, makes us. Don't carry the weight of regret, transforming it into anger towards the God.' He glanced at the gathering of the Awoken Ones. 'Forgive his missteps. Perhaps they aren't missteps at all…' However, his words of solace fell flat on my ears. No convincing, urging, or persuasion could sway me now.

Unsettled by the presence of so many individuals, unnerved by the multitude of gazes fixed upon me, I rose and walked towards Anita, who was still grappling with her separation from Cherish. Once again, the others were ready to move forwards, unconcerned about the Human vessel that had been left behind. She was no longer of use.

'Please, don't follow me,' I stated, my tone sharp, my hand extended to pull Anita to her feet. 'Let's go.'

Leaving them all surprised, we walked away, descending towards the edge of the same forest where we had initially met Trusk. Noah seemed bewildered. Whatever reason I had for excluding him from that private conversation, it wasn't fair. After all, we had shared the recent past, the past beyond that, and more. In his mind, he was losing me once again. In my mind, I was traversing the path of surrender.

'How are you feeling?' I began, my hand still holding hers.

'How am I feeling? How are you feeling?' Once again, her defences were up. We could have spent more productive time discussing me.

'Cherish has departed from you… Right now, I'm more concerned about you. Remember what we thought? That hosts carrying Awoken Ones might be…bearing a heavy cost? Tell me you're OK.' I moved closer, locking eyes with her.

'I'm OK. I feel…OK. I actually feel free, if that makes any sense.' She smiled.

'I'm afraid I won't be as fortunate, Anita…' I turned away.

'What do you mean?' She was visibly anxious.

'Noah and I are creations of a spell. We exist not to carry, but to…be. Love is ready to emerge. And when it does, the spell will dissolve.'

'What are you saying? You'll vanish? Noah will vanish?' She grasped my shoulder, trying to force me to face her.

'There's a great war on the horizon. The Gods will confront Nothing once and for all. But in this near future, there's no longer a "me" and "Noah" together. There's only one of us, Love.'

Anita withdrew her hands and took a few steps back, halting amidst the dead trees that once bordered the edge of a vast forest. She appeared upset, angry, and wounded. As she was mentally thrust back in time, looking for an explanation, Anita was catching up fast, just as rapidly as she had lost Cherish. In an instant, she returned to our present, after navigating back to the origin of all that madness.

'No,' she declared firmly. 'This isn't right. None of this is right. We were seeking answers, remember? We were trying to help you resolve your nightmares…to then return to our happy life…' Tears welled up in her eyes.

'We were meant to do this, Anita. It was our destiny.'

'We're just pawns now. Is this what we've become?'

'I'm afraid we always were,' I responded, offering a smile as I approached her. 'But we're good pawns. Pawns for the greater good.'

'So, this is it. You're just going to let it happen?' Anita continued to resist the idea.

'It doesn't matter whether I allow it or not. It's bound to happen, one way or another, which is why I'm here talking to you about it, in private.'

'What else is there?' She was angered, but her curiosity was piqued.

'Once this is all over, Time will bring John back. I'll make sure of it,' I quickly added after seeing her sceptical look. 'And when he returns, he won't find me here to explain things, to tell him all the things I wanted him to know.'

'You're asking me...' Troubled emotions flickered across Anita's face.

'You are the Awoken One of Memory, after all.' I smiled.

'I was...' Her tone turned sharp. 'We broke up.' And amidst that strange, dying land, two smiles emerged. Silence settled between us, our minds communicating without words, asking questions, offering answers, yet our mouths remained still. We knew our paths would inevitably diverge. Anita was the only one I could entrust with the task of informing John about what had happened to me. To convey my love for him and the lengths I would go to in order to spare him from suffering.

'Now, let's go back. Noah must be worried that we left without him.' I embraced her tightly, summoning all the strength I had left.

'He doesn't know, does he?'

'No, he doesn't. Revelia told me about their vision when Iris's dome was shattered, propelling them a year into the future. That year is nearly up. Whatever is approaching, it's coming swiftly.'

'Daniel, you have to tell him!'

'I know… Let's go now…'

Our journey back to the group was unhurried. Anita's mind wrestled with the myriad events set to unfold from that moment onwards. The prospect of an impending conclusion loomed large and nebulous. What would be left in the aftermath of the war remained an open question. A few steps from the others, she stopped again and turned to face me.

'What will happen? Who is going to be left…after?'

'You mean, when this is all over?'

'Yes. Let's say Love comes back, and you and the others will face this gigantic, evil threat. Will there be anything left standing? You said it as if I will still be here, able to tell John all the things you won't be able to.'

'Yeah, I'm not really sure. But I've seen Love do it before—saving the people of Earth, saving their lives and memories.'

'What if they fail? The Gods, I mean. Will you be born again? Will Cherish come back to me?' In Anita's words there was more than fear. She had grown fond of her connection with Cherish. Somehow, she had seen in the Awoken One that other half she could not find in anybody else.

'I'm afraid this is a plan you can't make this time. We have to hope it will work out.'

'If you get to be born again, and I survive, I'll make sure I find you! I'll be your Praetorian! I promise this to you.' And Anita's hands found mine once more.

Upon our return, Noah had rushed to us. In his mind, he was left behind in the stories, the secrets Anita and I told each other. As he moved closer, I briefly reassured him.

'I'm sorry, Noah. I didn't mean to leave you behind. I needed a moment alone with Anita. I needed to let out this huge pain I feel inside.' It wasn't fair, and he hadn't changed his feelings about it, but I eased his worries enough for him to wrap his arms around my shoulders.

It was strange how my relationship with Noah had evolved in a matter of months. I was terrified by the idea that I could fall in love with him, betraying John. I felt attracted to him in so many ways that it was beyond comprehension. At some point, I had rejected the idea, pushed him away, only to pull him close to me once again. Just a few days before, we were lying in bed, close to each other, travelling through the ancient past. But now, in the secret of my own thoughts, I finally came to understand what I truly felt for him. He was a part of me. His half of the God was joining my half, resonating with it, magnetizing it. We were hosting a soul that had been torn apart, and its pieces were finding each other, calling out to merge once more. I wasn't in love with Noah, I wasn't dreaming of an unchallenged lust. I was responding to a call that we were destined to answer. Like Anita just said, we were pawns, but moved for a greater good.

'I'm really sorry, Daniel. I didn't want this for us, for you. I wish we could erase it all,' he said.

'It's going to be alright. We will pull through.' And I hugged him back. 'We need to find some time alone soon. I need to talk to you.'

'Is everything OK?' he asked, briefly glancing at Anita.

'Define OK? Yes, I just want to be alone with you for a little while. We've been running, fighting, surrounded by so many people. We need to be alone now.'

'Daniel,' Health interrupted, 'I'm afraid we have to leave at once. The master of destruction might show his evil presence any second now.'

'The rite must happen in the same land where Love's node once stood and where Love crashed down after the fall,' Cherish chimed in. 'By the large stones where Iris's dome watched over the sacred spot.'

'There is nothing left in there,' Revelia said, with Trusk silently agreeing, nodding his puffy head.

'What we need is the sacred ground. That's all. The rest is only smoke and traditions that came much later,' Cherish continued. 'Like Health, Love needs the energy that was dispersed in those lands. His core has penetrated the very roots of that place. This is why Daniel and Noah were born there. This is why Iris was holding the dome in that exact place.'

'Daniel,' Anita whispered, 'you were not just born in Ireland. You are actually from the same place as Noah?' Incredibly, she was still seeking the same answers she'd talked about just a few minutes earlier.

'At last, we are closing the circle,' I said.

In the sweep of her arms, Cherish called all the Awoken Ones to the same act. One by one, they turned into bright flickers and disappeared within my body. Noah looked at me, once more perplexed. Although we shared the same purpose and were two exact halves of one God, the Awokens were moving in and out of my core only. I was the one who had gone solo in some of our visions. But I knew why. Revelia had given me the final hint through a secretive confession. In the glimpse of the future, one of us was still walking the lands of our world. It was no coincidence and it was not cruelty. It was the only way through.

Once all the magic disappeared within my heart, the Gods moved into a circle. In the middle of that embrace, Anita, Revelia, and Trusk were getting ready to be moved again. In a snap, the landscape suddenly changed. The ashy, rough Runae was replaced by large trees, branches scattered everywhere, mixing with the aftermath of Noah's home's explosion. The once upside-down tree was reduced to a dead bush, its branches crushed into themselves; there was no life left. A few of the stones were still standing, their familiar marks still visible. Upon our arrival, the Gods turned around, their eyes wide open, their hands ready for battle. The enemy had stood there once; Death himself had turned that place into a replica of his own court.

There was no Harpy left to watch the area, no scout roaming around looking for enemies. They were all gone, as gone as Iris and her dome. We were free to act, to move swiftly. The milestones towards that goal had been challenging, painful, and full of misery. Strangely, the most important step was coming to us unusually quietly. If that was going to turn the war in our favour, it wasn't showing any hint of an upcoming fight.

The three Gods moved beside a few of the big rocks that were still standing in their positions; they were ready to initiate the final spell. With his clepsydra out in the open, Time glowed a bright green, bending space and rewinding the centuries, shifting to a time when the ancient site was still intact. Twelve large, grey pillars appeared, taking the place of the bare ruins we had seen in their future. Inside the inner circle formed by the silent stones, four more, smaller and wider stones surrounded a reborn tree. With Health's hand on its side, a golden light infiltrated its essence. Its roots planted in the ground, its branches unnaturally enlarged, myriad pink flowers multiplied on its top, like a bright, magical crown.

After a few moments, a veil formed between us and the sky above. Its glowing, transparent surface spread in all directions, engulfing the space around us; its edge travelled far, moving towards the same green grass Health had brought back to life. As its touch met the ground, a sudden flash dispersed among the old trees. In the exact place where Iris's magic once stood, a new dome was formed, stronger and brighter than before. We were safe, frozen in time, unreachable by evil.

'May the power of the ancient ones keep this space obscured from evil,' Time declared, 'Outside of time and space, it will not keep Nothing away from us, but it will make us invisible to his wicked army.'

'Daniel, Noah,' Soul added, 'the moment has come. Please stand by the tree.'

Soul's words struck into our hearts like merciless blades. We had taken thousands of steps towards that very moment, often unsure where we were headed. We had learned who we were and who we needed to become again, yet we still weren't fully prepared. I needed to talk to Noah, there were so many things to say.

Deep inside, I hoped he wouldn't go back to his usual self, rushing into what was next. It was as if he could read my mind—Noah looked at me, challenged. He wasn't ready, as I wasn't. There was more to unfold, more to do, more to say before we could awaken Love, or so we thought. We both briefly glanced at Anita. She had been our guide, our help, our sanity since the start of our journey. But she couldn't speak a word. In her eyes, I could see myself talking to her in Runae by the forest. Somewhere, deep inside, she was telling me to wait a little longer, to plan things properly, to weigh the decision carefully.

'No,' I blurted out without thinking. 'Not yet.'

'Daniel, it has to happen now,' Health replied with a soft smile.

'We can't do this. Not before I talk to Noah.'

Under the stunned gaze of the Gods, I grabbed Noah's hands and led him away, far from their ears and sight.

Stopping at the edge of the new dome, I felt that a final confession needed to happen, within the secrecy of that renewed prison. We were following the steps of our written destiny, but we were going to walk it with our heads held high, fully aware of what lay ahead. Noah needed to know.

'Suddenly, I'm not ready for this. Is this normal?' he asked before I could speak.

'It is for me. It has been for me all along, and now it is for you too.'

'I know. You've always been telling me to wait…even now, in this late hour, you told even the Gods to wait. I have to admit, you're stronger than me.'

'I told them to wait not because I want to. You're becoming me now, just as much as I'm becoming you. I want to move forwards. I know we have to, but not before you know what I know,' I said, moving a bit further away, letting a flat, large rock become the keeper of my confession. We were mirroring ourselves back in time, sitting on a bench in one of Rome's many parks.

'I knew you had something going on. Tell me, please,' Noah said, sitting beside me, his eyes locked on to mine.

'You saw what happened between Cherish and Anita. We wondered what would become of the two of them once the Awoken One woke up. I know what will happen to us two as well, now that Love is about to exist again.'

'Tell me…I'm ready.'

'We are the two halves of Love. We will exist as one, in the shape of one God, one body. However, one of us will have to remain here, alive. There is something the Gods had not foreseen.'

'There's a reason you've been going solo in some of our visions,' Noah interrupted, standing up. 'There's a reason why the Awokens and the Sevens came to you only. There's a reason why Dõron protected you more closely than she did with me. It wasn't just because of Athymos.'

'Yes…' I replied, turning my face away. Though I knew I was about to tell Noah he would be safe, it felt like I was sending him to die, sacrificing him for the greater good. '

'And so you got access to another secret? What am I missing? What are they missing?'

'The moment I came back with Eros, as I was desperately trying to convince myself John wasn't gone, I saw Creation. I saw her power, her making and the spell she cast on the Gods. It is all true. The artefacts are the beacon of their powers and, as they all have one, so did their mother, our mother.'

'Please don't tell me we are going after another amulet. I just want this to be over. I want to go back to our lives, together. I want to get back the ones we lost, get back your John, go back feeling free from all this pain and grow old beside you, Anita, Trusk, Revelia. Tell me we can…'

'We could, you could. But you have to do something for me first. I won't be there to guide you, so it's important to agree on this now.'

'I won't let you! You can't let me continue this alone!' His voice rose a little, his words trembling. 'We're in this together! We go together, or we stay together!'

'It's not about going or staying. It's about keeping one of us alive, Noah. Try to understand, I don't want to see you vanish into nothing!'

'Do I? Do I want to see you vanish into nothing?' he replied almost immediately. 'I know my attraction to you, our desire for each other, it's not what I thought it was before. I know it was Love calling from afar, telling me we're meant to merge our souls into one. But if one of us gets to keep his body, his life, why not you? You have John, Anita, people you're connected to. I have nothing and no one!'

'You do now. This has been your journey all along. Yours was to become the keeper, the one who will carry the friendships we've built, standing beside the people we care about the most. Helping them in the aftermath. My journey was the opposite. Learning to let go, learning the value of sacrifice in the name of Love. You had no one to love, and now you get to have many to protect. I had many, and I had to learn to let them go…'

'Are you saying this was part of our destiny? Learning these two ways of love? To have and to lose? Are you saying we were meant to take two different paths?'

'Yes, a part of it. We'll be together for eternity, but one of us will have the chance to return to their Human life. I didn't want it this way. Here, now, as I'm talking to you, I'm accepting the impending future. But I couldn't truly do it if you weren't going to embark on our next journey aware of what awaits us… Now, I need you to do something for me. To do something when I'm gone…'

'Will I remember all of this? Will you remember all of this, me?'

Noah was gradually coming to terms with his greatest defeat. He had wanted to move forwards all his life, and instead, he had to stay behind. In a cruel twist, I wanted the exact opposite. I wanted to stay behind, to follow like a shadow to John's bright soul, to be a friend in the background for Harry, to be a guest peering into Anita's life. Yet, I was being pushed forwards, forced to accept the leading role in the final act. My call to Love was to act. Noah's was to accept.

As he turned back and sat beside me again, his hands in mine, we connected one last time. In the sanctuary of our deepest secret, our minds intertwined, we summoned seven of the most powerful Awoken Ones. They materialized in our reality, appearing as transparent beings, white ghosts called upon when needed most. Agapei, Storgén, Prometheus, Eros, Philiat, Pragma, and Xena enclosed the two of us in a circle of emotions, their hands extended towards us, weaving a melodious blend of serendipity and sorrow. They manifested in our reality what Noah and I were feeling inside—our willingness to yield.

'Seven,' I said. 'The Gods are moving forwards without a vital piece of information. There is a reason why the Harpies—and Death most of all—could trace us back. There is a reason why he was entrusted with the evil deed, riding the carriage of destruction. Our artefacts, the Gods' artefacts, come from the same power. The same power Creation embedded in the four planets across the universe. The same power she infused her artefact with. Although the sceptre is back to its rightful owner, there is one more in their hands. Noah will have to continue this journey on his own. Yet love and hope will have to stay strong. It's time to act.'

'Daniel...' Noah whispered.

'I know. I love you, with or without Love inside me. Here and anywhere we will be. You will always be a part of me and in the hearts of the ones who stand by your side. Now, Seven!'

'Choose to give,' Prometheus said.

'Choose to stay,' Pragma added.

'For the ones we loved...' Storgén continued.

'For the ones we care for the most...' Philiat said.

'For the ones we never met...' Xena added.

'For the ones we cannot live without,' Eros continued.

'We do it again, for the greater good,' Agapei concluded.

My eyes and Noah's met again. Enveloped in a soft, warm light, we moved in an instant. From the far side of that quiet place to the very centre of the dome. Under the astonished gaze of Anita, Revelia, and Trusk, we found ourselves standing by the large tree, hand in hand, eyes locked on to each other. The three Gods were waiting for that precise moment. Long were their cloaks, shining were their faces; their power suddenly resonated with ours, growing in magnitude, stripping that world of every shadow.

Their artefacts floated and spun around an invisible centre of gravity; they called Noah's heart out into the open. Finding my shell, attracted to it, it settled on its core, touching the very white inside. Like a brief leap into my past, I saw John's grand paintings again, the ones I had seen with the eyes of my pure imagination, the Gods represented in their true powers, one by one. And now, we were painting the resurrecting rite with the colours of renewed magic, tipping over its final edge.

The Gods fused their nature with their power, transforming into luminescent, pulsating stars; embracing their ultimate destiny, they reached the far walls of the dome, penetrating the matter, surging from the very ground where Noah and I stood. A final glance at the one I cared for the most, Trusk was holding on to Revelia's hand, a look of worry on his face. Her eyes burned red, flames of raging fire, spilling the fierce power of prophecy into the space. Anita met my eyes in a final, fleeting glance.

Her tears flowing was the last thing Daniel remembered as he passed on the duty to someone else, someone with a greater mission. In the crumbling of his soul, as every single particle of his humanity dissolved into thin air, one final heartbeat shook the ground. Its roaring sound had a name: John.

Chapter Thirty-Two
Love

∞

An unstoppable blast of energy was released to every corner of the forest. Like hundreds of birds scattering in the skies, pink petals flew all across the dome, making it flicker and wobble between realities. Although strong, Time's magic was no match. Cracks appeared all over the surface, sending rays of light from the past to the present, and from the present to the future. Hanging on by a bare whisper, the dome was about to collapse again.

As the bright light vanished, one being was still standing by the naked tree. Noah's figure was holding on to the same spot, his hands still hanging in the air, holding someone who was no longer there. His eyes were lost in nothing, his expression dull; he had lost connection with Daniel and with his own power. Love's half had left him, setting him free, leaving him empty. The Gods had disappeared, taking Daniel with them to an unknown realm, and sending Anita into a whirlpool of desperation. In Revelia's arms, she was crying from a painful loss. Trusk moved a little away, his wings down, looking for Daniel, his eyes darting frantically from place to place, unable to accept the fact that his trusted companion was gone.

'Daniel?' His voice was low; its sound was broken. He moved close to the only one spared by the rite. 'Noah? Where is Daniel? Noah?'

'The future is becoming present,' Revelia answered. 'Trusk, this is what we knew would happen. Daniel is gone...'

Those last words struck Anita's heart like violent mauls from a restless beast. She was barely standing on her feet, her arms folded around her chest, her face immersed in darkness. Noah woke up, brought back by Trusk's hand, pulling him back to reality.

'It's gone... I don't feel it any more...' And he looked at his own hands, his heart robbed, devoid. 'I don't feel him any more. My head is empty. I can't feel Daniel's mind inside mine.'

'Where are the others?' Revelia went on, her eyes still shining like rubies. 'We can't stay here long. The dome is about to collapse!' A few seconds into the future was all the Leonty could master.

In the blink of an eye, the spell above their heads broke apart, like pulverized crystals. Time was ticking again; their breaths merged with the real world, and the four found themselves uncovered, in the open, in dangerous vulnerability. Their fates were soon to follow the same path the dome had taken; they would become easy prey for the evil that had sensed the surge of power brought by the rite.

'Trusk!' Revelia continued. 'Bring us under your magic. We need to disappear from sight, fast!'

'Here!' And the Chomp quickly complied, flaring up and raising his magic flame on top of his head; the four disappeared.

'How could they just…leave us?' Noah's sorrow from defeat was still evident.

'It's all they've been doing, after all,' Anita replied, her tone not judgemental, but filled with realization. 'They've been working towards this moment for centuries and centuries. We were only a small paragraph in the infinite book of the Gods.'

'It was Time who sent Varayal to its end,' Revelia said unexpectedly, walking slowly beside the others. They were leaving the dangerous place behind. 'He went to the past and took the tiara from Soul, removing his only source of power.'

'Runae's very same fafe…' and Trusk sighed heavily.

'But Daniel is different. Love is different!' Anita continued. 'If all of this has happened for a reason, I'm certain he will make sure everything and everyone will come back!'

'Love was not able to stop Nothing from sending the deadly meteor to Earth. He could only try to save the ones left…' Noah recalled one of his latest visions.

'What's going to happen now? Revelia, Trusk… You have no home to go back to. And probably neither do I and Noah. This is not how I imagined it would end.'

As the group turned the corner, exiting the woods, the solitary road Noah and Anita had seen before, on their way to the house by the lake, was still there. The old car was still parked on the side; its rusty look had worsened with time and continuous rain. Some of the strange stickers had faded away, turning yellow and grey.

'I forgot we borrowed this squeaky wrench! Niall is going to kill me!' Noah exclaimed.

'Do you think it still works?' Anita asked, as the Runae folks looked at the lifeless relic, puzzled.

'We can try…' Noah replied. 'Where do we go? Noah's Bridge?' And with a strong pull, the driver's door opened with a creaking sound.

Although old and parked there for a long time, the car could still surprisingly perform its magic. When it was turned on, Anita let Revelia and Trusk in. The two couldn't believe how strange that Human machinery was, and once a few bumping sounds echoed loudly and the wheels started to spin, they squeezed together in the back seat, terrified.

'Do we have somewhere to go?' Anita asked, holding on to the precarious seat. The car was sending all sorts of warnings.

'In town? I can get us somewhere,' Noah said, turning left, leaving the country road for a bigger, faster one. A few other, newer cars were speeding up.

'We can't let them be seen. It has to be somewhere safe!' And Anita turned around. 'You two, get down a little, make sure no one sees you. Actually, can't you use the Flare again now?'

'No,' Noah exclaimed. 'Don't! The radius of that thing is too big. It would make the car disappear completely. Not safe at all!'

But the two passengers were too confused to listen to any word that was said. They were pressing their backs against their seats, as if they could suddenly merge with the old fabric. Their faces were in shock, Revelia's eyes were shining red. She was searching for imminent danger while in that vehicle of death. Luckily, the forgot, borrowed gift resisted long enough to get them safely to Noah's Bridge. Right in the same spot where she had been taken, Noah turned off the engine, and after asking Trusk to quickly use his magic, he let the passengers out.

'We need to eat,' Noah said. 'Let's go to my house, I'll get some food for us right after.'

'What time is it?' Anita looked around, a few steps away from Noah's home. 'There is this strange light in the sky, this greyish haze all over…'

'I have no watch or phone any more. I only hope Time's dome wasn't like Iris's. The last thing we need is to have lost another year!'

They had not travelled through time again. Time's magic was about containment, a glitch in the flow of the hours. There was no ancient spell that anchored that place to a specific day. But the world around them had indeed changed. As if a powerful storm was approaching from the far east, the early hours of the morning were turned into a frozen, dark evening. Some people came out of their homes, their shops, gathering together on the streets, questioning the sudden, worrying change. From the backyard of Noah's home, some of his neighbours spotted him while looking at the far horizon. Through the kitchen window, Anita could see the distant lake and the tiny island in its centre. Something large and obscure was rumbling, rattling, electrifying the atmosphere. Unusual in that far southern place, rays of green and pink light moved across the sky from one part to another. Like a magical aurora, the unexpected northern lights were taking many by surprise.

'Pipes are open. Let's put the heating on, and then we could all use a shower…' Noah said, walking back in.

'What's going on out there?' Anita asked, getting Revelia's attention.

'Is this normal for your world?' she asked in return.

'Not really. Not here, anyway.'

Noah moved away, looking for a few things the unexpected guests might need. His home was simple; a few pieces of furniture sat alone, unable to fill the space organically. Here and there, some pictures collected dust. In a lonely corner, an old, metallic chair quietly stood. It was clear to Anita that this was where Noah's mother must have spent her last days on Earth. A side table nearby still displayed all sorts of documents Noah had pulled while searching for answers, looking for the artefact, his past, his future.

After Noah left the house to find them something to eat, a sad silence fell on the three left behind. As Anita showed them how to use the bath to get clean, they took turns, towels ready in their hands. In the meantime, their minds rewound the latest events, questioning their future. For a long time, it had felt like they were on a quest, with only one goal. Once achieved, they would come back home like heroes. But nothing turned out to be true. They had lost who they were, where they came from, where they were going, who they were going to be from now on. While Anita could still rejoice about being back on Earth, the other two were in a different situation.

'Are we going fo be living in fhis world now?' Trusk asked, looking at Revelia, who was drying his curly hair with a small towel.

'You should be going home where you belong. Your real home, the one that looks like the day Time brought everyone back.' Anita spoke before the Leonty.

'If he doesn't use his power to make it happen, there's not much to go back to. The only ones we still care about, they're in this house.' And to those words, Anita moved closer, taking Revelia's hands.

'If that's the case, you can stay with me! There is no way we are going to part ways unless you have a home to go to. And maybe even then...' she added, smiling. 'We have gone through so much together. We will always be together.'

Once Trusk was dry, Revelia took his spot, and with Anita's help, she managed to remove weeks of dirt, dust, and pain from her inked skin. Helping her dry her long hair, Anita asked:

'Is it something all Leonty have? Those marks on your skin...' And she ran a few fingers over Revelia's shoulders.

'In the last few yacs, yes. This is because we were the only ones left...' And Revelia moved her hair to one side, showing the intricate marks down her neck.

'The only ones left?'

'Yes. The only ones with magic in our veins. This is what it is. The power running through our bodies was made evident by the marks our skin. This is how our sister made sure we would be feared and respected. But Una exterminated every soul, every living being anyway. She didn't want *them* to fear us. She wanted us to fear *her.*'

'It must have been terrible. Daniel, Noah and I have seen in Una's mirror. We know the horrible things that happened to your kind... I can't even imagine the pain.'

'Yes. As I said to Daniel once, she was born evil. There was no way to hide it. There was no way to hide the massive power running in her bones.'

'Has she ever used it against you?' Anita asked, unafraid of getting too close to painful topics.

'She has. In the beginning. Over time, I learned to anticipate what she wanted and avoided putting her in a position where she needed it. Knowing how evil she was, I couldn't risk her manipulating my mind, controlling it. She could have asked me to jump right down from her keep, and I would have done it.'

'But your sisters couldn't resist her?'

'It wasn't possible without foreseeing the danger. Their steps were watched, counted; the trap was always ready to snap at my sisters' will. Demetra might have resisted, perhaps. But fear was Una's second-best power. A power that didn't require any magic.' And to those words Anita moved closer to Revelia, hugging her.

In between grief, loss and pain, Anita could see her love for her passing through. On the other hand, Revelia was discovering for the first time the power of a touch brought from love. There was no dark witchcraft, there was no manipulation in it. Friendship and empathy were showing themselves to her as if made of a new, surging magic.

'I'm back! OK, there's trouble coming our way!' Noah shouted from the hall, two large bags clutched to his chest. His face looked worried. 'Whatever this thing is, up in the sky, it's not natural!'

The four rushed outside through the backyard doors. To the left and the right, Noah's neighbours had multiplied in numbers. Friends and family had gathered to witness the strangest weather phenomenon they had ever seen in their entire lives. Feeling the pressure, Noah suggested they speed things up and get some food before being forced to run again. Whatever was happening out there could easily find them.

It wasn't too long before another powerful warning shook their hearts and every living soul at Noah's Bridge. Just as they were about to finish their meal, a thundering roar ran across the space, followed by a high-pitched blast that shattered all the glass windows. The four dropped everything on the table, terrified. The ground trembled under their feet as they rushed outside onto the main road.

Hundreds of people had preceded them, panicking and shouting in the streets. The skies turned purple, and in a vortex of elements, a point in the far east shone brightly, like the sun had grown ten times its size at sunset.

'This can't be good!' Anita shouted as she quickly moved to avoid people pushing and running for their lives.

'Revelia!' Noah yelled, witnessing some men and women looking right at them and shouting even louder. 'You're visible!'

But before Trusk could put his magic to use, another blast reached the lands, pushing them and everyone else to the ground. Cars joined the screams with their alarms blaring, and pieces of glass filled the air around homes and shops. Far away, invisible to Human eyes, the war between the Gods had begun.

'What's going on?' Noah said in shock, covering his eyes from the dust rising from the ground.

'It feels like that day in the Ancient Mirrors,' Revelia said, her long hair flying up, pulled by a mysterious gravitational force. 'The day of the Great Dawn!'

Cars started moving by themselves, dragged by an unseen hand. Some still had people inside, attempting to escape by driving, but the vehicles were unresponsive. Street lights and poles bent, their roots cracking the ground, and shop signs detached from their frames, moving towards the same bright point in the sky. As Anita and Noah were losing their sense of gravity, their feet floating in the air, they were about to join the large mass that had formed above their heads.

Suddenly, the hovering force gave up. It turned into a breeze, losing power and being mitigated by the protective power of the Chomp, who raised his hands above his head, the Flare burning bright. The shielding veil fell on his friends, reducing the impact of the new threat. As time seemed to flow backwards, the winds changed direction, the pulling turned to pushing, and everything that had been taken away moments before came back with rage and anger. Cars and items crashed to the ground and against walls, sending the few people left into a frenzy.

Someone had sucked out the very essence of their lives, everything they owned, and was now regurgitating it against their masters. With it, a surge of a large wave, water taken away from its resting place at the lake, was responding to someone's will, moving into the village, overcoming natural barriers, and crashing into buildings. The ancient bridge, the symbol of that old place, was shattered into raw stones and bricks by the explosion of the raging river. As if the nature swelled its molecules, its matter was enlarging and pushing against its own people, who fled to the far side of the land, running into the woods.

'We need to leave now!' Noah said, terrified.

'Can you pull us up?' Revelia asked Trusk, who was still holding on to his power.

'If's foo sfrong. I can barely hold my Flare!'

'I'll carry you this time,' Noah replied. 'We'll do it the old way, *run!*'

I knew I had left the greatest part of my life, of my being, somewhere down on Earth. Somehow, I knew they would still move ahead, determined to survive, determined to finish what I had asked them to do, even if I was gone. But my soul, my mind, my new will were put to a different use. I had finally come to do much more than just be. I was back to protect Earth, protect the Gods, and bring my true mother back.

Evil had a very different plan in store for me, for all of us. He had walked the lands of that and many other planets for a very long time, under a different name and different nature. Through the hands and eyes of the Harpies, he retained the role of a king for too long. Now that we returned in full strength, Nothing could not fight the war by proxy any more. We were too big of a threat. We had to be put down before attempting the impossible. With his core almost cleansed by Health and Love's spell, after lurking in the shadows for centuries and allowing his nullifying essence to eradicate the very magic of creation, he could finally face us all, his power vastly increasing, crashing against the Earth's atmosphere, pulling its waters, and moving its mountains. He had come to bring the last resisting world to its end, to bring us all into him, into the immensity of his darkness, into the wrathful, immortal, never-ending nothing.

∞

The End

The Power of Love
The Two

Epilogue
Creation's Sacrifice

∞

In their final moments together, Daniel never fully confessed to Noah the entire vision passing through the eyes of his mind. As the clock was ticking its final hour, the most important thing he had to share was Noah's next move, nothing else. But Daniel knew, and I knew how important everything was. Would I have troubled his mind with the details of what I had sent to my host? To what extent could Noah take it? No, he couldn't. Nevertheless, by the grace of a renewed knowledge gifted by my beloved sister, the story was finally told.

As it was long agreed, Soul, Time and I met on Talush, Health's protected planet, a world of immeasurable beauty and strength. A land of powerful beings, nature was embodying the immortality of her master. While everything around showed the pride and beauty of our mother, the threat of destruction and emptiness lurked in the shadows, already drawing near its adversary. The five of us had gathered deep within a vast forest. The trees were ten times as tall as we Gods, and the bushes and flowers spilled colours of magnificent vitality. At the very heart of the woods, roots and branches formed an incredible storm of beauty and strength. With only the sky as their limit, a gigantic, living structure sat peacefully in the green land. Everywhere, beings moved back and forth.

Following Health's instructions, they were preparing to resist an impending diabolical attack. Some of them resembled my beloved Humans from Earth. Their strong muscles defining their limbs, their hair long and shiny, they looked powerful and yet graceful at the same time. With deep, dark skin and sweat on their foreheads, they were organizing the counterattack to an ambush that had occurred in the recent days. In the polar regions of the planet, Nothing's army had taken advantage of the perpetual shadow to secretly construct a weapon of destruction.

'I heard the Hoonits talking about something in the far north,' Time said as he arrived. His face was shaded by concerns for leaving Runae unprotected, and he seemed visibly unhappy to be there.

'The one we don't speak of has come up with a new trick!' Health replied, moving beside Soul, who was silently observing the beings of Talush. 'People are falling seriously ill everywhere. The disease is spreading rapidly, changing and mutating before we can address and eradicate it!'

'It's more than just a disease!' Soul finally added. 'It's not only affecting their bodies. Somehow, it penetrates their cores, infecting their thoughts and souls from within. It's as if they have lost their own will.'

'It's what they were before you came into existence,' Creation interjected. 'Nothing is causing them to regress, undoing what we have done! This is how they were before you and your sister existed.'

'We need to move faster, Mother,' I said with a sorrowful expression. 'Somehow, these creatures have lost the most vital parts of themselves.'

'Time, Soul, Health!' Creation called, capturing their attention. We fell silent, our eyes and ears focused.

As we looked on, Creation extended her arms in the air, her hands up, summoning three shining objects from an unknown reality. Suddenly, the entire space around us froze. Every Hoonit in the far-below land stopped their work, captivated by the bright light emanating from the large wooden structure. Rays of warm light filtered through the branches, bouncing off thousands of leaves in an intricate dance of pure magic, leaving them spellbound. At the base of the tall structure, two pointy heads moved away from the same gateway they had guarded for years. Their rounded, large eyes gazed upwards. Their skinny, knotty appearance made them look like walking trees. On the tips of their heads, a similar tuft of hair popped up, standing alone.

'These, my children, are yours to keep,' Creation continued, her voice resonating from all around. 'They were forged from fire and energy, strong as your will, made of the same substance as you are. For now, they won't appear to have much power. But in time, they will become the key to our victory in this battle!'

'What are they meant to do?' Health asked, her eyes reflecting the same bright golden light emitted by the three artefacts.

'If I succeed, these will preserve your lives. It's essential that you never part from them, ever! Allow them to become a part of you, an extension of your power, of who you are.'

'There are only three…' Time interjected, his eyes ever keen for scrutiny. 'Where is the fourth one?'

'I already have mine,' I replied, materializing a reddish stony diamond resting on a white shell. 'I assisted Mother as she infused them with her true power.'

'Your brother gave them shapes that he felt were right for each of you. I think you can guess who gets what,' Creation added with a brief smile.

As our gathering had been primarily planned by our mother so she could share her intentions, her sudden departure caught me off guard. Her plans felt clear before, yet I couldn't comprehend why she chose to withhold the true nature of those artefacts from my brothers and my sister. As they were now, they were merely decorative objects without any power or magic. Without Creation's spell, they remained empty vessels for a magic that, if in danger, had nowhere to go.

'So, is this it?' Time wondered aloud as our maker suddenly left. She had smiled once more, handed the artefacts to their rightful owners, and then departed, dissolving into nothing.

'I don't understand what they're supposed to do,' Soul added. 'I don't sense any power or essence emanating from them.'

'Love?' Health turned her attention to me, as the other two Gods had done before her, awaiting an answer.

'I'm not entirely certain of Mother's exact intent. She said they are meant to protect us in times of peril. Somehow, she found a way to bind our energy, our true essence, to these objects. In case we die, we should be able to return through them,' I explained, revealing the truth all at once.

'But they're not yet…ready?' Soul inquired again. 'What is lacking?'

'To defy the laws of matter, she must have discovered something quite peculiar,' Time speculated.

'Does it really matter?' Health's enthusiasm remained undiminished. 'We have finally a way through! This is what we needed to defeat him!'

'At what cost, sister?' Time's question quickly dampened her renewed joy. 'What's the catch?'

Health wasn't allowing our brother's pragmatic viewpoint to mar the significance of that news in her mind. She was steadfast in believing that could be the turning point in our long-awaited triumph against evil. A few moments later, the master of time departed from the gathering, hurrying off. He wanted to return to Runae, completing a spell he had set in motion without our knowledge. In his mind, that was the way forwards. As us three walked through the breath-taking gardens surrounding Health's kingdom, Soul began to speak.

'I've been contemplating something,' he began. 'What if the worlds we've sworn to protect could do more than merely exist? I've been thinking about what you said, Love, during our last meeting. Perhaps there is good in granting them power of their own.'

'Do you still fear it might dilute our strength instead of amplifying it?' I replied, handing a flask containing a mysterious greyish fluid back to a Hoonit who looked at me in return, with pride.

'I do, but I also see how it could enable them to fight for what is rightfully theirs,' Soul continued, smiling at the same Hoonit who poured some of the magical liquid onto a small plant, transforming it into a tree within seconds.

'We need to ensure that we, and they, are prepared for what lies ahead. I'm certain Mother's plan will work, but what if it demands a heavy toll?' Health mused, moving her hand near a massive tree, as if inviting us to enter it. 'After all, even with the creation of these nodes, these passages…what exactly are we preventing?'

'You know well, sister,' I replied. 'These weren't created to prevent Nothing from attacking and destroying us, but to make it impossible for his armies to pour from one world to the next. Remember, we can't sever the magic connections between our worlds. They stand at the four corners of the universe, each holding the edge of Mother's making. Our magic and so the evil magic could flow in and out of this very planet if it weren't for this node.'

'That's exactly what I mean,' Health responded energetically. 'We've been thinking too narrowly. I truly hope Mother's new trick will have far-reaching effects. She must have found a way to do more than this.' And with a circular motion of her arms, she created a passage through the thick bark, cutting it as if it were fragile paper. 'Please, promise your next visit will be soon. I have a terrible feeling that something is coming, and it's coming soon.'

Upon those worrying words, Soul and I departed, each returning to our respective worlds, carrying the weight of an uncertain future on our hearts. Little did we know, it would be the last time we set eyes upon Talush in all its splendour and strength. As we moved through the passage, a thunderous roar erupted from a distance, causing the magical walkway to flicker and then shut down entirely. Caught off guard by shock and surprise, Talush was devoured by rage and magic; a massive wall of fire began to spread across the lands. Health's expression turned horrified as she was thrust to the ground by a powerful surge of energy. From both the west and the east, the sounds of screams and rumbles reverberated loudly. Hoonits everywhere ran for their lives, unable to confront the enemy who had descended with full force, his grasp crushing the core of their planet.

The newfound delight Health had experienced just moments before was obliterated. In mere moments, dreams and hopes were dashed by the diabolical will of Nothing, who finally revealed his true form. A vast, ominous shadow began to extend across the sky, transforming day into night and bringing a frigid, deathly sensation. Small stones and lifeless leaves scurried about on the ground, gradually lifting, pulled by an eerie, compelling force. As that power intensified, Health's feet lifted from the burning soil, raising her into the air. Animals, plants, Hoonits, and all living creatures floated, powerless to resist. Trees were uprooted from their homes, their foundations shattered. Dwellings and buildings followed suit, crumbling into dust as their structural integrity dissolved. In the petrified gaze of the God, everything began to disintegrate into a thin, dark substance. Cells and molecules were ruthlessly torn apart, dragged by an unrelenting, malevolent intent. As Creation's masterpiece was rewound to nonexistence, our mother appeared by Health's side. Flickering with magic, her hands on my sister's shoulders, she gazed at her with a mix of terror and determination.

'There is no time!' she urged. 'You must leave now!'

'No, Mother!' Health retorted with fury. 'I won't abandon them. They… They all are my children to protect!'

'I haven't completed the spell! You are still mortal,' Creation stated, pushing her will upon her daughter. 'If you stay, you'll be lost forever!'

'The very reason I exist is precisely the reason why I can't leave them behind.'

However, the odds were set against Health's determination. The ground and sky began to warp. Like wax exposed to excessive heat, everything melted away, drawn towards a dark point in the distant atmosphere. They were on the brink of becoming part of the same matter as a black hole that materialized out of nowhere, consuming every particle in its path.

'My child, this is beyond repair. You must go. I need to initiate the rite of power now, releasing the enchantment onto your artefacts. Please, make your way to the node and reach your brother Soul!'

Urged by our mother's plea, Health summoned enough power to wrest herself from Nothing's grasp; her course was clear. She had to reach the colossal tree before its magic could be overwhelmed and extinguished, entangling her in Talush until its end. Creation vanished with a snap, her physical nature left behind, transitioning into her true form of pure energy, ascending above the world and soaring towards her adversary. Her power, immensely potent, pushed her between evil and Talush, her eyes ablaze.

'I warned you before!' she cried out into the void. 'I am the future; these worlds and my creation are things you cannot take away!'

'Your existence defies me, defies all that should be,' a voice replied. Something was forming before the God. 'You shall return to me, and with you, every abomination you've crafted…'

'No! Your time is over. This is the era of existence!'

A colossal being manifested in front of Creation. Twin hollows stared back at her. His mouth was like a vortex, spinning and drawing life from all around. The God of every making appeared minuscule, like a tiny radiant point into the darkness of the universe. Her determination unwavering, her power paled before the King of Obscurity. As the gravitational pull intensified, a spear-like power shot forth against Creation, who struggled for her life. In the attempt to progress with her plan, she willingly drew Nothing closer who stripped her of her power like flashes of fierce flames. In the fleeting span of a moment, just before the enemy could strike her down, Health interposed herself between them, absorbing the blow into her essence.

'No!' Creation screamed, stunned by her daughter's fate. The God of Health was pierced through, torn into shreds of energy. 'This is not how it shall be!'

With raw power born from grief and desperation, Creation's energy surged tenfold. Her hands outstretched into space, she reached every trace of Health's remaining essence, reassembling them before her enemy's eyes. As the weak and barely surviving God materialized once again, Creation whispered:

'Listen to me, run to Soul and heal. Warn him!' Creation's head turned towards her daughter, sheltering her once more. 'As all fades before coming back, nothing dies but only transforms, as pure life regains its purpose, my plea is set. May my energy find its rightful hosts through their magic. May their creations preserve their essence until they can reunite!'

Health's sceptre appeared in the darkness of the final hour, shining brightly before Nothing's eyes, who'd just witnessed yet another unexpected defiance. Creation released the full power of her being into space, reaching the edge of the universe, flowing into the Gods' artefacts, piercing evil like thousands of poisoned thorns. With a staggering blow, Creation transformed her life into a potent weapon, a spell of hope, an invocation of faith and eternal existence. The mother of everything that existed made the ultimate sacrifice. Everyone's path was laid out once and for all.

As she vanished, a promise was forged. A new chapter of a never-ending war was written in secret; the new era began. She had given away her life to protect her children and everything she had made, inflicting her will right into her enemy's heart. In the empty space left by Creation's disappearance, her own artefact was floating dead. Its light gone, its covers shut, Creation's amulet was defenceless, ready to be taken by evil hands. Health had just reached the node when the bright, motherly light pushed on her weak shoulders, causing her to slip through the node. The last thing she felt, passing from one world to the next, was her maker's final breath and wish.

The other side was not more welcoming than the one she had just left behind. If Talush had been torn apart, Varayal was burning alive, consumed by raging fire. Whatever Nothing sent to the worlds, he had done it on both planets simultaneously. The sky was red, the lands raged under an intense battle. Soul stood at the centre of a large valley, close to three tall towers. His home under attack, it was the only place still standing. The people of his world had gathered under his protection, fighting for their lives against the evil's army. Countless bodies lay dead or floated in the nearby river. Some were being resurrected in a different form, returning as spirits standing beside their protector.

With her back to the planet node, the doors closed shut. The tree on the other side turned to dust, erasing the passage through time and space. Unable to return to her own world, Health was rushing to support our brother with the little energy she had recovered when something unusual caught her attention. Something else had entered those lands. Only a few miles back, someone else had used the portal to come to the rescue. The familiar essence of our other brother reached her senses through the miles in between them. In her mind and her heart she was certain of the reason why our brother appeared in time of need:

despite his resistance and opposition, Time had come to stand beside his siblings, completely unaware of his mother's fate.

Faced with the choice of continuing her run towards the battle or rush to meet her brother, something else stirred Health's emotions. I was calling her from afar, troubled and confused. My silent cry penetrated her mind. My voice was strong, as if I had doubled my power. My presence echoed through space and time. Health could feel my heart beating twice. In between the pages of history, I was resounding from both her time and my future. Two versions of myself existed in the same reality, one on Earth fighting in protection of my world against Death and the rocky bullet he was riding towards Earth, and the other on Varayal, split into two beating hearts, desperate, broken and fragile.

'Love, is that you?' Health asked, her voice barely audible amidst the deadly sounds of war. Her weak essence shifted through realities. 'I can hear you. Where are you?' But there was no answer. All she could feel was a distant echo of a lost brother who could not hear her.

Counting on the arrival of Time in support of Soul, she rushed back to the node. If our brother had come to save Soul, she had to do the same for me. Ready to traverse myriad miles, Health opened the door of Varayal and left. Contrary to my sister's beliefs, Time's arrival was not for Soul's sake. His magic was spreading across the burning lands, manipulating the ticking of every second. Not in his own present, the God had come from the future. Like me, he appeared as a double, with two different bodies and two different wills. One, the same one Health had known since the beginning of their existence, clung to his stubborn desire to protect Runae, the world he had sworn to safeguard. The other, an older version of himself, had come to Varayal to exploit his brother's misery. Master of everything that was and would be, Time knew he had entered a loop of events that had to unfold. He was on a single mission: to take the Tiara of Souls away from his brother, the same artefact that had just been transformed into an everlasting spell by our mother, to achieve a greater good.

Accompanying him was a being from his world, a Leonty, suspicious and gifted with a piece of her master's magic. She would catch a glimpse of Time's plan without fully grasping its meaning. At the moment of their appearance, she sensed the presence of my sister, just before she departed. Unbeknownst to any of us, I, my brothers and my sister, were existing and alive in the exact same place and time. Different versions of ourselves missed the opportunity to be together once more.

The only chance we were going to have for the next thousands of years was lost. In our failure to find each other, the Gods would endure pain, imprisonment, apparent death, and oblivion. When Health left Varayal, history was rewritten. She would reach me just at the end of the battle against the enemy, saving me from a fatal blow by transforming Nothing's act into a merciful spell. Time, walking through the lands of Runae, would soon follow the same destiny—enslaved by the Crimson Queen through the power granted by her master.

Creation's sacrifice became an unending agony. Instead of rendering us immortal, the spell froze us in an eternal state of defeat. Ages would pass, with us Gods striving continuously to revert our present and our past, only to repeat our actions over and over again.

The Power of Love
The Two

Ross J. Kinnaird

About the Author

Ross Joseph Kinnaird was born in a far land something like 1000 years ago. He moved to Italy as an infant and grew up in the deep south, shaped by the sun and the wildness of the sea. After moving to Ireland in 2010, he began collecting and organizing the many stories he had written. They all seemed to have one theme, one soul. With the Celtic magic that his new home brought to him, Ross finally saw his novel taking shape through the mystical eyes of his mind. And so, 'The Power of Love' became the journey of a lifetime, perhaps spanning many lifetimes.

In the realm between reality and fantasy, he fused together the diverse ways life presented itself to him. Through a literary roller-coaster of emotions and feelings— pain, sorrow, happiness, friendship, and love—Ross J. Kinnaird wrote the many stories we tell ourselves in our never-ending search for greater meaning.

'Art, feelings, music, emotions have always been the strongest part of me. I was only a young teenager when I started transferring my busy mind onto paper.
As the years passed, life and experiences enriched my soul to a point where The Power of Love finally took form.
With the strongest connection to what I saw life as, the story of Daniel, Noah and Anita became an extension of who I am, of who many of us are.'

R. J. Kinnaird

ISBN: 978-1-0686863-3-7

For more info on The Power of Love Series

www.thepoweofloveworld.com

The adventures of Daniel, Noah and Anita continue in:

The Power of Love – The Three

First edition: December 2023

First Print: December 2023

Edited by Imogen Howson – Inkwell

Cover by Ardel Media